The Memories We Made

William Bergeron

Meadow Blossom Flowers—Madison, WI
ISBN: 978-1-7388675-0-9
eBook ISBN: 978-1-7388675-1-6
Library of Congress Control Number: 2023902275
Title: *The Memories We Made*
Author: William Bergeron
Digital distribution | 2023
Paperback | 2023

This is a work of fiction. The characters, names, incidents, places, and dialogue are products of the author's imagination, and are not to be construed as real.

Dedication

To Benjamin, for always cheering me on and pushing me forward.

To my dad, for giving me the initial drive to start writing.

To Émile, who gave me the first push to tell this story.

To my friends, family and colleagues who encouraged me to keep going.

You are all my inspiration…

Chapter 1

What just happened?

Even if classes were over and we were walking to the nearest bar, I couldn't help but get lost in thought, the monotony of my feet hitting the pavement at a steady pace a faded music to my ears. I couldn't believe the events that had just transpired and kept going over it in my mind, trying to find any reason to dismiss it as a prank. I came up blank in that regard and continued staring at the floor, the sound of my friend's laughter in the background sometimes reaching me. The hot air of the late spring evening blew on my face and coursed through my whole body, making my shoulders slump down even harder than they already had. I sighed and went over the events again while shaking my head, fumbling a piece of paper in my pocket, scared and apprehensive to even look at it again.

So many questions and so little answers. Why now? Why me? What could possibly have brought her eyes to me? I wasn't even sure how that made me feel. A cocktail of emotion was brewing inside me and the end result was still a mystery. I finally looked up after a few minutes of staring at the ground, hands still in my pockets and loosely following my friends. Spring was ending and the trees shone with color all around the city, but all I could see were the grey sidewalks and the black roads. Cars kept loudly going by us, adding to the sound amalgamation that formed all around me. I couldn't think straight anymore. Was that because I thought too much? Was it truly something that could be explained with exterior factors or was my mind simply too foggy after trying to process what just happened?

What just happened?

The question had a nice ring to it, but since it didn't have an answer, I rejected it and tried to ignore it. But like a persistent bug, it kept coming back no matter how many times I swatted it away. What was the point? I couldn't answer or chase it away. Would I be stuck with it for the rest of my life? I wasn't too much of a fan of that prospect, but what else was I supposed to do? Talking with my friends could be an idea, surely, or perhaps they would laugh at me instead. Was it a gamble I was willing to take? After a few seconds of blankly staring at the buildings going by one by one as we continued walking down the street, I internally nodded to myself.

◊ ◊ ◊

As summer break was drawing near, the busy life of Lone Oak University seemed to slip away a little more every day. Students with no more classes stopped coming to school and as the week went by, the corridors became more and more barren, plunging the entire building into a sea of silence. "Exam season" was a term on every student's mind, either causing stress or shining a glimmer of hopefulness for the summer break. There was only a little more than a week left to the entire semester and most couldn't wait to be home after a few painful weeks of studying. Today was Wednesday evening and I had just finished my second to last class.

As the clock ticked over to indicate the end of the class, the parting words of the professor couldn't reach many of the students who bolted out of the class. I wasn't as excited as they were, seeing as I had another class on Friday, but I nevertheless rapidly got my things and head out to the door. I shot a glance at my friends sitting at the back, looking to see if they were coming, but they seemed to be in a heated discussion about something and most of them hadn't even started to move. My head turned to the professor who simply smiled at me and nodded before slumping down in his chair. He seemed exhausted which, to be fair, was completely justified. His material was very good and you could tell he put a lot of effort into his classes, but they mostly went underappreciated by his students. I smiled back at him and turned around, intending to go empty out my locker before Friday's final class.

Lone Oak University didn't have many classrooms and most of them were on the second floor, spanning the entirety of the building. This class was no exception and while the majority of students took the central staircase to go down, I usually took a different route. Both to avoid the traffic and the noise it made. I wasn't too much of a fan of crowds, especially when no one could move like sardines in a can. I much preferred to go down the staircase at the end of the second-floor hallway. Not only was it much quieter and out of the way for most, but it led directly to my locker so it was a double win for me. As I reached the crossroad and all students turned to the main hallway, I slipped away from the crowd and reached the doors at the end, alone. I sighed and rolled my eyes in annoyance. Even that little time it took for me to get from my class to here was too much, so I didn't even want to imagine going through the whole group every day. I sighed sharply and pushed the doors open as they clanged with a heavy metallic sound that resonated in the staircase for a long time.

My footsteps echoed as I made my way down. Arriving by the door at the bottom, I heard voices behind me and glanced over at them. Three students, squatting down, were looking at me, eyebrows raised, like they waited for me to get on with it so they could resume whatever business they were doing. With a shrug, I opened the door and walked directly in front of me to my locker. Along with four others, they were the only lockers in this area. Apart from these five, all of them were in the middle wing of the school, but by some pure miracle, I was assigned one that was so out of the way I never even met the four other students that were given lockers near mine. I didn't even know if they were still going to this school. The lockers didn't seem occupied, but then again, neither did mine so how could I know? Still, the fact these lockers even existed was a little weird. Did the school somehow order too many lockers and had to make room somewhere for these five? The thought seemed ridiculous, but management was certainly capable of screwing up something like this, as they demonstrated on multiple occasions, so while it certainly was bizarre, I never gave it much thought. It just kind of made me laugh a little every time I thought about it, but I was glad to have been assigned a locker this out of the way.

I quickly input the code on my lock and it sprung open. The locker door squeaked. That was also something different about these lockers. Since they were so out of the way, they weren't as maintained as the others. I opened my backpack and started to put in all the books I didn't need anymore. English novels, math homework and a few straggling pages. I only left one for my last class. My eyes stopped on the coat still hung at the back of the locker. The days had been getting hotter for a good month now, but I always neglected to bring it back home and so it stayed there. I didn't have much of a choice now so I reached out to grab it, but just as I was about to stuff it in my bag, I heard a voice to my right.

"Hi, Jack!"

A feminine voice. That wasn't any one of my friends. Plus, they wouldn't call me Jack, maybe more "dude" or "buddy", but definitely not by my name. I turned around to look at who was calling me. I could recognize her anywhere. Camille. She had long blonde hair that flowed to the middle of her back. Two strands on each side of her face, one side almost covering her bright green eyes and her genuine smile seemed to radiate joy. Was it because of her hair color that resembled the sun or because of her general demeanor, I couldn't say, but every time I saw her, I couldn't help but smile. Today was different, however. She was talking to me. She never talked to me. We only had one class together and we only spoke on one occasion. Well, I couldn't say anything then, so that wasn't much of a conversation at all, making this even more of a surprise. Realizing it had been a few seconds and that she was looking at me, I snapped out of it.

"Oh, um, hi, Camille…" I said, embarrassed. *Why was I embarrassed?*

"I hope you don't plan on wearing that in this weather," she teased.

It took me a few seconds to realize I had my coat in my hand, which I promptly stuffed in my backpack before turning back to her.

"Oh no, I just forgot it in my locker. No, wearing that would be asking for trouble, especially since the weather is so hot and I would overheat for sure. I mean, some people still wear coats, but I don't, but like I said, I just forgot it in my locker."

Camille chuckled a little and put her hand over her mouth.

"Don't be so nervous, Jack," she said, laughing a little. "I just had something to ask you." My mind raced to figure out what she could want with me and I drew a blank. There was nothing that made sense to me, we never talked to each other, she was basically a stranger to me. One that I couldn't keep my eyes off of, but a stranger nonetheless. The only thing we had in common was our French class, but even then, she had other friends in that class so if she wanted notes or anything like that, she could just ask them. Why come to me? Plus, how did she know where my locker was? "Are you okay?"

Her question made me snap out of my ruminations and I made eye contact with her. She looked puzzled, like she couldn't figure out why I was acting the way I was. My eyes immediately shot down, my nerves taking over my body.

"Yeah, yeah, don't worry about me," I answered nervously. "What was it that you wanted to ask me?"

"Well, first of all, could you look at me when we're having a conversation?" Her tone wasn't mean or annoyed, more encouraging. I looked up again and she smiled at me. It nearly made my heart melt right then and there. My stomach almost turned on itself. "That's better, isn't it?" she said with a chuckle. I could only nod and form half a smile. Words couldn't come out of my mouth even if I wanted them to. "Are you ready for the French exam next week?" she asked, trying to contain her laughter. I felt bad thinking it must have been at my expense, but I tried to ignore it as best I could.

"Uh…yeah, yeah, I am. Why?" I answered, stuttering.

"I am having a little trouble with the material from the last few classes and I could really use some help. Would you be willing to help me study for it?"

"Well, sure, but couldn't you have some of your friends help you with that?"

"They're not available tonight or tomorrow. You're the only one that can help me with this," she quickly responded, a glint of confidence transpiring through her speech.

The only one? Surely other girls in the class would be willing to help her and it would be way less awkward than with me. This was the longest conversation I had with a girl that wasn't my mom in a long time and my legs were pretty much ready to give in. I had talked to girls before, that wasn't the issue, but I seemingly couldn't do so well when it came to her specifically. I was almost amazed at myself for still being conscious at this point.

"Okay, well, um. Yeah, I can help you study, if you really want to. So, when do you…"

"Tomorrow. At my place. After supper. Here."

She reached for her pocket and handed me a folded piece of paper. I carefully unfolded it to reveal an address and a time. The handwriting was simply beautiful, I couldn't help but compare it to mine and realize how much better it was. Honestly, I'm surprised people can even read me sometimes. Hers was on another level. After a few seconds, I looked up and Camille was gone. Stunned, I investigated my surroundings, but there was no trace of her. I peeked around the corner into the corridor leading to the middle wing of the school and there she was, walking away so fast you could almost say she was running. I could swear I heard her giggling, but that might also have been the echo of her footsteps in the corridor. I didn't think to call out to her until she took another turn and got out of vision. A familiar voice snapped me out of my thoughts.

"Yo! What are you doing, dude?"

I turned to my right to see my friends walking towards me from the other staircase. Seems like they finally settled their argument or whatever they were talking about in the class. Realizing I still had Camille's paper in hand, I quickly folded it back up and stuffed it in my pocket as I closed up my locker. My friends finally caught up to me. Chris gave me a slap on the back.

"We're heading out to the bar, you coming?" he asked, sliding his hand on my shoulder.

"Um, yeah sure," I answered. "But I won't be staying too long, cause…"

"Cool, come on, let's go."

They all started loudly talking about something else and started making their way to the exit. I couldn't help but grab my backpack and follow them. Fortunately, they didn't ask me anything on the way to the bar as I was completely lost in thought. Funny how you can still walk and follow a group while thinking of something totally unrelated. I couldn't get over why Camille was asking me to help her study. It's not like she really struggled with anything, she was consistently getting good grades and answering correctly in class. Somehow, I didn't think she was being honest about needing help to study.

◊ ◊ ◊

No matter how many times I thought about it, the situation wasn't getting any clearer. Why was it so conflicting? I was glad when, for a moment, I managed to think of something else as we finally reached the bar. Due to its proximity to the school and the fact that most drinks were cheaper than the competition, it attracted a lot of attention from students and it was generally pretty busy and today seemed to be no exception. We made our way inside and sat down at one of the only available tables. Glancing over, we recognize a few other students sitting there. Seems like we weren't the only ones celebrating the end of classes. Of course, that wasn't my case as the question crept up in my mind and the piece of paper fell into my hand again. I absent-mindedly turned it between my fingers, focusing on the texture of the paper sliding across my skin and silently hoping that would somehow help my cause.

It didn't.

The waiter soon arrived to take our drink orders after we sat down. I remember asking for something, but I didn't even know what. After a few minutes of chatting, he came back with all of our drinks and told us to let him know if we needed anything. With that, he left to tend to other tables.

"Hey, man, what's up? You've been out of it since class ended. Something wrong?"

I looked up at my friends. They were all staring at me, glasses almost empty as I had still not started mine. How much time had passed since we sat down? I didn't even know. I couldn't take my mind off Camille's request. Why was I so obsessed with that? Yeah, girls didn't usually talk to me out of the blue like that and that was a little weird, but she asked me to help her study. What was so weird about that? Wasn't it a totally normal thing to ask to a fellow student?

"Yeah, it's just um…I got invited to a girl's place tomorrow and uh…"

"Oh, very nice," Michael said, cutting me off. "Whose?"

"Camille, a girl in my French class," I answered.

"Wasn't she the girl you were talking to me about the other day? That's great news, man. So, what did she invite you for?" Chris pried.

"She wanted help to study for our final class on Friday and the exam next week."

"Study, huh? Something tells me you're not going to study at all," Vincent chuckled.

"Yeah, you got that right," Chris seconded.

"What do you mean?" I asked, uncertain to what they were alluding.

"Dude, from what you told me, she clearly doesn't need a study buddy. Plus, she has other friends in that class who could help her. Why would she ask you of all people to help her?"

That kind of hurt, but he was essentially saying what I was thinking. She did give me a reason though.

"She said that all her friends weren't available, so I was the only one who could help her," I said.

My friends laughed a little. I wasn't sure if they were laughing at me or not, but I for sure didn't know how to react.

"So, that was an excuse. She's clearly into you and wants to see you alone outside of school. Meeting for the first time at her place is a bold move, don't mess it up. You got this, dude!"

They all cheered me on for a few seconds and I couldn't help but put a hand behind my head in embarrassment.

"I don't think she means it like that, at all. There's just no way that's true."

"Sure, man. Whatever, you do you," Michael said with a slight chuckle.

Eventually, they moved on to another subject. Even though I was sitting right next to them, I couldn't hear what they were saying. I took my first sip of the night, lost in thought again. Could Camille really be inviting me over for more than just studying? From what my friends were saying, it certainly appeared that way, but I couldn't fathom the idea that she could be into me. I was the reserved one, sitting at the back of the class, barely able to talk to anyone else than my friends. We hadn't even spoke before. How could she possibly know who I was? My heart raced every time I was around her, that much I knew, but I couldn't decipher her intentions from what little interaction we had this morning. This was so unusual to me, everything was completely new and, this time, I couldn't learn about it by looking it up online. I'd have to go there tomorrow and figure it out by myself. The thought alone was making me nervous again. What would I say? How do you even start a conversation with someone that's basically a stranger? Before I knew it, I had finished my drink and everybody else was getting ready to leave. I absent mindedly paid the bill and walked out of the bar. We said goodbye and promised to keep in touch. They all teased me about Camille and asked for news real soon to which I responded that it surely wouldn't be interesting to hear how my study session went. With that, we parted ways as I was going left and all of them were going right. Tomorrow would be one exhausting day; it couldn't be anything but.

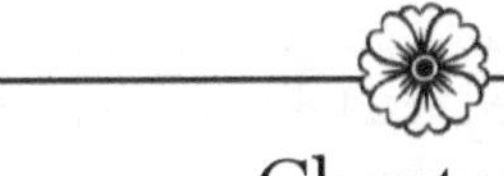

Chapter 2

I hardly had any sleep that night. I kept hearing Camille's voice in my head, her invitation and how she looked so beautiful. I couldn't get my mind off her. Plus, with everything my friends had said, I didn't know what to think anymore. Did she really mean to invite me to study or did she have another reason like they were alluding? I turned around, trying to get into a more comfortable position on my bed, but it seemed like everything was bugging me; from my clothes to my sheets. How do you tell the voice in your head to shut up and let you sleep? After what felt like hours, I finally fell asleep.

I woke up the next morning completely exhausted. My head hurt and my eyes were itchy as if I stared at a screen for way too long. I slowly turned around to look at my alarm clock. 8h12 a.m. I stretched, trying to wake my muscles up from their slumber. As soon as a clear thought could be formed, all the conversations the day prior came rushing back and I let out an audible sigh. What was I going to do? I rubbed my face with one hand. Eventually, I got up and went to open the drapes to let some sunlight in my room.

It wasn't a very big room by any means, but it was enough for me. I lived in modesty, didn't have too many fancy things and enjoyed having everything organized. In one corner of the room was my bookshelf with a little bit of everything in it from fantasy and science fiction to historical books. Resting on top of it were a few souvenirs I brought back from various trips I did when I was a kid. Right next to it was a desk where I liked to do my homework and other writing assignments. A couple of papers were messily scattered on it. I'd have to get to that soon to not lose anything. My school laptop was also on it, still open. Seems like I had forgotten to close it last night and left it on. Opposite of the desk was my bed. The sheets weren't my primary color of choice, but they had been given to me by my parents a few years back and I hadn't felt like changing them yet. Right beside it was a little brown nightstand where I liked to keep my keys, wallet and other important things to bring when I went out. The white walls were a little bright at times, times like now, when the sun was shining right on them and reflecting the light into my eyes. I squinted a little as I made my way out of the bedroom.

Right outside the bedroom was the living room. As I always did, I gave it a glance as I walked by. I don't know why I had to peek every time I passed a door or a room, but it was something I couldn't control. Was it to make sure everything was still there? Then why did I do the same thing in classrooms at school? At some point, I stopped trying to hide it and just did it. Nothing ever happened by me peeking anyway. A few steps later and I was in the kitchen. Not the biggest kitchen and definitely not used to its full potential, but it was sufficient for me and I quite liked its quirkiness. It was in its own bubble, small and somehow productive. I didn't know a lot of recipes and wasn't a great cook by any means, but it's something I learned after a while. Cooking for myself was something I had a little trouble with, because of lack of skill or pure laziness, I wasn't sure, but I always found it better to cook for others, when friends came over for example. There's something about cooking for someone else that makes the activity more enjoyable. I made myself a quick breakfast and sat down at the kitchen table, reminiscing again about my meeting later with Camille.

Before I realized, I was staring into nothing and my breakfast had become cold. It was now almost noon and I had gotten no work done. I was a little behind on my preparation for my other classes and wanted to get it over with before tonight. Hastily, I ate what was now the saddest meal I had in a long time and went back to the desk in my room to tidy up those papers and make some space. I had to make sure to get prepared for my philosophy class exam as it was the first one next week and also the one I felt the least prepared for. After all, this was the class I had the most trouble in and I wasn't sure why. Maybe those types of books just didn't resonate with me or maybe it was the way the teacher was approaching the subjects. Regardless, I needed to take some extra notes on the last few classes and make sure I knew what was going on if I wanted a good grade on the exam. I organized the papers into one pile I set on the left and sat down in front of my laptop. I opened a writing software and stared at a blank page. The cursor flashed and flashed, a single black line in a sea of white. I didn't know why, but nothing was coming up and I couldn't focus. After a while, I took out one of the books we had to read for the class and tried to study that instead. I realized after reading the same line four times in a row this probably wasn't working either. I sighed again. Seems like there was nothing to be done until tonight.

Camille was occupying all of my thoughts. Every time I tried to get away, she would pull me back in with her golden hair and charming eyes. Every time I thought of something else, her voice would resonate in my head to distract me. Her laugh would make my heart rate go faster. My eyes wandered to the piece of paper she handed yesterday. After a few seconds, I pulled up a map on my laptop and looked up her address and how to get there. She wasn't living too far, but it was a little bit of a ride in public transport. No matter. At this point, I knew I had to see her or I might fail all my classes.

◇ ◇ ◇

I didn't know when supper time was for her, but figured 7 p.m. would be a good time to show up. Not too late and not too early, just right for a study session of a few hours and then I'd go back home. No big deal, right? As the bus was reaching my stop, I hastily rang to let the driver know to let me out. The doors quickly opened and I made my way out. Camille's house was a few minutes of walking away and on I went. I didn't really know how I was able to walk, my legs felt like jelly and like they could crumble any minute. The weight of my backpack on my shoulders made them slump down like a flower wilting away under the heavy rain. It didn't contain much, but it was shockingly heavy in a way I couldn't explain. The sun wasn't quite setting yet, but was peeking now and then through the houses on the opposite side of the street, periodically blinding me. At least the weather was nice. It wasn't too hot, but definitely warm enough to avoid having to wear a jacket. Sometimes, a cooler wind breezed through my hair and hit my face. It was refreshing and also helped keep my thoughts in check. I didn't know what to expect and the unknown factor made me very nervous. Suddenly, I realized something in a brief moment of clarity. These were houses. She wasn't living in an apartment, so she was probably still living at her parents' place. What would they think of me? Would they be weirded out by someone like me hanging out with their daughter? How awkward would our first meeting be? I didn't think I could support having that kind of stress added on to this already nerve-wracking situation.

Finally, I arrived in front of her house. It wasn't anything different than any of the other houses in the neighborhood, but this one somehow scared me more. On the left side, there was a paved driveway which led to some stairs that circled back to the front door. Fortunately, there was no car parked and I breathed out happily. One less thing to worry about. Readjusting my backpack, I made my way up the stairs and found myself in front of the white door that separated me from Camille's home. All I had to do was knock. A simple thing, really. Yet my hand felt as heavy as stone and the door seemed so intimidating. It wasn't the first door I had knocked on, so why was this one any different? Eventually, I managed to lift my hand and knocked three times, almost as softly as a gust of wind. I waited for a few seconds, but nothing happened. I looked up and sighed nervously. I lifted my hand again and knocked three more times, but way harder. I heard movement inside and stepped away from the door, swinging back and forth on my feet. I felt like I couldn't sit still, like I had to move or else…or else what? The sound of the door creaking open snapped me out of my head and there, standing in the doorway, was the girl I had come to see.

Camille was radiant, as always. Her blonde hair flowing down her back and her green eyes made me melt in place. She was wearing a sunflower brown dress that contrasted well with her hair and made her stand out even more. The dress met her curves very well and stopped just under the knee, meeting up with her stockings. I stood there, dumbfounded and in awe, not wanting to look her up and down, but fighting with all my willpower to stop me from doing it anyway. When she saw me, a genuine smile formed on her face as she gestured for me to enter.

"Come in, come in. I was beginning to think you weren't going to show up."

"Should I have come sooner?" I asked, genuinely looking to know if I was in the wrong. After all, I couldn't possibly know when supper time was for her and her family as it might be different from mine and she had neglected to tell me a precise time. If ever, the thought barely crossing my mind, that I would have to come again, I'd love to be at a more convenient time for her.

"Oh no, no, I was just saying. I, uh, kind of left in a hurry yesterday and didn't make sure you were actually on board with it," Camille said, with a hand behind her head and a little grin on her face. "Well, don't just stand there, come on inside, we're not going to study out there, are we?"

Camille almost pulled me inside the house. Practically tossing me aside, she closed the door and locked it. I took a few seconds to take in my surroundings. There was a living room on the left, stairs leading up in the middle and the dining room on the right. That was all I could see before she dragged me up the stairs with her towards what I could only guess was her room. I almost tripped a few times while going up due to the sheer speed Camille was going. Before I could react or say anything, we were now in her room with the door closed, sitting on her bed side by side. Never would I have dreamed of this scenario. I would have thought we were going to study on a table downstairs or in the living room, but I couldn't possibly have imagined being alone with her in her room the first time going to her house. Who was I kidding? The thought definitely crossed my mind, but I chose to ignore it due to the impossibility of it actually happening. Yet here we were. Funny how these things happen, sometimes.

We sat there in silence for a few moments during which I looked around the room, backpack still around my shoulders, but now resting on the bed sheets like me. The walls were a mixture of blue and green, not quite pastel, but close to it and the dwindling light of the sun passing through the window at the back of the room formed what appeared to be dancing shadows. It wasn't the biggest and it didn't have much in terms of furniture. Near the window, a white desk contrasted with the surrounding colors. It seemed a lot messier than mine, but I didn't want to pry any further than I already had, so I turned away. On another wall were two sliding doors, most likely hiding a closet and, from the lack of it in the actual room, a dresser. Opposite to that, a bookshelf, smaller than mine and less garnished, completed the scenery. What was curious about it was one side was reserved for books and the other contained boxes of various size that appeared to be for puzzles. Did she particularly like doing them, I wondered? The bed we were sitting on was almost in the middle of the room, not quite tucked in any corner, which was weird to me as Camille would have probably gained some space by moving her things around a little. But she was probably comfortable having things sorted this way, the complete opposite to me. And this silence that lasted for an eternity certainly didn't help me in any way. Finally, her voice shattered it as she brought me back from my observations.

"So, um, I was thinking we could maybe watch a movie? What would you like to see?" Camille inquired, looking at the floor as if the wood panels had any answers. She seemed timid, not unlike me, but not like her greeting at the door and her enthusiastic run up here. Why the sudden attitude change? I guess I wasn't in any place to talk either.

"A movie?" I asked. "Shouldn't we be studying for the exam, as you said? Isn't that why I'm here?"

Her hand went up to her face, almost hiding it from me. I caught a glimpse of it and it seemed redder than what I remembered.

"Yeah, of course, um…we'll do that later. I just need to relax a little and I usually do that by watching a movie. Plus, this is kind of awkward and maybe that would help ease the situation…for you I mean," Camille stammered.

It wasn't that I didn't like to watch movies, I actually quite liked it, but it just didn't seem to be what we ought to have been doing at that moment. Perhaps she really wanted to put me at ease? I definitely wouldn't object to it; my stomach was probably about to give in from sheer nervousness, but I still secretly hoped that we could just get on with the studying portion so I could get out of her house. Not because I didn't like being near her, but my nerves could only take so much and I had to look after myself, didn't I? Why did I want to leave and stay at the same time? Weren't those two opposite feelings? Before I could even answer, she presented me with three options by handing me movie covers. I shakingly took them and looked at the titles. None of them I had ever heard of and my mind couldn't even figure out the genre from the titles or the covers. It was like it had stopped functioning and couldn't process even the simplest of tasks. Randomly, I selected the middle by pointing at it and Camille seemed delighted by my choice. She snatched the movies back, almost startling me by how assertive her movement had been, and she got up to get her laptop that was sitting on her desk. She also took out a little tray that could be used to hold the computer up. I was still sitting straight up, seemingly paralysed from head to toe, as she moved around the room and prepared the movie. Before I knew it, it was starting and Camille was now behind me.

"You can lie down, you know," she said with a slight chuckle. Almost like a robot, my head slowly plumped down on her pillow.

I could feel her weight in the mattress. She wasn't far from me, but not too close either, keeping a fair distance between us. I was both glad and upset that she did, like an undecided toddler. Her bed was a little bigger than mine, but even then, it seemed too small to my liking. It was a really conflicting feeling, both wanting to be closer to her, but being so nervous about it and wishing she wasn't. My mind couldn't pay any attention to the movie at all and I found myself lost in thought before long, wondering what I was even doing here in the first place. Sometimes, I felt Camille change position and move and I would shudder every time as if she were about to hit me or something. But the hit never came and instead she lay back down, perfectly content in watching this movie I had picked, but had paid no attention to since it started.

After a while, I felt something pressing on my back and then something on my arm. It took me embarrassingly long to figure out it was her own arm and my eyes widened in shock. That meant that…what was pressing against me was…I felt her leg's touch and her head almost bumped mine. There was no doubt about it. She was cuddling me! A shiver shot down my spine and I started to shake, which was weird considering it was nearly summer. I wanted to turn around and ask her what she was doing, but something was preventing me from doing so like an invisible hand holding my head into the pillow. I couldn't move a muscle, some few tons weighing down on my entire body. I was frozen in place like an icicle, doomed to lie still without ever being able to get out. I felt her breath caress my cheeks and the sound of her voice as she whispered.

"How are you feeling?"

I couldn't even come up with an answer. It was like her question took away any form of thinking my mind could possibly have and I felt a little overwhelmed. How was I feeling? Could I even be honest with her and tell her that even her presence made my stomach turn and she was the reason I was shaking from nervousness? I knew I had to say something, however, and my brain defaulted to the only thing it still knew.

"Uh…yeah, yeah…I'm fine. Yeah. Perfectly fine," I said, voice cracking to top it all off.

I felt her arm move towards my legs as her hand wandered across my chest. I braced myself, closing my eyes in anticipation, but nothing came. I could only think of what she was doing and couldn't come up with an answer. The sound of the movie, only ignored before, was now completely out of the equation as I was totally focused on her hand and the path it left behind. It stopped a little on my hip as if looking for validation it never got. After a few seconds, it resumed its descent towards my crotch and, as it was getting a little too close for my comfort, I jumped out of bed, nearly knocking down the computer tray and her computer along with it. I found myself looking straight at her as I felt my cheeks burning. She was a little stunned by the sudden movement and we made eye contact for a brief moment. I peered into her eyes, seeing both confusion and disappointment with a little pinch of shock. In the moment, I didn't quite understand why she was feeling that way and resigned to flee the scene as fast as possible to hide the shame of the situation. A little more abrupt than I intended, I opened her bedroom door and stepped outside, looking for any other room I could reasonably hide in. Luckily, the bathroom was in sight almost directly in front of me and I practically sprinted towards it. I only regained some semblance of composure as I closed the door and locked it, panting heavily. As I turned to the side, I noticed my face in the mirror above the sink. Come to think of it, I hadn't even shaved before coming here and the hair that covered my face was in such a state. My forehead was shining under the yellow light of the bulbs above me. My light-brown hair was also a mess, perhaps from lying down or from the sudden rush that came over me, but it was always so hard to deal with that it didn't strike me as odd. My shirt was sticking to me like a spiderweb, my pants felt heavy on my hips, I wanted to take them all off and breathe for a second. I went over to the sink and leaned on it, heavily breathing and trying to relax. What had just happened? This wasn't a study session, after all. She clearly had some other intent, but I just wasn't prepared for that at all. Well, my friends did tell me, clearly, and I had chosen to ignore them, my mind rejecting even the slightest possibility they could be telling the truth. And the truth it was. Was she acting on true feelings or was this her way of trying to make me comfortable? If it was the latter, it clearly wasn't working. Just as I was getting everything back under control, a knock resonated on the door. I instantly froze, staring straight into the mirror, silently hoping it wasn't her, even though I knew that was impossible. Maybe it would have been less embarrassing that way.

"Are you okay?" Camille asked from behind the door with a tone of genuine concern. Her knocks were gentle, almost like she restrained herself from fully knocking, for reasons I didn't know.

"Yeah, I'm…I'm coming out," I answered shakingly, taking another deep breath before turning around towards the door.

My hand reached the lock and turned it slowly. With a *clack*, it slid aside, unlocking the door. Moving down, I seized the handle and, just as slow as the lock, turned it to open what little separated me from Camille. With a creak, the door revealed a new scene before me. Standing just outside the bathroom was Camille, now in her pajamas, looking both concerned and shy. As soon as she saw me, her eyes went straight to the floor and her right foot was resting on her toes as she balanced back and forth like she couldn't sit still. For a few moments, I couldn't take my eyes off her, she was the very embodiment of cuteness and yet, the most embarrassed was most likely me. Why did she change into her pajamas? Did she expect me to stay here all night? The mere thought brought back all the feelings I tried to suppress in the bathroom and they went straight to my head. Without a second thought, I bolted towards the stairs, straight past her, and started going down as fast as I could.

"Wait!" Camille called out behind me.

I didn't stop. With the front door in sight, I quickly opened it and got out. I could only hear Camille call out to me one more time, but it was too late. I was already out on the sidewalk, running from this moment, from my feelings and from her house.

Why? Even I knew I was a shy kid, not even considering myself a man at this point, and when it came to matters of the heart, I was as inexperienced as a baby trying to walk for the first time. After all, yesterday was practically the first full conversation I had with a girl and that was awkward enough, but to be put into this situation today was more than overwhelming. I certainly felt something for Camille, that much was certain, but I was still confused as to what it was, what it meant, if it was the same for her or not. How could I be sure? I might never have an answer to that question, but I asked myself it anyway.

I ran for a while before realizing I had no real idea how to get back. I looked up the public transport schedule online and found a nearby bus that would take me close enough to my apartment. It was only then that the absence of my backpack on my shoulders was felt and with a facepalm, I sighed heavily. A complete idiot. I left my backpack at her house and there was no way that I would go back there now, not after this. Not tonight anyway. I had to get out of here, go back home and drown myself in embarrassment. Then, and only then, was there a chance of me looking to get my backpack from her.

Chapter 3

When you've been going to school for more than a decade, you start to get accustomed to the feeling of leaving the house with a backpack on. The weight on your shoulders is reassuring, like you didn't forget anything back at home and you're fully prepared for the day ahead. Having that suddenly taken away was not only weird to me, I felt almost like I wasn't whole, like a part of me was missing, forgotten or perhaps left behind. As the school drew closer and closer, the weight missing from my shoulders seemed to shift into my heart. The fear of the unknown is a very strong feeling. I had no idea how I would get my backpack back and the thought of having to face Camille now was the most terrified I had been in a long time. What would she think of me now that I ran away from her like a scared infant? Would she even dare talk to me anymore and simply keep my things?

I got into the school by the doors closest to my locker, wanting to limit the amount of time I would be in the building. I passed by a few students squatting in the staircase, the same as two days ago, but this time they seemed to pay more attention as they surely noticed the lack of a bag on my back. Or was that my imagination? I felt like they wanted to say something, but I simply walked faster to pass them and didn't make eye contact. As I opened the door to reveal my locker in front of me, I noticed a white paper stuck on it. A note, perhaps? I approached it and ripped it off, carefully reading it. *If you want to get your backpack, meet me at my locker. Number 294.*

The note was from Camille, no doubt about it. Even though I hadn't seen it a lot, I could recognize her handwriting anywhere. Her locker was on the other side of the school, but that wasn't the biggest obstacle. I had almost resigned myself to forget about the backpack and carry on with my day, hoping to avoid talking to her even though we were in the same class. Maybe she'd want the same thing and everything would work out perfectly. But the note made me hesitate. This seemed like the perfect opportunity to figure out what she thought of me now, to put this whole thing behind me, return to being the quiet kid at the back of the class that minded his own business and that girls didn't want to talk to. Torn between two feelings, I decided to go meet with her and hoped she would be alone.

A few minutes later, I was nearing her locker. I almost turned back a couple times and practically dragged my feet the whole way, but I was here. My heart was beating way faster than it should have, threatening to burst out of my chest at any moment. Finally, amongst the many rows of lockers that formed the main common area of the school, I saw her and her friends, waiting in the second to last row. As she saw me, she motioned me to come with her hand and held up my backpack. Stupidly, I turned around to see if she was really talking to me. Who else could she be talking to? It was mine, of course she was talking to me. I approached timidly, both intimidated by the fact all her friends were standing with her and by the awkwardness of our situation at that moment. They looked at me with big smiles on their faces, silently taunting me and I did my best to ignore them. I stopped when I got near, but not too close either. It was like I felt safer with a certain distance between us. Eyes down, I waited for her to start talking, mainly because I didn't know how to even start this conversation.

"I think you forgot this yesterday," Camille said while holding up my backpack. Without a word and barely looking up, I nodded and held out my hand to take it. The sudden weight on my hand almost made me fall, but I managed to regain my composure before making a fool of myself in front of everyone.

"Th-Thanks," I said nervously. I didn't know what else to say. I slowly put it on and the familiar touch put me slightly more at ease.

I saw her motion to her friends at the corner of my eye, but I kept my gaze to the ground. Her friends moved away to another row of locker, leaving us alone. I felt her hand on my chin and, with her help, finally looked at her. She didn't seem angry. In fact, she smiled at me. A smile I couldn't quite understand. It looked…amused, almost like when looking at a dog doing a silly trick. Her reaction confused me. Why was she so cheerful, always so beaming with happiness? I couldn't make sense of it. I wasn't angry or anything either, of course, more like frozen in place, incapable of doing the simplest thing like looking her in the eyes while she was so assertive in her demeanor. She exalted confidence from every fiber of her being and, while I wasn't exactly intimidated, it was a very different feeling compared to what my friends made me feel.

"You had better not forget it next time," she said with a slight chuckle. She leaned back and crossed her arms. "So yesterday happened, huh?" She waited for a few seconds and, after my lack of answer, leaned forward with an incredulous look on her face. "What happened back there, Jack?"

"I...I... got nervous and...and... didn't really know how to react so I ran away...I'm sorry, I just...this is all new to me," I struggled to say. I was sort of hopping in place, uneased and uncertain of the situation. It was like I couldn't sit still, wanting to run away again, but some force attracted me and almost forced me to stay.

"I think you need to get out of your head and just let go," Camille answered. "What did you think I invited you for yesterday?"

"Well, to study for French class, was it not?" I asked.

"It wasn't to study, Jack." She paused for a second, almost hesitating. For what, I didn't know. "I like you and wanted to spend some time with you. Wasn't that obvious?"

"No, it wasn't," I answered while shaking my head and looking down again. I caught myself and looked at her instead. "Like I said, this is all new to me. I genuinely thought you wanted some help to study and that's why I said yes."

"That would explain certain things," Camille said, leaning back again. "How do you feel about me, then?"

What did I feel about her? She had to have some sort of magical ability to ask the most awkward questions ever. I couldn't even begin to figure out what I was feeling, especially not now. It was true that I felt some attraction to her, but since I had nothing to compare it to, I couldn't truly know what it was. Was it simple attraction? Love? Companionship? Just a crush or perhaps a girl I found really pretty? The lines between all these were very blurry to me and I couldn't decipher on which side Camille landed on. To be put on the spot like this was almost enough to make me turn back, for real this time, but I resigned myself to do at least one thing right. I looked at her directly this time and, with the last shred of confidence I was able to conjure, I became the boldest I had ever been with a girl.

"I'm not sure I have an answer for that question yet. Could I have your number? It's just that with summer approaching and the exams coming up, if you wanted an answer, I think that would be the best way to talk." I stopped talking, already saying way too much for what my request was. Camille looked surprised, then amused and then something else I couldn't figure out. Her gaze changed, eyeing me up and down while biting her lower lip, and she held out her hand to me.

"Sure."

I patted all my pockets, forgetting where my phone was for a moment, caught in heat of the moment, still hooked on that last expression I didn't understand. I was beginning to panic as I couldn't find it. My chance would be ruined if I didn't take out my phone, like, right now. Finally, the familiar rectangular shape fell into my hands and, with a lot more trouble than it should have been, I unlocked it, opened a new contact and handed her my phone to input her number. She took it, almost greedily, and input it so fast I was taken aback when she handed it back to me a whopping three seconds later. With some hesitation, I took it from her and looked at it for a moment. A few seconds passed while I stared at the screen, not processing what I was seeing. It was as if the phone had been foreign to me or a brand new one I had just bought from a store. Either way, I couldn't believe it. Camille had really given me her number! A small victory, but a victory nonetheless. I looked up from the phone and met her eyes as she smiled at me. I felt my cheeks get warm and my face got red. This time, there was no stopping me. I swiftly turned and started going towards the right. I heard Camille shout out to me.

"French class is not that way, Jack."

How red from embarrassment can I possibly get? I didn't have the answer to that question, but I couldn't imagine someone being redder than I probably was at the moment. I stopped immediately, as stiff as a tree planted in the middle of the corridor, my mind all blurry and holding my breath. My entire face felt like it had been lit on fire and my hands, clutching the shoulder straps of my backpack, were starting to slip. I turned around and, almost running at this point, walked as fast as I could away from Camille's locker while hearing her and her friends giggle a little behind me. I sensed the gaze of every student in the vicinity on me. Was it really the case? Maybe not, but there was no way I could tell with my eyes fixed on the floor.

Not even two minutes later, I was sitting in class, well in advance. Luckily for me, the classroom was open before it started and there were no other classes before mine so I could just walk in, sit at my usual desk at the back of the class and try to get it together before anyone else showed up. I was completely alone in the otherwise empty classroom and, with my backpack resting on my desk, I pulled out my phone to look through my contacts. I didn't have to scroll far, Camille was near the top after all, but as I got to her name, another one popped up on the screen. Chloe. I sighed a little, the name sending my thoughts into yet another spiral.

Chloe was a long-time friend. I met her in high school, in the first year to be exact, and we became friends in the first few weeks. Luckily, we were always in the same class and could rant about our professors, homework, exams and everything else school related to each other. I used to go to her house, back then it was her parent's house, to study together for upcoming tests. I wondered if she was still living there or if she had moved out. For a while now, we had lost contact and didn't speak to each other for what seemed like an eternity, but was realistically more like a year at this point. The circumstances were still tricky, but I had a disagreement with her choice of boyfriend at the time and we had a small fight about it that didn't get resolved in the best way. On one hand, I missed my friend and the good times that we had together. There was a time where we could tell each other anything. I told her about my crushes and she would laugh at me and I would advise her on hers. She usually had more luck in that department than me. On the other hand, she did some things that were kind of messed up and that was how we lost contact. I still thought about it from time to time, but that was almost a year ago now. I felt like I was over the whole thing, yet I was clearly not if the simple sight of her name could affect me like this. How we managed to avoid each other for a year while going to the same school was nothing short of a miracle, even if a part of me still would have liked to see her again. Why didn't I? What was stopping me? Then, I noticed Camille had sent me a message. I didn't even notice that it was sent a few minutes ago and I quickly opened it. It was quite simple, really. Just a smiling emoji with its tongue out. The sight of it made me smile as well. I definitely felt more comfortable talking by text than in front of her, yet I couldn't seem to type a response. I only noticed then that the classroom had filled up and, as I looked up from my phone, I saw Camille and her friends enter through the door at the other end of the room. She met my eyes and winked at me. I quickly hid behind my backpack which earned a slight chuckle from her. That awarded me another text. This time, it was still an emoji, smiling but with its eyes closed. Fortunately, the professor walking in and starting the final class of the year saved me and made me turn off my phone. Perhaps I could distract myself from all this ordeal by listening to the lecture.

I couldn't. The professor might as well have been talking in an alien language for all I knew. It all sounded like distant gibberish to me, barely audible from the back of the class. Somehow, it felt like I was underwater while sitting down, swimming aimlessly in my mind. All around me, the events of the past few days kept bouncing around, almost taunting me and I had trouble knowing what was fiction from reality for a moment. Did those things really happen or was it all a dream that I had yet to wake up from? The touch of my backpack's fabric on my hands, the coolness of the desk and the hard wooden seat of the chair confirmed that I was not lost in a fantasy or a nightmare, this was real life. I tried to look at the board behind the professor, but the image seemed to blur as if my eyes couldn't function properly. I did not need glasses, I was certain of that, but couldn't explain what was happening either. Then, my gaze set upon Camille, sitting a few rows ahead of me in the middle of all her friends. One of them, I didn't know her name, looked at me for a second before poking Camille on the shoulder with a pencil. Surprised, Camille turned around to look at her and she pointed directly at me. My eyes met hers and, for a moment, time froze and everything around me disappeared. We were pretty far apart, but I could remember those eyes anywhere. I wasn't so nervous, sitting all the way over here while she was over there. Up close, it was different. One, two, three, four seconds passed as we stared at each other, uncertain of what to do next or what was even happening right now. Then, with a genuine smile, she broke off the eye contact and turned to her friend. I saw her whisper something inaudible to me and her friend silently laughed. She then turned around to tell her other friends and soon, the whole group turned around to look at me. I've never hid faster in my life, covering myself behind my backpack, hoping they would stop staring at me and restart paying attention to the actual class going on. I felt my phone vibrate and jumped a little from my seat. No doubt it was her sending me a message. I couldn't open it right now, though, could I? No, impossible, I was already on edge, there was no need to put myself through that. But what if it was important? How important could it be? Couldn't it wait until the end of class? What if she asked me a question and wanted an immediate answer? Even with all those questions, I left my phone alone and instead checked the analog clock ticking above the door. Only fifteen minutes had passed since the start of class. With a muffled sigh, I resigned to wait. This class seemed to go on forever and I couldn't wait to get out of here, go home and try to move past this stressful week.

◊ ◊ ◊

The sudden movement of the students gathering their books, moving their chairs and almost sprinting to the door pulled me out of my thoughts. Was the class over? I looked around in confusion for a second and, since everyone was leaving, I figured it was. Camille and her friends, still in front of me, didn't pay me any attention and simply left. I guess they got tired of looking at me after I didn't come out from behind my backpack for the entirety of the class. Understandable, really. Who would want to stare at that? I waited a minute, letting everyone leave before me. Not that I was attached to this class, far from it, but I didn't want to move in a crowd and wanted to avoid talking with Camille and her friends if possible. I didn't know how I could face them after what happened earlier at her locker and in the class. They must have thought I was such a loser with no hope of redemption.

After everyone else had left and only the professor was sitting at his desk, working quietly on some papers, I got up from my seat. My legs were numb and my neck hurt from the weird position I was in. I rubbed it with my hand, the coldness of it soothing the pain a little. Then, with a single motion, I put on my backpack and started heading towards the door. I couldn't wait to get out of this place. With classes being done and only the exams left, I could already taste the summer vacations. If only they could get here sooner. My phone shifted in my pocket as I walked and I remembered the text I got from earlier. I took it out and checked the notification. As I suspected, it was a text message, the little red circle above the chat icon indicated it so. Who was it from? Well, there could really only be one person. I opened up the message. I looked next to Camille and... nothing. She didn't send me the message. Then who did? Right under her name, the little red icon was visible. It was Chloe. I looked at my phone, almost in shock. Why did she suddenly text me out of the blue, in the middle of class? What did she even say? After all this time, it had better be something important, a long heartfelt message, an outstretched hand looking to rekindle a lost friendship, or maybe...

Hey

That was it. A simple greeting sent over two hours ago with only the unread mark as a response. I was standing in the middle of class, immobile, staring at my phone like it was a foreign object I didn't know how to operate. How could I respond to this? It had been almost a year now, a year of no contact, no messages, no phone calls, nothing and she was breaking that silence with a simple "*Hey*"? The sheer audacity almost made me want to scream, but then again, I was kind of silently hoping we could talk again. The fault was not all hers, though, as I had made no effort to contact her either. I was telling myself she wouldn't want to talk to me after what I said back then and figured if she wanted to, she could always message me back and I would answer. Except now that she did, I couldn't. With another sigh, I closed my phone, resigning myself to deal with this matter later, once I was home and comfortable in my chair or in my bed. I was now the last one in the class, probably by a few minutes at this point, and as I started walking again, I looked to my left towards the professor, willing to nod to him as a final goodbye before next week's exam. He was focused on his work and didn't look up to me and so I walked out the room. Classes were now completely done. I should have been ecstatic, overjoyed or maybe only relieved, yet the sight before me made me feel otherwise. Camille and her friends were standing nearby, seemingly waiting for someone. That someone could only have been me as I was the only one still here. As soon as I walked out, Camille, who was leaning on the wall to my left, got up and made her way up to me. Her friends, gathering on my right, nodded at her and she nodded back. Soon after, they left, leaving me and her alone. Well, with the professor behind me, of course, but he was probably too absorbed in his work to hear anything.

"Hey," she said.

"Um, hi," I answered back nervously. What was even going on?

"Listen, I know we didn't get off on the right foot. What happened at my house… we can forget about that. You said you didn't have an answer for me and I get that, but would you like to go on a date with me?" she asked.

The request came at me like a wrecking ball I never saw coming. It seemed like she jumped a few steps by asking me out and I couldn't quite believe she did. Did she really just do that? She said it with such confidence, like it was no big deal, but I could never do something like that in a million years. She was staring straight at me, pressuring me for an answer while staying silent. It was so sudden, so forward and I didn't have time to prepare for it at all. The question bounced around in my head, almost like I couldn't understand it, and it took me a while before I could even process what she said. Coming up with an answer, however, was a completely different story. I seemed to stare at her, no sounds coming from my mouth even if I wanted to. It was like I had suddenly gone mute or forgotten how to speak. I felt my heart pounding in my chest as if it wanted to burst out. My stomach was stiff, my entire body was stiff. I didn't know how long we stood there for, it seemed like an eternity to me and perhaps it was the same for Camille, because she answered her own question for me.

"Look, I know a place we can go tomorrow around eleven. Sound good? I'll text you," she said, her voice a distant sound.

Then, I felt something wet on my cheek, but only for an instant. What was that? I looked up and met her eyes. She didn't keep eye contact for long and, turning a slight shade of red, she ran to my right, clutching her book that she kept in her hands for some reason. Wasn't that weird? Why didn't she put it in her backpack? I held my hand up to my cheek, feeling the wet skin on my fingers. What just happened? I couldn't wonder for long as a deep masculine voice came from behind me as he cleared his throat. I jumped in place, startled and moved aside while turning around. The professor was looking at me, eyebrows up, silently questioning me. I guess he was wondering what I was doing standing alone in the hall instead of going home which was a valid question, to be fair. I didn't have to answer him, though, as he said, nonchalantly, and while walking away.

"You had better get home, mister Bradley. Unless you plan on studying for the exam in the hallway, I suggest you find somewhere slightly more comfortable."

With that, he left and turned the corner leading towards the nearest exit. I was left there, dumbfounded and overwhelmed from everything that just happened. One thing was certain, the end of the year did not go as I had planned. Was it for the best or for the worst? I hadn't decided yet on that answer, but I had a feeling I would soon find out.

Chapter 4

I nervously checked my phone for the twentieth time in the last five minutes. I'm not sure what I was expecting, time wouldn't have jumped hours ahead in the brief seconds between me checking. The relentless fidgeting with my phone almost made me miss my stop, but I rang the bus driver just in time. With a skip in my step, I got up to the doors and, as the vehicle slowly and noisily came to a stop, I stepped outside. Immediately, the sun attacked my eyes and I had to cover them with my hand as the bus left. I looked around for a bit and, finding nothing that stood out in terms of landmarks, looked again at my phone for directions. Opening my map, I moved around in a circle until it pointed me in the right direction. Travel time indicated a few minutes to walk. Not too bad. When the pedestrian sign lit up from across the road, I started making my way towards where Camille told me to go.

I didn't really know this part of town well. I didn't usually wander off too far from my home and this being a twenty-minute bus ride, I had scarcely visited this area. The roads were very busy, people were walking everywhere, cars were trying to make their way, it was all a little chaotic. Several restaurants had tables lined up outside fenced in with wooden structures ornamented with hanging lights tied in a ribbon. Some parts of the road weren't accessible to cars and in those section, you could walk freely in the middle of the street. Despite this, it was still very noisy as numerous conversations could be heard from people eating outside or just hanging about in the sun. I didn't like crowded places, but this was somehow different. There were a lot of people, but there was ample space to move around still, and, against all odds, I found myself quite enjoying my walk. I looked around at all the shops on each side of the street. Most were restaurants, but there were also clothes shops with little stands on display on the sidewalk, some odd store that seemed to have a little bit of everything piled up in a huge mess you could view from the giant window in front and even a few bookstores. Growing up, I really enjoyed visiting those and grabbing anything that caught my interest. I was an avid reader once, but I seemed to have lost the drive that once got me to pick up books and take the time to immerse myself in the stories they told. I always said to myself I had to go back to reading and, seeing those stores, I thought to myself that this time, I would. However, there was some other place I needed to be. According to my map, it should be really close now.

I noticed the cat sign from afar and concluded that must be it. Getting closer, I started to look around for Camille and it wasn't long before I spotted her waiting in front of the café. I sighed nervously. The walk almost made me forget why I was even here. This was my very first date and with Camille no less, but I was afraid I wouldn't know what to talk about. We hadn't really spoken to each other for a long period before. Would I be awkward? Would I annoy her into leaving? What would I do then? Subconsciously, I had started to walk towards her and her voice snapped me out of my thoughts.

"Jack! Over here!" she said, waving her hand at me. She was leaning against the wall near the door to the café, but was now standing straight, hopping in place like an overexcited bunny.

I made my way over to her and, as I got close, couldn't help but stop and stare. She was wearing a beautiful sunflower-covered yellow dress that paired marvellously well with the weather, contrasting the grey sidewalks and the wooden structures around. Her beige purse was hanging from her side, her left hand holding it in place. Her other hand was occupied holding her straw hat in place when the slightest breeze passed between us. Finishing it all, she also wore little brown sandals that left her feet mostly uncovered. Her outfit was so simple, but it was perfect for her. I was in awe. Compared to my simple plain black shirt, jean shorts and running shoes, she was the height of fashion. Suddenly, our eyes met as she leaned her head down to meet my gaze.

"Like what you see?" she said with a slight smile.

"Oh!" I said, snapping out of it. "Yes, I mean, yeah, I mean I didn't mean to stare, it's just that, um…you're really pretty." Instinctively, I closed my eyes and my hand reached out to the back of my head, rubbing my hair in embarrassment.

"You're not looking too bad yourself," she nodded approvingly. "Shall we go in?" She gestured towards the door to the café we were standing right next to. It took me a few seconds, I didn't really know why, but I shook my head.

"Yes, of course. Thanks."

She opened the green wooden door to the café and we made our way in. Straight away, we were assaulted by a little kitten. It must have been a few months old at most, as it meowed at us loudly, wanting to be pet. Camille went straight down to give the kitten what it rightfully deserved as a waitress soon came in to check us in. Suddenly, Camille turned and looked at me with an anxious look.

"Oh my god, I didn't even ask you, are you allergic? Are you okay with cats?" she said with her hands blocking her mouth. I didn't need to hear her however; her eyes were enough to tell me what she was saying.

"Don't worry about that, there's no problem," I answered with a little wave of my hand.

"Thank god," she sighed heavily in relief. "I was beginning to panic a little over here." Curiously, her tone and attitude didn't quite fit the words she was saying. She wanted to sound nervous, but completely missed the mark in that regard. I noted it but didn't comment on it. What good would that have done? Perhaps it was all in my head as well and I didn't want the date to get off on a bad start. I was already apprehensive about the whole thing and there was no need to bother with petty details like that if I could avoid it.

The waitress showed us to a table near a small window on the side of the building as Camille waved goodbye to the kitten. There, a cat structure was almost overlooking our table and on it sat two cats. One of them looked directly at us as we walked over. It was a golden orange color and seemed young and energetic, but also very small. It was clearly older than the kitten that greeted us at the door, but it must have only been a year old. It didn't get up at all, preferring to stare at us, the slanted yellow eyes piercing into our souls. The other one, a bigger black cat, was sleeping next to the first one and didn't move a muscle as we sat down, even when we dragged our chairs, making loud creaking sounds. I guess it must have been used to the noise of the café and wasn't paying it much attention anymore.

Now that we had sat down, I looked around at the café interior. Much like the outside, it had a very strong wood feel to it, almost like a cottage lost in the deepest parts of the forest. Huge wooden beams spanning from one side of the roof to the other towered over our heads. Here and there, they descended into columns, outlining doors and different sections of the shop. In the front of the shop, multiple tables were disposed in a lower level illuminated by the shining light coming from the giant façade window. Along the edges of the walls, some cozy red benches were installed, their color popping out from the otherwise brown aesthetic. Wooden chairs padded with red cushions also contrasted with the decor, all lined up in a very organized way, at least when the café was empty. Now, it was very crowded, almost every table were taken by various individuals, some couples, some people simply reading a journal and others just looking for a little drink on this hot day. Completing the scene were the cats running around. Some wanted attention from the guests, some were plenty satisfied with sleeping in the most unlikely of places while others sat in corners and preferred to look at everyone from a distance.

We were seated in a section that was slightly higher than the ground floor. Along the edges of the wall, right after the corridor that served as the entrance, several tables, including ours, were tucked in and only allowed two people to sit at a time. In that general area, there were multiple cat towers and other toys where the furry friends could play and spend all their energy. One of them, a large grey cat with a tiger pattern, was repeatedly swiping at a pink ball that sprung back and forth every time he hit it. I couldn't help but smile at it. It looked like it was having fun, that's for sure. Sometimes, I wished I could turn my brain off and let go, but there was always something going on in my mind, some thought that needed more attention than necessary, a task that needed to be done at home, a homework I couldn't forget about, an essay that was due, an evening out with my friends planned in the near future. If I could only play like that cat was, life would be much simpler.

Across from our table span a large counter where the staff could take and deliver orders as well as communicate with the kitchen in the back. On the counter, there were multiple desserts and other pastries on display. They all looked very good, but I wasn't feeling like having something sweet. Perhaps Camille would want one, though. Above, on a giant beam of wood, a blackboard with the menu written in chalk spanned the entire length of the counter. From where we were, we could just look up to see all our options, but we also conveniently had small hand-crafted menus on our table.

I glanced over at Camille, who was already studying it intensely, and realized I hadn't even started to figure out what I was going to order. I shook my head to snap out of it and took a hold of the menu in front of me. Even if it was written in plain English, it seemed as though the words were dancing on the pages, taunting me. Was it the nervousness kicking back in, or did I suddenly become unable to read even the simplest of menus? Even the numbers at the end of the lines were switching places and even if I blinked, the words didn't come back. Just as I was struggling to get a hold of myself, the waitress came back, armed with a pad and a pencil, ready to take our order.

"Are we ready to order?" she said with a smile. Her voice snapped me out of it, and, out of panic, I dropped the menu on the table. I looked her at her and sighed in relief when I saw she was looking at Camille.

"Yes, I'll have a lemonade, thank you."

"One lemonade," the waitress noted as her pencil danced on her notepad. "And for you, sir?" she asked as she turned around towards me.

Her question took me a little by surprise. Who else was she going to ask it, though? I was the only one left, but I wasn't ready to order. I hadn't even begun to figure out my options yet. Panic crept up like shadows on a setting sun and I thought of the first thing that came to mind.

"A coffee," I almost shouted. Even the sound of my own voice startled me. I couldn't bear to look at Camille, she must be so embarrassed of me.

"And what size would you want your coffee?" the waitress asked, completely oblivious to my struggles. I was trying to keep it together, for my sake more than hers or Camille's, and I wasn't exactly succeeding.

"A small one, thank you," I said, wishing this entire conversation could start again. For a first impression on a first date, I was making a fool of myself. The waitress repeated my order as her pencil resumed its dance. When she finished, I was expecting her to leave, but she was still standing there. Why was she still here? Our order was done, was it not?

"Would you like anything to eat with your drinks? We have a wonderful selection of desserts, some lemon cakes or maybe some fresh fruits?" the waitress offered.

I sensed Camille look at me. I could feel her eyes on me and in that moment, they felt as though they weighed a thousand tons. All I could do was shake my head from side to side, barely noticeable. I hoped that was enough and the sound of her voice confirmed it.

"Oh, you know what, a lemon cake would be lovely! I'll take one!" Camille answered.

"I think someone might like lemons, don't we?" the waitress asked.

"I absolutely adore lemon-flavored stuff. Guess I made that a little obvious, didn't I?" Camille joked. The waitress laughed along while I sat there awkwardly. I didn't know if it was appropriate for me to laugh as well or not, the nervousness was gripping me tightly and holding me in place, preventing me from doing anything. I hoped the feeling would pass soon.

The waitress probably looked at me at some point, but I blanked out and didn't hear her at all. Perhaps she and Camille exchanged a few more words, but I was gone in another world, trying my best to come back to my sense. Eventually, she left, leaving me and my breaking conscience with my date. If anything, it would all be over soon at this pace. "It's awfully hot today, isn't it? I thought I would melt getting here I was so hot." Her voice snapped me out of my torment, and I looked straight at her. She seemed very lax, smiling at me. Her left hand tucked her hair behind her ear, and I couldn't help but smile back. She was as cute as the day I first saw her, many months ago. Then, I had dreamed of being in this exact position, but had resigned to forget about it, telling myself there was no way a girl as popular as her would dare to go on a date with a guy like me. We were in two different leagues, miles apart from each other, and yet here we were. I was glad to have this chance, even though I felt it slip away by the minute. I rose back in my seat, maybe a little too suddenly as she seemed a little startled.

"Yeah, the bus ride here was infernal. Even with the windows open, I had trouble breathing," I said, confidently and uncharacteristically. She seemed surprised. By my answer, probably not, but by my delivery most likely.

"Jack?" she said, leaning on the table and looking straight into my eyes. Should I have felt fear or comfort in that question? It was hard to tell, but I resigned to answer regardless.

"Yes?" I answered shakily, uncertain of the tone I was supposed to use.

"Relax. It's just me, there's nothing to be nervous about. I know this is your first date, but I promise I won't bite, leave or whatever. I'm here to have a good time with you." She sounded genuine and her words appeased me, even if only a little. Perhaps there was a chance for me after all. I only had to seize it, grab it with a hand and pull it towards me. It felt as though my shoulders dropped down a few meters as all tension in my muscles vanished. I took a long inspiration, eyes closed and holding it for a few seconds, before releasing it and opening my eyes back up. They met with hers. She smiled at me. I smiled back. I was fine. Everything was fine.

"Better?" she asked with a slight chuckle.

"Yeah," I answered.

"You know, you're kind of cute when you get nervous," she said with a smile and a head tilt. "Maybe you should get nervous more often."

"Are you joking? I'm already on edge enough as it is, there's no need to pile it on even more." She laughed at my response, and I joined in with her. It was a much-needed outlet, most of my awkwardness washing away with the sound of our laughter. After a few seconds that felt like forever, we slowly regained our composure, and I looked back at her. "Why did you choose this café in particular today?" I asked out of genuine interest. Did she have a thing for cats? Was she a regular here or was this the first thing that popped up on a *Top ten places for a first date* tier list?

Camille looked to the side in a pensive expression, seemingly rummaging through her mind for something. Was she trying to remember the answer to my question? It took a few seconds, but she eventually turned back and stared at me with her beautiful green eyes. Every time I met her eyes, they seemed to hypnotize me, and I couldn't look away. Not that I would want to anyway.

"I used to come here a lot as a kid. I really liked petting all the cats and making many friends and my parents would always take me here on the weekends after going shopping nearby. It was a good time..." she trailed, looking a little bummed out.

"Was?" I simply asked, prodding her to open up more. Was I pushing too much on a sensitive subject?

"A few years ago, suddenly, my parents became allergic to cats. Well, not really, but they had reactions when meeting cats like sneezing and getting a runny nose, stuff like that. So, they stopped bringing me here. But I could never detach myself completely from this place. Everything here makes me feel at home, surrounded by all these furry friends. Don't you think so?" she asked, tossing me back the ball I had thrown at her.

"It's actually my first time in a cat café, I must admit. Well, it's my first time on a date, so almost anywhere would be my first time. Though, I got to say, you did choose well. I can understand why you love this café so much." It was clear in my eyes that she had very good memories here and that she was sharing a part of herself in bringing me here. I wasn't well versed in the stories of the heart, but it struck me as a very trusting act for almost complete strangers. While it was true she was very forward, with what she tried last time I was at her house, I didn't feel like someone else would do the same thing with me. It was like she was already opening up, way faster than I was, even though nothing was going on between us. Nothing yet, anyway. Was that too quick? Should I be more trusting of her already because of it? Was that what I wanted? I wasn't even sure anymore.

My train of thought was interrupted by the creaking of the chair I was sitting on. In a slight panic, I looked left and right, trying to identify if it was going to shatter under me, but saw nothing of the sort. Instead, a black and white cat was rubbing its head on the wooden legs, clearly wanting to be pet. My hand instinctively went down to pat it on the head and it responded to me with a loud meow. I heard Camille snickering and turned my head to look at her.

"It certainly seems to like you," she commented with a smirk. I continued patting its head with containing my laughter. It was true, I really liked cats. There's a whole debate about being a cat person or a dog person and my answer to that is that I'm neither. I just like animals in general and am comfortable with most of them, given they are friendly. I wouldn't want to fall face to face with a wild bear, for example, but if it was friendly and liked to be pet, then why not? I pondered if Camille was the same or if she only liked cats for a few seconds and decided to ask her.

"Do you like other animals aside from cats or are you only a cat person?" I asked, still rubbing my hand on the softest fur I had ever touched. The cat purred loudly after every touch, now standing on two legs with its two front paws resting on my jeans. It had its eyes closed and I smiled at it before turning back to Camille to hear her answer.

"You know, I think I prefer cats, but I couldn't refuse a dog if it wanted to be pet," she answered with her right hand rubbing on her chin. "I think I also have a soft spot for ducks."

"I like cats, but I could see myself living with a dog, a lizard, anything really. Having a companion like that, it's something else, isn't it?" I trailed. I spoke quietly, almost like I didn't want Camille to hear or perhaps because I didn't want to remind myself of my previous losses. She seemed to pick up on that.

"Did you lo…"

Camille let out a little surprised cry as another cat, this one slightly larger than the previous ones jumped on her lap with absolutely no bother. It looked up straight at her and they held eye contact for an instant that seemed to take forever before the cat decided to lay down on her legs. She looked at me with a look that made me melt. Her eyes seemed as if she was about to cry, from happiness I assumed, and her mouth was distorted into what I could only describe as a deflated balloon. Yet, I knew she wasn't upset even if her entire face wanted to tear up and she was doing everything she could to hold it back and make it look like she was fine. I could only smile at her.

"It certainly seems to like you," I said, returning her own words against her. She started to laugh and I could swear I saw a little tear in the corner of her eye, but I joined in her laughter and lost sight of her. The cat didn't seem to mind the commotion at all and even started to purr loudly. Camille scratched its ears softly, earning herself the quietest meow.

For the next few minutes, we seemed to be lost in a sort of trance, both looking at the cat in complete silence. Neither of us wanted to disturb it, even if it didn't seem to be bothered by movement much, and we couldn't find anything else to say. It was like the simple fact that a cat got in the middle of our conversation made us forget how to talk. Starting the conversation back up would be difficult and awkward and, in that moment, I think neither of us wanted to be the one to break the ice. Luckily for us, our order came to save the day.

"Alright, folks, one lemonade and a lemon cake for the miss and one small coffee for the sir. I've also brought some milk and cream and there's already sugar on the table for you, okay?" said the waitress with a genuine smile. She glanced over at Camille's lap and saw the cat sitting there undisturbed. "I can see you got adopted by Luna. She's the favorite around these parts. Everyone loves her, though I got to say, she doesn't sleep on people's lap often so treasure this moment, my dear. It's the little things that make our day." With those words, the waitress left us with our furry companions and returned to her occupations.

"Luna, huh?" Camille said, looking down lovingly at the cat. "I understand why you're the favorite." Suddenly, the cat decided to leave and hopped back down. I managed to finally get a good glimpse of it. She was a marbled cat, grey on the top and white and brown on the belly. After walking away from us a little, she sat and turned to face me. Her eyes seemed to pierce deep into my soul, yet I also saw some mischief in there. She was certainly playful and very pretty. She had small patches of brown fur around her mouth, making it look like she had a little bit of a coffee sip which matched well with her being in a cat café. Camille's question made me turn away from Luna.

"Why did you order a coffee of all things?" she asked with a slight chuckle. "Isn't it already hot outside? Didn't you want a cold drink to freshen you up?"

"To be honest, I think I panicked a little back there," I answered with a laugh. "I just ordered the first thing that came to mind."

"I guess that makes sense. Still, what a terrible choice in this weather," she commented, shrugging.

"Hey, we're still in a café. At least its thematic," I said, defending my very questionable drink choice. I knew it was bad, but I couldn't admit defeat in front of her.

"Sure, Jack. Sure," she ended with another laugh. I couldn't help but join in. I felt a lot more comfortable now that a few minutes prior. We were talking, we were laughing, we were making some friends, everything was going a lot smoother than I had anticipated.

I didn't know how much time had passed since we came in the café, but most people had already left and we were among the last ones as the sun was setting down, tainting the entire shop with an orange coat. The previously busy atmosphere was now reduced to a few quiet conversations that could scarcely be heard coming from the downstairs area. Most of the cluttering coming from the kitchen had stopped as the closing time was getting closer. I hadn't realized it was already this late. Time had flown by so quick in Camille's company that it felt like an instant, like we were in an entire new dimension reserved only for us. A dimension where time didn't exist, and we could talk however long we wanted. That being said, our conversation was now dead silent, for a few minutes now. I distracted myself by looking at the cats running around the café, the staff taking a much-needed break and the busy street now starting to slow down. I noticed Camille was fiddling with an empty milk cup I had forgotten to put on the plate that came with my coffee. Feeling a little bit of that nervousness coming back, I ventured forth.

"Camille?" I asked softly. She raised her head to look at mine. Her eyes looked almost tired. Could she be bored? Was I not interesting enough, and she was now reconsidering her date choice? For a while now, she appeared to be thinking of something else, her responses shortened and brief where she had previously gone into greater detail and been inquisitive about things I said. Why had this change occurred? Was it to do with me? She seemed uncertain about what to say most of the time, like she was waiting for a question to pop up and it never did. I risked myself by asking, the anticipation driving me crazier by the minute. "Is something wrong?"

She sighed heavily and let the milk cup go, pushing it aside near the sugar container. She looked back at me. I could tell something was bothering her, she didn't feel the same as when she came in. "Look, Jack, I had a great time today. Honestly. I'm just wondering if…you have an answer for me yet? Because I don't want to go forward with this if you don't feel the same way."

Her question took me a little by surprise. An answer for what, exactly? Was she referring to what happened at her house or perhaps what she asked at school? It had to be, didn't it? We certainly did have a good time today, we seemed to have some chemistry at least. I didn't really know how to evaluate that, however. I had never been in a relationship before, was this a sign of a healthy relationship or was it simply a grace period where everything seems nicer than it really is? Did I really like Camille, or did I like the idea of being with her? After all, I was a little bit of a loner, hidden away in the back of the classroom while she was in the spotlight, shining bright for everyone. She was popular and I was the opposite of that. She didn't seem to mind, but was that simply a facade? It was undeniable I was attracted to her, most of the guys in our class would be, I could only assume, so what gave me the right to be with her instead of another? I suppose the answer was she had chosen to go on a date with me and not another guy, so that had to count for something, right? Then, a text message cropped up in my mind. Chloe's message. I still hadn't answered it yet, but it made me doubt myself for a second. She was a long-time friend, and we spent a lot of good times together, kind of like Camille now. Was I also attracted to her? Was it the same thing? We hadn't talked for months now, and she messaged me out of the blue. Could I really pass up this chance with Camille even though I knew nothing about what Chloe wanted to talk about? Why was I even thinking of that right now? How was it of any relevance to the current events? I shook my head internally. No, I couldn't. I might know nothing about love and the stories hearts can tell, but I would never if I didn't take this chance. My mind wandered to one particular day where we had an assignment in my French class. Pairs were selected randomly, and it just so turned out that I was paired with Camille and one other girl. I felt so nervous back then, I couldn't even say a single word of the entire period and ended up talking with them only through the assignment. Communication was very hard to say the least, but it was the best I could muster. To say I had a crush on Camille would be an understatement, before I had resigned myself to try and forget her, that is. She must have thought I was such a weird guy then and yet she had invited me on a date with her. Back then, I thought it was my only shot, the one and only chance I would get to talk to her and ask her out and I couldn't do it. I let it come and go without interfering and now, a second chance presented itself to me. Another shot at gathering the courage I didn't have then, another shot at standing up for myself. Frankly, I didn't know if it was right of me to think of it like that, but I decided to go through with it anyway. I looked back at Camille and met her eyes. They were now reassuring, concerned, lovely. I couldn't help but smile at her.

"Yes, I think I do."

She closed her eyes for a moment and sighed again. This time, however, I could tell it was in relief. She extended her hand towards mine and, realizing what she was doing, grabbed her with my own. She smiled again, the biggest one I had seen yet, and we walked together towards the exit, leaving our furry companions behind. It didn't matter. Nothing else mattered. For once in my life, I felt genuine joy at the thought of us sharing many more moments like this and enjoying every second of it in each other's company.

Chapter 5

And so, the exam week came and went. Lone Oak University, once the busiest establishment for miles around, became almost like a ghost town. There were only one or two classes taking exams at a time and some of them weren't even full. The once quiet hallways of the last week were even quieter now, almost echoing whenever someone took a step. I stood in front of my locker, gathering the last of my things before leaving for the summer break. I stopped for a second, taking it all in, as this was most likely the last time I was going to use this locker. Next year, I would be assigned another one and the comfortable locker hidden away that I currently had would be nothing but a fading memory. Finally deciding to close the door, I walked towards the staircase behind me. The doors opening resonated for a long time, even more than usual, a lingering feeling of nostalgia in the air. I made way to the door leading outside but found myself incapable of opening it. I didn't really know why, but this being my final exam of the year, leaving for the summer break tied together with the fact my summer was not going to be the way I had planned made this all a mess in my head. I thought back to the beginning of the week, when I took my French exam.

◊

Camille sat in her usual spot, just like the rest of us. For some reason, the teacher didn't bother putting us in alphabetical order or rearranging the room layout in any way. I guessed he really trusted us not to cheat or something. Quickly, he passed us the exam and I got right to it. We might have had a lot of time, but it could also drain very quickly, and I didn't want to mess around with this one. I was prepared, of course, no thanks to the *studying* session I had at Camille's house last week, but even so, I knew that taking my time could also backfire in these types of exams. After a while, I didn't know how long exactly, I looked up at Camille's seat and realized she was gone. I was a little surprised. I didn't expect her to finish so quickly, not that I doubted her abilities or anything like that, but I thought of myself as a pretty good student and even though I was almost finished, I wasn't totally done yet. How long ago did she step out of class? I got back to my exam, proof-reading more than anything and finally got up to turn in my copy a few minutes later. The teacher nodded silently as I handed in my paper and I went right for the door, backpack on my shoulders and trying not to disturb the other students. The door creaked loudly as it opened, and I wondered how I didn't hear it at all when Camille got out. Was I really that concentrated? Perhaps I had simply tuned it out to focus better. In the corner of my eye, I saw someone sitting on a bench nearby. They turned their head to face me as I stepped out and got up with a big smile. We walked away for a bit after nodding towards the end of the hallway.

"So, how did it go?" Camille asked enthusiastically.

"Well, worse than you from what I can gather. How did you finish so quickly?" I answered, also investigating.

"That's because of the multiple studying sessions I had, you know," she joked, jabbing me gently in the ribs.

"Yeah, I bet," I said sarcastically.

Instinctively, my hand moved towards her as we were walking, silently begging for her to grab it. Even though she didn't look, she noticed and soon after, our hands were locked in together. I forced myself to look in front of me and try to hide the biggest grin on my face, but to no avail. Everything around me seemed to melt away into darkness and I could only feel her hand in mine. I don't even know how I kept walking straight or knew when to turn.

"I didn't know you liked holding hands this much," Camille teased in a pretty loud voice. I instantly stopped and recoiled, looking around to see if anyone had heard her. Of course, nobody did. We were the only ones in the hallway and probably the only ones walking around in the entire school. Plus, exams weren't being held in this part of the building. Camille laughed a little at my embarrassment and then tugged gently on my arm. "Come on, let's go."

We were almost at the school exit now and before we reached the door, I spoke up. "Do you have anything else planned today?" I asked, with my other hand rubbing the back of my head. I didn't know why I always did that when I was embarrassed or nervous, it was kind of an automatic reaction I couldn't control even if I was aware of it. Camille stopped and looked at me.

"Do you?" she asked back with a slight grin on her face.

"Well, I thought that…maybe we could…you know…hang out together," I managed to say in the lowest voice I could possibly muster. Camille smiled even more and got really close to my ear.

"Yeah, I think we can do that," she whispered. She retreated and let go of my hand as she walked towards the door. I shuddered a little. Sometimes, she was really intimidating, and I didn't quite know what she was insinuating, but I got the general idea. I lightly jogged to catch up to her.

"Hey, no funny business, okay!" I said while running.

"Yeah, yeah, whatever, mister," she dismissed with a laugh. I soon joined in with her as we crossed the doors leading out into one of the best days yet.

◇

I snapped back to myself and realized I had been standing in front of the door for quite a while now. That was a few days ago and since then, Camille and I had been texting a lot. We were both comforting ourselves for the remaining exams to come and simply talking about whatever came up; the new games I was playing, the books she had read, movie and show recommendations, stories about silly past family gatherings and so on. It felt like we had already started to build something together, something I didn't fully comprehend yet, something mysterious but inviting. I wanted to know more about her every day and almost all my thoughts were of her. Even now, as I was exiting the school, I had stopped to think of Camille. My girlfriend. The concept still sounded funny to me, like a joke that went on for way too long that had started to morph into reality. At times, it felt like a dream, a distant illusion while at other times, she was standing next to me, holding my hand, and I knew it was genuine. Funny how the mind sometimes tries to play tricks on itself. I reached for the door and gave it a push, officially ending my first year of university as I stepped outside into the warm sun.

An instant wave of heat crashed on my shoulders. While it was shining bright in the afternoon sky, the sun rays hit as hard as a ton of bricks, and I slumped a little under the pressure. The asphalt of the courtyard seemed as hot as molten lava and I didn't even want to know how hot the metal bars of the bike racks were. When glancing ahead, my vision was slightly distorted as the heat rose from the ground, creating the illusion of water puddles on the ground. I reconsidered my decision to walk home for a moment, but ultimately carried on with my original plan and started to walk down the road that led to my apartment. It was around a thirty-minute walk so I knew that, by the time I would be home, I would surely need a shower. Yet, I still wanted to do it, simply to finally take in the fact I was done for school for three months and to start my summer vacation the right way. Adjusting my backpack, I soon turned onto a very familiar street.

The school was in the best parts of the city and adjacent to it was one of the richest neighborhoods in the city. The roads were completely straight, you could see the grey sidewalks stretch for a few hundred meters before coming to a stop. On either side of the street, rows of three-story houses rose from the ground, symmetrical and identical to their neighbors. They were all made of red bricks and had grey tiled roofs. A great number of windows occupied most of the facade. The lawns were all green and well-maintained and so were the hedges that acted as fences on either side of each house. A garage big enough for two cars completed the luxurious look. One of these days, I would have a house of my own. One where I could live with the family I would have, one where none of us would miss anything. However, I wouldn't want a house in this neighborhood. I had no interest in showing off my wealth and buying something this expensive. I wanted something a little more personal, more unique and not this copy-pasted look that every neighbor would have. I would want a house that I could call mine.

I reached for my water bottle hanging off the side of my backpack. The heat was striking a little harder than I had initially thought, and I silently thanked myself for filling it back at school. I didn't usually carry it with me but brought it today for some reason. I guess I subconsciously knew about the temperature of the day before even stepping out. Or maybe it was a fluke and I got lucky. Either way, I took a big gulp and a wave of coolness rushed through my body. I was only a few minutes into my walk and already the thirst was manifesting itself. I just hoped I had a big enough bottle and continued my way. Eventually, after reaching the end of the road, I turned right towards a small shopping center.

There were only a few shops, hardly a shopping center really, mainly some hardware store, a clothes shop, a convenient store and, most importantly, *The Tower*. It was a restaurant that popped up about a year ago and everyone was talking about it. They were famous for their hamburgers that stacked up high and, supposedly, they were also very good. I had never gone myself, but often wished I would drop by, just to see what the fuss was about. But I never did. I didn't really know why, I guess the opportunity to go there with someone never presented itself and I sure didn't want to go in alone. I found it weird to go dine by yourself, something about it was awkward to me. Going to get breakfast was about the limit for me, but sitting down at a table to enjoy a steak and wine? The thought would never cross my mind. The overwhelming aroma coming from *The Tower* pulled me in like a fishing rod reeling in the biggest fish of the pond. My feet didn't obey my command and marched straight towards the door. At the last second, I stopped myself in front of the door, unable to go in. The giant glass windows, imprinted with the logo; a tower of stacked hamburgers somehow spelling the name, was like a giant before me. I could see the inside of the restaurant, the staff rushing and trying to serve everyone, the customers deep in conversation sitting at every table and even the kitchen, at the very back, with more steam floating around than a sauna. I felt the pulling sensation again, my heart longing for it, for the experience. It called to me. I refused. Almost begrudgingly, my feet went back to the street, and I resumed my walk.

After a few more minutes of walking, I came across one of my favorite hangout spots; Sapphire Park. It was the biggest park in the city covered in blue daisies and blue daffodils, hence the name. They were arranged to form lanes that surrounded the entire park and, when the winds blew hard, you could find petals covering every inch of ground and grass. The park was very busy and numerous groups were scattered here and there; some were sitting at tables and enjoying a late lunch, some were playing soccer in one of the clear spots of the park and some were simply lying on the grass, not quite tanning but under this strong heat, it wouldn't take long for the skin to change color, so they had better watch out. Along the edges of the park were giant trees measuring two dozen meters high casting their shadow on benches dispersed in regular intervals. As I made my way through the ground hardened by the many footsteps that came before mine, I spotted a free bench and, on a whim, decided to sit down for a while and enjoy the fresh air and the surrounding scenery. Setting my backpack down at my feet, I took out my water bottle again and its content rejuvenated my drying lips. I closed the lid on the bottle and set it down beside me. Even though Sapphire Park was surrounded by roads, you didn't hear the cars much. The roads weren't very busy at this time of day and the sound of laughter coming from the kids playing nearby drowned what little you could hear of any engine. Bright and colorful, right in the middle of the park, was one of the biggest playgrounds I had ever seen. There were about ten different slides, what looked like a giant spiderweb made of red ropes all tangled up, dozens of stairs and other various games crammed into the multitude of walls composing the structure. I couldn't count the number of kids running around, but judging from the sound of their laughter, they were having a lot of fun. I couldn't help but smile. Often, in family gatherings, they would ask me if I wanted kids in the future and I always responded negatively, but I wasn't so sure of my stance now. Why was that even a question my relatives asked me? I didn't even have a career yet, I barely knew what I wanted to do with my life, let alone bring another human into this world. However, the more time passed, the more I became accustomed to the notion of having a family and getting my own house and everything related to that. Perhaps I was influenced by the variety of media that seemed to push this as the norm and the goal to achieve, yet it also felt natural to be yearning for all this. I still wasn't exactly sure of my decision, though. I turned my attention to several groups in the very back of the park, laying on picnic blankets in the heat of the sun. They certainly seemed to be having fun. The simple thought of food made my stomach growl, and I realized I hadn't eaten anything for lunch yet. I had better get back to my apartment and cook myself a nice meal. Maybe I had some leftovers in the fridge I could heat up else I could just make something quickly. Just as I was about to leave, I heard a voice to my left.

"Jack?"

I turned towards it, curious. It had a familiar ring to it like I had heard it before many times, but I couldn't exactly pinpoint who it was. My gaze set upon her, and my eyes widened. She was wearing a white shirt with the long sleeves rolled up and a red skirt held unto her waist by a small black belt. Her black stockings paired well with her shoes of the same color while her fiery-colored hair made her attire pop out even more. It was sliding to the right of her face, as it always had, and was tied behind her head, carefully avoiding the glasses that rested on her nose. She looked very surprised to see me, but so was I to be fair. I never thought I would randomly run into her, in the biggest park of the city no less, yet here she stood in front of me. For a moment, I couldn't figure out what to say. It seemed like words wouldn't come out of my mouth and I had to force myself to answer her.

"Chloe," I said with an equally surprised tone. "I wasn't expecting to run into you."

"Neither was I," she almost whispered to the ground. An awkwardness floated between us as we both didn't seem to know what to say. It had been so long since the last time we spoke, and it wasn't on the best of terms either. No wonder a tension seemingly palpable rested between us as the silence took its place once again before she broke it once more. "You…didn't answer my message," she said, looking back at me. Her tone almost indicated a question, like she was looking for a reason why I didn't, but I didn't have one.

"I meant to, I swear, it's just that…this past week has been kind of crazy and it's really overwhelming me a little," I admitted. I wasn't lying, not anything of the sort, I fully meant to respond to Chloe, but I had forgotten to do so and the past few days with Camille had been great, and it had slipped my mind. Being here, right now, she made me realize I should have taken the time to at least acknowledge her text from last week, but it was too late now.

She leaned forward with an incredulous look and readjusted her glasses with her left hand. The movement made her hair shine in the light of the sun and, just for a moment, I admired her beauty. But her mocking voice brought me back down to Earth.

"Crazy, huh? What, did the exams really give you that much trouble? For someone like you, they should have been no problem, right? I bet you studied hard for them like you always do," she said in a mocking tone.

Studying. Of course, I had studied for the exams, but the simple mention of the word brought me back to that evening at Camille's place, how I panicked and ran away. We were supposed to study back then, even though that was never Camille's intentions, but how was I to know?

"Yeah, I did study, of course. You got me, but…no, that's not it, exactly," I answered with a hand behind my head, embarrassed.

I didn't want to say everything to her, it was so sudden and even if we were best friends once, that time had passed once she cut contact with me for the past year. Things were not like they were back then, a time where we could tell each other secrets and could trust in the other. I longed for it, sometimes, when the night had fallen and the dreams hadn't taken me yet, but over the course of the year, I had learned to confide in myself and take care of it on my own.

"Surely then it's your job giving you extra shifts you didn't ask for again, right? They were always down to give you the absolute worst hours they could, didn't they?" she asked.

"Actually, job has been kind of on the low side lately, so that's not it either," I answered, letting my words hang in the air like I had something that followed, yet didn't. She seemed to pick up on that and probed me further.

"What is it, then? If it's not school or your job, what else could it be? I don't think your friends would do something bad to you and you don't have a girlfriend, so…" She let her sentence run and then looked at me straight, waiting for an answer that didn't come. I made an awkward smile and stared at the ground, wanting to get out of this situation as fast as possible. "Don't tell me…you have a girlfriend?" she asked with her hands covering her mouth. There was another long pause, a pause that seemed to last a lifetime, a pause that only I could break. And the only way was telling her everything, the truth of what happened in the last week.

"Uh…yeah. I do," I finally answered, still looking at the ground. I rose my head up to meet her eyes and was taken aback for a brief moment. Chloe looked…upset? The faintest glimpse of tears appeared at the corner of her eyes and her mouth was trending downwards. Barely perceptible, I saw her hands close into a fist and wondered what it could all mean. Before I could say anything, however, I was interrupted by her hands clapping loudly. I was startled a little and looked down at her hands, then back up at her face. She was now all smile and any trace of sadness had vanished, leaving only joy in its place.

"Oh wow, that's great! Congratulations! How long has it been?" she asked, excited.

"It's only been around…a week," I said, definitely not as excited as her to be revealing this much.

"Oh… so it's brand new then. Who's the lucky girl?"

I hesitated. Chloe was my friend, a long-time friend, once the only one I had, but this relationship was so new I didn't know if it was right to be telling everyone about it. I hadn't even told my parents or even my friends yet and I almost talked to them every day. If I hadn't bumped into Chloe today, how long would it have been until we spoke again? Was it right to tell her this much, given these circumstances? Did I want that? I cast away those thoughts and decided to just tell her. After all, it's not like Camille and I were hiding our relationship, I just omitted to mention it to most people. Was that deliberate or not? I wasn't quite sure.

"She, uh…. her name's Camille. She was in my French class this semester."

"Oh…I see."

That was her answer. I frowned a little at it. What was that supposed to mean? Did she know her or something? She once again appeared upset, but it was really hard to tell. She had joined her hands in a similar way to how people pray and held them close to her chest. Of all the things she could have said, this contrasted so much with her attitude a few seconds ago that it made me suspicious. I shook my head and investigated.

"Is there something wrong? Do you know her?"

"It's nothing."

"No, really, tell me. What's wrong?"

"I said it's nothing, forget it," she said in a more direct tone. It almost seemed like she snapped which took me a little by surprise. I didn't know Chloe to be quick to anger and the sudden dryness of her answers left me speechless. Once again cutting me before I even started talking, she continued. "Listen, Jack, I… I'm really sorry about pushing you away. I was wrong and my feelings were confused, and I didn't know what to do. But you were right. Kyle really was an ass, and it took me a long time to realize that. I think… there was a bit of a misunderstanding, and it got out of control. I'm sorry I didn't reach out to you before…I… I wish…" She paused for a second, taking a deep breath before continuing. "I wish this distance between us didn't exist, I wish we could go back to how things were last year, how they always were between us. Can we do that? Can we go back and pretend we never drifted apart?"

I took a few seconds to process what she just said. What misunderstanding could she be talking about? Everything was crystal clear to me so what could possibly cause some confusion there? I wasn't totally disinterested to know, but her proposing to rekindle like this was... out of the blue. After all, that was also what I wanted ever since she pushed me away for Kyle, but that all happened last year. Now, I didn't know exactly what I wanted; what Camille would say about this. Last year, I had no one in my life, but now things were different. The bond I once shared with Chloe had been severed already and I didn't know if it was possible to tie it back together anymore. It's not like I wasn't willing to try, but at this very moment, I couldn't answer positively. I looked at her, expectantly, even though I knew my answer would disappoint and it was all my fault.

"I'm sorry, I... don't think I can do that at the moment." I looked down, unable to keep eye contact with Chloe any longer. I could sense her gaze on me and the emotions rushing to my eyes. This wasn't how I had planned to reunite with her, this wasn't my intentions at all. This was all messed up.

"I understand."

I looked back up at her. She also seemed to be holding back emotions, but I couldn't be certain as I was really concentrating on keeping mine inside. I was surprised by her answer. I thought she would have protested more, tried to convince me, argue with me, but she was simply accepting my decision. Something that, a year prior, I couldn't do.

"Well then, I guess I'll uh... see you around. I'll text you soon," she said turning around and starting to walk away.

"I promise I'll answer this time," I almost shouted back. I didn't know how much my word was worth to her at this point, but I felt compelled to tell her regardless. Was that wrong of me to assume? Chloe stopped in her tracks and turned around, the saddest smile garnishing her face. Then, with her hands in her pocket, she walked away on the shadowy dirt path, raising little patches of dust behind her. All around me, the sounds of laughter and conversation seemed even louder than before, and I sat back down on the bench for a moment. I stared in front of me at the fountain and got lost in the movement of the flowing water. Something about water always calmed me, be it the ocean waves or a simple pool, it reflected the sky above and the most beautiful thing nature had to offer in my opinion. I didn't know how long I stayed like that, but it must have been a while because my butt was sore from the hard wood planks I was sitting on. Only being about halfway through my walk, I still had some ways to go, and it wouldn't help to be walking around with sore muscles. I got up and stretched my arms and legs, grabbed my backpack and went on my way, crossing runners or cyclers on the dirt path, kids playing with various balls and several people reading in the shade of the trees. Even as I crossed them, I didn't see them for my mind was occupied by something else. I kept thinking how Chloe reacted when I mentioned Camille. It seemed odd to me, but I couldn't put my finger on it. Did they know each other somehow? We did all go to the same school after all, but I didn't know everyone there. I would have to ask Camille about it. Maybe she could enlighten me on this whole situation.

Eventually, after a few more minutes of walking, my apartment complex finally came into view. If I was honest, I almost didn't notice it. In fact, I didn't even know how I got where I was, my legs seemingly walked on their own while my mind was drifting away in confused, incoherent thoughts. The conversation with Chloe still resonated in my head. *"Oh...I see,"* she said. I didn't know what I was expecting her to answer, but that certainly wasn't it. I always had a hard time deciphering emotions from conversation alone and this one was no exception to the rule. Chloe sounded sad, yet excited. Upset, yet bouncing up for joy and congratulating me. What was that all about? Even as I opened the door and took the staircase up to my apartment, the answer to these questions didn't come. Lost in thought, I climbed up as a force of habit, not even realizing what I was doing. I took out my keys and unlocked my front door, opening it up with a loud squeak that resonated in the empty hallways connecting my apartment to the neighbors. I stood there for a second, contemplating the luminous mostly barren rooms before me.

Finally, I set foot inside, taking off my shoes as soon as I closed the door and locked it. Immediately as I got in, I breathed in the familiar scent of home. Every home has one, that distinctive smell that hits you as soon as you come back after a while. It's a smell that's hard to describe and it's also different for other people coming over to visit. Only the people in that living space can truly experience it. It was good to be back home after finishing all my exams, yet I still had this lingering weight on my shoulders and, while my backpack was admittedly still on my back, setting it down next to my chair lifted no pressure at all. It slumped down heavily with a bang, pushing my chair a little as I sat down on it. I turned on my computer with a slight sigh. As it was booting, I rubbed my face, trying to wash away this feeling that hung around my chest, but to no avail. Maybe some browsing on the web to get my mind off things would help me put this conversation past me. I opened the browser and started a video while also logging on to social media. There, an image that pretty much took the entire screen space popped into view. It was of a beautiful night sky and a shadowy forest, a scene taken right out of a fantasy book cover. In big bold letters, a date was highlighted and under it, a small description of what it was could also be read. I leaned back in my chair, wondering for a moment. It didn't take me long to figure out what I wanted to do and, soon afterwards, the phone was dialing. It didn't ring long, but it certainly felt like it as I was very anxious for her to pick up. Soon, her voice came through to my right ear.

"Hello?" she said.

"Hi, it's me," I said, nervously. This wasn't the first time I had called her, yet it still made me nervous every time. I didn't like phone calls much.

"Oh, hi Jack! How is it going? You all finished up with exams?"

"I'm doing…well, it's uh…yeah, I'm doing fine. Yeah, I'm all finished with the exams. Hey, listen, I have something to ask you."

"Yeah, what is it?"

"There's this ad I just saw about an opportunity to go stargazing this weekend. It's been a while since I went myself, but I figured it…might be nice for a…. date or, you know, yeah. Um, do you…?"

"Yes! Yes, of course I want to go! When is it?"

I smiled a little at her excitement. Camille had always been forward with the dating aspect of our relationship so far and it felt nice to be inviting her this time. I felt she liked it too and was delighted to be going on something like this. I hadn't gone stargazing in a long time, a few years now, but I was adamant on making this a fun experience for both of us. After all, our first date went well, I couldn't let her down with this one. I made sure to tell her the date and time and she wrote it down carefully. Afterwards, there was a little awkward silence that lodged itself between us. Even though we were far apart and speaking through phones, I could feel the conversation slipping away. I didn't really know what else to say. Just as I was about to say something to hang up, she broke the silence instead.

"Jack?" she said, asking if I was still there.

"Yeah?" I answered quickly.

"I…" There was a little pause. A pause that took centuries to finish until eventually, she resumed her thought. "Never mind. See you on Saturday!"

Before I could say anything back, she had hung up the phone. I was left a little speechless for a moment. That was a little sudden to end the conversation like that. What did she even want to say? Nothing I could really do now and sending her a text asking what she wanted would be rude, I thought, so I let it go. Afterall, we were going to see each other soon enough and it was going to be one of the best nights of my life, I could feel it. I didn't know how, but I did. The conversation prior to this one had vanished from my mind as it was purely focused on the next few days and preparing mentally for another date with my girlfriend.

Chapter 6

We took a bus to get to our destination; a grassy hill located on the outskirts of town. The area wasn't developed yet, and I hoped it wouldn't for a while, because this was one of my favorite spots to go stargazing. I had gone multiple times in the past, but I never anticipated it quite like this time. Even as the lights went by and the streets flowed under the wheels of the bus, I couldn't help but move in my seat a little. It was the first time I was going with someone other than my dad, it was also the first time I had invited someone on a date. Needless to say, I felt a little pressure on me to make the date go as smoothly as I could, task I didn't know if I was prepared for.

The bus was nearly empty. Apart from Camille and I, there were only three other people. There was a guy at the back listening to some obnoxiously loud music and, even though he had headphones, we could hear the beats of his song from where we were. Across from us, another man seemed to have just gotten off work as he was still wearing his uniform. He was staring out the window, probably lost in thought about his day or perhaps looking forward to a day off tomorrow. At the front, a woman was talking to the bus driver who was enthusiastic about finally having a conversation. Most people in public transport kept to themselves and it was rare to see someone engaging with the drivers. It was common courtesy to thank them as you get off the bus, though, but I never really got involved any more than that. Even then, it took me a few times to finally get you were supposed to say thanks. The first few times, I silently got off and, while nobody said anything, I could simply feel something was off. My head turned to look at Camille. She was looking away through the window as well, her gaze fixated on a constantly moving point outside. Her long blonde hair covered her ear and cascaded on her shoulders, meeting the bus seat a little. When she felt my eyes staring at her, she turned around with a sly smile on her face. Her eyes met mine and she looked away for a moment and, when she turned again to face me, I answered with the most genuine smile I could. She smiled back while closing her eyes and silently held out her hand forward. I felt it move on my lap, as slow as a snail, like she was timid about it. My hand met hers and our fingers tangled as we both enjoyed this quiet moment.

We got off the bus a few minutes after that. Since it was on the outskirts of town, the hill in question was a few minutes of walking distance from where we were. Hand in hand, we started moving towards it. I felt like I wanted to say something, like this moment was going to get awkward if I didn't start saying something, anything, yet I also enjoyed the simple fact she was present, walking with me with her hand in mine. I felt like this physical contact brought us closer together. Normally, I didn't really like other people touching me unnecessarily, but holding hands with my girlfriend was an exception to this weird quirk I had. I felt like it was different, like it meant something more than the physical contact and that made it okay in my mind. I wondered what she was thinking right now. Was she thinking the same thing? Highly doubtful, I knew, but I wondered still. It's a simple activity, walking, but it's a lot more enjoyable when you get to share it with someone you like. Even this silence right now was something I would rather not break. Not until it was time, anyway.

We reached the hill soon after. Climbing to the top was a lot more difficult that I remembered, but the sheer sight unfolding before my eyes as I got to the summit was worth it. Even though it was mostly dark outside, the lights of the city in the horizon were like a reflection of the sky above, a multitude of yellow dots in a sea of black. We stood there for a few moments, recovering our breaths and looking out at the sights all around us. I knew I wasn't in shape, but this activity made it all the clearer to me that my cardio could really use some work. Perhaps I could go for a run around my neighborhood some other time. I took out the blanket we brought from my backpack and spread it on the grass, pushing it down with my weight as I laid down on it, soon followed by Camille who let out a huge sigh as her head hit the blanket-covered grass.

"That was way harder than I thought," she said with a laugh. "I don't know why, but I pictured the hill you were talking about to be a lot smaller."

"Actually, I thought the same. From memory, it didn't go so high, but then again, my memory isn't the best," I replied jokingly.

We shared another moment of silence with each other. The sort of tension I felt earlier was now gone and I was simply comfortable lying next to her, even if it meant not doing anything. Camille broke the silence again.

"The sky is so pretty tonight," she said. I could tell she was looking up with a great sense of wonder from just her tone of voice alone. I looked straight up to evaluate her statement and found out she was correct. There were no clouds floating about to block our view and more stars than it was possible to count swarmed the black night sky. The moon, not quite full yet, was shining bright among them, covering us with its light.

"It really is," I answered, trailing off my sentence. "This reminds me of when my dad used to take me stargazing when I was little." I heard Camille turn her head to face me, but I continued looking up. "Every year, he would take me here, on this very hill and we would look up at the stars together. Sometimes for hours. It was one of my favorite things about summer vacation. Everyone kept talking about going on trips abroad or going camping or just hanging out at their friend's place to play games, but I was always focused on this. I never got to spend much time with my family, they were always busy, so this was one of the only times where my dad would do an activity with me. Ever since he moved away a few years ago, I tried coming back a few times, but it simply isn't the same without someone else tagging along…" I stopped myself from talking any further as I realized I was monologuing, almost talking to myself. "Oh, I'm sorry, I didn't mean to ramble on," I said as I turned to face Camille. She smiled at me with a little shy smile.

"You don't have to apologize. Besides, I did talk about when I was a kid back at the café, so it's only fair that you talk about yourself here."

"You're right, I'm probably just overthinking it because I'm still a little nervous. It is only my second date, after all," I said, trying to justify my actions for no reason. Suddenly, I felt Camille's shoulder hit mine as she scooted over next to me, startling me a little. She giggled shyly and I felt her hand wander up to my chest and then retreating to her side. As I felt her fingers move away, I almost wanted to tell them to come back, to stay, but somehow, I couldn't. Instead, my mind decided to ask one of the questions that floated around inside it for quite a while now.

"Hey, Camille?" She turned back towards me as I actively avoided her eyes until I had finished my question. "There's something I'd like to ask you. Actually, I've wanted to ask you for a little bit, but I couldn't find a good time. Um…" I paused for a second, gauging her reaction, but she kept silent. I felt myself swallow and decided to proceed. There was no turning back now. "What made you approach me initially?"

The words floated in the air and faded into nothing. Camille had heard them, I was sure, but she didn't answer. Should I not have asked her that? Did I break the moment we had just a second ago? Why did I have to mess up everything all the time? Hesitantly at first, she answered my question.

"When I first met you, I thought you were kind of weird. We had the group project together and the only thing you did was nod at everything I said, and you didn't even say a word. You did your part, but that was pretty much it. No interaction at all. Yet, after that, I couldn't stop stealing looks your way, observing what you were up to and wondering what was going through your mind." She paused for a second and looked away, trying to find a way to articulate her thoughts. Her feet were moving around on the blanket, messing it up with each swipe. She put her blonde hair still visible in the moonlight behind her ears and turned back to me. "I waited a long time to see if these thoughts and feelings were real and when I couldn't figure out if they were, I decided to just go for it and ask you directly. As soon as we talked at your locker, though, I knew. Knew that they weren't fake, even though I was extremely embarrassed at the time."

"You certainly didn't act like it," I said, teasingly. "If anything, you seemed so confident in yourself that I was intimidated by you."

"Did I look intimidating as I ran away as soon as I gave you my address?" she asked.

"Not exactly, no," I answered with a laugh.

"There you go," she concluded, joining in my laughter.

I let the conversation die down a little, more for my sake than hers. My heart was pounding in my chest, I felt like I had just come off the harshest rollercoaster of my life. The cool air brushed against my skin and made the blades of grass all around us dance and sing. Above us, the tree leaves rustled, almost sounding like rain, but there were still no clouds in sight. I turned to face Camille once more, somehow, I couldn't stop looking at her and then looking away like it was some sort of prank. She turned too and our noses could almost touch we were so close. I looked into her eyes and saw nothing else than a reflection of my own feelings like two giant mirrors piercing through my soul.

"You know," I started, my voice as soft as the wind, almost like I didn't want her to hear it. "I actually had a crush on you the very first day I saw you."

"Really?" she asked, both surprised and curious. I felt like there was something else in her tone but couldn't quite put my finger on it.

"Yeah…The first time I saw you walk in that room…it was almost like time froze still. You were wearing your striped shirt; you would wear it often on Fridays I noticed, and when you walked in, you had this sort of aura about you. I couldn't take my eyes off you. And then, we made the slightest eye contact and I looked away instantly. You probably didn't even notice me back then, but I sure did notice you. I just…never had the courage to ask you out like you did with me."

"I'm not sure if I should be creeped out or find you cute," Camille laughed at me.

"A mix of both, I guess," I said, joining in her laughter. She nudged closer to me, resting her head on my chest. Instinctively, my arm went around her behind her back, cradling her close to me. After a few seconds, I realized what I was doing and froze, my hand halfway down her back at this point. I didn't know what to do. Was this okay? Was it too forward? Was I making her uncomfortable?

"Don't be so stiff, Jack. Relax," she said, not even moving her head at all. My muscles loosened up and Camille moved her head a little to signify her appreciation. We laid there for a while, our breathing slowly synchronising itself as we stopped thinking about it. It really was a beautiful night and now that the sun had set, it would soon be high time to spot shooting stars. As I was about to mention that to Camille, she went ahead.

"When are we going to see shooting stars?"

"It should start really soon, actually. I was just about to tell you, too, you were too fast for me," I teased a little. "There was one more thing I forgot to tell you. My dad and I used to play this little game when we went stargazing. We would look up at the sky and count the number of shooting stars we would see in a given time. Whoever saw the most would win. What do you say we do that too?"

"What does the winner win?" she asked, suddenly very curious about the whole thing. She perked up, backing away from my chest and standing on her elbows, looking directly at me.

"Um, we usually just declared a winner, there wasn't really anything to win, per se," I answered.

"Alright then, what about this; whoever loses has to kiss the winner."

It took me a while to process what she had just said and even when the words reached me, they just didn't seem to make any sense. Then it hit me, and I stood up, now sitting on the blanket.

"Kiss? You mean like a real kiss? Like on the lips?"

"Well, yeah, where else would you kiss?" she answered like it was the most obvious thing in the world.

She had given me a peck on the cheek before, but never a full kiss and the simple possibility that she would kiss me for the first time was enough to make my heart burst out of my chest. I almost couldn't contain myself and answered a little too excitedly.

"That sounds like a great idea!"

"I knew you'd like it," Camille chuckled. "But I'm not about to lose to you, mister, even if you do have more experience than me. Better watch your back," she threatened with a finger.

Just as she was finished, I caught some movement at the corner of my eye and turned towards the sky. The first shooting star of the night flew by and disappeared in an instant, leaving me smiling. Camille looked puzzled and confused, but before she could even ask, I looked back at her smugly.

"One," I said, trying to contain my laughter. Camille turned around to face the black sea above and, seeing nothing, she turned back towards me.

"That's not fair! That doesn't count!" she pleaded.

"Oh, I believe it does. How does it feel to be losing?" I asked her.

"You'll tell me at the end of the night, won't you?" she answered with a challenge.

It was on. Now normally, if both people are paying attention, they can count the same amount of shooting stars go by as there was no rules stating they count only for the first person to see them. And so, Camille and I were staring at the sky, the stars shining bright and the moon even brighter, trying desperately to distract the other by shoving them aside or making them talk about something else. The conversations flowed really well, even better than the other time at the café, and I learned a lot about Camille.

She usually wore dresses as she found them lighter than pants and more comfortable. She didn't like winter because of the cold and the snow and would rather spend some time in the sun than inside, freezing under a blanket. Her favorite color was yellow. She didn't like seafood and preferred to eat simple, easy to prepare meals rather than cooking something that took hours to make. Her absolute favorite flavor was lemon, a fact I had already experienced at the café. She was well-off and liked to spend on herself to buy clothes whenever the summer arrived and would usually go shopping with her friends once a week.

In return, I told her a little about myself. I liked autumn the most because the tree leaves were changing colors and taking a walk through a forest during this time was a sight to behold. My favorite color was green and, just like her, I didn't really like extravagant meals. However, unlike her, it was mainly because of my laughable cooking skills and I was living on my own. I told her how my father had left a few years back and the situation not being the best with my mother, I decided to rent an apartment and live by myself to finish my studies. I liked hanging out at the bar with my friends, though I wasn't a heavy drinker. I liked to go out and make plans with other people but was also perfectly happy being at home every so often. We talked for a while, but the distraction strategy didn't work. Both of us saw the exact same amount of shooting stars. But it didn't matter. Because I was going to win off the very first one and was secretly hoping that Camille would forget. Right now, the score was 7-6 in my favor. Time was running out. In just a few minutes, the alarm I set on my phone would ring, sounding my victory and Camille would have to kiss me. As the clock ticked on, my heart pounded faster with apprehension. I had never kissed anyone before and wanted to make a good impression, but I didn't know how. Was there even technique to it or was I just overthinking things, as usual? Probably the latter, but what if it was the former? Would Camille be disappointed? *Hold on a second*, I thought, *she's the one who has to kiss me, not the other way around! She should be thinking about all this stuff, not me!* I could sense she was getting restless, moving around on the blanket. Perhaps she was also getting nervous? I silently smirked. She was kind of cute, in a way, acting all tough and confident, but deep inside, she was as nervous as I was. Or so I thought.

In an instant, she jumped on me, straddling me around my waist, pinning me down by holding my shoulders to the ground. I couldn't even react and, while she wasn't the heaviest, she put all her strength into keeping me down. I let out a startled gasp and my legs flailed around aimlessly. Under us, the blanket was getting pulled by my feet dragging it around.

"What are you doing? I can't see anything," I said in a slightly more panicked voice than I would have liked.

"Exactly, if you can't see anything, you can't see any more shooting stars," she said so confidently like she had just figured out the best strategy for this game.

"Well, you can't really see the sky either, right? How do you plan on winning like this?" I asked with a snicker.

Camille let go for a moment and I took my chance. Gathering all my strength in my left arm, I pushed us so we would roll to the side, with her now under me and myself on top in the same position she was in before. The maneuver surprised her too and she let out a little scream mixed in with laughter. I wanted to keep her on the ground as well but didn't want to apply too much force on her either, so I ended up going in the middle. She didn't really struggle to get loose which I found weird. If we both couldn't see the sky, then surely that meant I would win, right? Was she intentionally throwing the game? Did she have another plan in mind? By now, there was only a minute or so left, my alarm would ring, and it would be over. What could she possibly do in this position?

Just as I was wondering all these questions without answers, her face suddenly brightened up and a giant smile plastered her face. I was thoroughly confused now.

"Two more!" she loudly exclaimed. "Two more just flew by!"

I turned around, still on top of her, but the starlit black sky stared back at me with no traces of any shooting stars. I scanned it again, desperately trying to find anything, but either my eyes deceived me, or they had gone by already as I turned to face Camille again, empty-handed. Then, in perfect comedic timing, my alarm rang, signaling the end of the game. She had won. I couldn't believe it. How could this have happened? It was almost poetic, in a way. I was overconfident and lost to chance, a well-timed misfortune, some would say. Although, even losing in this situation was nothing alike true misfortune, as it was either kiss or be kissed. There were certainly worse punishments out there.

"I win," said Camille with the biggest grin on her face. "Now you have to kiss me." Her voice was simply the cutest, a mix of confidence and embarrassment which made her blush as the words left her lips. Her lips. I was staring at them, incapable of taking my eyes off them. Slim, inviting, wet, red like fire and intimidating. I was just now realizing that she had put on lipstick, making them pop out even more than usual. Did she somehow plan this? No, she couldn't have, how could she have known that we would play this game?

I didn't know much in the matter of kissing, but from what I did see in various forms of media, they usually close their eyes while they do it. Apart from that, it was entirely foreign to me. Camille's blonde hair was scattered about on the blanket, and I looked straight into her eyes. They, too, were inviting me, almost pleading me to get closer like a siren's song to a boat's crew. I felt her hands move along my back and push me down lightly. I realized I had let go of her shoulders and she was now back in control yet didn't move. I lowered my head, slowly getting closer and closer to her, our breath now syncing up. I also knew to come at her in an angle, rather that's what they would do in movies, and so I did the same. My vision got dark as I closed my eyes, now hovering above her lips, taking a second to gather the courage to finally give my first kiss.

Until she took it first.

Her hands pulled me down onto her, wet lips now caressing my own. The contact sent an electric shock in my entire body and, while I did open my eyes in surprise, I closed them just as quickly. The sensation was entirely new, nothing I had ever experience before. In that moment, love seemed to spill out of my heart and channeled into my lips. My arms that used to be tense, loosened up a little and my hands moved up to caress her head. She seemed to attack me, like she was hungry for something, her head moving in some sort of circular motion as she kissed me again and again. I could do nothing more than try my best to respond, but it felt like trying to tame an animal. Ferocious, hungry, wild. Just as I was getting into her rhythm, something strange entered my mouth. Something foreign, unknown, something I wasn't expecting. My mind stopped for a second, trying to figure out what it was until I realized it was her tongue. She was trying to find mine, trying to dance with it as our lips were locked into one another. I responded, moving it to meet hers and they twirled around each other. Yes. I could get used to this. If this was kissing, then I wanted to kiss her a lot more. Why hadn't we done this before now? I guessed that I was more to blame on this one for my lack of experience, but now that I had a taste of it, I didn't think I could let it go. Suddenly, her tongue retracted, and our lips parted ways. I got up slightly to look at her and noticed we were both panting. Her eyes were shining as she stared into mine. I could see the love spewing out from her and she must have seen the same in me. She smiled the most genuine smile she had ever given me, and I tried to smile back. It was probably a horrible, disfigured grin as I was barely able to formulate any coherent thoughts, let alone concern myself by the look of my face.

"Was that your first kiss?" she asked in a soft voice, almost like a whisper as if she didn't want even the trees to hear her. I took a few seconds to process what she said.

"Um…yes, it was," I answered in embarrassment. I thanked my luck that it was dark outside, and she couldn't see my skin clearly. I was probably even redder than a tomato.

"Not bad for a first time," she said as she winked at me. "Did you like it?"

"Very much, yes. I'd…like to kiss you again, for sure," I answered hesitantly, not sure if the words I was saying were appropriate or not.

"I certainly feel that," she said with a smug tone. What did she mean by that? She could feel that? I was very much confused as she started to move her hips up and down, making me look down there myself. Then, I saw it and blushed. The bulge in my pants had grown…a lot since we started kissing and it was now resting on her stomach. My heart stopped for a second, panicking and unsure what to do. Should I apologize? I should probably get up, right? What if she was now disgusted by me? Before I could get off her, she rose, her head now very close to mine. I felt her hot breath on my ear, and she got close.

"We'll keep that for next time," she whispered gently. She backed off and looked at me, smiling with a wink while trying to contain her laughter. I must have been making some dumb face or something, but I didn't care. I got up promptly and stood as stiff as a stick, extending my hand towards her to help her get up which she took it without hesitation. She got up and bent over to pick up the blanket from the grassy hill, shaking it a little to blow off the blades of grass that stuck to the bottom, and folded it back into a little square. Meanwhile, I was stood there, incapable of moving, seemingly joining the trees that stood over us even though I had no leaves, no branches and no bark. Camille's voice pulled me back in.

"Jack, come on," she said, inviting me over with her head. My legs moved on their own and I walked towards her, still processing what she had just said and everything that just happened. I still couldn't get over the kiss and how it felt. In that moment, I sensed we were connected like never before, like she shared a part of herself in that kiss, like her feelings mixed with mine had formed something new. It was truly a night to remember.

On the bus ride back home, my thoughts wandered back to the final moments of the game. The part where she said she saw two shooting stars. Did she really see them? Did it matter? It did not. I was simply happy that it happened at all and, even though the ride was mostly silent, it was almost like I could hear her thoughts whenever we made eye contact. When we parted ways, she kissed me again. It was less electrifying, less vigorous, but just as lovely. I thoroughly enjoyed these small moments now as they let me switch my mind off and live only in the present, forgetting about all of life's troubles, if only for a short while. Whatever the case may have been, it was always worth it. However, all good things come to an end, and we split up for the night. I was already longing to get her company again and even though I didn't know when that time would come yet, I eagerly awaited it.

Chapter 7

We arrived at the busy park as the sun was shining at its highest point in the sky. The hot rays hit us hard as we made our way onto the grassy field before us. Scattered about, numerous tall trees offered some much-needed shade where most people were sitting already. There were also a few picnic tables all around the park, some were moved into a more comfortable spot while others laid in the sun with nobody around them. A few dirt trails snaked their way through the park, dividing it into sections and providing clear paths to cross it. Some people were walking along them, trying to keep moving under the hot sun, while some were hiding in the shade and waiting for the heat to pass. Some were using bikes to get around, raising little dust clouds as they rode through, carefully avoiding the pedestrians walking at their own pace. Along the paths, sturdy wooden benches were dispersed and offered a place to sit for anyone wanting a short break, to read a book or simply admire the scenery. A playground surrounded by a giant sandbox was in the center of the park and there were many kids running around in the area, causing an understandable ruckus which awarded a slight smile on my face.

I don't know if we got extremely lucky or found a spot nobody else wanted, but we managed to snag some space under one of the trees just on the outskirts of the playground. We settled down and I let my backpack drop to the dirt floor covered in various roots, grass and pinecones. Camille put down the picnic basket she had been carrying and grabbed one of the corners of the blanket I had brought in my backpack. Together, we unfolded it and carefully laid it down, trying to avoid any of the bigger roots jutting out of the ground. Camille opened up one of the sides of the basket and started taking out everything one could need to make a sandwich; some butter, mayonnaise, mustard, some ham, some turkey, some chicken, freshly cut tomatoes, lettuce. I couldn't believe how much stuff she had brought, but then again, it was probably better to have too much than not enough. I took out the little cooler bag from my backpack. I didn't even know how I got it, but I found it in my apartment not too long ago and figured now was probably the best opportunity to use it. From it, I took out two drinks, one for me and one for Camille. I still had another one, just in case, but I figured one for each of us would be enough.

"This spot is great, isn't it?" I asked as I set down the drinks on the blanket.

"It really is, I don't know why nobody else wanted it," she wondered aloud. "Do you think it's because of the playground nearby? The noise, maybe?"

"Hard to say, I don't think it's that bothersome," I answered while shrugging my shoulders.

Camille finished taking out all the condiments for the sandwich and turned around to look at me, finally noticing the drinks in front of me. She studied them for a few seconds, then turned her gaze to me with a puzzled look on her face.

"Didn't you say you bought the drinks?"

I looked at her with an even more confused look on my face.

"I... did?"

"Did you forget about my drink, then? I don't see the iced tea that I asked for."

My heart skipped a beat as I looked down at the drinks before me. There was an orange Crush for me and what I thought was an iced tea was in fact a yellow can of Fanta. I knew for a fact that the other can I had wasn't iced tea either. How could I possibly make a mistake this dumb? She would not be happy about this...

"It seems I confused your drink with this Fanta," I said, slowly like that would make it better. "Um, do you still want it? I also brought a can of..."

Camille sighed heavily in disappointment while rolling her eyes. I could tell simply by the sound that she was really annoyed, and I didn't know what else to do at this point other than staring at the dirt.

"Fine, give me the Fanta," she said with a voice as sharp as a recently edged knife. I handed it to her and, as she grabbed it, nearly took my whole hand with her too. "You really need to find a way to remember things better, because this is getting ridiculous now."

I pouted, but she was right. I had a hard time remembering that kind of stuff and, even though I made a list of everything I had to buy, including the drinks, I only put *Drinks for picnic* on my list and that didn't quite help when I got to the aisle in the store. I could have texted her to ask what she wanted, to make sure, but I didn't want to bother her again about it as I had already asked once before. My eyes were glued to the ground in what could only be described as shame, but I found that to be a little bit excessive.

Embarrassment, maybe, but it's not like I did anything extremely wrong, right?

"I'm sorry, I didn't mean to buy the wrong drink for you, I'll make sure to text you next time to confirm," I said more to the blanket than Camille.

"It's fine, but now you won't get any ham. Ham is only for the good boys," she teased.

"What? That's not fair! I like ham the most!" I said in protest as I got closer to her, trying to yank the ham pack away from her. She laughed at me and held it close to her while turning around, preventing me from getting any. I tried to get a hold of it, but she was now curled up, fully protecting the ham like her life depended on it. Well, two could play at this game. I grabbed a hold of the tomatoes she had cut for herself and went to the other end of the blanket.

"Well then, you don't get any tomatoes," I teased back. Camille turned around as fast as a deer that hears the hunter and looked straight at me. If her eyes could kill, then I would surely be her first victim.

"You don't even like tomatoes," she said while squinting her eyes, holding her breath and folding her arms in the cutest pout I had ever seen. After a few seconds, she lifted her head up towards the top of the tree. "Fine, you can have your ham. But in exchange, I get my tomatoes."

"Sounds like a deal to me," I said, getting closer to her as we both started laughing at the absurdity of the situation.

The rest of the sandwich making process went by smoothly. Finally with our lunch in hand, we sat side by side, looking in the distance at nothing, appreciating the breeze with the sound of people enjoying their days fading in the background. We ate in silence at first. I don't know if it was because Camille was still a little annoyed at me or for another reason, but I let her break the silence in her own time which she did soon after.

"This really is the best kind of weather, isn't it? The sun, the breeze, what more could you ask for?" she said looking up at the clear, blue sky.

"Oh yeah. I'm glad we came here today on our day off work. Speaking of which, how is that going for you?" I asked, wanting to move the conversation a little further.

"Well, nothing too exciting happening. The usual clients coming in and screaming about anything and everything, complaining the pumps aren't working or we don't have their specific flavor of chips, you know. I am kind of tired of it, but you have to make money somehow, right?" said Camille, gradually slumping her shoulders as she talked.

"Yeah, that sucks. At least you get some nice regulars to brighten your day, right?"

"Of course, just as there are bad clients, there are also good ones. There's this really sweet old lady that comes around at the same time every week and she is the most caring person I've ever met. Plus, I usually get shifts around with Tom, so that also helps me get through it all."

"What do you mean?" I asked out of genuine concern. I didn't consider myself of the jealous type, but the way she said it seemed weird to me. Was the glint in her eye there because she mentioned the old lady before or was it something else?

"Oh, he just does his job really well and we can joke around a lot while still getting all the work done. When I'm paired with others, they're so stoic and rigid, almost like I'm working with robots. It's weird."

"I can get behind that. My coworkers are also the reason why I stayed at my job for so long. If it weren't for them, I think I would have quit a long time ago," I said in agreement.

"Job is getting you down too?" she asked.

"Yeah..." I answered with a sigh. "You know, I'm fine working on the weekends when school is going on but working during the summer really gets me down. I feel boxed in while there's all this great weather outside and I can't be a part of it," I explained while motioning to the park. My job was monotonous, just stocking shelves, completing transactions, processing movie returns. Most of the time, the store was empty, and I was the only one there. Then, occasionally, a co-worker's shift would overlap with mine and it would be the best time of the day. Unfortunately, that didn't happen very often.

"I feel the same way, which is all the more pleasant spending the day with you," said Camille while resting her head on my shoulder. I awkwardly turned my head to try and look at her and she smiled at my attempt. I only caught a glimpse of it at the corner of my eye, but that was enough for me. Even though we hadn't finished our sandwiches yet, I leaned in for a quick kiss and she eagerly met me halfway by shifting her head, our lips briefly touching and parting with a smooch. I smiled as I backed up and she lifted her head to take another bite. We enjoyed another moment of silence before she broke it again. "When I think summer is almost already over, I can't help but feel a bit sad. There are so many more things I wanted to do," she said with a pout.

"Well, there's still the rest of July and almost all of August left. That's plenty of time, right? I know we have to work, but surely there will be more opportunities like this in the upcoming weeks. I'm sure of it. Besides, school starting again doesn't mean we can't enjoy more days like these. We'll find some time."

Camille turned her head to look at me. I could feel her gaze on me, this feeling of being watched lurking at the back of my head, but I continued staring forward with a slight smile.

"You know, Jack, sometimes you do make sense. Only sometimes, though," she teased with a little snicker. I turned to face her, and she looked away, clearly containing her laughter as her shoulders bopped up and down, her neck getting visibly redder by the second. I moved to the complete opposite side of the blanket to her, my back turned towards her and my head looking straight at the tree that provided us with shade. I let out an audible *humph* and raised my head, pretending to be offended and looking forward to her taking the bait. I took another bite of my lunch; I was almost done at this point. Camille didn't respond to my fake out and so, a minute or so later, I turned back around to face the playground again. After all, it was a lot more interesting that looking straight at bark for the rest of the picnic.

We finished a few minutes later and only the drinks remained, almost empty too. We both looked on as kids ran around playing a game I didn't really know. One of the kids had his eyes closed and was chasing the others while shouting something I couldn't quite make out. Then, all the other kids would respond and quickly run to some other part of the playground. Quite a few times, one would let out a quick frustration shout, but I didn't understand why. The game seemed to be over when all the kids would get caught by the one that had his eyes closed and then they would switch who had to catch the others. It sounded like a lot of fun and I found myself almost wanting to go back to my childhood to play this game with my friends at the time. Then again, I didn't have that many friends, but I'm sure we could have made some good times.

"Jack, can I ask you a question?" Camille said in a clearly nervous tone. It took me a little by surprise. What could she possibly be so nervous about?

"Uh, yeah, what is it?" I answered with concern.

"How do you feel about kids?"

It was going to be one of those conversations. Of course, I never had one myself, except when my parents asked me, but I felt like it was different now that it was my girlfriend. I had watched a few movies with conversations like these and they either seemed to go very well or very poorly depending on the answer. Should I answer truthfully or try to guess what she wanted to hear? That could potentially backfire in a spectacular way and, if I was being honest with myself, I didn't know what her view on the matter was and trying to figure it out in a split second was a little bit mad. So, I went with the truth.

"Well, they can be a little bother sometimes, but they can also be the cutest thing. They're so innocent all the time, they don't know anything. They used to annoy me a lot more, but as I get older, I can't help but smile at them."

Camille shook a little, rubbing the blanket on the dirt below as her feet moved all over it. She let out a sigh and looked down.

"How do you feel about having kids?"

Honestly, even though I expected the natural follow-up to her first question, it still took me by surprise. It was probably good to ask these questions early on in a relationship, I thought, because if the other person wasn't on the page, it would be kind of hard for both of our futures to align. We had gone on several dates at this point, was I supposed to ask this earlier on? The thought didn't even cross my mind, but now that she mentioned it, it was certainly important. Of course, I had thought of the answer to that question before someone else asked it, but for some reason I couldn't say it. The words kept jamming in my throat. Was I afraid of her response? If it was different from hers, would things end here? Could we move forward if our views diverged on this subject?

"I… want to have some, but definitely not now. School is not over; I'm barely scraping by in my apartment and my job, and I don't think I would be ready to take care of a baby. Are you… are you thinking the same thing?" I asked.

She took a while before she answered. Every passing second dragged on for an eternity, like a clock that would not tick over or an alarm that kept on ringing no matter how many times you turned it off. My heart pounded in my chest, threatening to burst out at any moment. The apprehension was the worst part of it all. We had never talked about this, never even mentioned it and the sheer thought that we could have divergent views and things could end right here, right now was enough to make me pass out.

"I definitely want to have kids. It would be wiser to wait, but I feel ready even now. While it would be a challenge going to school, work and taking care of a baby, I'm sure I could do it. But, if you truly believe what you said, I am willing to wait," she answered.

I had my doubts about her being able to go to school, take care of a child and work all at the same time. I couldn't even work out a good schedule for just school and work, let alone having another me to take care of. However, her response sent a wave of relief down my entire body and my muscles, all tensed up from the anticipation, relaxed all at once and I slumped down a little.

"I am so glad you said that," I said. "Honestly, I'm not sure what I would have done if you had said you didn't want any," I continued while laughing a little. "Though, I don't think we're at that stage in our relationship yet, considering we haven't..." I trailed.

I felt Camille get close to me in an instant, almost lightning fast. I didn't know it was possible to move with such speed. She got really close to my ear and whispered something, her words traversing my body like a jolt of electricity.

"Should we do something about that?" she said. She backed off a little, her head still very much close to mine, but allowing me to turn towards her. Our eyes met and she bit her lip slowly. I had seen that look before. Then, she had said to save it for next time. This was it; this was the next time. I could feel her restraint from pouncing on me right then and, as I nodded positively, she packed everything so fast I don't think I blinked once before she was done. She took my hand and almost dragged me all the way to her house. Granted, the park wasn't far, it was right down the street, but I still felt like a pet that didn't want to be walked that gets dragged along the way. However, it wasn't that I didn't want to, but she was going so fast my feet could barely keep up. She fumbled with her key like she was drunk and couldn't figure out where the keyhole was or what key she was supposed to use until, finally, the door to her house opened. I, of course, had been here a couple of times already, but simply couldn't get out of my head the very first time I crossed that door and the chaos that ensued in her bedroom that evening. However, now was different, very different. This time, I was ready, or so I thought.

I didn't even have time to gather my thoughts until I was literally yanked inside by what felt like a magnet pull and tossed to the side, my back against the wall next to the front door. It slammed hard and, as I looked up around, still a bit confused by all the sudden movements, something grabbed my hand and started dragging me along upstairs. Sudden reflexes kicked in and my feet lifted themselves to climb one stair at a time. My brain caught up with everything that was going on and I just had to speak out.

"What about your parents?" I said in a shaky voice as I stumbled to get up one set of stairs. Without missing a beat, Camille's hand grabbed harder on mine to pull me up while marching forward, an unstoppable force with nothing in its path. Her voice, which I almost didn't recognize in the moment, answered back in a dismissive tone.

"I wouldn't worry about them" was all she said, and I somehow understood I shouldn't bring it up any further. Were they inside the house or were they gone? I had no idea, but Camille seemed certain she wouldn't be bothered and what else could I do but go along with her? Yet, the tiny part of me that wanted to protest, just to make sure, was somehow stronger than everything else.

"But…" I couldn't finish my sentence before I felt us finally getting up the flight of stairs that separated the first floor from the second. Her room, a hard right after the stairs, had its door open and Camille dragged us both inside in a flash. The blue and green walls surrounded me and almost filled me with a sense of familiarity, but there was nothing familiar about this situation at all. Sure, Camille made a move on me in this room a few months ago, but then, I had fled the scene while now…I didn't think I could even if I wanted to. A few moments later, I felt the room spin on itself as I tumbled downwards, the ceiling now straight in front of me. Something soft cushioned my fall and I took a big breath to gather my bearings. Before I could even react, Camille climbed on top of me, the luring shadow of the hunter over the terrified prey. I let out a gasp that quickly got swallowed by our lips interlocking into an electrifying kiss. My hands instinctively went to her back to bring her closer to me. I knew about this now. We had kissed a few times since our first one, on the hill under the stars, and I had had some practice. However, just like our first, she had this insatiable hunger that possessed her, a lust she normally contained inside that she only let out in a few chosen instances, and this was one of them. Her soft, wet lips kept moving around mine, her tongue fighting for dominance over my own to which I gladly submitted. My hand clutched her back and moved down towards her cheeks. They surfed over clothes and reached them, gently caressing them as she shook her hips in the same motion as her kiss. Time seemed to have stopped. I didn't know how long we spent like this, kissing with as much passion as we could, shaking the bed a little with every sway her hips made. All my senses were focused on her, her weight, her lips, her legs, her breath, her breasts. More than once, I thought about moving my hands underneath her shirt, but I stopped myself, not wanting to be too bold and ruin the moment until her hand took mine and put it under her shirt herself, squeezing gently to tell me what to do. I did as I was silently told and cupped both of her breasts. This was the first time I held a girl's chest before, and I was discovering the wonders of playing with them. The shape, the size, the weight, the softness of pressing them, the buds that gradually hardened and became more prominent, the smoothness of the skin and their bounciness as they moved around in accordance with her own motion.

Her lips parted with mine and her head moved towards mine as she whispered in my ear.

"Seems like you're ready to go." Ready to go I was. I couldn't remember a time when I was this hard before and her being on top of me didn't help relieve my pain. She shifted her body and moved downwards, her hands trailing on my chest, getting lower and lower, making random shapes as they went along. I let myself drift for a moment, taking deep breaths as I was focusing on her hands until I heard the familiar sound of a zipper. Clothes were pulled from my hips and soon after, my member sprung out for her to see. The sudden movement and cold air spread through my body in a flash as it fell back on my belly with a low thud. I opened my eyes and looked down at Camille as she grabbed it with both hands and popped the head into her mouth. The sudden warmth and wetness earned her a moan as my eyes closed by themselves and my head fell back down to the bed. I could feel her tongue moving around the head as her hands moved up and down, soon joined by her mouth. The sensation was unlike anything I had ever experienced. I had pleasured myself before, of course, mostly by watching videos and movies, so the act itself wasn't unknown, but never could I have imagined it would feel like this. My mind drew a blank as all I could think of was the gradually building pleasure she was working so passionately to do. She was making weird sounds, but I could barely hear them, they were almost muffled like I had tuned out every other sense but the touch. Some saliva dripped down the shaft from her mouth which she caught with her other hand cupping my package. Suddenly, with no warning, I felt her head taking in way more of me than she had before and the spongious feel of her cheeks touched every part of my manhood. My panting turned into a deep moan that gradually became louder until, finally, she came back up for air and released her hold of me. She took a moment of respite before going back to town which only accelerated my breathing. I could feel it. It was coming. This time, however, it felt like I wouldn't be able to contain myself and would explode everywhere. My breathing quickened again. The sloppiness of her mouth, her hands jerking me, and the sounds seemed to accelerate into a crescendo. My breathing quickened. I felt myself reaching the final act until suddenly…

Everything stopped all at once. She moved away from me, her lips left my member, her hands trailed off and I was left in complete silence. I waited a few seconds, uncertain if she was going to resume what she was doing and was simply taking a break, but nothing came. Curious, I opened my eyes and started to look down. I didn't make it very far until her legs surrounded my head and pushed me back to bed, her folds now directly over my mouth. I heard her laughing at me.

"Couldn't let you have all the fun, now, could I?" she teased as she made small back and forth motion with her hips, rubbing herself on my face. I took the hint and let my tongue explore her body fully. I had never seen a girl naked before, not in real life anyway, but while this couldn't let me see Camille, it could let me feel her. My mouth covered her womanhood as my tongue slid across her folds, gently massaging them as she had done to my member. The wetness of my mouth soon covered her and spread across to my cheeks as well. I didn't mind. Then, my tongue found the top of her slit and, every time I would pay attention to that spot, she would tense up and moan. I made a habit of licking that spot every little chance I got and the whimpers she would make made me that much hornier. I stayed on the surface, not willing to dive into her just yet, kissing and exploring every little part of her as she slowly made rocking motions on my face. Her juices mixed in with mine and the taste got on my tongue. I wouldn't say I liked it, but every moan she pushed, every time her legs tensed up around my face, every breath she took, every gasp she made, made it worth it in my mind. After thoroughly focusing on every exterior part of her, I plunged inside her folds, earning a bigger moan this time. I infiltrated her, my tongue a greedy explorer looking for gold in her mine. And gold I struck. Was it from her own arousal or from my saliva, I didn't know anymore, but my cheeks were now covered in wetness, yet that didn't stop me. Her legs tensed up harder this time and she held her breath for a few seconds as she moaned loudly. Finally, she sighed, and her muscles all relaxed at the same time, almost crushing me under her weight. She stayed like this for a moment before removing herself from me. Even I was panting at this point. She got off and went to the other side of the bed. She lowered herself, her breasts resting on the bed while her bottom was high up in the air. I turned around to look at her and she looked back with a wink. Nothing more had to be said. She was right there and was inviting me to take her. My member throbbed at the idea, standing proud and clearly filled my envy. I stood from the bed and positioned myself behind her. Uncertain, I held my shaft in my hand, guiding it and easing it into her. However, from this angle, I couldn't see very well, and she guided me towards her entrance.

"A little lower. A little more. That's it, right there."

Once I knew I was at the right spot, I pushed myself forward a little and instantly went inside her, her wetness enveloping me instantly. The sudden warmth of her insides took me by surprise, and I moaned in pleasure in unison with Camille. We stood there for just a moment before my hips resumed their movement on their own. My hands instinctively grabbed her by the hips and pulled her into me as I was pushing against her. If I thought her mouth felt good, it was nothing compared to this. This time, I was pressured from both sides, her walls tightening up around me with every motion I did. The texture was also very different, in a way I couldn't describe with anything else than divine. I wasn't quite used to the motion, and something felt a little uneasy about it at first, but I soon found my footing and began to go a little faster. Camille stuck her face in the now messy blankets to muffle her moans which, even then, were pretty loud. I was also panting heavily, holding back that edging feeling that kept creeping up and up. Each time I hit her cheeks, the sound of flesh hitting flesh resonated in her room and I didn't really know why, but it turned me on even more. I was mesmerized by her bottom bouncing in quick intervals, creating a ripple effect that seemed to electrify her entire body. Her left hand was clutching the sheet as hard as she could while the other was under her, frantically moving around. I was reaching my limit very soon but, as I went to warn her about it, she stopped and moved forward on the bed, turning around to lie down on her back, facing towards me. She lifted her legs up, clutching them with her arms around her chest, her womanhood on full display for my eyes to see. This time, I could see it in its entirety, and I couldn't help but stare. Under the light, it shone a little, inviting, eager for me to go back to it and Camille was giving me full access. I got closer and got on the bed, on both knees, standing over her. I looked at her folds again. I had explored it earlier with my tongue and was now devouring it with my eyes. I wanted her. I wanted her more. I lowered myself, my body completely over hers as we locked eyes together. Hers were shining too, shining with envy, with anticipation. They were talking to me, silently pleading me to take her again. She wanted me too. My member naturally found its way to her entrance, and I couldn't resist but to plunge back in her, triggering another moan from both of us. She closed her eyes for a second but opened them back up to stare into mine. I began moving my hips, back and forth, back and forth, slowly at first. Our eyes never lost each other, and we didn't blink. Our panting synchronized; her hips moved in unison with mine as we continued to stare into each other, reaching to the deepest parts of ourselves and showing it to the other. A wave of heat came over me and I let out a huge sigh. I couldn't hold on any longer. I accelerated, by will or by instinct, I didn't know, but she seemed to enjoy it a lot as her moans became louder too. It wasn't long before the familiar feeling of reaching climax overwhelmed me and I quickly pulled out of her. I throbbed a few times as a small pool accumulated on her belly while a jolt of electricity bolted through my entire body. I had reached this point before, of course, but never to this extent. I realized I had been holding my breath this entire time and let out a sigh of satisfaction and backed off from Camille who was already reaching for nearby tissues. She wiped herself clean and threw the tissue in a garbage can I had never noticed before, tucked away in the corner of the room. She moved around, resting her head on one of the two pillows on her bed and motioned me to come closer. I lied down beside her, and she cuddled me, her left leg on top of mine and her breast resting on my chest. Her head was tucked in near my neck and my left arm cradled her, slowly moving up and down her back. I had never experienced this feeling at any point in my life. Was this the purest form of love? Of lust? I didn't want this moment to end, I wanted it to stay forever. I wanted us to stay cuddled up like this for all eternity, yet I knew that, eventually, we would have to move. The thought of it made me sad and, if it wasn't for the overwhelming joy that continuously spread through me, I could almost have cried. A few moments later, we were both drifting asleep. Never had I felt so safe to fall asleep in my life and, even if she was resting on me, I felt protected and an immense sense of trust from the bond we had just formed.

◇ ◇ ◇

I slowly woke up, my eyes still heavy and pressing me to go back to sleep. It took me a few seconds to remember where I was. The texture of the pillow, the feel of the sheets and my naked body all brought me back to Camille's room. I got up on my elbows, scanning the room and looking for her. She was nowhere to be found. The walls stared back at me in the still bright bedroom. I turned around to check her alarm clock. 3h56 p.m. The summer sun was still not anywhere near the horizon, yet the room seemed a lot darker than what it was a few hours ago when we came in. I guess I was too focused on the moment to pay attention to this sort of thing. The door, which had previously been wide open, was now closed and an eerie silence pressed on in the room. It felt like waking up disturbed what little peace was left and, for a moment, everything appeared unfamiliar. Now that I thought about it, this was the only time I was in Camille's room alone for an extended period of time. I wasn't one to go around snooping, but I would be lying if I said I didn't think about it. My eyes panned across blue and green walls to the wooden floor where my clothes were scattered about. How did they even get there, I wondered, as I didn't remember tossing them aside or anything of the sort.

72

With a little grunt, I stood up and gathered them all, silently dressing up. As I was putting on my underwear, I thought about everything that happened a few hours prior.

The details were a little blurry to my still foggy mind, but I distinctively remember the passion that inhabited us both. I could still feel everything she did, the pleasure it brought me, and I couldn't help but smile. But that smile faded a little when I realized a crucial detail that went overlooked in the heat of the moment. We hadn't used any protection. The thought of it slammed down like a ton of bricks and my heart stopped for a second. After all this talk about kids, was this her way of forcing me into it? Did she do this on purpose or was this a genuine oversight from the both of us? I was partly to blame, of course, but I felt like my inexperience almost excused me a bit. As quickly as it came, that line of thinking vanished, and I resolved myself to us being equally to blame in this scenario. I only hoped that she wouldn't get pregnant from this. I started to make my way to the door but stopped midway through reaching towards the handle. Taking a deep breath and calming down a little, I opened it and looked to the bathroom, not far from her bedroom. The door was open. She wasn't in there. Surely, that meant she was downstairs, doing something else, I didn't know what, but the fact she had woken up before me and let me sleep in her room made me smile. I still couldn't believe she cared as much as she did for me and, making sure to be as quiet as possible, I started making my way down the stairs.

Not even all the way down, I heard the familiar sound of a knife hitting a cutting board coming from the kitchen. I turned left as I reached the ground floor, passing through the dining room and swerving around the table. Stopping around a small wall that delimited the kitchen area, I leaned to my right to look. There she was, her back turned to me and entirely focused on whatever she was cooking. I could tell from the laces tied behind her back she was wearing an apron. Her blonde hair flowed all the way down to just above her butt which I gladly peeked at. Even if it was now covered, it was still one of the best I had ever seen. I silently walked, almost as if I was in a kid's cartoon, and went behind her. I put my arms around her and hugged her from behind, earning a startled scream from Camille as she clearly panicked for a second before realizing it was me. She calmed down and turned around to face me.

"Why did you do that, you startled me," she whined with a laugh.

"I don't know, I felt like it," I responded with a smile. "What are you making?" I inquired as I looked at what she was cutting.

"Actually, you're just in time. I was cutting some cheese and a few apples for an afternoon snack. You want some?"

"Yeah, that sounds great!"

She leaned in to kiss me and I met her halfway. The smooch sound still made me chuckle a little inside, but I contained my laughter with a smirk. She rolled her eyes and turned around to grab the plate she had set on the counter. We made our way back to the dining room and sat at the table. She was in the best seat, the one that had extra leg room while I was diagonal from her, not quite next to and not quite facing. She put the plate between us and started picking up pieces of fruit to snack on.

"So, how was your first time?" she asked with a smirk.

I almost choked on the piece of cheese I had taken. I did not expect that question at the table. Maybe in her room, sure, but out in the open like this, it felt too personal to talk about. However, I was not about to not answer her.

"It was fantastic. I didn't know sex could feel this good, honestly. I mean, the videos I watched made it seem like it felt good, but you never really know for sure, right?"

"Right," she agreed, prodding me to go forward with my thought process.

"I wasn't too sure about it at first, I guess I doubted myself and figured I would lose it instantly, but I'm glad that didn't happen. What about you? I know it wasn't your first, but..."

Camille snickered as she stuffed a piece of cheese into her mouth. "Yeah, I guess you weren't *that* bad," she teased. When she looked at me, she couldn't control herself and started laughing at me. I couldn't see how my face, but I guess it was funny. I joined in her laughter. Was it a nervous laugh or was it genuine? I didn't really know. She put her hand on mine and looked at me straight in the eyes. "It was good. Really good." Her words reached my heart with a wave of heat. I'm sure now my eyes were reflective of my feelings.

"Thanks, that means a lot." She nodded with another smirk and resumed her snacking. We sat there for a while, eating in silence. I was delaying what I wanted to say. Was this the right moment to bring it up? Was it better to wait a little? No, it had to be now, surely. I did not want to have this conversation, yet I knew it had to happen one way or another and talking face to face would be way better than texting or calling. I knew that much. I took one last look at her. Her messy hair was almost shining in the light coming from the giant window in the dining room. Even while she was eating, her profile was a thing of beauty. I sighed a little, which caught her attention, and she turned around to look at me inquisitively.

"There's…there's something I want to talk about," I started hesitantly. I could feel her eyes straight on me, looking at me with both curiosity and apprehension. She had no idea what I wanted to talk about. "The sex…it was…really good, truly, I never felt anything like it before, but I can't help but feel like we…" I stopped myself for a second to gather my thoughts. They didn't come at all, so I went back to improvisation to try to get my point across. "We didn't use protection and, because we had just talked about kids, I was wondering…"

"No." I looked up at Camille, who was staring back at me with serious eyes. I had scarcely seen her this concentrated before. All her attention was focused on me and what I was saying which made me at least slightly relieved. At least she was taking it seriously. "You're wondering if I deliberately didn't tell you to use a condom to have a kid with you, is that what you're trying to say?"

"Um…yeah…yeah, that's what I'm wondering," I said with a weak voice. Why was she so intimidating now? Her eyes were as piercing as an arrow, her expression locked between anger and what appeared to be sadness, but I wasn't sure. I couldn't look at her for long and stared at the table, her gaze still longing on me. I felt ashamed to even ask, but how was I supposed to know?

"Jack, look at me," she almost commanded and I did as I was told. In that moment, I think she could have asked for anything, and I would have done it. "I will never, and I mean never, do something like that to you. I've heard stories of that happening to people and that is not okay. Do you understand me?" I nodded. Disagreeing with her now would be suicide, anyway. "What happened back there was pure passion, a heat of the moment oversight. If you want to, I will make sure to remind you next time."

Those words came to me as a relief. She didn't resent me enough to bar the possibility of a next time, but at the same time was also telling me she could remind me to put one on in a way that made me feel like I really should do it myself.

"If that's any consolation, today is a safe day for me. And you pulled out, remember?"

I did remember that much. However, I had heard it was still possible to get pregnant even if the guy didn't finish inside, which still concerned me. What if it did happen? What if she thought it was a safe day, but it wasn't? I knew there were some pills girls could take to avoid pregnancy, and even though I didn't think it was a good idea, I felt like I had to bring it up.

"Would it be too much trouble for you to get one of those pills at the pharmacy? You know, the ones that prevent you from getting pregnant at all?"

"Jack, I'm telling you, it's a safe day. There's no need to get that, there's no risk."

"There's never no chance of it happening."

"I think I know how my own body works. Yes, there's absolutely no chance of me getting pregnant. Why are you so insistent about it?"

"I just want to make sure, Camille. I'm not ready to deal with that sort of thing and, as much as I want kids in the future, it can't happen now. Can you just do it this one time, please?"

Camille sighed heavily and rolled her eyes. "Fine. I'll get the pill tomorrow. You happy now?"

Happy would not be the word I would use to describe this situation. After the wonderful moment we had spent together came our first real argument. Well, if you could even call it that. It was enough to ruin the mood, though, and I felt really uncomfortable in her house all of a sudden. I needed to get out. Needed to gather my thoughts. I got up from the chair and started to walk away.

"Where are you going?" Camille asked in a concerned tone. I could hear she wasn't mad at me, and her tone was probably more aggressive than she wanted it to be, but the question still felt like an attack.

"I… I just need to… I think I should go," I stuttered, barely able to get words out of my mouth as my emotions threatened to surface.

"You don't have to go. I thought we could watch a movie or something together tonight. You don't want to?" she asked, also getting up from the table. I walked up to her front door and held the handle in my right hand. I turned to face her. Her face which previously was as cold as ice and as stern as a parent correcting their child was now riddled with concern and disappointment. I couldn't bear to look at her any longer and looked down, trying to escape her eyes.

"It's not that I don't want to, but… I'm sorry." As soon as the words left my mouth, I opened the door and went out, closing it behind me with a little more force than I wanted. I lingered on her house entrance, unsure if that was the right move or not and started walking towards the nearest bus stop to go back home. Was I right to do what I did and to bring it up? I felt like I needed to, needed to know if that was her intention or not, which I was glad it wasn't but maybe I had hurt her feelings in the process. Even though she didn't show it at the time, perhaps even the fact I had this thought hurt her more than she would like to admit. I couldn't shake the feeling that I had messed up and was only hoping that I would be able to talk to her again soon. Funny thing to hope when I had just left her house, wasn't it? Maybe I could call her tonight, after we would both have calmed down from it all. Would she answer me? I did rush out of there on a whim, maybe it would have been better to stay and talk thing out more. All these doubts in my head kept bouncing around as I got on and off the bus and walked home to my apartment. As soon as I came in, my phone vibrated in my pocket. Curious, I closed the door and took it out to check what it was. A text message.

I love you

Conflicted wouldn't begin to explain how I felt while reading those three words. Such simple words with a very deep meaning. Normally, they would have made me feel ecstatic; my crush and now girlfriend confessing her love to me, what else could I wish for? Any person would feel warmth and love when receiving those words from their partner. And I did, I truly did, but the bitter conversation we just had tarnished the meaning behind them, like she was just trying to buy peace or did it out of guilt or anger. I didn't know anymore. To add insult to injury, this was the first time she ever said them to me, and it wasn't even in person. I couldn't help but feel disappointed, both in myself for insisting the way I did in our prior conversation and in her for wasting her first declaration in the form of a text message. Couldn't she have done it to my face, while we both looked at each other, after sharing a kiss? Why did she wait so long to send it, too? What was she feeling right now that made her do it?

Despite all those unanswered questions and pointless doubts, I knew one thing for sure. I loved her too. I couldn't be experiencing these feelings if that weren't true.

Chapter 8

"Yeah." I paused for a second, listening. "Okay, cool, see you in five." I hung up the call and lowered my phone as I turned to Camille. "They said they'd be here in about five minutes," I said.

"Nice," she answered with a slight smile. She looked around for her purse, grabbed it and put it on her shoulder. Her blonde hair swung with her motions and, even now, I still couldn't get over how beautiful she was. She looked at me with her emerald eyes, both piercing my soul and comforting me at the same time.

"Ready?" I asked while smiling at her.

"Oh yeah, I've been wanting to go to the beach for so long, I almost can't contain myself. I feel like I could just start dancing at any moment," she said enthusiastically.

"Show me, then," I said with a nod in her direction. Much obliged, she started a little dance, her arms close to her chest and just shaking her hips from side to side. It wasn't much of a dance per se, but it still made me laugh. I leaned in for a kiss, which she gladly gave me and as I opened my eyes, they met hers. "Nervous?" I asked, more of a statement for myself than a question.

"I think if any of us two is nervous, that would be you," she answered laughing.

"Probably, yeah."

It was true. This would be the first time my friends would meet Camille. My girlfriend. The first one I ever had. They had heard me talk about her in text messages, of course, but we never had a chance to meet in person this summer. Everyone has been busy with work and our schedule never lined up before today. Some of my friends did already have significant others, Chris and Vincent were already taken and I had already made their girlfriend's acquaintance, but this time, it was different. Would they tease me about it or would they just greet her and that's it? What would the other two guys say? I didn't know what their reactions would be and that coupled with the fact it had been almost three months since we last saw one another, I was apprehensive about the whole thing. Perhaps a little too much, from what I could tell from Camille's demeanor. After all, if she wasn't nervous, why was I?

A honk coming from below us took me out of my thoughts. I looked down to see the familiar black van parked right in front of my apartment. That was them. I turned to Camille.

"That's them. Do you have everything?"

"Everything is in the bag there," she said as she pointed to a large bag on my bed. It had our towels, sunscreen, goggles, basically anything one would need when going to the beach. "I got my purse and my phone, I'm all good to go!" she finished with a smile. She was clearly very excited about this trip.

I grabbed the bag and we quickly started making our way down. As soon as we got out of the building, Michael and Chris came out to greet us.

"Jack! My man, how are you doing?" said Michael, the closest to us. "It's been way too long, man," he said, extending his fist towards me.

"You're right about that," I said, answering with a fist bump. "It's good to finally see you guys."

Chris joined the three of us and we greeted each other the same way as I did with Michael. Both turned to Camille.

"Aren't you going to present your lady?" Chris said with a smirk.

"Oh yeah, uh… Michael, Chris, this is Camille. Camille, this is Michael," I said pointing to the right. "And this is Chris," I said, this time pointing to the left.

"Very nice to meet you," Chris said, soon followed by Michael. They both quickly nodded down as well. It seemed like a code between guys that you nodded down to greet someone you don't know and nod up to greet a friend. Nobody had taught us this, but we all did it. I didn't know if that applied only to my friend group or if it was guys in general, but it was still a strange phenomenon to observe.

"It's very nice to meet you too," Camille answered with a giant smile. "Honestly, I can't wait to get there, the beach is calling to me."

"It sure is, I feel it too. Shall we go?" Chris asked with a jingle of his keys. It was more of a rhetorical question, and we all started moving towards the van. Chris opened the trunk for us to put our bag in and we all got seated. Camille and I were in the back, she was on the passenger side, and I was behind Chris. He turned the keys, starting the car as the engine roared. He looked at me in the rear-view mirror.

"No funny business in the back, yeah? This is my parent's car and that wouldn't be right."

"Chris!" I said, flustered he would even think to say that out loud. Michael and Camille started laughing, soon joined by Chris as well. I could feel my face being red-hot and we didn't even make it to the beach yet. Camille put her hand on my shoulder which made me turn towards her. She simply winked at me with a smirk, and I returned to my pouting. This wasn't going my way, but at least she was integrating well with the group, I suppose. The van started moving and off we went. Michael turned to us, looking especially at Camille.

"You seem a little familiar. Were you in my English class last semester?" he asked.

"I don't know, in which class were you?" Camille answered.

"207. We had our classes in the left wing, second floor, just passed the library. On Tuesday afternoons."

"Yeah, that sounds about right. Sorry, I never noticed you were there," Camille said.

"Not at all, I didn't notice you either. Well, I'm glad we finally met," Michael concluded with a smile.

"Likewise," she said, also smiling at him.

The entire exchange made me smile too. I saw that I had nothing to be nervous about. Camille was clearly already making friends with mine and didn't seem out of her element at all. If the situation was reversed, however, and I was meeting her friends... now that would be a disaster. I had already seen them once, when I went to get my backpack I had left at her house the first time, and while we didn't interact at all, I only remember them laughing at me while I was at my most embarrassing moment and that didn't feel too good back then. Plus, they looked kind of smug after the following class, but I'm sure they were fine, after all they were Camille's friends and if she was my girlfriend, how bad could her friends be? However, the simple thought of meeting them was bringing back the same feeling I had when first going to Camille's house; the stomach turning and the heart beating so fast it threatened to pop out of my chest.

"We should get there in about ten minutes. Vincent and Sam are already on their way too, they should arrive just before us," Chris said, still looking directly in front of him. I thought it was weird how drivers could do that, like they were talking to the window in front of them but addressing people in the back. As I didn't drive, it was a complete mystery to me how they managed to do all these things at once. Maybe one day I would learn how to drive, but classes were expensive, and I couldn't afford a car anyway, so it didn't quite make sense to me to start now.

Michael plugged in his phone to the van with a long blue cable and started playing some tunes. The familiar sound of electric guitar and drums filled the entire car as Michael pumped the volume up. We could barely hear each other without screaming. Honestly, I was still surprised how Chris was able to keep concentrating on the road in these kinds of situations. Surely, the music at this volume would be super distracting, but he kept on looking forward and the van didn't swerve at all.

"This is my jam!" Camille said from my right. I turned around to look at her. Both her arms were up in the air, not extended fully, and she was dancing excitedly to the rhythm of the song. Well, dancing as much as the seatbelt around her chest and waist allowed her too, which to be fair, was a lot more than I thought possible. Her eyes were closed, she wasn't paying attention to anything else but the vibes all around us. Even Michael didn't look like he had heard her as he didn't turn around to answer her. I leaned in a little closer to her, making sure to avoid her occasional swinging arms.

"You like this kind of music?" I asked, both in surprise and excitement at the same time.

"Oh yeah, I could listen to this all day," she answered without missing a beat and with her eyes still closed. I returned to my spot, a giant smile on my face. If there was one thing that I wasn't expecting, it was Camille listening to the same kind of music that I did. I never asked what she liked in that regard and frankly, I didn't really know what I did expect her to say, but the fact we had once again something in common reinforced the idea in my head that this relationship could really work out. Sure, we had the occasional disagreement, as all couples did, I assumed, not that I would know firsthand of course, but it was still going well for both of us. The rest of the car ride was spent in silence from my part, but Camille soon joined Michael in singing loudly when the next song rolled over.

◊

Just as Chris said, we arrived about ten minutes later and parked the van in the massive parking lot overlooking the beach. We got out as Chris popped the trunk open, revealing all our bags. Since we didn't have that many, they were all messy and rolled around during the ride, but it didn't take long to gather everything back. I took our bags in my right hand and stepped back to allow the other guys to take their stuff, taking the chance to look around.

The beach area was separated in three zones, so to speak. First, the parking lot where we were overlooked the beach from a fair height and extended over a fairly large area. Over to one side, multiple shop were lined up, offering food, clothing and other amenities to anyone in need. Going down from the parking and around the shops, some staircases hugged the small hill to link the two, allowing people to move from the beach to the shops and vice versa. From what I could tell, the beach was packed today as there weren't many spots in the parking lot still available. After all, it was a bright sunny day and, just as the thought crossed my mind, a wave of heat spread through my body as the sun rays pressed down on my shoulders. Sunscreen would be a must before going into the water and I was silently relieved we brought some. Michael's voice brought me back.

"Vincent said they'd be waiting around the pastry shop, so let's go over there to meet up with them." When he mentioned the pastry shop, I could feel Camille's eyes light up beside me even though I wasn't looking at her. I knew they offered some delicious treats, but surely getting one just before swimming was not the brightest idea. I took her hand in mine and she turned around to face me, almost drooling on the floor.

"We can go there later, yeah?" I said and she nodded aggressively, having a hard time containing herself. She gave me a quick peck on the cheek and jumped a little in place. I never knew she could get so excited over a dessert, but then again, I was kind of looking forward to it as well.

"Are you guys ready to go?" Michael asked. We nodded that we were, and Chris locked up the van before we started making our way to the shop area. As we gradually got closer, the aroma started hitting us, taunting, inviting, but we resisted the temptation as much as we could. It was progressively harder and harder, yet we remained strong. It eventually went away when Vincent and Sam came into view as they waved at us to get our attention. They also came towards us to meet us halfway. I didn't realize how many shops there were before we got closer, but now that we were standing just in front of them, it was surprising. Not quite like a mall, as it was mostly little shops and businesses, but the amount of them lined up beside one another was still impressive. It looked like there was anything someone would need, from shoes to clothes to food to beach-related items like sandcastles mold and beach balls. I wondered how they were keeping business in the winter as nobody would come buy beach balls when it was colder than a freezer outside. I didn't really have time to wonder any more as the other guys joined us.

"Yo! How's it going folks!" Vincent greeted. "Doing good, I hope?"

"Oh yeah, especially today. Did you guys wait long?" Chris asked.

"No, no, just a couple minutes. Tried to catch some shade under the shops there, but the sun is relentless today. Anyway, I see we have a newcomer to the group?" Vincent said as he looked at Camille.

"Yes, Vincent, Sam, this is Camille, my girlfriend. Camille, this is Vincent and Sam," I said, presenting everyone like I did for Chris and Michael.

"It's nice to meet you two," Camille said with a little nod.

"Nice to meet you," Sam said with a nod. He was never one to bring that much attention to himself and he wasn't about to start now.

"You sure seem to have landed a good one, Jack," Vincent teased with a little smirk. "Never knew you had it in you."

"Vincent!" I exclaimed, feeling my face getting redder and redder, and it wasn't from the sun either.

Everyone laughed in unison. Vincent winked at me as I looked away, trying to hide my embarrassment. It went away as soon as Camille clutched my arm and, with a smile, gave me another kiss on the cheek. She seemed a lot more comfortable than I was which I guess was a good thing. When everyone regained their composure, we started walking towards the wooden staircase leading down towards the beach. With Camille by my side, we were closing the march and, as I got closer to the stairs, I lingered a little to admire the view.

The lake spread out far and wide, wide enough that we couldn't see the other side even standing where we were. A sturdy see-through wooden fence surrounded the edge of the hill, encasing the parking lot and the shop area in a little pen. Stretching for what seemed like kilometers on either side of the shops, the sandy beach lit up under the sun, its yellow sand reflecting the rays back into our eyes. It was somewhat crowded; it was hard to spot a place where we could lay down our stuff while not being uncomfortably close to another group. The calming sound of water was covered by laughter and general conversations erupting all around. The heat was somewhat hidden by the very slight breeze that picked up, but it was clearly not enough to cool me down. I still couldn't wait to take off my shirt and shorts to reveal the swimsuit I had underneath and rush to the water as fast as possible. Camille, noticing me staying behind to admire the view, turned around with a puzzled look, but a simple smile told her everything I was thinking at that moment. With a slight movement of the head, she invited me to resume our descent and I obliged. The sand-covered wooden steps creaked under each of my steps, and I wondered how they would hold up to someone heavier than me. I was a pretty skinny guy and weighed almost nothing. Nonetheless, it was also kind of comforting in a weird way to hear the creak sound, like stepping in a very old house. The only difference was the smell which wasn't the best right now, but I couldn't identify where it was coming from. Was it the group standing next to us or maybe the one that was grilling something in a portable barbecue? Was it simply the smell of the lake? Was this how a beach usually smelled? I had never paid enough attention every time I went, so I genuinely had no idea. I covered my nose the best I could and powered through, following the other four guys that were way ahead of us now.

A few moments later, Camille and I caught up to them as they had just started setting up their stuff. Beach towels were laid on the sand, a cooler was set down near them and a small beach umbrella was secured. I hadn't even noticed they had brought all this stuff. Those were probably Sam and Vincent's stuff, because they were clearly not in the trunk of the van. My shoes were already filled with sand as we joined up with them; I couldn't wait to get them off.

"Ah, there you are, you two! We thought we had lost you," Chris said.

"Jack lingered a little to watch the beach," Camille explained. "Where should we put our stuff?"

"You can just lay your towels there or put them against the cooler there. Don't worry, I'll keep watch over everything," Sam said with a smile.

"Oh, you're not going to swim?" I said with a little surprise.

"No, swimming's never been my thing. But I still wanted to hangout, so here I am! I brought a book, so it's all good. Rather you have a good time than have somebody else sulking and being unable to go because they have to watch the stuff," Sam said.

"That's very nice of you, Sam," Camille said while setting down her purse near the cooler, under the shade. "Don't try anything, I'll know," she said teasingly with a finger pointed at him. He laughed a little and she joined him for a few seconds before she turned to me.

"You ready?" It was more of a rhetorical question, because she didn't wait for an answer before starting to undress. We, of course, had planned to put our swimsuits underneath our clothes to speed up the process and not have to go into a bathroom to change. The sight of her removing her shirt and skirt, even if there was something underneath, brought me back to that night, the night where we made love for the first time. We hadn't done it since, partly because of what happened last time and possibly a lack of time on my part. I had to take extra boring shifts at work whenever I could to pay for school and my apartment which unfortunately left me with very little to work with. The day at the park was a few weeks back now, and I was really craving that intimate feeling again. I was constantly entranced by her, following her movements like an overly curious child, simply standing there in the sand and not feeling anything in my feet. Though, it wasn't like we weren't seeing each other at all. I did go to her house a couple times since that night, but we were usually too tired to even think about anything else than watching a movie or something, eating a frozen dinner as well. Yet, those nights were still very enjoyable to me. I liked to simply cuddle up with her. I just wish sometimes we could…

"Are you going to swim with your shirt and shorts on or…?" Camille asked with a smirk. I looked down to see I hadn't started to undress at all, and she was already done. She was applying sunscreen to her arms and legs, and I had to break away the eye contact to focus on me for two seconds. I was like a hungry animal stalking a prey, incapable of not staring, embarrassing really. I removed my shirt in one motion and brought down my shorts soon after, revealing my light blue swimsuit. When I looked back up, Camille was done putting on sunscreen, but she turned to me with the bottle.

"Could you apply it to my back?" she said.

"Sure," I answered, taking the bottle out of her hand and pouring it in mine. She turned around and took her hair in her hand, bringing it to her front and exposing her entire back to me. Even seeing her from behind, I couldn't help but stare a little. Her neck, her shoulders, the little green strap of her swimsuit. I put both hands on her, causing her to shiver just a little under the sudden coldness of the liquid and massaged it to her entire back. I didn't have time to do much before I felt a hand reach down to my crotch and grabbing a hold of me. Her head turned slightly towards me.

"Did you get hard?" she teased with a whisper only I could hear. My friends were right there and here I was, getting gripped by my girlfriend out in the open in a public place while applying screen to her back and having flashbacks of our first night together. Understandably, I was conflicted about the whole thing.

"I can't help it, seeing you in a swimsuit is…making me have a few thoughts," I said, trying to justify myself. I wasn't doing a good job.

"Thoughts of what?" she said, slightly bending forward so her butt was rubbing on me as she did little circular motions.

"You're not helping," I said in a soft voice, mostly a thought that somehow came out of my mouth. She laughed at me and stood back up. I finished applying sunscreen to her lower back while trying my hardest to hide the now obvious bulge in my swimsuit. That was the only thing I hated about them. With no underwear and the stretchy material, swimsuits really did a poor job of hiding boners, so I generally tried to avoid getting one whenever I went swimming, which wasn't always easy and especially not now. Granted, Camille was standing in front of me, which was a start, but what would happen when she'd go away?

"All done," I said, gently tapping her shoulders. She turned around to face me.

"Thank you," she said with a smirk. She leaned forward and kissed me softly and backed away, looking straight at me. "Try to calm down before going swimming, yeah? Wouldn't want your friends to know you got this excited in public," she said, always laughing straight in my face.

The situation was not funny. Michael's voice grabbed our attention.

"Are you guys all done? Because we're going!"

"Jack will stay a little, but he'll join us shortly." Camille turned back towards me. "Don't make me wait." With that, she joined up with Chris, Vincent and Michael as they headed towards the lake water. I sat down, knees to my face and trying to hide my face. Sam was right next to me, and I had hoped he didn't see all of me when Camille had moved away. I did my best to hide my boner from everyone else and tried to think of something, anything, that would make me calm down. But it was no use, my mind kept wandering back to her touch, what she said, the other night, the moment she undressed. Maybe if I looked around and got distracted by something else, it could help?

I got up a few minutes later with the bottom half of me not reporting for duty. It was very hard to think of something else, almost impossible and I didn't know how I managed it, but I did. I turned around briefly to look at Sam. He was reading his book and wasn't paying attention to me at all. I wondered if he had even noticed I was there. Regardless, the water was now calling me, and my body was answering excitedly under this torrid heat. I rushed towards the edge of the beach while carefully dodging other people that were building sandcastles, playing volleyball or just laying down to soak up the sun. As soon as my feet touched the water, I felt a wave of coolness shivering through my entire body. I continued walking down the sandy underwater slope until, eventually, I was up to just above my knees. While it was refreshing, it was also kind of cold, if I was honest with myself. Normally, I only swam in heated pools and, while that may have altered my perception of what cold water actually is, swimming in a lake was definitely not the same temperature. It would take me a moment to get used to it before I could dive completely and soak as much as possible and so I stood there, rubbing water around my arms and chest, trying to accustom myself to the temperature before going in. I must have gotten distracted, because I never saw her coming. A loud splash of water on my right took me by surprise, but I didn't have time to turn around until my arm got pulled straight down into the lake, sweeping me off my feet and submerging me completely. The cold water attacked my face in tiny icy needles and a muffled scream turned into bubbles that rose to the surface. My hair was floating all around me, I could feel it, but I didn't want to open my eyes to see it. I had heard that opening your eyes underwater was bad for them and especially in the ocean or in a lake. I didn't know if that was true or not, but I wasn't willing to take the chance. Finally, my feet found the sand under me, and I pushed myself out to the surface, taking a deep breath and coughing a little when I did. My hair was covering my face and I couldn't see from who the laughter in front of me was coming from. But I recognized it quickly enough.

"Why did you do that?" I asked, swiping my hair to the side to allow me to see again.

"Because you took way too long to get here and I didn't want to wait any longer," Camille said, slowly getting closer to me. I had regained my composure when she reached me. She was squatting down in the water so only her head was out. Seeing a little head moving about was kind of funny, especially when she made different expressions and faces to me, and she seemed very small when she finally reached me. She had to look up to see my face, which was a feeling I really wasn't used to, but meeting her eyes in that moment made me slump down too and I sunk to her level.

"Hold me," she said, spreading her arms underwater to allow me to grab her. I went in for a hug and she jumped to get on me. Her arms were locked around my neck and resting on my shoulders while her legs were crossed around my lower back. Her chest was pressed against mine and her mouth was close, so close, I could almost hear her breathing through the noise all around us. Being like this brought back the feelings I had tried to supress only a few minutes prior, and I really tried to not get excited, but it was no use. The electricity of the moment was palpable, our breathing was synchronized, yet there was this tension that separated us. We couldn't break it. Was it because we were in public, and we couldn't give ourselves in too much? Maybe, and if that was the case, it made me a little sad. I would have given a lot to go back to her room right now. Did she feel the same way? I leaned in for a kiss. I didn't have to lean very far, because as soon as I moved, her lips met mine with ferocity, like a hungry wolf finally eating after days of hunting. Her hands moved up to the back of my head and pressed lightly, bringing me closer to her. One of them started moving around in my hair. I had learned recently that I really liked the feeling of her doing that and, since I had never experienced it before as it's not something that my friends and I did, I had never known. The contact of her hand made everything around us go blank. I could almost ignore the cold water moving about around me, the sound of swimmers coming back up for air, the sound of laughter coming from people playing with balls and frisbees, the sound of casual conversation. Finally, our lips parted, and I stared into her eyes. Full of passion, full of love, full of excitement, full of life. I didn't know how mine were, but hers made my heartbeat faster and filled me with an indescribable heat.

I realized I had been walking without knowing. My legs were moving on their own, carrying Camille around with me, dodging every other swimmer that came around us while being distracted by her at the same time. By now, we were a fair distance from where we were initially, and I was about to go back when she got off me with a loud splash. After a few seconds, she came back up to the surface.

"I'm going to go make a few laps around the lake. Do you want to come with me?" Camille asked.

"Oh, I'm not that good of a swimmer, I think I would only slow you down. I'll be returning closer to our spot and just chill there," I answered while pointing to the area where we came from.

"Alright, I'll join you there soon!" Faster than I expected, she turned around and dove underwater, swimming away like a dolphin. I was kind of worried as there were multiple swimmers around and it was hard to see anyone that was underwater, but I figured she would be fine and started making my way back to Sam, or rather the area in front of Sam. I never liked to swim for long, I preferred to go for quick swims and go often instead, but I had just gotten in so it would be a little while still before I got out. On my way, I crossed a lot of different people, some mothers bathing with their child in their arms, some that were throwing some kind of missile object high in the air to catch it back up and even some that were just laying on their back, floating about to the current of other people moving next to them. I spotted what seemed like a couple, holding hands and walking on the edge of the beach. I wondered how nice that would be to do with Camille. Such a simple thing, really, but it had a certain charm to it, I found. A few months ago, I never would have even thought about it that way. After all, walking on the beach alone didn't bring anything exciting when you could play a sport or do a sandcastle instead. I wasn't much of a beachgoer anyway, but now that I had someone else in my life, I found there were some things that I saw in a different eye. Funny how a few months can change your perspective like that. A light tap on my shoulders took me out of my thoughts and I turned around to see who it was. Camille's head was halfway in the water, her mouth barely hovering over the edge. She was looking at me with a look I had rarely seen before and, at first, I didn't quite know what it was and what it meant. She soon enlightened me on that.

"Already back?" I asked her.

"I've lost my top…" she mumbled, barely audible. The fact she covered her mouth underwater probably didn't help.

"You what? I can't hear you."

"I've lost my top," she said a bit louder, but still quiet enough that only I could hear. I instinctively looked down at her chest. I couldn't see very well because of the troubled water, but the emerald tint that used to be there was clearly missing and her arms were held close to her body.

"How, what happened?"

"I was swimming around the edge, like I said, and the straps at the back must have loosened up. There was a loud splash and a wave crashed near me and nearly swept me away. I dove underwater to try to avoid it, but the current took my top off and it drifted somewhere. I don't know where it is," she explained.

Well, now wasn't this a predicament. I knew how embarrassing that must have been for her and was desperately trying to think of a solution, but the fact she went looking for me indicated she hadn't thought of anything either. Did she bring another swimsuit perhaps? Would it be possible to search for the one she lost? Although she probably didn't want to swim half naked in public, understandably so.

"Did you bring another pair with you?" She shook her head to say no. I looked up to search for an answer. I doubted the clouds had any input on the matter, but nothing came. Until I remembered the shops we passed by earlier. Was there a shop for swimsuits? I remember seeing a clothes store, but none of the front displays had any. Surely, when the business is next to a beach, you would sell some swimsuits, right? Maybe I could go there. I looked down at Camille who was now starting to get a little emotional and panicky. After all, I wasn't the one in this situation, but I understood.

"I remember a clothing shop up on the hill when we arrived. There might be some swimsuits for sale, do you want me to go buy a new one for you?" I offered. At this point, it was the best I could come up with. She nodded enthusiastically.

"Yes. Please hurry." I didn't bother to respond and started making my way towards our setup where Sam was. The way back seemed to stretch for miles. Was the beach always this long? I could feel the staring gaze of Camille lingering at the back of my head like a hunter stalking its prey. Only, this time, she wasn't much of a hunter. I struggled to get out of the water and finally landed on the sandy beach. My feet instantly became covered, and it only got worse as I walked towards our setup. On the way, I passed a group of kids that were making a giant sandcastle along with a working moat coming from the lake. It was quite impressive, but I unfortunately didn't have time to linger and admire it. Camille was waiting for me, so I pressed on and finally reached Sam, who was still reading calmly next to all our stuff. When I approached, he took a bookmark nearby to save his page and turned his attention to me.

"Back so soon? I thought you would stay in there longer," he said.

"Oh yeah, I just wanted to… look at the shops we passed earlier. I'm going there now," I answered in a tone that probably revealed my uncertainty.

"You ought to enjoy the water while the sun is still up. We can swing by the shops later if you really want to," he proposed, oblivious to the urgency of Camille's situation.

"I'm just going to have a look around. Probably won't be too long. I wanted to get out of the water anyway, so it's alright."

"If you say so, man. Good shopping, I guess," he said with a little laugh. He opened his book back up, diverting his attention from me as I was getting dressed. While we talked, I had shaken all the sand from my feet and put my socks back on, also putting on a shirt at the same time. I dried my swimsuit the best I could and grabbed my wallet sitting in Camille's purse. I wondered how much women swimsuit cost. I had never bought one before, but surely it couldn't be that expensive, could it? After all, there was barely any fabric to a bikini, it's not like they were shorts, right? My thoughts isolated me from the rest of the beach, the sounds fading in the background and the sensation of sand under my feet the only reminder of where I was, and I sorely focused on getting to the shops as fast as possible. I had accelerated my pace without even realizing it, but the little sandy dunes made it hard to get a footing and I almost tripped a few times. From far away, I could still feel a pressuring gaze coming from behind me and I couldn't help but imagine it was Camille, stalking me like a hawk. I always found that feeling weird, the feeling of someone looking at you while you do something else. It's often an unpleasant thing, which I sometimes experienced even while I was alone at my apartment, like somebody or something else was watching me, even though I knew there was no one else in my home. Your peripheral vision convinces you something is there when there is not. Most times, I can't help but turn my head to look, but there is never anything there.

A little while later, I had reached the wooden steps leading up the hill. Every step creaked under my weight as I made my ascension. Were they about to completely bend and shatter or was the creaking noise not an indication of the weakness of the wood, but the sound of the planks that had been worked for many years, maybe decades? Nevertheless, it was somehow reassuring, like a constant reminder of the progress I was making until, finally, I made it to the top. I looked back towards the beach, turning around slowly, and tried to find Camille. I spotted her quite easily. She hadn't moved an inch since I had left and was clearly looking back at me. Without making her wait any longer, I set my sights on the shops again. The clothing shop soon came into view, and I hesitated for just a second before entering. I was going to shop for a bikini. A girl's bikini. Was it even appropriate for me to be looking at those? I shook my head to chase away those thoughts. Even if it was inappropriate, there were no other options, anyway, so it couldn't be helped. I opened the door which greeted me with the sound of bells, announcing my presence, and made my way inside.

My eyes scanned the shop floor for the swimsuit section. It was obvious, right in the middle of the store, and I wondered why they didn't showcase any in the front display. Surely, you would want to advertise those instead of general summer clothes, but then again, I guessed it kind of made sense. Customers would probably know they sold swimsuits, but not other clothes. After all, here I was, the living proof of that thought. But there was no time to waste. I beelined it straight to the women section and, as soon as I got there, got a bit overwhelmed. There were so many designs, shapes, sizes and colors. Men swimsuits were so simple, shorts with a different color or design. That was it. But here, there were simply too many choices. How could I choose one? I picked up the first one in front of me and read the label.

Oh no

I couldn't stop staring at the words written on the tiny label. Cup size. I instantly felt a ton of bricks fall on my shoulders. I didn't know. I didn't know Camille's cup size. If I took one too small or too big, it wouldn't fit and it wouldn't be much better than what she had now. I racked my brain, trying to remember something, anything, a moment where she would have told me, a label on one of her bras or swimsuits I would have read, but nothing came. I never paid much attention to that kind of detail, figuring she would probably be buying those kinds of things herself. I put down the one I had in my hand in defeat and stared at the piles of different ones laid on the table in front of me. So many to choose from, so many possible errors to make. Which one would fit? Then my eyes set on someone else, standing across from me, also browsing the same section. A woman. I felt both a wave of relief and of nervousness. Was I about to ask a stranger to help me figure out the cup size of my girlfriend? What other choice did I have? It's not like I could buy them all and figure it out later, I had to make a choice now and be quick about it. I went to take a step towards her, around the table, but stopped right away. The woman seemed familiar, and I looked back at her one more time. My eyes widened.

Chloe.

I didn't know how to react. Relieved it wasn't a stranger or concerned it was Chloe, of all people. Judging from our last conversation, she wasn't too fond of Camille, so helping her was probably the last thing she wanted to do and it's not like I could say the shopping was for me. I had no choice. Like a dog with its tail between its legs, I made my way over to her. She seemed to notice me approaching, because she looked up from her browsing and our eyes met. She froze, only for an instant, but long enough for me to notice.

"Hi," I said with a hand at the back of my head, looking away.

"Um… hi," she said in a confused tone. "What are you doing here?"

"My friends and I came to the beach and um… well, some things happened and here I am," I answered shakily. She must have thought I was lying, because even though I was looking away, I knew she was raising her eyebrows in disbelief.

"In the women swimsuits section?"

"Yeah, well, I also came here with Camille, but she couldn't make it in here with me and now I have to get her a swimsuit, but I don't know her sizes and I'm afraid I'll screw it up and make it even worse than it already is and…" I blurted out, not letting Chloe get a word in. She had to cut me off.

"Okay, okay, slow down. What was that about Camille? You need to buy a swimsuit, but you don't know her sizes? What does that even mean?"

"Well, you know." I gestured to my chest area, pretending to grab some imaginary breasts. "Her size."

"Right. So why are you telling me all this?"

"Well, I figured since you're a woman, you'd probably know better than me." I sighed, realizing the dumb idea that it was. How would she know better than me? I was Camille's boyfriend, and she was a stranger to her. Rather, someone she didn't appreciate much, from what I could tell from our previous conversation. There was no way she would help me.

"Alright. Listen, I'm doing this for you, okay, not for her," Chloe said while going to the other side of the table. She started mumbling to herself and I couldn't understand anything of what she was saying. She picked up a few swimsuits and tried them on herself, which I thought was weird, because if she was helping me, then the swimsuits weren't meant for her. I also didn't quite understand why she was so dismissive of Camille. Had she done something to her in the past? I caught up to Chloe who was constantly moving around the table, looking at different models and still muttering something. As I got closer, I managed to hear the words *bigger* and *tight*, but that was all.

"Hey Chloe," I said to get her attention. She looked up at me. "Why do you dislike Camille so much?" Chloe put down the swimsuit she had in her hands and sighed heavily, closing her eyes and lowering her head a little. She took a few seconds, possibly to gather her thoughts, and looked back at me.

"That's really none of your business, is it? Now, if you want me to help, can you drop the subject? And answer this, does she like a swimsuit with some support or not?" I didn't know the answer to that question. In fact, I didn't even really understand what she was saying and the first part of her answer kind of threw me off. There was obviously something going on between the two and if Chloe wasn't willing to answer me, maybe I'd have to ask Camille directly. Lost in thought, I didn't realize I left Chloe hanging until I saw her gesturing towards me in expectation of an answer.

"Um… I… don't really know, so I guess we'll go with support?" I answered with a question. I really wasn't helpful, was I? Chloe sighed and rolled her eyes. She handed me one of the swimsuits near her. It came with both a top and bottom, of course, and for a second, I wondered if it was possible to only buy the top, but the idea was so ludicrous that it vanished instantly. Of course, you couldn't, what was I thinking? I grabbed it from Chloe's hands and her arms slumped down like she could finally let go of something as heavy as a ton of bricks. She turned around from me and started walking away.

"I'll be going now. See ya." With that, she made her way to the door, leaving me stranded there, still processing what just happened. Why was she so mad, all of a sudden? I knew we hadn't really made up, at least not completely, but she was being very hostile for someone who was my closest friend at one point. It made me a little sad and, somehow, I knew it came back to Camille. I'd really have to ask her about it when I got back. The thought snapped me out of it, and I looked down at the swimsuit I had in my hand. I quickly made my way to the register. I was worried the cashier might think I'm a weirdo for buying women's clothing, but she paid me no mind, almost reciting her monologue and the price by heart or reading from a script. I paid, grabbed the swimsuit and went out the door in a minute. I had to get back to my girlfriend as fast as I could.

It's something I had never realized before, but I always looked down whenever I walked. I'm not even sure why, was it to constantly see where I was going? Then, wouldn't it be better to look straight ahead to avoid running into someone? Did I have to physically see my steps to remember how to walk? That made no sense. Was it to avoid making eye contact with anyone walking the opposite direction? That might have partially to do with it, but what was so wrong about eye contact? It was a little awkward, sure, but nothing I couldn't deal with. I really didn't have an answer to those questions, but when I realized I did look down, I raised my head to see ahead of me instead. And there she was, leaning on the wooden fence, looking out to the lake and the beach. I slowly approached her, leaning right beside her.

"I'm sorry," I started. "I shouldn't have asked."

"Don't worry about that. Is the swimsuit okay?" she asked, still looking ahead. She seemed to be avoiding my eyes.

"Yeah, it should. Thanks for the help, by the way. I didn't have the opportunity to say it before you went out." Chloe smiled a little fake smile and looked down.

"No problem." Her voice was shaky. I didn't understand why, but I didn't probe any further. Even as oblivious as I was, I knew when to drop a subject.

"School is starting soon, isn't it?" She answered with a little positive hum. "Listen, last year without talking to you was…kind of hard. I missed you; I missed what we had before. I know you said it to me before and I said I couldn't do it, but if we keep it to the school, I think it would be fine. Do you think we could…?" I asked.

"I doubt it, Jack. I seriously doubt it." She stood back up from the fence and I copied her, turning towards her. A light breeze picked up and swept her red hair to one side and she held her glasses in place. She looked straight at me with defeated eyes. I didn't quite know how to react and simply stood there, barely more than a scarecrow in a field. She put her hand on my shoulder and I gave it a quick look before returning to meet her eyes. "Goodbye, Jack." Her hand returned next to her, and she turned around, walking away from me. I wanted to tell her to stay and explain what she was thinking, but no words came out. It was like I was completely paralyzed and couldn't move my body even if I wanted to. Eventually, when she was now far away, I regained control, but it was far too late. Plus, I had to get back to Camille. I was very late. My gaze lingered on Chloe, shrinking as she got farther and farther, until I couldn't tell her apart from anyone else. I turned back to look at the lake, sighing a little before descending the familiar creaking wooden steps. I'd really have to ask Camille what all that was about.

I barely stopped at our stuff to undress and hide my wallet. Sam didn't lift his eyes from his book, and I was glad he didn't. There was something about having this swimsuit in my hand, open to the eyes and judgement of everyone that didn't sit right with me. Would they think I'm weird walking into the water with a girl's swimsuit in hand? I hoped they wouldn't get any ideas like I stole it from someone or something like that. But most of all, I didn't want any questions from Sam or any of my friends. I wanted answers from Camille and that's where I went, barely a few seconds after I had stopped to undress. She was in the same spot I left her, she hadn't moved an inch and simply went along to the small waves while everyone around her swam, played and splashed. She, however, was looking straight at me with undecipherable eyes. There was a hint of relief, hidden way back, and what seemed like… anger? Why was she angry? Was she even angry or was I imagining things? I reached her after the cold water hit me again. I thought of stopping to ease myself into it, but Camille's expression made me reconsider and I just went for it. It felt like a rush of sugar or a lightning bolt coursing through my veins. I was keeping the swimsuit top out of the water for reasons that didn't make sense, after all, it was going to be wet anyway, so why bother?

"Here you go!" I said enthusiastically.

"Took you long enough," she said as she snatched it from my hand. "I was freezing out here." She plunged the swimsuit into the water, making a small splash that sent water directly towards me. She brought it to her chest and tried putting it on. Her hands were desperately trying to bind the little clip together around her back, but it looked like it was missing just a little bit of length to the cords as if it was too small.

"Do you need any help?" I offered, moving my hands towards her.

"I've been putting on swimsuits and bras for a lot longer than you, I don't need any help," she responded rather aggressively. I backed up a little, shocked at her response. Why was she like this? Was it something I'd done? If it was, I had no idea what. She finally clipped it together and straightened her back while getting up and out of the water. My eyes locked straight into her chest and even I could tell that it was way too tight to be comfortable. She tried adjusting it, but there was nothing to be done. "Ughh, it's way too small, Jack. What were you thinking?"

"I tried, okay, I never bought a swimsuit for a girl before. Why are you so mad about it?"

"Because it feels like something is constantly pressing against my chest and it's the opposite of comfortable. And who was that you were talking with up there?" she asked, looking directly at me. If I wasn't in water, I might have caught on fire from her eyes alone.

"I met my friend in the store and she counselled me into picking this one," I said, still unsure of why she was so accusatory towards me when I had done her a favor to try to save her from an embarrassing moment.

"She?! Oh my god, Jack, what are you saying? You met up with a girl up there behind my back?"

"It's not like it was planned or anything," I said, subconsciously raising my voice a little. "She's been my friend since high school, I've known her longer than you."

"And who are you dating?"

I looked at her in confusion. What did that have to do with anything? It's not like I was dating Chloe or anything, we had barely spoke and she didn't seem interested in me or Camille at all, so what was the big issue here?

"I'm dating you…? What do you mean? I'm not dating someone else behind your back, that's absurd."

"Oh, Jack…A guy and a girl cannot just be friends, that's impossible. If there's truly nothing going on, then never talk to that girl again. It's a rather simple request, right?"

"I'm not going to stop talking to her just because you don't like that I can have girl friends, what are you saying? You're not making any sense right now!"

"Then I guess this relationship isn't that important to you, is it? I'm not asking for much here, just stop talking to her behind my back and everything will be fine."

"You would break up with me over this? Seriously?"

"Yes."

We stared back at each other for a moment that appeared to last a lifetime. Neither of us wanted to budge and we didn't even blink. We kept eye contact until, finally, I looked down in defeat. I liked Chloe a lot, as a friend, and I really wanted to reconnect with her, but I also didn't want to lose Camille. What if I lost my girlfriend and then Chloe ditched me like she did last year? I'd be left alone again, and I didn't want to go back there. I looked up to meet her eyes. They were still on fire.

"Fine. I'll stop talking to her," I mumbled reluctantly. If anything, I was trying to end the conversation to move and didn't want to linger on the subject any longer.

"See, wasn't that easy? We could have avoided this entire thing if you had just said yes the first time," she said while moving around her swimsuit. She was desperately trying to find a way to make it more comfortable, but after a little while, she gave up. "Why did you have to get it so small?" she mumbled to herself. I heard, but I let it go. I didn't want another fight and just wanted to enjoy the rest of the day.

That was a hard thing to do. From that point on, Camille was irritable, snapping at almost anything and I found myself just avoiding her most of the time, going around for a swim or returning next to Sam before going back in the lake. Sometimes, I'd see one of my friends wandering around from a distance, but everyone was seemingly scattered about. I was sitting on my towel next to Sam when I sighed a bit more heavily than I would have liked. Without lifting his eyes from his book, he broke the silence between us.

"Everything okay?" he said, out of genuine concern. I could tell from his voice. Sam was always a very caring person, very in tune with how others felt around him and would always try to help whenever he could. This time, however, I really didn't see a way he could assist me.

"Not really, no. Camille and I had a little fight and we're kind of avoiding each other right now," I answered, looking down between my legs at the towel motif as if it had the answers to my questions.

"Well, it's not really my business and I don't know her very well, but she'll come around. Just give it a couple hours or a couple days," he said, finally looking at me while putting a bookmark between the pages of his book. I sighed again. She was the one mad, but I was the one running away so who would come around then? My mind wandered to Chloe and what Camille said about her. Was it true? That a guy and a girl cannot be friends? Did I make the right choice? How was I supposed to let her know I couldn't talk to her anymore after both she and I had tried to reconnect somewhat? I rubbed my hand over my face, trying to grab all those thoughts and throw them away, but it didn't work.

"Yeah, I hope so…" I said, letting the words linger in the air. There was still so much to say, but I didn't know if I was ready to talk about it to anyone. Sam seemed to respect that and went back to reading, but I knew he was still available if I ever needed it. I smiled through the sad expression on my face. I was glad he was one of my friends.

The sun was going strong for most of the day but, just like every other day, it started going down on the horizon, tainting the sky with orange and red stripes. If it wasn't for the awkwardness between us, I could have pointed it out to Camille and we could have admired it together, but right now, that seemed impossible. We just had the minimum amount of interaction while packing up our stuff and making our way back to Chris' car. Just as he was opening the trunk and starting to put his stuff in, a hand landed on my shoulder, and I turned around to see who it was. Sam was standing there, in silence, and just nodded at me. I didn't know how he communicated so much from a simple nod, but I understood everything he said and nodded back. He seemed satisfied with the answer and said his goodbye to everyone while waving his hand. My eyes lingered on him, walking back to Vincent's car which was parked a little further away and I smiled. I could always count on Sam.

The trip back was spent mostly in silence. Was it because everyone was tired or did they feel the tension between Camille and me? I didn't know, but no amount of music could appease the palpable friction. Chris tried to initiate a conversation, but only got simple responses and understood now was not the time. There was only one question that got more engagement from Camille.

"So where am I dropping you guys off? To your place?" he asked me by looking in the rear-view mirror.

"Actually, you can drive me back to mine," Camille said. She leaned forward and gave him her address and he nodded. It was on the way, anyway, so it didn't really matter to him. It mattered to me. I was a little disappointed at her response, both because I wished we could have spent the rest of the evening together and chill at my apartment and because I wanted this thing between us to disappear. I felt like going our separate ways was not the best outcome but insisting now would most likely cause another fight and I didn't want to impose that on Chris and Michael. They had nothing to do with it and I didn't want them to see our personal conflicts either. The whole car ride, Camille was looking out the window, facing away from me. I kept stealing glances at her, but she wouldn't budge at all, not paying any attention to me like I was some annoying stranger. I resolved myself to do the same thing. I wondered what she was thinking in that moment, but no answers came.

Eventually, we reached her house and Chris parked right in front of it. He popped the button to open the trunk and Camille quickly got out of the car. I was about to do the same, but she looked at me with furious eyes and I understood immediately. She wasn't in the mood to even talk it out. Perhaps this was worse than I thought, but I couldn't understand why and what the problem was. I just happened to take a size too small for her swimsuit and talked with a friend of mine for a few minutes. What was the big deal? Camille got her things out and walked next to the car, leaning in to talk to Chris and Michael.

"Thanks for the ride," she said in a dry tone.

"No problem," Chris answered, lifting his hands from the wheel to salute her. She didn't respond and simply turned around, walking away from the van. We waited until she got in her house and started driving away. Somehow, it was even more tense when she wasn't here. "You want to talk about it?" asked Chris by looking at me through the mirror.

"Not really, no," I answered. "I'd rather not."

"Alright, man. Just know that we're here for you if there's anything," Michael said, turning around to look at me.

"Thanks, guys," I said absent mindedly, still looking out the window. The streets went by until we had reached my apartment. I slowly got out and walked to the back of the van to get my things. I didn't know why, but the bags seemed heavier than this morning even if she had taken out her stuff. I heard a car door opening and closing and sighed, looking down. Michael put a hand on my shoulder.

"Don't let it get to you, man. I don't know what happened, but you'll get through it. If you manage to get some free time next weekend, maybe we could meet up again, yeah?"

"Yeah, that sounds great. Listen, Michael, I... I don't understand why she's mad, how am I supposed to fix it if I don't understand?"

"The greatest mystery of men, that is. She'll come around and tell you. Just make sure to listen when she does, yeah? Course, that's advice coming from me, so take it with a grain of salt."

She had already told me her reasons, but they didn't make sense to me. Was I supposed to just accept them and move on? Is that what it meant to be in a relationship? That's not what it appeared like to me, but it was my first and only relationship after all. Perhaps I was wrong to think this way? I thanked Michael by nodding down and walked away from the parked van. I went inside the door leading into the building and turned around to salute my friends. They waved back and drove off. I lingered in the doorway for a few moments, lost in thought, but they were as empty as they could be. It was like thinking without thinking, a permanent blank that didn't go away. I didn't know what to do. Should I call her to try and talk things out or let things cool down until she reaches out to me? What about Chloe? Was I supposed to just let her wonder why we couldn't talk anymore? Should I talk to her anyway, regardless of what Camille was saying? All these questions bounced around in my head with no answers in sight. I quietly got my keys out and went up the stairs leading to my apartment. As I opened the door, I was struck by the sudden darkness of it all. Even if it was the same as I left it this morning, it felt cold, uninviting, empty. I stepped inside regardless, put aside the bag next to the front door and closed it behind me. I fell in the bed just a few seconds later, hoping that sleep would take me rather than spend an entire evening wondering what would happen in the next few days, but my hungry stomach had other plans and kept grumbling, preventing me from getting any sort of rest. This was not going to be a fun end of day.

Chapter 9

We had decided to meet up at the bus stop just a few minutes away from school. It was now the end of August and, just like almost every year of my life, school started up again. The heat of summer was slowly fading away but was still very strong today as the sun shining above cast down its rays straight on us. There was no breeze to be felt and the humidity made clothes stick to the skin. I was wearing the lightest shorts I could find, simple jeans cut just above the knee and a green shirt. I usually wore black, but it didn't feel like a good idea with this weather and as soon as I stepped outside, I patted myself on the back for a decision well made. Next to me, Camille was wearing a light white blouse and a long skirt that covered a good portion of her legs. Purse in hand, her long blonde hair was tied up with a little bow, desperately trying to prevent it from sticking to her exposed neck. We thought of putting on sunscreen before coming but felt like it would smell a bit too strong, especially in a closed classroom, and dropped the idea. My neck was burning, and I was silently rubbing it from time to time, hoping I wouldn't get a sunburn. I didn't usually get them, or rather it was very hard for me to get any even without sunscreen, but today was different. It must have been the hottest day of the entire season, with barely any exaggeration. Adding to the fact I had my backpack pressing down on my shoulders and weighing me down, it felt like I was carrying a ton of bricks even though it was mostly empty. The fact we were both exposed waiting at the intersection for the light to signal us to cross didn't help either.

"Are you excited for another school year?" I asked, trying to pass the time with a little conversation.

"Honestly, I think I'm just glad to be getting out of work. I'm fine with working every weekend, one or two days a week, but working full time? I cannot be asked," she answered in a whiny tone.

"I feel exactly the same, actually. I'm always a little bit nervous starting a new year. What type of professors will we get? Ones that give a lot of homework or ones that are more casual about teaching? Will they be nice or severe? You kind of never know before going into it, right?"

"You really worry about school way too much," she laughed a little. "Just go the class like normal and everything will be fine. There's no use asking these many questions. You can't answer them anyways."

"You might be right," I said, nodding approvingly. The light turned green, and the pedestrian sign lit up. We both made our way across the busy boulevard and took to the path leading to the school.

From afar, the building wasn't all that impressive, but it was still larger than the surrounding ones. Shaped like an old manor, it had a left and a right wing closing in the middle section, forming an incomplete square shape. Most of the classes were in the left wing and there were multiple rows of classrooms lined up side by side. It was the busiest part of the school and today would be no exception. Even though my locker was in the left-wing last year, it would probably be moved to the middle section, and I hated the thought. The front part of the school had the main entrances, two double-sided doors separated by staircases leading up to the second floor. The cafeteria was straight ahead as soon as you came in and both to the left and right were rows upon rows of lockers. I hated to be packed in a crowd while I was trying to leave, so last year's locker was the perfect spot for me but given that there were only five of them tucked away back there, the chances of me getting it again were quite low. Perhaps I could get one next to Camille's? The right wing was the least busy part of the school, because it was mostly occupied by the gymnasium. Some classes could be held on the second floor, but not as many as the opposite side for the high ceiling of the gymnasium took out a good chunk of the available space. Straight in the middle of it, on the second floor, was the school library. I enjoyed spending time there, especially in winter when it wasn't practical to go outside unless you wanted to study out in the cold and found it to be a quiet spot where I could work on anything I wanted in relative peace. Sometimes, a group of students would come in and make a little too much noise for my liking, but they would get told off by the librarian quickly enough that it wasn't too big of a problem. I didn't know why but reading in peace at home simply wasn't the same as being at school. Maybe it was the fact that other people around were doing the same thing and we were all silently encouraging each other, like runners keeping pace with runners in front of them in a never-ending cycle of motivation. I had only been to this school for one year, but it already felt like a second home, of sorts.

In front of it stretched a giant courtyard for a few hundred meters. Right in the middle of it, a giant oak tree cast its shadow over a circular patch of grass surrounded by small grey rocks. Judging from the shade, the grass must have been fake, because it was impossible for something to grow without any sunlight, but students didn't seem to mind as a lot of them gathered under the tree to study and read in their spare time. As it was the beginning of classes, the courtyard was crowded and there were no spots left under the oak. What was surprising, however, was the sheer lack of other trees on the entire school grounds. Perhaps they wanted to honor the name Lone Oak University, but was that taking it a little too literal? The grassy fields cut by the stony paths made for a nice aesthetic and walking on them brought out a feeling of nostalgia. Weird considering it was only my second year, yet it felt comforting at the same time.

As we continued walking and the building got closer and bigger, the previously small students now became regular-sized, and the sounds of conversation started reaching us. It was mostly gibberish, and I couldn't make out anything from them, but there was a general sense of joy hovering over everyone there like they were all happy to be back. I looked around, trying to get a feel of the place and take it all in until some familiar red hair caught my attention. I stared a little, trying to figure out if it was really her, and right as I was about to call out to get her attention, Camille interrupted me.

"Hey, is that Ginger I see?!" she asked, excited, looking straight ahead. Chloe looked up from her book and her eyes shifted downwards as soon as she saw us. Camille walked a little faster to get to the bench Chloe was sitting on and stood next to her. "Didn't know you'd be back after last year! How has your summer been?"

"Hi, Camille," Chloe said, still looking down. When I got close, she lifted her head to look at me, but quickly went back to staring at the ground.

"Are you in class 201? I can't wait to sit next to you this year, too!" Camille said, pushing Chloe on the shoulder which caused her to grab for her glasses to hold them in place. She readjusted them quickly.

"No, I'm in 202," Chloe sighed. "I'm sorry."

"Oh, so you're in Jack's class, then? I guess it is fitting for a nerd like you," Camille said, laughing and looking at me for validation. I couldn't let this go on any longer.

"Why are you acting this way?" I asked her, staring straight at her with confusion and, if I was honest, a little bit of disgust.

"I'm just talking to my friend Ginger here. What's so wrong about that?" Camille answered while putting a hand on Chloe's shoulder and shrugging at the same time.

"You're being unnecessarily mean to her. And her name's not Ginger, it's Chloe," I said firmly. Chloe looked up to me and I shifted my eyes to meet hers. She was silently pleading me to make this stop, I could feel it, and I intended on doing just that. I never thought Camille would be capable of doing something like this and I thought less of her for it. I couldn't believe she would bully someone, let alone my friend. But it all made sense now, why Chloe was disappointed as soon as I mentioned Camille. I felt sorry for her, but also was completely baffled by Camille's behavior and couldn't articulate any coherent thoughts. I simply stared back and hoped she would understand what she had silently tried to tell me twice already.

"What, do you know her or something?" Camille asked.

"Yes, she's my friend from high school and you had better stop bullying her. Why are you doing this, anyway? Did she do something to you?"

"Was she the one you talked to at the beach?" Camille asked again, ignoring my own questions.

"Yes, but what does that have to do with anything? Why do you resent her so much? There's no reason for this. I thought you were better than this."

"Oh, well if you were talking to her back there, then you can forget what I said about not talking to her anymore. There's no way someone like her could end up with someone like you, so there's really no problem."

Chloe quickly got up and started walking away. I looked at her shoulders as they went up and down. No doubt, she was crying. Camille turned around to watch her as well.

"Hey, where are you going, Ginger? We were just talking!" she shouted, her words piercing the heat to reach my fleeing friend. I grabbed Camille by the shoulder and turned her around, using perhaps a little too much force than I would have liked. She grunted from pain and looked at me, confused and in shock. "What are you doing? You hurt me."

"Never do this again," I warned, firm and direct. I felt like my eyes were throwing knives just waiting to strike.

"Oh, come on, it was all in good fun. She'll be fine," Camille dismissed with her hand.

"There's nothing fun about this. I thought better of you."

"Whatever." Camille turned her face away from my staring eyes and wiggled her shoulder free. I let go, looking at her for a few seconds before turning around and quickly following Chloe inside the school. If there was anything I could try to salvage, I would, but I felt hopeless. Surely, now, Chloe would hate me. How could I ever stand in front of her again after what Camille had just done? Why didn't she tell me she was being bullied before? Why? There were no answers to my questions, only Chloe could hope to enlighten me on them, but would she even talk to me now? I hoped so as I opened one of the double-sided doors Chloe had gone through and found myself inside, looking to either side for any trace of her. She must not have gone far. I had to find her.

I swung my head back and forth, hoping to catch a glimpse of her fiery hair. That was how I normally found Chloe as the monochrome walls of the school interior made her pop out even more. I guessed that wasn't a good thing if Camille was always being this mean whenever she saw her, but I didn't have time to think about that. I couldn't see past the locker rows in the doorway, and I moved up towards the cafeteria to stare down both corridors leading to each wing. Students were looking at me, I could feel their gaze on me, but I couldn't worry about them right now. Chloe wasn't in the corridors, and it didn't seem possible that she would run into the cafeteria sobbing like she was, so I figured she must have been at her locker. But which row? I decided to follow my instincts and went right. Some little voice in my head was telling me this was the correct direction, but what if it was wrong? I had an urge to talk to Chloe right now, a feeling like this couldn't wait until after class. What if she was on the left side and the classes start and I missed my chance? No, she would be here, I knew it. I didn't know why, it was more wishful thinking than anything, yet I convinced myself to go forward regardless. I ran past a group of students standing in front of the cafeteria and some others sitting on benches nearby. I almost bumped a few others that were coming in the other doors, but I managed to dodge them just in time. Finally, I reached the lockers and proceeded to look down each row. Then, at the end of the final one, I saw her sitting down, her face hidden in her hands and knees up to her chin. I approached her slowly, trying to slow down my breathing which had gotten a lot faster. She didn't react at all when I got close.

"Chloe…" I started, uncertain of what I was going to say, what words I needed to say, what words she needed to hear from me.

"Go away," she answered through tears.

"Chloe, listen to me…"

"I said go away! I don't want to talk to you right now."

"What Camille did was wrong. I don't know how long this has been going on, but there's no excuse for it. I'm not going to say she didn't mean it, because she did, but regardless, I'm sorry this has happened to you. If there's anything I can do…"

"Like you didn't know about it, you jerk."

"Truly, I didn't. I'm also sorry for not being there for you when you needed me. I…"

Chloe stood up in a flash and looked straight at me. She was crying still, but her eyes were that of anger. It took me off guard.

"Not there? You're the one who cut me off completely when I started going out with Kyle!"

"Woah, hold on."

"Do you have any idea how long this has been going on? It's already been a year, a painful year of torture, every day, she would find me and insult me, berate me, call me names, whatever you can think of and you just say you're *sorry*? Add to that the fact you started going out with her? What was I supposed to do, come to you to say that your girlfriend was being a bully? Would you have listened to me? It's not about you, Jack, don't try to take the moral high ground here. Your girlfriend is mean and there's nothing more to it."

"She made a mistake, Chloe, she…"

"Don't defend her, I don't want to hear it. One day, she'll do the same to you. She will break your heart in two and when that day comes, don't come crying to me. If the last year is any indication, you don't even care anymore anyway."

"You know that's not true, I…"

"You almost had me, you know? When we met in the park and at the beach? You almost made me think you were trying to reach out and you could have changed her, somehow. How naïve I was to think that. You can never change her; she is and always will be a bully"

"She doesn't bully me. Did you do something to her?"

"Don't try to flip it on me! How dare you try to blame me! I did nothing to her!"

"Look, I know you don't want to hear it, but Camille is a good person. She bullies you and that's wrong, I agree completely, but she must have a reason for it. I'm just trying to understand it to be able to make it stop. Do you understand? I'm trying to help you."

Chloe looked down for a second, in thought. Her tears had slowed down, leaving traces across her cheeks and making her eyes puffy. She readjusted her glasses as she looked up at me.

"There's no reason for this. There's no excuse. You can try to reason with her, but that will never work, because she's just an unreasonable person. Believe me, I tried. Regardless, if you keep going out with her, I don't want to see either of you anymore."

Chloe turned around and walked away from me, leaving me standing among the lockers, alone and confused. She kept mentioning there was no reason, but it didn't make sense to me. Camille, the one who went stargazing with me, the one with whom I had my first kiss, shared my first time, the one who I went on countless dates with, was bullying someone for no reason? It simply didn't fit in my mind. Surely, there was a piece missing and I intended on finding what it was. If Chloe didn't have the answer, then Camille would. I also turned around, focused on finding her. I saw Chloe walking away at a fast pace and figured I would wait a little bit before going to not make it look like I was going after her. Then, my eyes landed on the giant clock hanging up on the wall just above the cafeteria. Classes were about to start, and I knew I wasn't in the same one as Camille. I'd have to catch her afterwards. I silently cursed, frustrated at my inability to do anything about the situation. Why did Camille keep this from me? Why did Chloe not talk to me about it? Why was I so incompetent? The sound of people moving around took me out of my thoughts and made me follow them like a sheep following the herd. My class was on the opposite side of the school, but I still had time to make it. As I walked, I avoided the looks of everyone else and kept my eyes glued to the ground. How could I look anyone in the eye, now? My girlfriend was bullying my friend and I didn't know about it at all. How could you blame the ignorant for not knowing? Well, I was certainly blaming myself, because if this would cause me to lose Chloe forever, then... I couldn't let this happen. I fully intended to get to the bottom of this and figure out the real reason why she was bullying her. Before I knew it, I was standing in the doorway of my class. I stood there for a second, lost and confused, like I didn't know how I got here. I heard a voice behind me telling me to move aside if I was just going to stand there and I shifted to the left to let them pass. Two girls, clearly annoyed, went past me. I looked at them, then at the entire class. I scanned the room, looking for an empty seat. There was only one left, in the back row next to...Chloe. Why was fate so cruel sometimes? I walked across the room and sat down, trying to avoid meeting Chloe's eyes, but she didn't even look up, ignoring me completely. I guessed it was better this way. I took out my phone and texted Camille.

Meet me at my old locker after class. We need to talk.

Just as I was sending the message, the professor walked in and greeted the class. This was going to be a long lesson.

◊

"Hey."

Camille's voice reached my ears and I turned around to see her. Just as I said, we were meeting at my old locker, away from any others that could be hearing our conversation. She stood there, not quite leaning on the wall, but close enough that it could appear so. I couldn't decipher if she was annoyed or just talking normally, but I was inclined to believe the former, just in case. She kept looking down, avoiding my eyes, and I was doing the same.

"Hey, you came," I said, trying to talk in a softer voice. Camille nodded, but kept her eyes glued to the floor. "Listen, I know what you're going to say, but this is about Chloe." Her eyes shot up and stared at me directly. If she wasn't annoyed before, she was now. I could tell from her body language that, not only did she not want to be here, she most certainly did not want to talk about Chloe of all people.

"I don't want to talk about her," she said firmly.

"I know, but we have to. I have to know why you're being so mean to her. Camille, you're a nice person, I know that, or else I wouldn't be going out with you, but this isn't right. Why are you doing this?"

"It's all she deserves after what she did," Camille answered, her tone shifting from annoyance to anger. I was confused by her answer as Chloe never mentioned anything to me and she said she hadn't done anything. Something didn't add up, but I didn't know who was lying.

"What did she do? She said she didn't do anything" I said, trying to get an answer. Camille rolled her eyes and shrugged animatedly.

"Of course, she didn't tell you, why would she? You want to know what she did? She cheated on my brother with some douchebag named Kyle and sent him into a depression that he still hasn't recovered from. She destroyed him completely. Did she tell you that?" Camille asked, getting angrier and angrier by the second.

"You have a brother?" I asked out of genuine shock. She had never mentioned him and I never saw him from all the times I went at her house. I had met her parents, of course, and we had dinner a few times with them, but there wasn't a single mention of a brother. Was she making things up to frame Chloe? How can you hide the existence of a close family member like that? It's not like I was her boyfriend for long, but I figured in a few months she would have said his name or just casually mention the fact she had a brother, but there was nothing. Nothing came to mind.

"Of all the things to get hooked up on, it was that. Really? Yes, I have an older brother, his name is Max and that ginger girl ruined his life. Pretentious glasses-wearing..." Camille's insult got lost in a whisper.

"You never said you had a brother," I said. "Why did I never see him at your house before?"

"Oh, my god, this is not what's important right now! He's not living at my house, he moved out after the breakup and is doing much worse since then, but he refuses any help. The fact is, it's all your friend's fault that he's like this now and I'm simply making her pay on his behalf. That's it, nothing more, nothing less."

I took a few seconds to think. If what Camille was saying was true, then Chloe was clearly in the wrong for what she did, there was no denying that. And it did make sense with what I had heard a year prior. I knew she had a boyfriend when she started going out with Kyle and she didn't mention breaking up with him, so I called her out on it. She didn't appreciate the insinuation and we had a big fight that led to us not talking for a year. If that previous boyfriend was indeed named Max, then everything could be true. However, Camille might also be lying and trying to bully Chloe for no reason, or rather, for another reason. Chloe claimed that she didn't do anything, but Camille was claiming the opposite. Who was lying and why? It's not like I trusted one more than the other, one was a long-time friend and the other was my girlfriend. It did seem odd that Camille was suddenly acting this way when she never showed any sign of it when we went out for dates and she didn't seem to bully anyone else, but wasn't targeting one person specifically a thing bullies normally do? Even though I talked to both of them already, the answer was still blurry, and I couldn't make out the truth. Perhaps I would have to talk to Chloe again now that I had Camille's version of the story. Nonetheless, the bullying had to stop, that much was still firm in my mind.

"I'm hearing what you're saying, Camille, but it all comes back to one thing; you have to stop bullying Chloe. It's wrong, it's not who you are, and I know you are better than this." Camille rolled her eyes at me and looked away.

"Why are you so protective of her? Why do you keep defending her?" she asked, almost like a mumble, but loud enough that I would hear it. And I didn't have an answer. Was it simply the fact she was my friend or was there another reason hidden behind it? Was I just doing what I believed to be right or did I have a subconscious ulterior motive? "What, do you love her or something? Yeah, right." Her words and tone made me confused, and I couldn't come up with a definitive answer. After a few seconds, Camille continued. "Look at how you're acting right now, you're ridiculous! You need to stop seeing and talking to her."

"I've said this before, I'm not doing that. If you continue to try and control what I do, who I can or can't see, bullying my friend, then this isn't going to work out." I blurted the words and regretted them almost instantly as Camille looked up straight at me, daggers in her eyes, staring straight into my soul. I could feel the sharpness of her gaze and we stood there in silence for a few seconds that felt like an eternity. I didn't understand what was so hard to understand about it. I just wanted her to stop harassing Chloe and I wanted to be able to talk to her. Was that so much to ask? I tried being assertive in my statement, both back at the beach and just now, but it only appears to have backfired in my face. Camille's face barely moved when she broke the tension between us.

"I can't believe you would choose her over me. I'm done." She turned around and slammed the doors, pushing them open with a loud bang and made her way next to the staircase to the door leading out of the school. I stood there, shocked, angry at myself for saying what I did, and regretting how this conversation ended. I didn't like to fight, I wasn't a confrontational person, but I stood firm for what I believed in. What Camille was doing was wrong, but was I ready to lose her and our relationship over it? Would Chloe even talk to me if the bullying stopped, or would she still ignore me? I rubbed my hands across my face and sighed heavily. How did it come to this? Where had summer gone?

◊

It was now two days later. I didn't have another class until today and kept clear of the school as much as possible. Camille and I hadn't spoken since the fight we had and although I reached out to Chloe, she hadn't responded to my messages. I was expecting as much, but it still didn't feel good to be ignored like this. I was both hoping I would and wouldn't run into her today, because I felt like we had a lot to talk about but was dreading having the conversation at all. I sighed a little as I made my way through the school courtyard.

The weather had been nice this week and today was no exception. Although not as hot as Monday, the sun was still shining bright high up in the sky. A nice breeze cooled me down every now and then, making the heat a little more bearable. Under the giant oak in the courtyard, countless students were sitting in its shade, enjoying the outside while avoiding the heat waves of the sun. As much as I liked summer, this type of heat was simply the worst. I liked it better when a little jacket was enough to feel comfortable outside, but summer wasn't here to last much longer so I figured I might as well enjoy it before it goes away to make place for autumn.

As I reached the main part of the courtyard where the oak stood strong, I noticed Chloe sitting on a bench, facing away from me. She was in the exact same spot as Monday, but this time, I was alone; Camille wasn't here. I had to talk to her, not only to tell her the full story, but to say that I knew what

110

happened and to try and make amends to regain our friendship. I walked up to the bench and shyly greeted her.

"Hi," I said, unsure of how I should start this conversation. How could a simple greeting be this hard to figure out? Chloe lifted her eyes from her book and met mine. She only looked at me for a second before loudly closing her book, picking up her purse and walking away. I didn't react immediately, I definitely wasn't expecting that kind of response, but I couldn't let her get away before at least saying what I had to say. "I know about Max and Kyle" I said, hoping that would grab her attention. And it did. Chloe turned around halfway, like she was unsure if she wanted to really proceed with this talk or if she just wanted to ignore me.

"You've known about them for a year now, what about it?" she asked in an annoyed voice. She didn't want to talk about them, that much I was certain. Yet I had to.

"I learned something recently that might be important to you. Max is…Camille's brother," I revealed, praying she would take it well. What did that mean, I wasn't even sure, but I was hoping to avoid a blow up or Chloe getting angry at me.

"Okay, so?" she asked, not following what that meant. It was like she didn't care at all.

"Chloe, when you broke up with Max, it sent him in a very bad depression and he still hasn't recovered from it. Camille is blaming you for that and that's why she's taking it out on you. Do you get what I'm saying?

"I really couldn't care less about Max right now. And I don't care what her reason is, she's still a bully and you're still her boyfriend. I don't want anything to do with you anymore. Please stop talking to me."

Chloe turned around, preparing to walk away, but stopped in her tracks when she spotted a blonde girl coming her way from another direction. She grunted in frustration and stood there until Camille arrived next to us.

"What do you want?" Chloe asked Camille in an aggressive tone.

"What are you doing here, Camille? You don't have any classes today, do you?" I asked.

"I'm still not talking to you," she answered while looking at me. She turned around to face Chloe who avoided her eyes by looking down. "Listen closely, because I'm only going to say it once. I still hate you for what you did and I will never forgive you for it, that much you can be sure. However, I am willing to ignore you instead of being mean. Don't get any ideas, it's not for your sake, but for Jack's. Speaking of which, Jack is MY boyfriend and whatever you think you're doing or planning, you need to cut it out and leave him alone. Got it? Good. That's all."

And with that, Camille turned around and left, leaving both Chloe and I speechless. We looked at each other for a moment, still processing everything Camille had just said. She came in like a hurricane, devastating us with her words and leaving a wreckage behind. Did I hear her correctly? She said she would stop bullying Chloe…for my sake? Was it because of what I said last time we spoke? I was relieved, not for me, but for Chloe. I've been wanting Camille to stop harassing her ever since I knew about it which, granted, was only two days ago, but I felt like I gave it an honest effort and, finally, I was successful.

"That wasn't so bad," I said out loud, looking in Chloe's direction. She simply huffed and readjusted her glasses before turning around and leaving. I had hoped it would make things better between us, but I guess she needed more time. There was only one thing I didn't quite understand about what Camille had just said. She said to stop doing whatever Chloe was planning or something along those lines. What did that mean? What was Chloe trying to do that affected Camille so much that she felt the need to point it out? It also involved me somehow, but Chloe was actively trying to avoid me for months now, rather she didn't feel interested in talking to me in the slightest. Then, what was Camille trying to say? I felt a wave of heat rushing through my body and I snapped out of my thoughts, realizing that Chloe was long gone, and I was standing directly in the sun, taking the full brunt of its assault. For some reason, standing still was worse than walking, as if being mobile somehow dodged sun rays. If anything, it should be worse because you're moving around, right? I shook my head a little and started moving towards the school. I sighed, thinking of both Camille and Chloe. A few months ago, things were so simple. Camille was almost a complete stranger, a girl in one of my classes I had developed a small crush on and Chloe wasn't talking to me at all. I had a few friends and no drama of any kind. While now, it seemed that drama was following me everywhere I went, hiding in my shadow and biding its time to strike at any moment. Why were relationships so unnecessarily complicated? Maybe I needed some time off, like an evening out with the guys at a bar or something. I took out my phone and opened our group chat. I typed out an invitation and within minutes I had a few replies, scheduling a meet up on Saturday. At least I could always count on them to support one another when something was going on. I wondered how Chris and Vincent were doing it. They both had girlfriends of their own. Were they also caught up in some drama like I was? Thinking about it, why was I the only one to bring my girlfriend along on that trip? Sure, it was for her to meet my friends in the first place, but now that I thought about it, it really was odd, wasn't it? I'd have to ask both guys, I suppose. Both were coming on Saturday, too, so then was a perfect opportunity. I couldn't wait for the weekend to arrive, and it was only the first week of school.

Chapter 10

The week went by and soon enough Saturday was here. Camille and I hadn't really talked since Monday and while I tried to reach out, she didn't respond to any of my messages, so I figured I'd let her cool down and let things go for now. I didn't bother sending her a text this morning for that same reason. I missed her a lot, but I didn't know what else to do and thought that night would a good opportunity to ask Chris and Sam about it. Maybe even some of the other guys could pitch in ideas as well. And so, here we were, at the bar sitting around a table with beer in hand talking about random stuff that happened that week, school starting again, what kind of classes we had, how strict the professors seemed and so on. Despite my drama troubles, I tried to let it go and join in the fun, laughing with everyone and just enjoying my evening.

"So, how's it going with Camille?" Chris asked, looking at me while waving his beer around. Every pair of eyes turned to me and I felt myself shrink in my seat. I wanted to say everything was good, simply to get out of the center of attention, but I simply couldn't get myself to lie like that.

"It's… not going so well. We aren't talking right now, there's been some drama, I don't want to bore you guys with it and it's a little personal so, yeah, that's about it," I explained looking down at the table.

"That seems to happen an awful lot, huh?" Michael commented.

"Hey, I told you to keep that to yourself, man," Sam said to Michael.

"Guys, stop, he doesn't need this right now," Chris said, trying to prevent an argument. "Well look, man, if you want to tell us a little bit about it, then we can maybe try to help you, but if you keep it bottled up, there's not much we can do."

"Yeah… I know," I sighed, contemplating telling them everything or only parts of it. I lifted my eyes from the table and they wandered all across the room. The bar wasn't very well lit and the dim atmosphere brought some comfort to the various tables with the low-hanging lights over them. The wooden feel of the place reminded me of an old cottage deep in the woods and you could almost smell it if it weren't for the kitchen right next to us.

Between us was a giant wood counter with numerous stools with green cushions. There were a lot of banquettes scattered all along the edges of the bar, including the one we were sitting on, and their emerald cushions made the wood finish pop out even more. The bar wasn't that busy tonight, surprisingly so for a Saturday night, and the chatter of conversations only rose to a manageable volume. Some parts of the walls were made of stone and hanging on each one was a painting that illustrated the history of the bar. Most of them seemed to be really old, the colors fading from the canvas by each passing day while some of them were vibrant like they were done yesterday. At the very back, hidden and tucked away was a fireplace that roared slightly, bringing a little bit of heat to the front of the bar where most costumers sat. I was glad to be surrounded by friends in this sort of place, because recent events were kind of throwing me off and I didn't quite know how to respond to them. Their counselling, for good or for worse, was comforting.

"Um…where to start…So, you guys know about my old friend Chloe, right?" I asked. They all nodded positively, prodding me to go on. "I finally talked to her again at the tail end of last semester and another time at the beach. I won't go into too many details, but Camille doesn't like her and was being mean to her, telling me I needed to stop talking to her. I said that wasn't an option and she thinks I'm choosing Chloe over her. Obviously, this is not what's happening, but yeah, I don't know how to resolve this."

"That does sound like a delicate situation. In any case, you need to set boundaries with Camille and make them clear. You're allowed to have girl friends too," Chris said.

"Man, if I had a girlfriend and she wouldn't allow me to see or talk to other girls, that wouldn't work out in a heartbeat," Michael commented.

"I actually had a similar issue at the beginning with my girlfriend," Vincent said. "I managed to convince her that I wasn't going to cheat on her with every girl I talked to and that it was okay to have friends of the opposite sex. It took a while, but she understood. Now, it all comes down to if Camille even wants to understand."

"She is very firm about what she believes in and a pretty direct person in general," I said. "I'm not sure I'll be able to…"

"Maybe you could show her what you mean, somehow? Convince her of your intentions, right? Like going somewhere with both…ah, no, that wouldn't work, they don't like each other, I forgot," Chris said.

"I feel like there's an element of trust missing here," Sam said. "She clearly doesn't trust you enough for you to talk to other girls. Have you done anything to earn or lose that trust?" he asked. I never really thought about it, but maybe it was something on my side. Did I do anything to earn her trust? What would that even be? We went on dates together, we even had sex, would you have sex with someone you don't trust? It didn't add up in my head, but surely there was something to it if things were on thin ice between us. We had our fights here and there, but I thought it was normal for a couple to have them occasionally. Perhaps I could do something on that front, but what? Just as I was about to vocalize my train of thought, my phone vibrated in my pocket. I took it out and checked to see who was calling me. It was Camille. We almost never called each other; I preferred texting as I felt like I could choose my words better to say what I truly mean. Phone calls made me nervous and sometimes I would say the wrong thing and that would lead to a completely different conversation. The sight of her name almost made me want to ignore it.

"Speaking of which, that's her," I said, shaking my phone in my hand in their direction. "Should I answer?"

"I wouldn't recommend not answering it. Trust me, you don't want to miss a call like this, especially now that you guys aren't on best terms. It's fine, man, just answer it. You can go farther if you don't want us to listen in," Chris said.

I silently thanked him and got up from my seat while answering the phone and bringing it to my ear. I walked away, getting closer to the hidden fireplace in a section where nobody was seated. I liked to pace back and forth whenever I did call someone, but I tried to restrain myself here.

"Hello?"

"Hey, are you coming home soon?" she said, almost in a panic like she had to say those words as fast as possible. The question took me a little by surprise. As far as I recalled, we didn't plan to meet up today and I wasn't sure what she meant by home. Did she mean my place or hers?

"Did we have something planned today? I'm out with the guys at the bar at the moment," I said.

"Are you serious?" There was a slight pause where none of us spoke. It clearly was up to me to respond, but her tone indicated that she wouldn't like what I was about to say.

"Uh… yes? Is there something wrong?" I asked.

"You absolute jerk!" she shouted at me while hanging up the phone. The end of call tone resonated in my ear for a few seconds as I stood there confused. What just happened? Why was she so mad all of a sudden? It felt like I had done something to her, something about today, but I didn't understand what. I was racking my brain, trying to remember something, anything, that would be linked to today, but found nothing. Today was…September 3rd. Was there an event on September 3rd? I opened my calendar app on my phone, but the day only had one thing: going out with the guys. I liked to schedule any events, dates, or evenings on it, but there clearly was something missing here. Something about Camille and today… I tried to recall previous conversations, perhaps ones where we told each other things to know one another better like favorite colors, hobbies and such. Then, one sentence jolted to my mind.

My birthday is on September 3rd. Don't forget! she had said to me once.

I did not just do that. I was such an idiot. I quickly got back to our table where all the others looked at me with anticipation, but I avoided their questioning looks. I didn't have time. I quickly slammed a 20$ bill on the table to pay for my drinks and bolted out of the bar. I heard Michael shouting at me in the background, but his muffled voice couldn't reach me now. My mind was spinning the fastest it had ever spun. I ran all the way to the nearest bus stop that would take me close to Camille's house and looked at my phone for the time. Luckily, the next one was scheduled in two minutes and, just as I was lifting my eyes from the phone screen, the bus loudly turned the corner at the end of the street. I sighed in relief, but my heart didn't get the message and started pumping even faster. There were a thousand questions bouncing around in my head and making me dizzy. What would Camille say? How could I mess up this bad? Can this bus get here faster? I calculated I would be at her house in minimum fifteen minutes, probably more like twenty. That was way too much, but what other choice did I have? The bus stopped in front of me and opened its doors. I've never gotten on a bus this fast before. I quickly paid and went to sit down at the back. Unconsciously, my legs were moving all around, I must have looked like I was on drugs or something, but nobody was really paying any attention to me. I kept looking at my phone, looking at the time, desperately begging the bus to go faster, but it was in vain. There is this sinking feeling that takes over when you realize you're going to be late and there's nothing you can do about it. It grabs your heart and rips it out, a kind of nervousness that takes hold of your body. I was so focused on keeping myself contained that I almost missed the stop. Signaling the driver to stop the bus, I got up and stood at the doors closest to the back, running out as fast as I could. Camille's house was about a five-minute walk from here, but I was intending to go a lot faster than that. My legs were moving on their own, seemingly gliding across the sidewalk under my feet. My breath got rough and loud, and my legs started to hurt, but I couldn't give up now. Soon enough, completely exhausted, Camille's house appeared into view. I climbed the few steps leading to the front door and rang the doorbell. I took a moment to catch my breath, bending down a little to rest my hands on my knees. No answer. I rang the bell again. No answer. My phone vibrated once in my pocket, and I took it out to see Camille had sent me a message.

Go away

At this point, I was pretty sure she wouldn't open the door. Luckily for me, she had given me a key a few weeks back in case she wasn't home and I wanted to wait for her inside. I took them out from my pocket with a jingle and started browsing through them. I've never had to use it before, so it would take longer for me to find it, but I was certain I had one. I scrambled through them one by one until I found it, put it in and turned the lock with a heavy chonk. I pushed the door open with a loud creak, announcing my presence louder than I would have liked and closed it behind me. I stood in the doorway for a few seconds as souvenirs came back to me. The way she dragged me up the steps in front of me, a dinner we had with her parents in the dining room to the right, a cozy evening we spent in front of the TV on the left. Here, the house was silent and cold, almost like nobody was home, but I knew that wasn't true. I started making my way up the steps to the second floor and stopped in front of Camille's bedroom door. Even through it, I could hear Camille sobbing, even if it sounded like she was trying to be quiet. I knocked on the door.

"Camille…"

"Go away!" she shouted, her voice cracking from her sobbing. I had never heard her voice like that before and it felt like needles ran through my heart. It made me sad as well, I didn't enjoy this situation at all. But it was my fault and I had to pay the price. Unfortunately, it seemed Camille was paying even more.

"Camille, I'm sorry. I didn't mean to…Can you open the door?"

"I don't want to see you right now. Go away."

"Can we at least talk it out? I made a mistake, but let me redeem myself by…"

"I don't want to talk either. Leave me alone and get out of my house," she interrupted. Her sobbing continued even though now she tried to muffle them in her pillows. My hand limply went down from the door, and I stood there, in front of it, completely hopeless. What was I supposed to do? Barge in? Force the door? That wouldn't be right, and she would hate me for sure. Leave? Wouldn't that make it worse or seem like I didn't really care enough about her? What other choice did I have? I rubbed my face with my hands, trying to come up with a solution and only one thing seemed to fit the bill.

They say sleep is the best counselor. That's what we both needed, I thought. She needed to calm down and I needed to figure out how to make it up to her and assure her I'd do better. I looked up at the white door, a barricade between Camille and me, a separation preventing us from expressing ourselves fully, a plank of wood that appeared to be a mile thick.

"I'll be in the guest room." I paused for a few seconds, trying to gather my thoughts and what I was going to say next, but there was only one thing I could say. "I'm sorry." I stopped myself before saying another word. I wanted to tell her I loved her, how much she meant to me, but that wouldn't have been right. I might not have a lot of experience in relationships, but even I knew in that moment that saying those words would bring out a storm of negativity and it was probably better to let it die down. I would have plenty of opportunities to tell her that in the morning. In the morning. Was I really planning on sleeping over tonight? Was that a wise decision? I didn't think she would do anything in my sleep, but a week prior I thought I knew Camille and then all this bullying situation came out and I wasn't sure about anything anymore. I turned away from the door and walked to the end of the hallway towards the guest room. The door opened without a sound, and I stood there, looking back one last time before closing it behind me. While I should have been restless and trying to come up with a solution, I couldn't help but yawn as soon as I was alone in the room. I was exhausted from both the roller coaster of emotions that had taken over me and my running here in a panic. I crashed down on the bed and looked at the ceiling for answers. Unfortunately for me, there was nothing written up there that could help me, only white paint that stared back. Even the ceiling seemed to be angry or maybe that was my imagination running wild trying to justify what I did. How could I forget something so important? I was never good at remembering stuff, that much I knew for a fact, but I thought I was pretty good at remembering birthdays and important events, things that only come once a year, that sort of thing. Apparently, I was mistaken and that had cost me a great deal. I looked at my phone and was surprised at the number of messages I had. In my panic, I hadn't noticed all my friends had texted me asking what I was doing, where I was going, asking if I was okay. I didn't feel like answering back and sighed heavily. I had messed up, badly, and was hoping for Camille to forgive me. Only time would tell and, even if it wasn't that late, I forced myself to sleep. It took a very long time, but eventually managed to clear my thoughts enough to lose myself in the dream world. It wasn't going to be a good night, that much I expected, but was still hoping to get at least some rest to talk it out with Camille the next morning.

I hazily opened my eyes. It was still night, and the room was pitch black. I couldn't see anything, but still looked around in confusion. I knew I didn't wake up by myself and felt some movements on the opposite side of the bed. I wasn't a light sleeper by any means, sometimes it was like I heard and felt everything going on in the room subconsciously, but that was unusual to say the least. There was clearly something in the bed with me and I didn't recall Camille having any pets. Just as I was about to call out to whoever got in with me, her hand reached out and rested on my chest. There was another shift and suddenly, her leg was on top of me, and her chest was straddling my left arm. Her head came to rest next to my neck, tucked in the space between my head and shoulders. I tried to move my arm gently as to not wake her up or make sudden movements and managed to slip it out of her grasp. It went down her back and almost all the way down to her butt where I pushed her slightly towards me. I wanted to feel her more, I didn't want to let this unexpected moment go. In that instant, I almost forgot about what happened, but reality caught up to my still hazy mind and questions started appearing suddenly.

Why was she here? Why did she do this? Perhaps I was reading too much into this and she wasn't that mad about yesterday's events? That last one was a bit of a stretch, but just like anyone can dream anything at night, my heart wanted to hope she would forgive me. And the fact she was here now, cuddling and sleeping with me, surely that meant something, right? I could feel her breathing on my neck as it gradually slowed down and she fell asleep once again. I restrained myself, trying to stay awake, but not really sure why. To be certain she wouldn't leave or maybe to enjoy this moment because I knew something would happen tomorrow? Her hand took me out of those thoughts as it suddenly moved from my chest downwards. I was a bit ticklish and tried to contain my laughter as she grazed on my bare skin. Her hand stopped right on my crotch, cupping both my member and my balls. I was startled but couldn't move an inch as she was resting on me, and she would surely wake up if I reacted. Was she really asleep, though? Maybe she was just pretending to see what I would do? In any case, my face became red in the darkness of the room, and I shifted my entire body on its side. She was now cuddling my back and I tried to make myself small to fit between her arms. Like on instinct, they grabbed me from each side and pulled me back to her. Her breathing was now down my neck and with every warm breath, I felt a heat pulse through my body. Even though her hand wasn't there anymore, my member started getting active. I shook my head. We couldn't. Not now, certainly, it wouldn't be right. I tried to calm down and it took a very long time, but I got there. Just before falling asleep too, I wondered was all this meant. Perhaps she wasn't that mad at me after all...

I slowly opened my eyes as the curtain of sleep slid back, letting the morning sun hit my face. It took me a few seconds to realize where I was, my mind still not totally back from the dream world. I turned to look beside me, but there was nothing. Even the sheets were neatly tucked in like nobody was ever there. Was it all a dream? The previously pitch-black room was now lit by daylight, and I looked around, trying to see any trace of Camille's last night passage, but found nothing of interest. Like a ghost, she seemingly came in and out without leaving so much as a hair behind, which was very surprising considering her hair length. The bookshelves on my left and the desk on my right didn't have anything either. Otherwise, this room was as empty as can be. I sighed a little. What was I going to say to her? I already apologized numerous times and she didn't want to hear it. What made me think she would want to hear it now? They say to never go to sleep angry and to always talk it out before going to bed, but if one side never wanted to hear what the other had to say, communication was hard. I completely understood how she felt, though, and when I thought about people forgetting my birthday, I felt disappointed too so I couldn't blame her for her feelings. I slowly got up from the bed and got dressed up with the same clothes as the day prior. They felt colder to the touch than I thought they would. I made the bed on my way out and stood in the doorway thoughtfully. I stayed for a few seconds and finally turned away from it, fully intending to figure out myself what happened last night. I went up to her bedroom door to find it open and empty. The curtains were still drawn at the back window, leaving the room in shadow even though morning had come. She must already be downstairs, I figured, and so I went down the stairs to look for her.

She was sitting at the dining room table, munching on some toast while looking at her phone. I wasn't a heavy walker, I tried to avoid making any unnecessary noise when possible but even I made the stairs creak a little under my weight. Yet she remained glued to her phone, either oblivious or clearly ignoring me. I was more confident it was the latter, as sad as it made me.

"Good morning," I said, trying to initiate a conversation. It didn't work as she continued scrolling, sometimes taking a bite of her breakfast. I was hungry too, yet not at the same time. I didn't want to eat toast right now, I wanted to hear her voice, I wanted her to say it was alright, I wanted to feel her lips on mine, I wanted… But we don't always get what we want. I turned away from her and walked to the kitchen to make my own breakfast. She didn't stop me, didn't even make a sound or movement at all. I popped two pieces of bread into the toaster as well and turned around to watch her. Whenever someone was watching me, I felt their eyes on me after a few seconds. It was a weird feeling, that one, almost a lost instinct of some kind and I didn't quite understand it. It's a little tingle you feel on your neck or your back, almost like their eyes were burning your skin by staring. I didn't know if others also had this feeling and if they did, Camille was doing a fantastic job of ignoring it right now. I wondered what she was thinking about at that moment. It took a few minutes of complete silence besides her occasional munching until, finally, my toast popped up. I breathed a sigh of relief and finished making my breakfast with my back turned. When I was done, I walked back to the table and sat across from her. There was a tension in the air between us, almost palpable, frozen solid like a glacier and I had nothing to break it. The room felt smaller, the seat wasn't comfortable under me, even the sound of silence was annoying. I knew I had to be the one breaking it but didn't know how.

"I'm truly sorry for what happened yesterday. There is no excuse, I messed up and I hope you'll be able to forgive me," I said, looking down at the table, unable to maintain eye contact with her. But there was no response. I lifted my head; Camille was eating without a care in the world, almost like my words hadn't reached her. It felt like I was a ghost, trapped in another dimension capable of seeing her, but unable to talk to her. She kept scrolling on her phone while I was over here battling inside myself to apologize correctly, and she wanted none of it. "Talk to me, please." I paused a few seconds. "You can't keep ignoring me like this, it's not helping…" I sighed, more talking to myself than to her. Yet, that caught her attention.

"I can't? Who are you to say what I can and can't do? And you know what's not helping? Your constant forgetfulness. It's like you can't go on two seconds without forgetting what you just did. It's annoying, it's bothersome and it's cumbersome mentally. Do you have any idea how it is to be with someone like this? I have to remember twice as much because you can't be bothered to remind yourself of the most basic stuff. You are so selfish and inconsiderate of others around you. How is it even possible to forget a birthday? Especially since I've been talking about it directly to you and you always responded positively so what gives? I even took specific care to ask my parents to be out of the house last night so we could spend the evening together and then you went out with your stupid friends instead? I just can't deal with this anymore. You ruined everything and then you have the gall to come up to me this morning and say, 'Good morning'? You know, when I first asked you out, I didn't think you were this much of a jerk, but I guess we never know for sure, huh? What do you even have to say for yourself?" she finished, her eyes staring daggers at me. If they were real, I would have long been impaled by now but, luckily for me, I was still alive to tell the tale. Or not.

Even though it was my turn to talk, the words just wouldn't come out. Hers shocked me far more than I thought they would and cut through me like a hot knife through butter. It was like she grabbed my heart with her bare hands and squeezed it out of my chest. However, she was completely justified in her anger. I really did mess up and hurt her feelings, I knew that, but it seemed to go way back than just yesterday. Why didn't she tell me it was bothering her this much then? I wanted to ask her, but now was not a good time, unless I had a death wish. I had no answer for her question, so I responded with one of mine.

"How can I make it up to you?" I asked, my voice dying down to a volume that could be considered a whisper.

"Make it up to me? By remembering literally anything, Jack! You get errands wrong, you get orders wrong, you get gifts wrong, when you remember them that is, I have no idea how you even function in society. How it's even possible to live like this, I simply don't understand. You need to get that sorted out, Jack, because I am done, I can't go on like this and with you constantly being unable to do even the simplest things." I felt like a porcupine with a thousand needles piercing my skin. I would have made a good iron scarecrow, if anything, yet I was still breathing. The truth was hard to hear, but it often is. I knew I had to say something, but if I was honest, I had trouble containing myself and not breaking down right in front of her. I took a deep breath and tried to calm down, looking down and, after a few seconds, up at her.

"I will be better, I promise." Camille seemed disinterested by my comment and looked away towards the window. "Can I… can we… hug it out?" I asked. I needed her in my arms, I needed her to tell me she understood, to tell me she would support me as I tried to support her. I needed to feel her skin on mine, her body heat to melt the chill in my heart, I needed her to tell me it was alright, to whisper in my ear that everything would be fine. I wanted to go back to that hill and to that café, to the places where I could see her smile and be happy.

Camille got up from the table, pushing her chair away. It scraped the floor with a loud screech, but she ignored it and went to the kitchen. I stared blankly at the wall in front of me, processing what she just did and trying to contain my disappointment. If she wasn't ready for a hug, there was no chance she would do anything I had hoped for. I looked down at my toasts, getting colder by the minute. No bite had been taken and they were sitting there, taunting me. I wasn't hungry after all. Camille came back to the dining room but didn't sit down again. She simply stood next to me.

"I think it would be best if you would leave," she said with a voice and a look as cold as ice.

"But I..." I tried to protest, but she cut me off.

"I don't want to hear it. Gather your stuff and go."

I got up from the table and she stepped away from me. I looked up at her and she looked away, avoiding meeting my eyes. I reluctantly turned to the front door and walked slowly. I had no stuff to gather and only put on my shoes before looking back at her. She still wasn't interested at all, and I sighed a little. The sound of the door opening broke the silence between us. There was only one thing I was still wondering but couldn't bring up during our talk.

"Listen, I know I messed up. Big time. I don't know how to go on from here and I don't know what last night was, what it means, but this hasn't changed how I feel about you. I love you. And I hope there's still a chance the feeling is mutual."

I stepped through the door and closed it behind me without waiting for her response. I took out my phone from my pocket to look at the time and heard noises coming from inside. I listened closely. Camille was clearly sobbing and trying to contain her tears but wasn't doing a very good job at it. Was it wrong of me to be relieved in that moment, knowing that she still cared, even a little? Perhaps it was, but it brought me some form of relief still. Not at the fact she was crying, of course, but that she felt something towards me, enough to make her cry and, if I was honest, I was containing myself for a long time and almost lost it too. The tears threatened to flow at the corner of my eyes, but my phone vibrating in my hand snapped me out of it. I looked at it to see who was calling.

Chloe.

I debated answering for a moment. Should I just ignore it or was it better to pick up? What would we even say, after everything that happened, it still felt like there was a ravine between us. Was it from the emotion that I just went through or from a feeling I always had deep down, I didn't know, but I answered the phone as I was stepping down from the stairs leading to Camille's house. I wasn't sure what this conversation would lead to, but it surely would be better than the previous one.

Chapter 11

The wind swept away the red, green and yellow leaves from the trees around us. Autumn had always been my favorite season for this exact reason. Whenever I went into an area full of trees and wildlife, the very sight of the multi-colored forest brought out a feeling of peace within me. The temperature was just perfect with a jacket on and it was the best time to go outside for a walk in my opinion. The ground was starting to change as well, slowly getting covered by star-shaped foliage and its green grass slowly fading to a less vibrant color. While it wasn't quite autumn yet, Sapphire Park always seemed to change color faster than other parks. Autumn was the preparation for winter, my least favorite season, but there was something about seeing the shift from summer that made it even more beautiful in my eyes. Trees could change color completely and remain proud and, subconsciously or not, there was something there that I strongly resonated with.

"The weather sure is nice, isn't it?" I said out loud. An orange leaf fell off a nearby oak tree and drifted in the wind. I followed it for a while, but eventually lost it when it finally landed on the ground among others. I smiled a little and turned to my left.

Chloe was silent for the most part; she didn't say a word yet except in response to my greeting. Even if I was upset with what Camille had said to me, the sight of Chloe somehow appeased me a little and, just for a moment, I had forgotten everything. I wished that moment could last forever, but the memories caught up to me soon after. But whenever I looked at her, I couldn't help but smile. Her hair was the same color as the surrounding leaves and the wind made it go sideways sometimes. She had to hold on to her little hat whenever the breeze picked up.

"I don't like autumn very much. All the life slowly gets drained away until everything freezes in winter," she said, looking straight ahead.

"I know," I answered. She had already told me that years ago. "You prefer spring, right? You always were a fan of flowers..." I trailed. Chloe nodded with a slight smile.

"Yes, I think there's something to them that I can't quite explain. They go through so much hardship in winter and only if they get through it can they properly bloom. I think that's wonderful."

"Quite a poetic one," I said, laughing a little. Chloe simply smiled after hitting me in the shoulder and looking away. We gazed at the park that had now changed drastically. Sapphire Park didn't quite live up to its name at this time of year since it was more the color of rubies, but winter would soon bring back its name to its former glory. There were not as many kids as the last time I was here, which was surprising for a Sunday morning, but the quietness had its perks. It felt really relaxing to be here and the fact Chloe was sitting next to me was even better.

"Is there something going on? You sounded a little down on the phone and I can see something is troubling you on your face, even if you try to hide it," said Chloe. She was sharp, always had been, but it surprised me every time.

"Thing aren't going that well with Camille right now. I messed up something big and she hasn't forgiven me yet," I answered. I wanted to tell her, but not everything at the same time. Wasn't it curious how I felt comfortable sharing things as personal as this, but not the exact reason? Deep down, I knew it was because I was ashamed, but I didn't want to face it.

"Oh, that sounds bad. What did you do?" Chloe asked. I was surprised by her inquisitiveness. I thought anything to do with Camille she would brush aside, but she sounded genuinely interested. I hesitated. Perhaps it was better for me to keep the real reason to myself, at least for now.

"I... don't really want to say, sorry," I simply said, hoping she would drop the subject. She seemed to get the hint and looked away, readjusting her glasses at the same time.

"Sorry, I didn't mean to put you on the spot there. If it's worth anything, I hope it gets better between you, for your sake and not hers." She sighed and turned to me. "You know, I still cared about you even if we didn't talk to each other. What I said back at school, I..." She hesitated to find the right words. I was simply listening, not pressuring her and letting her figure out what she wanted to say. "I didn't mean it. I thought you had changed, thought you were siding with her and was lying to me to hurt me even more, but I know now that I was wrong. You're still the Jack I knew even a year later and I'm sorry for treating you the way I did. You only wanted to reconnect and help me, didn't you? I shouldn't have associated what Camille was doing with you, it had nothing to do with you, so I apologize for that. I still don't like the fact that you're dating her, but I respect your feelings for her and as long as it makes you happy, that's all I can hope for."

I couldn't stand to hold eye contact any longer and looked away. I didn't know if she wanted to make it sound that way, but it almost felt like a confession. Chloe was a very good friend of mine, there was no doubt about that, and we had met in the first year of high school, back when I was more interested in school than girls. Meeting Chloe was a turning point of my high school years, she made me see the world another way and, as we grew older, I off course noticed her growing up as well. Was it friendship or more? I couldn't say, but I was glad to hear what she said. If anything, I was glad to get my friend back. Our prior conversation popped in my head; everything related to Max and Kyle and how Max was Camille's brother. However, I didn't know what happened exactly from Chloe's perspective and I was pretty curious about it. I wanted to ask her, but was it the right time? The right place? Was there ever going to be a right time and place? After all, these events were part of the reason why we drifted apart for a year, so wasn't it warranted to know exactly what happened and why? It felt like I had a puzzle with a few missing pieces, and I couldn't make out what image it formed without them. Camille had given me her pieces, but Chloe was holding the last ones. I knew this wasn't going to be a pleasant conversation, surely, but I needed to know.

"Chloe, there is something I'd like you to tell me." She turned to me, waiting for my question. "What exactly happened with Max?" She turned away and sighed. Even if I couldn't see her face that well anymore, I could tell her expression and demeanor had changed. While I knew it would have this effect somewhat, it still saddened me to see her like this. Readjusting her glasses, she took a deep breath and looked straight ahead at the bare playground in the distance.

"Max was… my first boyfriend. We met in school after we were seated next to each other in science class. At first, we couldn't talk to one another at all, and we only focused on the class homework and did our own things separately. But he approached me one day, apologizing for bothering me and asked for help on a particular question. I don't exactly know why, but it made me really happy, and I helped him figure it out. The smile on his face when he finally understood was all I could hope for. I think I must have fallen for him then. Looking back, I didn't know how to say it to him, though, and we kept on like this for almost a year. I think I was too afraid to tell him, and I figured he wasn't feeling the same thing if nothing happened after an entire year until the last week of school came. He confessed to me then and I said yes." Chloe smiled a little as she recalled the events. I looked at her in a different light. Was it the light of day causing this or were my eyes deceiving me? There was something about her now that seemed…different. Not a bad different, though, and I wasn't sure what to do with this feeling. Chloe continued, ignoring my silent thought.

"We started dating the next summer. At first, I really enjoyed spending time with him. It was usually at my house and whether we were playing something or watching a movie, I was happy just to be around. I started wanting more, to go out on dates at a café or go hiking or just taking a walk outside, but he refused every time with terrible excuses. I tried talking to him about it, but he didn't want to listen to me. Sometimes, when we had a day together, I had to remind him to eat and bring him his food or else he wouldn't eat at all. He never offered to help me cook and preferred to stay in my living room doing who knows what. Plus, I knew we were just dating and everything, but after a while I started to desire more physical contact and he wouldn't do anything, even if I wasn't subtle about it. In that way, Max kind of destroyed my self-confidence and I kept asking myself questions about if I was good enough and why he didn't want me, that type of thing. Looking back, he probably had something going on in his life and he maybe tried to fill the void with me, but it didn't work, and he didn't know how to end things. I did find it odd we would only see each other in school or at my parent's house. He would never invite me over to his parent's house, so maybe that had something to do with it. Or maybe that's just me trying to find excuses for him when there aren't any. Regardless, things between us weren't going great and that's when I started noticing Kyle."

"Kyle was a guy I met at work. We used to get numerous shifts together and we gradually started talking more and more. Kyle could tell something was happening to me as I became sadder and sadder over the course of a few weeks, visibly so, and he asked me numerous times to tell him what was happening. Even though I had my problems, I didn't want to burden him and since they were personal, I kept them to myself. But I cracked one day and decided to tell him everything. He just listened to me, not interrupting even once and when I was finished, offered me some advice. I tried to patch things up with Max, but I think things were long gone by then and Kyle had already occupied the place in my heart that Max once had. But I knew I had to do the right thing and broke up with Max before going back to Kyle the next day and asking him out. Perhaps things were rushed a little, I can't be sure, but they didn't last long either. I had only dated Max for a few months and breaking up with him stung less than I thought. And that's when you come in."

Chloe turned to face me, and I looked at her with inquisitiveness. I wanted to know what happened next, even if I knew the answer. She seemed to understand what I said even if no words were uttered, and snickered a little, looking back in the distance while shaking her head. It felt like the memories of that time weren't the happiest, but I was glad she was still willing to share them with me, however hurtful they may have been to tell. She paused for a few moments, probably trying to gather her thoughts, and then resumed her story.

"I remember we were at my parent's house doing homework and we had almost finished everything. You asked me how everything was going with Max, and I told you I had started seeing someone else. I remember you were confused, because I didn't tell you any of this as it was happening, and you asked me if I broke up with Max. I don't know why, but I hesitated for a long time, and I must have given you the wrong impression. I really did break up with Max at that point, but it had only been a day or so and he still held a place in my heart. My feelings were conflicted, and I couldn't come up with an answer right away even though it was obvious. You didn't say a word, packed up your things and left. I tried to tell you to stay, to explain everything, but you simply turned around and looked at me with disappointed eyes. You didn't say anything, but I felt your words cut deep in my heart. I couldn't hold you back to tell you the truth and you left. I cried that night, you know," Chloe said, looking at me with a sad smile like she was still containing her emotions. I was silent, listening how I had messed up yet again a year ago. I remembered these events too, from my perspective, and I did jump to conclusions at that time. I didn't remember what I was thinking back then, but it was wrong regardless. I looked back at Chloe, and she smiled at me, fighting back tears that welled up in her eyes before looking away.

"Every time I tried to reach out, I stopped myself because I thought you hated me and wouldn't even answer, so I wondered what the point of sending a message or giving you a call would be. I realize now that I should have at least tried and maybe we would have reconnected sooner. Anyway, so I continued dating Kyle for a while, but that too turned sour relatively fast." She paused again, probably wondering how to proceed. It was a lot to unpack, even for me, so I didn't blame her at all for taking her time. I was all ears, as she had been for me multiple times already. "With me, he was a very sweet guy, complimenting me and giving me gifts, opening doors for me, the whole thing. But it's the way he treated others that didn't sit right with me. He would curse at people, yell at them, talk behind their backs. It gradually became harder to work with him until one day I couldn't do it anymore and gave my two weeks' notice. I didn't tell him that though. They say to never date a co-worker and I realized then what they meant because the next few weeks were absolute torture. Subconsciously, I think I had given my resignation to the relationship too, but didn't tell him, which was definitely an error on my part. Still, we eventually parted ways and I found myself alone. I almost called you a few times but stopped myself before pressing the button every time. Things weren't going great, and I wanted to talk to you, but..." Chloe stopped, looking at the ground. She didn't seem to know what to say, but I figured she just needed a little bit of involvement on my part.

"Why didn't you reach out to me? I would have listened to you, the same way you listened to me when I had troubles. We always had each other's backs, what happened to that?" I asked, both for me and for her. I wanted to know, but also wanted to tell her she had my support, back then and even now.

"You walked out on me, remember? That doesn't exactly scream how open you were to conversation. I thought you never wanted to talk to me again. You didn't reach out either, Jack. I interpreted it as you were fine without me and didn't want me in your life anymore. It made me sad, but I figured that was who you were and that was that."

"I thought you were happy with Kyle and didn't need me anymore either. I guess we're both bad at communicating, huh?"

"We are."

We both smiled while looking away. Holding eye contact with her would have been too awkward in that moment and I couldn't bear to do it. I was relieved, however, to know Chloe didn't cheat on Max and my thoughts of her were wrong. I had judged her too fast and pushed her out of my life without letting her explain her story as she did now and, because of me, we lost one year of friendship together. Things weren't the same as they were, we clearly lost some of that complicity, that silent understanding that we had, and it was all my fault. I hoped to be able to put that behind us now and go forward with this, but a little voice in my head reminded me of Camille. She wouldn't approve of this, that was certain, and Chloe certainly didn't want to talk about her, but I was dating her so the subject would come around eventually. How could we avoid talking about her and not mention her? How could I talk to Chloe without Camille noticing? Wasn't that kind of cheating, in a way? I wanted to keep Chloe in my life, though, so I didn't know what to do. Chloe must have noticed my inner questioning because she looked at me and her stare eventually made me turn my head as well. My expression must have given it away, because even though I didn't say anything, she seemed to know exactly what I was thinking.

"You're thinking about Camille, aren't you?" she asked, her eyes filled with determination, staring back into mine. I held eye contact with her for a second but looked down. In shame or something else, I didn't know, but I knew she didn't approve of my relationship with her still. What was I supposed to do? "I still don't like that you're dating her, let's be clear about that, but I'm willing to overlook it if it means we can be friends again. Now the ball is in her court. Just remember what I said back at school." I looked at her with puzzled eyes and frowned. "One day, she will break your heart, Jack. I just hope you know what you're doing." I didn't know how to respond to that, but Chloe didn't wait for me to answer. She got up from the bench and started walking away, her red hair swinging from side to side like a dancing flame. She turned around and looked at me, her eyes both kind and compassionate.

"Nice talking to you again, Jack," she said, turning around without waiting for my response. I sat there dumbfounded, at a loss for words, unable to process what had just happened. I feared her words, what she meant when she said Camille would break my heart, scared of what it implied. I didn't want to think about that and chased those thoughts away. My relationship with Camille was on a rocky road at the moment, but we had those arguments before and always overcame them. I just had to find something to cheer her up, something she would like to do that we could do together. My head was spinning trying to figure out a place we could go until finally I remembered something she had said to me one day.

Isn't it weird how I like to go hiking, but never visited that mountain even though it's so close?

So simple I could laugh at myself for struggling to find it. We could go on a hiking date on the mountain. Hiking was one of those things I thought I liked but had never really tried before so I couldn't be sure. But if I liked taking walks in autumn, surely hiking would be no different or, at the very least, similar. So, I had the place figured out, now came the day. I thought Camille wouldn't be in the mood to even talk to me right now, so I figured I'd let things calm down for a while, then propose the idea and the day of would be a few weeks afterwards. That would mean it landed somewhere in October. Perfect, I thought, there wasn't a better timing for that sort of thing. The trees would be painted in many colors, the temperature would be exquisite and, most of all, it was an activity that Camille liked. That was the most important to me. I took out my phone to try and count the days and noticed I had a message from Chloe. It was just a simple smiley face with glasses on, but the sight of it sent doubts all over my body like an electric shock. I didn't know what this feeling was, but silently hoped it wasn't guilt over my rekindling with her, because I didn't want to deal with this right now. I pushed the message aside and resumed my task, but the thought of Chloe lingered at the back of my mind for a long time like a ghost taunting me from behind where I couldn't see. I finally decided I would ask Camille to go on the date two weeks from now and hoped that would be enough time for her to forgive me. I really needed to get her something for her birthday, though, even if it was late, and wondered what she would like. I never was talented at gift giving and I normally asked Chloe for advice when gifting my parents and others, but that would be inappropriate in this instance. I had to figure it out on my own, come up with the best gift idea in two weeks and give it to her on the date. Everything was looking brighter, and I nodded my head in satisfaction. I had a plan.

Chapter 12

The bus loudly stopped to let us disembark. As soon as we got out, the chill air of autumn hit us straight in the face. Today wasn't the best in terms of temperature, but it was the only recent day Camille and I had free with everything else going on like school and work. In the city, the wind wasn't as strong, and before we left, I was debating if I wanted to bring a sweater or not. Camille convinced me to do so. Another good move on her part. From the bus stop, we could see a parking lot stretching a long way with scattered cars here and there. The mostly black and white colors contrasted with the colorful leaves covering the ground all around us, getting blown by every breeze swirling around us. Seas of orange and red danced everywhere we turned, and I couldn't help but marvel at the sight. Autumn really was the best season, no contest, especially for these kinds of sceneries. Next to the parking lot was a building probably containing washrooms, but most importantly, there was a giant map of the different hiking trails we could take. I readjusted my backpack, tightening it around my shoulders and, after sharing a look with Camille, we made our way towards it. I shivered just as the wind picked up again, sending some more leaves everywhere.

"Good thing you brought the sweater I gave you," Camille said, smiling at me.

"Yeah, that was a good call," I answered. "It's actually really warm, I don't know how I got shivers there."

Camille shrugged at my comment and continued walking by herself. She soon stopped and turned around to look at me with a puzzled look on her face. I motioned her to come back as I undid the straps of my backpack and slid it off my back unto the ground. I was unzipping the biggest pocket when she arrived next to me.

"What are you doing?" she asked.

"I know I messed up last month, okay, and I know this isn't going to erase that, but I wanted to do something anyway. I'm not really good at the whole gift giving thing, but I figured you might like this one. Go ahead, take it," I said as I stretched open my backpack. It was a lot tighter than I was used to, mostly because of the box I barely managed to fit inside. It wasn't a big box, rather a long and thin one and I instantly saw the look of confusion pass on Camille's face. She took a hold of it and yanked it out of the bag, bringing it closer to her and holding it with both hands. I saw her eyes glimpse across the entire box until finally her eyes widened in shock. I knew she had realized then.

"You recognize the place?" She nodded that she did, but I said it anyway. "That's the cat café we went to on our first date. I saw you had a lot of puzzles on your shelf and figured you might want to keep that memory in another form. Do you like it?"

Camille didn't answer me and kept staring at the box. This time, I couldn't decipher what she was thinking at all. Was she trying to contain her excitement or did she hate the gift for some reason. Was she not into puzzles anymore and I got her something that made her look like a child? Did I mess up yet again? I internally sighed in frustration. Why couldn't I do anything right? Just as I snapped out of my thoughts, I met with Camille's eyes and noticed they were crying. She had a genuine smile painted on her face and streaks of salty water running down from her eyes all the way down to her chin.

"I love it!" She took another long look at the box, seemingly staring in disbelief.

"Why are you crying?" I asked in relief. I was just glad she didn't hate it.

"It's just…nobody has ever given me something this meaningful to me before and… I don't know what to say. Did you have this custom made?" she asked, wiping the tears off her face.

"Yes, I found a shop online that made different puzzles from a photo you send them. I went back to the café and took a picture of it from your perspective on the date back then and that's the end result. I'm glad you like it," I said, smiling too, incapable of containing my own happiness.

"That's so cool," she said between two breaths. "Thank you so much, Jack, that means so much to me," she continued, approaching for a hug to which I gladly responded. We stayed in each other's arms for a few seconds and before we fully parted ways, we looked into each other's eyes longingly. I leaned down for a kiss and her lips met mine. I didn't know how or why, but kisses were not made equal. This was the best one from the past few weeks, there was something about it that made my desire shoot up and I wanted to stay like this forever. But the chilly wind of the mountain got between us, and we separated. Camille was still smiling from ear to ear as she looked again at the box. "I've been into puzzles for quite some time now and I've always wanted to frame them, but I never knew how. I've got some scenery ones and some with cool animal shots on them, but none that made me feel that strongly about it. That has changed now. I'm definitely going to figure it out and frame this one" she said, more to herself than out loud, but I had to respond.

"I'll look forward to seeing the end result," I answered with a smile. There was a little pause where the only sound around us was the wind making the leaves dance.

"So, uh, as much as I like your gift, could you carry it in your bag?" she asked with a laugh.

"Oh, right, right. Yes," I said, grabbing it as she was handing it to me. I stuffed it back in the bag, closed it and put it back on my back, readjusting it before looking towards Camille again. She nodded happily and we started walking again towards the map displayed on the building. It was a lot bigger when we stood right in front of it, and it was a little overwhelming. Multiple colored lines shot all around a 3D transparent drawing of the mountain and seemed to cross each other multiple times across the entire length of the trails. Some trails simply circled the base of the mountain while some of them only went halfway to the top. From what I could understand, the green, red and blue lines all ended up at the summit but took different paths to get there. In the bottom right of the map was a legend indicating the name of each trail and the length of them. I knew we wanted to get to the top but didn't know if she was in the mood for the longest trail or a shorter one. Either way, it was going to be a little bit of a walk to get to our destination.

"So, which way do you want to go?" I asked, still looking at the map. "I reckon we could take the green line?"

"I kind of leaned towards the blue one because it goes around all the different lakes. I think that could be nice to see, don't you think?" she answered with a question.

"Yeah, we can go for that one, I don't mind. It's just a longer trail, so get ready to walk a little more."

"That's fine. Alright, let's go," she said, turning around towards the start of the trails. I quickly followed after taking one last look at the map but figured there would be indications on the way to avoid us getting lost. Plus, I could always pull up the map on my phone if there was ever any issue. From what I could understand from the wooden signs planted all around, most of the trails started here, but some of them started on the other side of the parking lot. Those must have been the shorter ones, because this sign was painted with a blue, red, green, yellow and purple line. I guessed they separated at one point up the trail, and we had to start here for now. We started walking on the uneven path littered with leaves and wood debris, hoping it wouldn't get worse the more we went up. It had rained two days ago, and the ground seemed a little wet still, so we had to avoid multiple patches of mud on the path.

There was something about the atmosphere of the trail that calmed me. The sound of our steps mixed in with the wind produced a melody I got lost in. Even though I was looking around, it was like I couldn't really see anything other than a sea of colors and felt at peace and relaxed. The fact there weren't a lot of people with us on this trail made the illusion even stronger. I didn't even realize we hadn't said anything in a while as I was too absorbed by the environment to think of anything to say. We had spoken between her birthday and today, but it was noticeably less than before. I thought it was my fault, of course, that she still wasn't over me missing her birthday, with good reason, but it still made me a little sad. I figured with the puzzle box I had given her today she might become more talkative or forgive me a little bit more than she did, but only the sound of dirt and leaves crunching under our feet broke the silence of the mountain.

The further we walked, the further we drifted apart. Subconsciously, we started to drift apart from each other, almost walking on the other side of the trail before realizing and coming back in a hurry. I felt saddened by it as I knew why this was happening, but I had hoped the gift I had given her would at least make her forget my mistake, even just for today. Not that the gift was only for this intended purpose, but I wanted to put that episode behind me, yet she didn't seem to be able to let it go. I guess that was wishful thinking on my part more than anything. After having to go back to her side a few times, I had an idea. I extended my hand towards hers and took hold of it. As soon as we made contact, she swung her hand back, avoiding my grasp. I figured she must have been scared by my sudden movement or something and tried to hold her hand again. She dodged mine a second time and I looked at her confused. She didn't make eye contact and simply continued walking in silence. I didn't know what was going on with her, but there was clearly something on her mind. I decided to let it go and stopped trying to hold hands. Maybe talking would get me more answers.

"It sure is nice, isn't it?" I said, looking all around at the trees. There was no response from her side and so I continued. "I always like taking walks during this time of year. It's my favorite season for sure."

"I know, you said that already," she answered dryly. My confusion was still present. What was going on? Why was she suddenly so distant? Did I do something again?

"Is there something wrong? You seem… distracted," I asked.

"No, nothing much, just walking normally," she responded. If anything, this was the furthest from a normal walk we ever had. Usually, we talked nonstop whenever we went out but today was different. In fact, it had been like that for a while now. The text messages didn't flow like they used to, our conversation barely revolved around anything else than school and work and we almost never had any moments to us. I knew something was up, but if she didn't want to talk about it, then there wasn't much I could do. I would still try to keep up a conversation though, but that had barely any effect.

Her mood seemed to shift when we first spotted the deer. I told her to stop quietly and pointed at the woods, leaning close to her face to do so. She didn't say anything, and her eyes followed my finger to the animal eating peacefully not too far from the trail. It was very hard to spot among the trees, its brown fur hiding it in plain sight. It was only because I saw movement out of the corner of my eye and looked that I was able to spot it. It wasn't doing much of anything, but it did spot us at one point and raised its head and ears, all senses in alert. I guessed it must have missed us before because we didn't make much sound as we weren't talking. After a few seconds, it lowered its head and continued eating, figuring we weren't a threat to it. I turned my head to look at Camille. Her eyes were practically sparkling as she stared at the deer intensely, studying its movement and admiring it from afar. She had a smile painted on her lips that wouldn't leave for any reason and she barely contained herself to avoid scaring it. The sight of it made me both happy and sad at the same time. I was glad she could feel these kinds of emotions still but saddened that they weren't about me. How could I bring this type of smile back into our relationship? Was that selfish of me? Shouldn't I just want her to be happy and the fact she was now be enough to satisfy me? We stayed around the deer, looking at it for a while before it decided to run away unexpectedly. Camille audibly sighed and looked sad for a second. She quickly got up and turned around to face me. I smiled at her, and she smiled back, but behind her smile was something hidden, I could see but not decipher. What could it be?

The ascension of the mountain took quite a lot out of us. We figured it wouldn't be that hard, but soon our calves were screaming in pain and our breath was rough. I was glad I brought a big water bottle along with me and we stopped to rest a little as we reached a large lake. Camille extended her hand towards me.

"Can you pass me the bottle?" she asked.

"Don't drink it all, now," I said with a joking tone as I handed it to her. She mocked me before pouring down the now lukewarm water into her mouth with a splashing sound. She drank a few gulps and handed it back to me. I took a few myself, putting the cap back on and sticking it back to my backpack. We still had a long way to go and it was running out faster than I expected. Camille was sat down on a massive rock that must have weighed a few tons and I sat next to her. We both stared straight at the lake, its movement coupled with the light of the sun making it shimmer lightly. The scene seemed taken from a movie and I couldn't help but wonder if this was all a dream. A few minutes passed in silence. I didn't know how she was feeling, but I was trying to come up with a way to start a conversation and words didn't want to form in my head. I was drawing a blank. There were so many things I wanted to ask her, though, why couldn't I just do it? What was wrong with me? Eventually, after a while, I managed to get a question out of my mouth.

"Listen, Camille, I don't know what's going on with you, but there's clearly something bothering you. I understand if you don't want to talk about it, but can you at least say if it's to do with me?" I asked, not daring to look her in the eyes and preferring to get lost in the water of the lake. However, I could still see her next to me and her head shifted down to look at the ground.

"It is to do with you, but I'm not sure what it is. I'm still trying to figure out a few things," she answered with a sigh. Her words put a weight on my heart and confirmed my earlier feelings. There was something there, something I did wrong or perhaps something I said that made her feel this way, but without any more clues, I was lost on what the cause was.

"Is there… something I can do to help?" I asked.

"Today helps. But unfortunately, this is something I need to do on my own," she said. Her phone made a noise, and she promptly checked it, making sure to turn it in a way I couldn't see.

"I understand." She sighed, still looking at her phone before putting it away. Something was troubling her, and that message didn't seem to help, but I didn't think prying would be a good idea, so I let it go for now. Perhaps I could ask about it later. She shifted her body towards me and leaned in, kissing me on the cheek quickly and got up, stretching with a loud grunt. I simply stared at her, unable to move and admiring her at the same time. I never noticed before now, but her blonde hair really did go well with the autumn colors and, for a second, she smiled at me and melted away my concerns. The storm that downed her mood seemed to have weirdly vanished and a shining sun now painted her face. I smiled back and got up too. Just as I did, I heard a piercing sound coming from behind me. I turned around to see what it was and almost had to duck down as a giant bird flew over our heads towards the lake with a loud screech. I followed it with my eyes and stared in disbelief. I looked over at Camille and she was just as much in shock as I was. We stood there for a few seconds before bursting in laughter.

"What was that?" I asked between two breaths.

"I think it was a hawk or something," she answered.

"That was crazy," I said, still laughing.

We calmed down after a few minutes and resumed our ascension to the top. The mood had shifted greatly and, while we weren't talking like we used to, there was a clear improvement. I didn't know exactly what was bothering her, but I was determined to do my best to try and fix it, whatever it was.

◊

Almost completely exhausted and barely able to put a foot in front of the other, we finally made it to the top. Our breath was short and coarse, my backpack seemed to weigh three tons and it was suddenly very hot in my sweater even though the wind had picked up. As soon as we arrived at a flatter surface, however, I felt an immense sense of relief in my legs and almost crumbled to the ground. I barely held on to the wooden fence nearby and forced myself to stand up and look around. There were multiple paths that lead up to the top, just like we saw on the map, and they all had their own little entry to the kind of plaza there. Grey rocks, covered scarcely with fallen leaves, covered the entire area with a nice pattern, alternating between straight and jagged lines all along the border. In the middle, a big fountain wasn't functioning, but still had a good level of water in. At the edge of the plaza, a solid rock wall about a meter high allowed visitors to take in the view without any risk of falling. As much as we didn't meet much of anyone during our ascension, there were now more than a few admiring the scenery and taking pictures. It was surprising we didn't even hear them while climbing as the sound of conversation was almost stronger than the wind. We took some time to rest a little, but I was getting very impatient to see the city from up here and I went ahead up to the rock wall.

To say I was in awe would be an understatement. When you walk in the city, you can't really take in how it looks as a whole, but up here, that was a different story. The roads, very squared and organized, split the scene in multiple rows while the parks and trees painted it in various colors, contrasting the massive amount of grey that layered the city. From here, we could see everything. Sapphire Park especially stood out like a sore thumb among the rest of the view as its size in comparison to other parks was almost overbearing. It seemed to cover at least two or three times what I thought it did and, not far from it, you could see the school. My apartment was close as well and I spotted it really easily. I tried to find Camille's house, but somehow it was out of view. Turns out, we couldn't see everything in the city, but a good chunk of it, nonetheless. Just as I was lost in thought, Camille arrived next to me and leaned on the wall just like me and we stared into the distance in silence for a while, the wind blowing in our face and messing up our hair. I was glad I was wearing the sweater she gave me because even if I was getting hot during our climb, it was now a lot colder up here and the wind had a bit of a chill to it. After all, we were already in October and winter was just around the corner. I wondered what this view would look like during all the seasons. Would the park stick out as much as it did right now if it was covered in snow? I figured everything would be coated in a white veil so it would almost look the same, but perhaps not. I would have to come back to the top in a few months to see about that. The passage of time was a concept I could never grasp fully. It seemed like it just flowed by in a flash, the seasons succeeded to one another, the school years came and went, and the cycle repeated. It had been like this for a few years now, but this year, something had broken it, had shattered the monotony of this life. And she was standing right next to me. I turned to look at her and she did the same as our eyes met. They were not the eyes I was expecting to see. They weren't in awe like mine, they weren't the surprised or cheerful eyes one could assume she would have. Instead, they were cloudy, undecipherable and grey. Did that have to do with what we talked about on the way here? I was apprehensive to bring it up again even if the question was burning my mind, but I decided to let it go for now. In due time, perhaps she would open up about it. Maybe it wasn't the right time for it, but I really wanted some pictures and couldn't wait any longer.

"We should take pictures of this view, it's incredible," I said, looking over at Camille. She had turned back, staring at the city spread before us.

"Go ahead, I'm not going to stop you," she answered. I took out my phone and immortalised this moment a few times before turning around, pointing the camera at her. At first, she didn't notice it but after a few clicks, her head turned, and her eyes widened as she realized. "Hey, don't take pictures of me!" she said in an angry tone. I didn't know if she was truly angry or simply playful and I went with the latter.

"Oh, come on now, I have to capture every beautiful aspect of this scenery and it just so happens that you're part of it," I teased, hoping that would go well. She just sighed and turned around, showing me her back. I guessed she wanted to discourage me from taking pictures this way, but her long blonder hair stopping just above her butt was a perfect view and I didn't stop myself from snapping a few more. Then, a thought crossed my mind and I just had to say it out loud. "I know, we should take a picture together." Camille turned around faster than a lightning bolt and stared daggers at me. I smiled at her and looked innocent.

"We are not doing that," she said.

"Why not?" I answered with a shrug. "It'll be fun, come on, come closer." I snuggled up to her and held up my phone as far from me as I could, trying to take a selfie with both of us in the frame. Suddenly, I had more respect for all the posts on social media with these kinds of pictures because it was really hard to find an angle where we looked good, were in frame and centered with nothing else around. Just as I was fidgeting with it, trying to find the perfect shot, I heard a voice coming from directly in front of me.

"Do you guys want me to take your picture?" the man said. I lowered my phone and a man probably in his early thirties was standing there, arms half-folded with his hands in the air with an inquisitive look in his eyes. My face lit up, that would be perfect, the shot would be miles better if someone else took it. I enthusiastically gave my answer.

"Yes, thank you so much!" I said to the man.

"No, there's no need," Camille mumbled. I turned to face her with a confused look. I wondered why she said that and perhaps I had heard her wrong.

"What did you say?" I asked.

"No, nothing," she answered, shaking her head. I decided to drop it and walked up to the man and handed him my phone. I went back next to Camille and put my arm around her. I put on my best smile and looked directly into the camera.

"Alright, we're just going to need the lady to smile a little bit more," the man said with the phone held horizontally, his arms completely outstretched. It took a few more seconds before he continued. "Ok, here we go." We stood still for the camera to snap some pictures and when the man stood up and lowered my phone, I went up to him to retrieve it.

"Thank you so much," I said with a nod.

"No problem, are the pictures to your liking?" he asked while motioning to my phone. I looked through. He had taken a few to be on the safe side and they all appeared fine to me.

"Yes, they are. Thanks again, we really appreciate it."

"Glad to hear it. Have a good day."

The man left to stand farther away on the plaza while I went back to Camille. I skimmed through the pictures again and showed them to her.

"Which one is your favorite?" I asked.

"I don't know," she sighed, looking anywhere but my phone.

"You're not even looking at them," I grumbled. Camille sighed again and turned around to look through them with me. She wasn't smiling in most of them, half between some sort of grin and grimace. There were even some shots where she was looking away, not even remotely close to the camera, but I simply passed them and didn't mention it. There was one picture that looked the best to me, and I showed her my phone.

"What do you think of this one?" She leaned over to look at it, but her emotionless expression turned to annoyance in the blink of an eye.

"Maybe you should answer that message," she said, turning around to show me her back. Confused, I looked at my phone to see what she was talking about. I popped open the notifications to see who had messaged me. Why? Why now of all time to send me a text? Why, Chloe? I tried my best to contain my emotions too so that Camille wouldn't hear anything and dismissed the text. Of all the times to send me a message, that timing was probably the worst it could have been. I didn't understand Camille's reaction, though, because she said she would ignore Chloe, but obviously she didn't just now. I lifted my eyes off my phone and realized Camille had walked away, leaning on the rock wall not too far from where I was. I sighed and followed her. I could see her eyes shift upwards for a second as I arrived. This wasn't going to be pleasant.

"I'm sorry, you weren't supposed to see that," I said.

"Why is that? Are you cheating on me with her? That's certainly like her…" she asked aggressively.

"No, there's no way I would cheat on anyone, especially you. No, she's my friend and we talk sometimes. We've been through this already, let's not go into it again."

"You're the one who keeps bringing her up."

"I thought you said you were fine to ignore her?"

"Of course, I'm not *fine*! I really have to spell it out for you, don't I? You never seem to understand, it's actually incredible. I'm fine with not bothering her at school, but when you keep texting her and everything, that's another issue entirely. Why can't you just understand I don't want you to talk to her at all?"

"And why don't you understand I'm not going to do that because she's my friend?"

"Ughhhh," Camille grunted, lifting her hands in the air and turning away from me. "I can't deal with this" she said as she walked off again. I sighed and looked at my phone, but nothing on the screen told me the answer to my question. What was I supposed to do? We already had this conversation multiple times and every time it ended badly. We simply couldn't agree on this particular matter, and no one wanted to give an inch to the other. I shook my head as I watched her get further and further away. I was confident she wouldn't leave and decided to let her cool down for a little while. I turned back to admire the view once again. Somehow, it wasn't the same anymore. The wind was colder, the leaves were taunting me and every time my eyes landed on Sapphire Park, I kept thinking about Chloe. Maybe it was a mistake to continue our friendship. After all, I managed to be just fine without it for a year, so what was another one? Maybe I'd be better to break it off with Chloe once and for all so Camille would be satisfied. Even the fact that the thought crossed my mind made me shiver. I thought it, but I didn't mean it. I couldn't. The sky had turned a different shade of grey than before, the city spread before me was bland and colorless. Maybe autumn wasn't my favorite season after all. Two arms hugged me from behind and held me tight. I was startled for a second, but there was only one person it could be, really.

"You scared me," I said, unable to turn around to face her.

"I'm sorry, Jack. It's just… I know what she does with guys and the thought of losing you to her is making me go crazy. I can't have her ruin both mine and my brother's life, but I pushed that burden on you and it isn't right. I like you and I don't want to lose you." She hugged me tighter, and I almost couldn't breathe. But I could feel only relief, relief that Camille was finally opening up with her feelings, that she apologized for stepping over the line. I couldn't see her face as it was buried in my jacket, but I really wanted to. I wanted to tell her how happy I was that she finally tried to reach out and communicate to fix things. I just didn't know how to say it and my silence grew heavier with each passing second. I tried to turn around and her grip loosened around me. I closed my eyes and sighed, grabbing her by the shoulders in a delicate way.

"Listen, there's something you need to know…" I started. "It's about…"

"Shut up and come here," she interrupted in a commanding tone while closing the small gap between us.

My lips were assaulted with hers and they locked into a deep kiss. The entire weight on my shoulders vanished instantly and I let myself go into it. My arms embraced her and brought her closer to me as my back rested on the rock wall behind me for support. We hadn't shared a moment like this for a long time and as soon as it started, I wondered why and wanted more. Her own arms crossed behind my neck and her chest pressed against mine. One of my hands caressed her back all the way to her head and I grabbed a bit of her hair. I played with it while losing myself in this kiss. How long had it been? I didn't know and I didn't care. After a minute passed that seemed to go by in an instant, she stepped away from me and looked me straight in the eyes. I could get lost in hers for hours, those bright green eyes that were angry just a few moments ago were now shining brighter than the sun. But she didn't have the same resolve she had a few seconds ago. She couldn't hold eye contact with me and was fidgeting around. I could see multiple emotions going through her face and she looked almost lost, like she didn't remember where she was or what she was doing. I grabbed her hand and she seemed to come back to her senses. I didn't understand what she was feeling deep down, but I couldn't shy away from my own feelings. I was overcome by this feeling of warmth in the cold winds of the mountain and couldn't look away. I smiled at her.

"I love you," I said.

"I know," she answered. There was a palpable pause after what she said. I thought she had something else to say, but nothing else came.

"Do you want to go?" I asked after a few seconds. She waited a few moments, debating, but finally nodded positively and, hand in hand, we started making our way down the mountain. The tension that was between us during our ascension seemed to have dissipated, at least a little bit, and I felt as light as a feather. The descent was much easier than the opposite and I finally thought we had figured it out. The trail winding down was also a lot shorter than the other and it only took us around fifteen minutes to be back at the base of the mountain. Considering the distance traveled, that was quite surprising, and we were both shocked when we saw the familiar building with the map on it appear into view. We thought it would take a lot longer than that to get back, but here we were. I checked my phone for the time and the bus schedule. It would only come in about half an hour, so we had a little bit of leeway before leaving. We decided to go hang out on top of one of the giant boulders that bordered the start of the trails. As soon as we got there, I got lost in thought again as neither of us broke the silence between us. I thought about what happened at the top. Would Camille ever accept me seeing Chloe? I get she had her motives with her, but to take it out on me was wrong in my opinion. If she didn't have to interact with her at all, what was the issue? I figured I would try to keep her presence on the low, make it seem like I wasn't seeing or talking to her, maybe that would be better? Could that be considered cheating in her eyes? Not romantically, but emotionally, like I was playing with her emotions and throwing them to the side and doing whatever I wanted, no matter the cost. Just like the past few weeks, I was torn between the two as I didn't want to lose either of them. I looked over at Camille. Her eyes were fixed on the horizon, looking into the small forest at the base of the mountain, and she wasn't saying a single word. She seemed pensive, as lost in thought as I was, but just like me, I could tell she wasn't thinking of the kiss we just had or the gift I had given her. No, something else was on her mind and I hoped it wasn't that message.

Before we knew it, we had waited enough and went to the nearby bus stop to leave. It soon came into view, and we got on board quickly. At this time, there weren't many people and we easily got two seats next to each other. I sat down, quickly followed by Camille, and shifted my backpack to be on my lap, hugging it close to me. I extended my right hand towards her, and it took a while after she saw it before she grabbed it. I looked at her and smiled, but she averted her eyes, avoiding eye contact. I frowned a little but made nothing of it. I tried breaking this oppressive silence.

"What do you want to eat tonight? I'm trying to figure out something, but I have no idea," I asked her.

"I think I'm going to head home, actually, sorry."

"Oh, you're not coming with me?" I said, disappointed.

"No, I'm sorry, it's just...I have things to do and I have to do them alone," she answered.

"Alright, cool, no problem. Then I guess I have to give you this..." I said, reaching into my bag and taking out the puzzle I got her. I didn't quite understand her reaction when she saw it again, but it seemed like a mix between confusion and anger? That seemed really odd, but I handed it to her regardless. She grabbed it with both hands and looked down and I could tell her mind wandered back to that date. I wondered how the cats we met there were doing. I checked outside to see where we were. There was still a little bit of time before she had to get off. Just as I tried to come up with a conversation subject, my mind drew a blank and no words came out. It was like I had forgotten how to talk and resolved myself to stay quiet for the rest of the ride. When her stop came around, she notified the driver and turned to me. I looked at her, meeting her eyes and saw conflict. She seemed to fight against something, I didn't know what, but she finally got up.

"Thanks for today, Jack. It was a really nice day."

"It was."

There was so much more I wanted to say, so much I needed to say, yet the words didn't come out. Just like that, in silence, she left and got off the bus. As it went away, I followed her with my eyes until she was nothing but a silhouette far away. I had a feeling something was off but couldn't quite put my finger on it. My thoughts haunted me the rest of the way and I almost missed my own stop. I quickly got back to my apartment, but even that had a certain feeling of unease I couldn't get away from. I was dragging it around with me wherever I went and didn't know how to make it disappear. I sighed and checked my phone. Chloe's message was still there, unanswered, and I didn't know what to do with that either. The rest of the day was spent debating whether I should call Camille or not and ultimately decided against it. If she wanted to be alone, she surely had her reasons and until she was ready to tell me about them, I was willing to wait.

Chapter 13

I hadn't felt this nervous since our first date. Tonight, Camille would be coming over to my apartment and I would cook supper for her. I wanted to make something interesting, not just boiling pasta and mixing it with store-bought sauce, but a meal she would enjoy and feel all my love through. The day prior, I went to the store to buy all I would need and found myself quite enjoying the experience. I bought plenty of stuff I had never bought before and just that aspect of cooking was making me happy. I always thought cooking for someone else would make the meal taste better, but I scarcely had the occasion to test that theory and, being a student still, the usual things I cooked weren't fancy at all. But tonight was different. This wasn't the first time she came over, of course, but a part of me wanted to go above and beyond for her now. Was it subconsciously because of something that happened prior between us? All I knew was I was in the kitchen for a while now, preparing multiple pots at the same time, cutting veggies and putting stuff on the stove. It felt like my head was going to overload and I had almost never been this concentrated before. I wasn't a great cook so even the simplest tasks took me more time than the average person and the result would often be subpar, but I hoped Camille could overlook that fact tonight and appreciate the gesture first and the food second. Before I had realized it, the light had dimmed, and I was almost cooking in darkness. As the seasons changed, the sun set a lot earlier than I thought and, before I knew it, it was dark outside and no natural light would occur until the next morning. Was I really in the kitchen for that long? I guessed so and walked up to the light switch to turn it on. The sudden flash of light blinded me for a second and I had to cover my eyes.

Ding!

The sound of a phone notification resonated through the entire apartment only filled with the sizzling of meat in a pan. I walked up to the kitchen table where I had set my phone down and grabbed it. Giving the power button a push, I checked the time. 6:28 pm. *That must be her*, I thought while unlocking my phone. A few seconds later, I read through the message she had just sent me.

I'm here, can you come down?

I glanced over at everything that was cooking on the stove. Most of it would be ready soon so I guessed my timing was on point, but I couldn't exactly leave it there and go down to join her. I was always told by my parents not to leave anything unattended on the stove and I was determined to follow that rule. I texted her back.

I can't go down right now, I have something cooking. Can you come up instead?

As soon as the message went through, I saw she had read it. Her response came in very quickly.

Please.

That was it. I wondered why she was so insistent on me going to join her instead of the opposite. After all, wasn't she supposed to come over? I walked to my bedroom to look out the window that overlooked the street. Through the numerous raindrops that covered it, I could see a familiar figure standing on the sidewalk, looking up at me. I could sense her gaze from that far away. Quickly, I went to grab my wallet and keys and rushed back to the kitchen to turn off everything. It wasn't ready yet and I just hoped that whatever she wanted wouldn't be too long or else it would become cold. Hurrying to the door, I almost didn't grab my coat. At this time of year, the air was getting colder and soon, rain would turn to snow and cover the world with a white veil. Even though it wasn't winter yet, you could feel it approaching, especially at night. A few seconds later, I had my coat on, locked the door and started making my way down the stairs to meet her outside.

The door opening made her turn around. She was wearing her usual black coat, some autumn boots and was carrying around a tiny umbrella. It only had room for one person though and, unfortunately, I had neglected to bring mine. Our eyes met and I smiled at her. She looked…sad? Or was it the rain that made her appear that way? Perhaps it was just an impression because her expression seemed to indicate otherwise.

The cold air hitting my face startled me as I walked towards her. The rain, although not the heaviest, was particularly fierce tonight. I was already feeling my coat getting wet and perhaps I had not chosen the right shoes. The left one had a small hole on the side of it and water was already starting to seep through, soaking my socks and making me walk in a weird way. I really had to get myself a new pair of shoes. Finally, I arrived next to her.

"Hi! How are you?" I asked.

"Oh, you know, the usual." She paused for a second. "What about you?"

"Same, actually. Um, did you not want to come inside?" I said gesturing towards the door. "I'm cooking right now and have stuff on the stove. I turned it off, don't worry, but it would probably be better than standing out here in the rain, wouldn't it?"

"Actually, I was hoping we could maybe take a little walk?" she proposed.

"You mean right now? In the rain? Can't this wait a little bit, at least until it calms down?" I responded, uncertain.

She seemed to hesitate. Even though she had an umbrella, it couldn't have been comfortable being outside like this. Plus, she had just come off work and probably wanted to rest her feet as she had been standing all day. The offer was tempting her very much, but she finally shook her head and looked me in the eyes.

"It will only be for a bit. Just around the block. It won't be long, I promise," she said.

She looked down for a moment, seemingly hiding her expression from me. Was she embarrassed? What was this about? I observed her for a few seconds. She was fidgeting with one foot, like she couldn't sit still and just wanted to go. She sometimes did this, and I wasn't sure was caused it, but I remembered she did the same thing on our hiking date a few weeks back. Was there a correlation? Perhaps, but I had never seen her like this before, not to this extent anyway. If anyone was nervous, it was usually me and even on our very first date, she seemed to handle it much better than now. What could possibly be going on that would make her feel like this? Camille wasn't afraid to tell me what she was feeling at any moment, she spoke her mind whenever she saw fit, a fact I sometimes had trouble with. The contrast of what she was then and now was as clear as night and day. She did have her occasional spontaneous demands and while this one stroke me as odd, I didn't see much point in arguing about it. If it truly was just going around the block, we would be done in ten minutes and then we'll go back to my apartment, have supper and get to spend a nice evening together. Without knowing it, I was also looking down and when I raised my gaze to meet hers. She was looking straight at me and trying to figure out my answer before I said it. With a shrug, I spoke.

"Alright, sure, let's go." Camille smiled a little and turned around quickly. She almost went without me, and I had to jog a little to catch up to her. We started heading towards the convenience store at the end of the street on our usual walking route. The silence was broken about a minute later when I finally decided to start saying something. "So, how was your day at work?" I asked.

She seemed startled by my question, like she didn't expect me to speak first. Maybe I got a little impatient but walking around in this rain wasn't ideal and she appeared to have something important to say. I figured she just needed a little push to start.

"Oh, um, nothing really happened. Standard day, you know. Although, there was this one guy who kind of pissed me off," she trailed.

"Oh yeah? What happened?" I inquired.

"He was roaming around the store for a while and when he finally came to pay, he kept asking me personal questions like 'do you have a boyfriend?', 'when does your shift end?', that sort of stuff," she answered.

"I hope you put him in his place, yeah?"

"I actually didn't really have time to. I answered quickly and tried to dismiss him, but he wouldn't go away even when the transaction was done. Luckily, my co-worker got him off my back."

"Tom, right? He's very proactive when it comes to you, isn't he?" I teased while giving her a little elbow bump.

She glared at me for a fraction of a second. I didn't meet her eyes, but I could feel the air suddenly getting colder. She didn't seem in a good mood; of that I was now certain. Did this guy really affect her that much? Before I could get too lost in thought, she spoke again.

"Yes, it was Tom. And he isn't proactive, he's just looking out for his colleague, okay?"

"Yeah, yeah, of course. I didn't mean to insinuate anything," I defended myself while raising my hands in the air.

We continued walking for a little while, eventually turning right at the street corner. It was a little busy at this time of day and I switched places with Camille to be the closest to the road. I always did that, which seemed to annoy her most of the time, but tonight she didn't say a word. I didn't mean anything by it, I just wanted to make sure she was safe in the event that a car would lose control and crash into us. In the grand scheme of things, it was probably pointless, but it gave me a slight feeling of control over something I really shouldn't have. I wondered if I was the only one that did that, it wasn't a conversation subject that usually came up, but maybe I was weirdly insistent about it. Nonetheless, I was glad to do it and even more so that she didn't argue tonight. She would usually always at least comment on it and sometimes outright refuse to move.

The rain had formed small puddles on the ground, and we sometimes had to dodge them to avoid getting our shoes wet. Plus, with my horrible choice of footwear, this would have spelt disaster for me. Whenever it rained, you could really see how bad the roads were. The rain didn't get properly swept to the nearest canals and stagnated in scattered spots, usually on the edges of sidewalks. If it was particularly bad, sometimes the entire width of the street could be flooded partially which made crossing it a nightmare. Luckily, we didn't have any of the problematic roads ahead, but even just looking around showed numerous giant puddles pedestrians could only cross by going onto someone else's lawn or by going in the street. On our way, we heard a cat meowing and hiding under a car. Camille commented on how frightened it looked and we stopped to try and get it to come out. It absolutely wanted nothing to do with us and stayed right under there, where it was dry. It was probably for the better, though, and we just hoped that the owner of the car would notice it before leaving, if he left at all. Driving in these conditions wasn't exactly the best and should probably be avoided if possible. Reluctantly, we parted ways with it and resumed our walk in silence.

After two more rights turns, we were now on the busiest road near my place. At every streetlight, numerous cars were lined up, their lights warping under the rain, creating an illusion of blurriness in my vision. It was as if the colors had somehow mashed together and were constantly moving as the signalisation turned green. We made sure to stand as far away as possible from the street to avoid getting splashed by passing cars. I could sense Camille was nervous. She would have spoken her mind by now, but her silence started to get me anxious too. She kept dancing from foot to foot, her walk as uncertain as she was, and she kept her head down most of the time. One could say it was to avoid walking in puddles and it wasn't that weird that she'd look to the ground, but something was up. I kept going straight, not wanting to continuously observe her, but there wasn't much distance left to our planned walk around the block and the final corner was approaching quite fast. I put my hand on her shoulder, making her stop. She turned around slowly and, as our eyes met, she looked to the side, seemingly avoiding me. I tried to sound as reassuring as possible.

"I don't know what you wanted to talk to me about on this walk, but now would be the time. Don't worry too much about it, everything's fine. You know you can just tell me anything, right?" I wanted to sound as reassuring as possible, but even my voice was shaky now. The feeling of apprehension didn't leave me, and my stomach was as solid as a rock in anticipation. Whatever she wanted to say, it wasn't easy for her, and it wouldn't be for me. What could she possibly want to tell me in this rain, though?

She raised her head and our eyes met again. Her eyes were puffy and red, and tears flowed down her cheeks. Without a word, she flung herself on me, embracing me with all her strength. It almost made me tumble down with her onto the street, but I barely managed to stay standing. Before I could say anything, she locked her lips with mine. The sudden kiss surprised me, but I let myself go, enjoying the spontaneous moment, and closed my eyes. I couldn't feel the rain, my wet sock, the ground, I couldn't hear the cars stopped nearby, the sound of the water drain, I couldn't feel anything except her soft lips. Then, just as I was getting over the initial surprise, I felt her tongue searching for mine. Lowering the last fragment of my guard, I fully embraced her. I don't know how long we stayed like this, it felt like forever and an instant at the same time. It felt different than the ones we had previously, that hunger wasn't present, that wild feeling she usually had had faded into nothingness, but I only noticed it when she eventually backed off. Still, I felt a wave of emotion crash in my heart and was overcome with warmth, like a heat current that swept through all my body. I couldn't help but smile at her, forgetting all that happened before this moment.

"I love you so much," I whispered to her, loud enough for her to hear, but low enough that anybody passing by would miss it. She was still in my arms, our mouths so close to each other, our breaths mixing in the cold air, numerous raindrops falling all around us. Even if I was soaking and her coat wasn't much better, I wanted to stay here forever, in her arms, close to her body.

"I want to breakup," she answered through the tears.

The words she spoke were like a gunshot to my heart. I was left speechless and frozen as they echoed again and again in my head. I looked at her with empty eyes and only saw rain and tears alike streaming down her face. I had so many questions. Why? How? Couldn't we talk about this? The way she said it was very clear to me; she had already taken her decision a long time ago and there was no going back. I felt hollow, like a part of me had just been ripped out and thrown to the side with no regards. My heart ached like a thousand needles piercing it over and over. After a while, I finally managed to say something.

"Are you serious?" I asked. I wasn't angry, rather curious and tried to convey that in the tone of my question, but I was an emotional wreck and, judging from her face, she wasn't much better.

"I am," she answered. "I'm sorry, Jack, but it doesn't work anymore. I need some space away from all this."

"Why?"

Camille sighed and put her hand on my cheek. I looked straight into her emerald eyes, these eyes that used to be so bright and shiny, so full of life and excitement with a glint of mischief, were now dull and devoid of light. I couldn't hold eye contact with her any longer and looked down, trying to contain my tears to not cry on her hand. I wasn't doing a very good job.

"We had some good times together, you know. The hill, the park, the beach. All those days, even if something didn't go as planned, were a blessing and I enjoyed every part of it. Everything that happened then… I wouldn't trade it for anything. But it doesn't work anymore. You set clear boundaries surrounding that other girl, and I respect that, but I can't live with them. Every time I see her, she reminds me of what she did to my brother, and I get angry. That's not good for me and I can't live like this. So, it's better that we part ways."

"I wanted to talk to you about that," I said, a last resort to try and steer this conversation back from the despair pit it was heading into.

"There's nothing more to say that hasn't already been said," Camille said firmly.

"But you're wrong, about everything she did to your brother," I said, pleading for her to listen to me. "She didn't…"

"Listen, Jack, I don't really want to hear you defend her. I know she's your friend, so of course you're going to take her side. Whatever she told you, it's not true. My brother told me everything that happened between those two and I don't see a way I could possibly forgive her. And if that means we must go our separate ways because of it, then so be it."

She paused for a moment, just a second, but it felt like an eternity. She pondered how to proceed while I was at a loss for words. How could I make her listen? She wasn't listening to me, like reciting a presentation she had practiced dozens of times. Even so, I saw the emotions on her face, the raw emotions, the tears and the sadness peering through the mask she was trying to put on. No wonder I couldn't get through to her; she had closed herself off from the outside world. This wasn't my girlfriend anymore.

"Jack, you like this girl," she continued. "Whether it be as a friend or more, I don't know, and you don't want to give her up, you made that abundantly clear. But I can't interact with her, she makes my blood boil, and she did something unforgivable in my eyes. I want to forget, I want to forgive, but I can't and knowing you will talk to her, laugh with her and tell her about us when you inevitably do something with her makes my heart ache just thinking about it. Do you understand? That's no way to live. If you don't want to leave her, that's fine, but then it means I cannot stay."

"There's nothing going on between me and Chloe, though, we're just friends, why can't you let that go?" I asked, my tone raising a little bit. I was frustrated. Flustered she wouldn't even consider my side, wouldn't even care to try and listen to the truth. She was ending things on a complete lie, a fabrication. Even as I wondered that, I couldn't tell who was lying anymore. "You're not even willing to listen to me about her…"

"You're right, I don't," she said while looking down. It seemed like she was ashamed of how she felt, but then why? Why reject the words before they even come out? If only she knew the truth, perhaps… Why didn't I tell her? Why couldn't I just tell her then?

"It has nothing to do with that, Jack. I'm not scared of you cheating and I don't think you are, even if she has a history of it." I winced a little at her words. "You're better than that and wouldn't do something like this to me. Even if it was only for a few months, I got to know you. And you got to know me. I know when you set your mind to something, you can do great things and you stick to your beliefs. I admire that about you, but it also means that other girl and I can't be both in your life, at least I can't. Don't resent me for this, Jack, okay?"

I took a few moments to process everything she had just said. All our previous dates flashed in my mind, all the laughs we shared, all the intimate moments we had, all the times we fought. Those emotions were real, those memories were real, and this heartache right now was real as well. Chloe told me Camille would break my heart eventually. Was this what she meant? How could she have known? I shook my head. That couldn't be possible. I closed my eyes, trying to contain myself, but I was never good at it. Was rain always this salty? I sunk to my knees, the puddle next to me splashing a little under my weight and my pants immediately became soaked. I didn't mind, I didn't even feel it. I looked down at the water and saw my reflection being warped by all the raindrops hitting the surface.

"What was the point of all this then?" I asked myself in a whisper. She caught what I said and squatted down to my level, putting a hand on my cheek again. The warped puddle returned to normal under her umbrella.

"There was never any point. Love isn't something logical, it's something you feel deep down in your heart. And feel we did, there's no denying that. Don't think of it like that. Cherish the memories we made and continue walking forward, wherever the road leads you next."

"I don't think I can do that if you're not walking it with me…"

"Jack," she said, grabbing me by the chin and lifting my head up. "Sometimes, there are crossroads in the paths of life and companions part ways. But that doesn't mean their paths will never cross again." She leaned in to give me a peck on the cheek and I couldn't react at all, her lips even wetter than usual leaving an imprint that got washed away just as fast. She backed up and I looked for her eyes, but she was looking down, avoiding my own. "I'm sorry." She practically whispered that last part, but I could hear everything still. She started walking away and, through the rain and the tears, I could hear her sobbing. She stopped after a few meters and turned around to look at me one last time. "See you at the next crossroad." With that, she began walking away for real this time. I extended my hand towards her, desperately trying to bring her back in my arms. I wanted to feel that warmth again, to feel her body pressed against mine, to cradle her, to kiss her, to share everything with her, to hold hands with her. But it all slipped away like the rain on my face.

I was really trying to contain myself, but just as a glass tends to overflow when filled too much, I burst into tears on the side of the road, soaked and overcome with sorrow. My heart ached more than anything I had ever experienced before, and I don't know how I managed to get back to my apartment in one piece. Everything was a blur, maybe caused by the tears or the rain, I didn't know. As soon as I opened my front door, I stood in the doorway, absorbed in thought. In front of me, I could see various memories playing, that one time we ran after each other in the hallway, the time we watched a scary movie, and I was more scared than she was, that time we kissed right in front of the door as soon as we came in. That last one lingered for a long time and it hurt the most. Never again would I feel her lips on mine, never again would I hold her in my arms. If my heart was in the depths, it somehow managed to sink even deeper and, by now, I didn't know how I would possibly recover it. I didn't even bother to take off my coat as I came in and crashed straight unto the bed. Quickly, the sheets absorbed everything and became wet too. I grabbed a nearby pillow, put it straight on my face and screamed as loud as I could. Screaming usually helped me get things off my chest, but not this time. This time, it only seemed to make things worse. I tried punching my bed, but to no avail either.

Ding!

I froze. I just now realized I had forgotten to take my phone with me when I got out. It was still on my desk, right next to me. All I had to do was reach out for it, but I was dreading what I was about to see on the phone screen. Would it be Camille? I don't think I could face whatever she would be saying right now. Shakingly and while trying to calm down, I grabbed my phone and opened it. I instantly recognized the icon. One unread voicemail. I tapped it and let the phone dial itself to my voicemails. A few seconds later, her voice filled the dark apartment.

Despite my heart being shattered in a thousand pieces, I smiled a little, trying to hide my sadness. After what just happened, a nice drink could do me good, but was I really about to go see Chloe now? Wasn't that just proving Camille right? Well, whatever, the deed was done, was it not? What difference did it make now? I opened my contacts and scrolled down to see Chloe. Just above her, however, was Camille. I must have stayed there, frozen, for a few minutes before finally tapping on Chloe's name and calling her. The ringtone rang a few times, but she eventually picked up. I tried my best to hide the fact I had been crying for the past few minutes and played it off as best I could.

"Hey, um, it's me. I'm free, so where are you going?"

I didn't even bother to change. I just went straight out of the door, looking for anything to change my mind off things. I didn't even bother cleaning up the small puddle of water that had formed from my dripping coat in the middle of my room. My apartment, once again, fell into silence. A dark and cold silence. A silence only broken by the sound of a ringtone. I had forgotten my phone again. On the desk, a screen lit up and the vibration caused a ruckus in the empty dark room. Her name was clearly shown, but there was no one to see or answer.

Chapter 14

The bus trip to get to the bar was the worst experience I've ever had to endure. Everywhere I looked, no matter if it was closely related or not, reminded me of Camille. The passengers, the sound of the rain hitting the windows, the movement of the bus, the empty seat next to me. I could almost feel her head resting on mine like it did so many times before, but its absence was duly noted now. I was trying my best to contain my emotions, to not burst out in tears in public and make a fool of myself in front of all these people, but it felt like giant claws had my heart between them and were squeezing tightly. The tears overflowed and ran down my face as I looked down to avoid any sort of eye contact. Perhaps going out was a mistake. Perhaps I should have stayed home. I tried to distract myself, but to no avail. It was like when a song gets stuck in your head and you try to get it out, but nothing works. This time, however, I couldn't get the vision of Camille walking away in the rain and, somehow, it always rained on my face when that image came up.

I was so out of it I almost missed the stop. It seemed to be happening a lot more recently. Tonight, though, there was a good reason for me getting lost in thought, but as soon as I stepped out, the rain started hitting my coat, a rhythmic reminder of what happened earlier that evening. I sighed heavily, wiping the tears off my face and made my way to the bar. It was only a few doors down the street from the stop and I was in front of it a mere minute after getting off the bus. I opened the big wooden door and made my way inside. As soon as I stepped in, the warmth of the place brought me some comfort. The atmosphere, troubled by noisy conversations, made the voices in my head calm down and allowed me to think somewhat clearly for the first time in the past hour. I walked down the corridor leading to the place and made eye contact with a waiter that came up to me.

"Alone for tonight, sir?"

It really shouldn't have, but the words made my shoulder slump. Did he really have to say it like that? I hoped he didn't notice and barely regained my composure.

"Actually, I was joining a group," I said softly, scanning the room in search of Chloe, but I couldn't find her.

"Okay, which group would that be?" he asked.

"Well, I am searching for them, but I can't seem to find them. There's a red-haired girl with glasses about my age in it, does that ring any bells?" I said. Maybe the description of Chloe would help him figure out what group I was talking about. Couldn't be easy, just for tonight, huh? The waiter seemed to think for a second and looked back at me.

"Yes, I think I know. They're not seated over here, they're in the section a little further down. Follow me." With that, he turned around and I quickly went after him. He made sure to grab what I assumed was a menu on the way and continued his little journey past a few tables and down some stairs until finally, he stopped in front of a long table. It could probably sit around thirty people, but only about ten were seated at the moment. He gestured towards the group as I arrived next to him. I once again scanned the room in search of familiar red hair and again, couldn't find her. I turned towards the waiter, but he had gone to tend to other matters, and I was left alone, overlooking this group of people I didn't know. They didn't seem to notice me just yet. I wondered if I was even in the right bar. Could I have heard the name wrong and came all this way to the wrong place? It wouldn't be the first time I messed something up and the present circumstances wouldn't help me think clearly. I thought back to the many times I got the wrong directions or forgot something important. The worst of all, her birthday. I was still not over how I managed to do that and the fact I was standing in a bar, just like that time, made the emotions come back in force. What would the group think of me, a stranger standing next to them, crying his eyes out? The creepiness factor was through the roof, but I couldn't worry about that right now. I was trying to not break out in loud sobs. That would have been the absolute worst and, if that happened, I didn't know how I could possibly recover. Although maybe that was a small blessing, but since this group was unknown to me, even if they did see me cry loudly, chances are I wouldn't ever see them again, so it didn't matter if I embarrassed myself. I calmed down a little, streams of tears drying on my cheeks, and searched my coat for my phone. I must have gotten the place wrong and was going to text Chloe to tell me the address of the bar again. I couldn't believe I was so forgetful, maybe Camille was right on that count. I knew I had to stop thinking about her, but everything around reminded me of our relationship, from little things like this to the bus ride to get here. Everywhere I looked, I could link it to something to do with Camille, a date we had, a moment we shared, little mimics she would do.

That made it much harder to process everything and, if I was honest with myself, I still couldn't quite believe what she said earlier. Surely, it was a mistake, and she would come around, right? After patting myself down for a few moments, I realized my phone was nowhere to be found and my heart, which wasn't feeling that highly to begin with, stopped. Did I drop it in the bus? Did I have it in the bus? When was the last time I had it? I couldn't remember, but panic started to take hold of me. First, the breakup and now this. It was a bit too much for me to handle and I was about to break until a hand landed on my shoulder.

"Jack! You made it!" she said. I turned around and saw Chloe, all smiles with shining blue eyes locked behind her glasses. She seemed to be radiating, I couldn't tell if it was the lighting of the bar or if she was divine, but the sight of her instantly made me calm down. I saw her eye me down from top to bottom and stopped to look at my face. "Are you okay?" she asked. I really wasn't but was much better than a few moments ago. I didn't know why, but I was compelled to hug her, and I almost pounced on her, taking her strongly in my arms. She almost fell, but credit to her, she held on. "Woah, what are you doing? What's gotten into you?" she said, taken by surprise by the whole thing. I couldn't answer as my face was in her neck. She was rigid at first, crisped and firm like stone, but soon loosened up and gave herself in to the hug. Normally, I would never do this, I don't think we had hugged each other since a few years back, but I needed this right now and she didn't back out. I was holding her body tightly against me and her warmth brought me comfort, a comfort I was desperately looking for. I could feel her breasts on my chest, but I paid them no attention. I was more focused on her hand rubbing my back, a gesture I didn't think I needed until she started it. I was certain she felt myself calm down too, but she didn't stop until I let her go a few minutes later. I backed away and looked her straight in the eyes. She rubbed her neck at the spot where my head was, and my eyes shifted to see what she was doing. She was wiping off my tears which had left a wet patch on her skin. Well, if I wanted to hide the fact I was crying, then that battle was already lost. I looked back up and she was still staring at me. "Are you okay?" she asked again, this time with a more concerned tone than before. Was it in shame or embarrassment, I didn't know, but my gaze shifted downward towards the floor.

"I'm sorry, I shouldn't have done that," I apologized, unable to hold eye contact.

"It felt like you needed it. I'm sure you had your reasons, but dare I repeat myself; are you okay?" she answered. I looked back up. That question wasn't formality this time, she genuinely was concerned for me. I faked a smile at her, hiding behind a mask of tears, a façade I had already constructed between my inner thoughts and the world outside. I wanted to tell her, but the wound was still fresh, and it hurt just thinking about it. I wanted to explain what had happened, maybe she could help me get through it just like we shared our pain for years, but I couldn't bear to remind myself of Camille any more than I had to and everything we experienced together. Not tonight, not here. I felt like she knew something was up, though, as my smile didn't seem to impress her at all.

"Yeah, yeah, I'm fine," I answered, looking to dismiss this conversation and bury everything deep. It was easier that way. Chloe looked at me suspiciously but didn't voice out her concerns again. I knew she didn't believe my answer, but I was relieved she didn't push the matter more. She nodded down slowly a few times, barely perceptible, and gestured towards the table.

"Shall we go then?" she asked. I couldn't refuse and followed her back to her group of friends. If at all possible, I wanted to avoid talking and thinking about Camille tonight and a group of friends and alcohol were just the things I needed to distract myself. We walked to the table deep in conversation and Chloe made a gesture to gather everyone's attention. It took a few tries, but eventually people noticed and started to quiet down. All eyes were fixated on me. In normal circumstances, I could have been embarrassed and blush, but not tonight. In fact, I wasn't even paying that much attention and only the mention of my name took me out of my head. I looked at Chloe who responded with a smile and turned back to her group of friends. Most of them nodded or waved, but one girl in particular seemed eager for me to sit with her. She was at the tail end of the group, too far to be engaged in any type of conversation and there was an open seat next to her. If anything, it would be easier to talk to just one person rather than a whole group and since I didn't know any of these people, I felt it would be difficult to mix when they were already talking for a while. I would probably be a bother. But not to this girl. Chloe tapped me on the shoulder and brought her head close to my ear. "I'll be over here if you need me" she whispered, her breath heating my skin for an instant. Even if it was nothing, I still liked it. It felt reassuring to have her so close to me and I nodded in response to her comment. I don't know why I didn't stick to her side, but regardless I made my way around the table to sit next to the other girl. She seemed excited when she saw me walk towards her, like she couldn't contain herself, and loudly dragged the chair across the wooden floor to give me space. I sat down, the cushion a little slimmer than I thought, and rested on the back with a little sigh. I closed my eyes for a second, but her voice made me open them again.

"Rough night, huh?" she asked. I turned to face her and took a quick look. I couldn't see her very well from where I was with Chloe, but now that I was up close, she was kind of cute. She had shoulder-length black hair that covered a part of her face, deep and dark eyes I could easily get lost in, a slim nose and a smirk painted on her face. The lighting of the bar made her hair shine a little and I swore I saw a glint of mischief cross her eyes for just a moment. She was absent-mindedly fidgeting with a straw in her empty cocktail glass while looking at me with both intense and calm eyes. I could tell she was somewhat feisty just from her body language, but I didn't know if I had the drive to have that energy tonight. I mostly wanted to forget, drown myself in some alcohol and maybe get lost in a conversation, but I wasn't sure. I wasn't sure of anything, I doubted myself for every little thing now and it was all her fault. "What happened?" she asked. Her expression had changed, from a smirk to a more compassionate look. I felt like I could trust her for reasons that still escaped me but bothering her with my burdens straight away didn't seem like the best idea.

"Nothing much, what about you?" I answered, looking to shift the discussion away from me. Maybe if she was the one talking, I could focus on whatever she was saying and not think back to blonde hair and green eyes.

"I can tell. Your eyes, they aren't like they usually are, are they? They have lost their spark and it's not because of the rain. What happened?" she insisted. How did she know all this? Did she just randomly guess right? Why did she need to know everything? We had just met, why did my problems concern her that much? I looked at her again. She was now serious, her eyes staring straight at me, piercing my core and seeing my very thoughts, or so it seemed. She probably just wanted to appear like she cared, but why would she? If it was Chloe, then that would be another story, but even then... I didn't confide in her either. Actually, perhaps the fact she didn't know me, or Camille would make her more impartial if I did talk to her about what happened. I needed to get if off my chest, to get my feelings out in words out loud, but was it right to push all of that onto this girl whom I had just met?

"I..." I said with a sigh. I still wasn't sure if this was the right thing, but I was committed now. "My girlfriend..." I choked up on the mention of her. Just the simple word made my eyes water, and I could have started crying at any moment. I loudly swallowed my feelings down and continued. "She broke up with me earlier tonight."

"Oh… I see," she answered. I didn't know what kind of response that was. Was she trying to be comforting, was she… disappointed? I was confused by what she said and must have made some kind of funny face because she started laughing a little. "Don't look at me like that, you look like a deflated balloon." The absurdity of her comment made me chuckle. What was that supposed to mean? How could my face appear to her like a balloon, it made no sense. I must have been even more confused because she started laughing harder. They say laughter is contagious, but I had scarcely seen this phenomenon in action with my own eyes. This time, however, she really dragged me into one that seemed to take weights off my chest. I felt like I could finally breathe, like all my burdens just flew away like birds in the sky, like maybe there could be still joy in my life without Camille. We finally calmed down and looked at each other, the remnants of chuckles still lingering at the corner of our mouths, threatening to come out at any moment. "I like you better like this. Your eyes are shining now," she said.

"You have a weird obsession with eyes, don't you?" I asked, more like a comment than a question. I wasn't in any position to talk either, I liked to focus on the eyes of a person too when I looked at them, it was one of the first things I noticed whenever someone new was introduced to me and the reason why I found her cute. Even if had the color of the void, her eyes expressed so much emotion, so much of her character it reflected on her entire personality. They say eyes are the mirror of the soul. Perhaps they were right.

"Well, you've been looking at them ever since you sat down too," she commented. I smiled a little. She had a point. I looked down for a moment and back up, making eye contact again. She lifted her eyebrows and smirked, proving her point. I continued looking at her longingly. We seemed to connect somewhat, understanding each other without words and there were already traces of friendly chatter even if we had just met. I never really talked to many girls in my life, Chloe and Camille were the main ones, but talking to her made me realize they aren't any more difficult to talk to than guys. It also made it clear I didn't know her name at all.

"I just realized I don't even know your name. Would you…?" I asked, but she cut me off before I could finish.

"Violet. Pleasure," she said, extending her hand towards me. I got confused on what I was supposed to do and looked at her, a bit embarrassed. She laughed a little and grabbed my hand to shake it herself. I shook my head in disbelief. Why was I so stupid sometimes? Of course, she just wanted to shake my hand, what else would she be extending her hand for? "Well, now that we got that out of the way, why don't you say we get something to drink? My treat," she proposed. I wasn't against the idea, but I was perfectly capable of paying for myself.

"I can pay for my stuff, there's no need," I answered. I thought she would like that I refused her offer, but it had the opposite effect.

"I said, my treat, no arguing," she said, firmly. I wasn't about to disagree any more than that and let it go. She signaled the waiter to come by and he quickly made his way to us. I heard them talking, but it was kind of distant. I was lost in thought again, somewhere deep and far away where their voices were muffled. Violet shook me a little and I came back instantly. I looked at her and she pointed to the waiter who was clearly waiting for me to order something. I didn't even think of what I wanted.

"Um…a pint of blonde, please," I blurted out in panic. The waiter nodded and went away. Violet tried to contain her laughter next to me, but some of it got out and I turned to see her covering her mouth with her hand, her shoulders moving up and down ever so slightly. "What's so funny?" I asked, a little harsher than I would have liked, but she seemed to pay it no mind.

"You were totally caught off guard," she said between breaths in a higher-pitched voice than before. "The way you said it was just the funniest thing you said tonight."

"Well, there's no need to laugh that much about it," I grumbled, and she laughed even harder. I wasn't really upset so I joined her. After we calmed down a little, the waiter came back with our drinks, and we got to talking.

After Camille had broken up with me that evening, I had difficulty imagining life going on without her. I was used to having her in my life, texting her whenever something funny came up, talking to her, hugging her, kissing her. All of that went away at the snap of her fingers and I fell into a void, some place where I didn't know what was up and down and everything appeared to be misplaced. The painful walk back to my apartment and the bus ride to get to the bar weren't much better either. It was like I lived inside my mind and my body was simply a shell somehow walking on its own. I was hiding, trying to protect myself from any other form of harm that could come my way. But meeting Violet, even for a moment, made me forget everything that happened. My mind had chased away any bad thoughts, any sad feelings related to Camille and banished them to make place for laughter and this new girl. Even if we had met a few minutes prior, I felt comfortable with her, like meeting an old friend, but it was a different feeling than Chloe, too. I was relaxed, but there weren't past events together we could lean on, there wasn't a familiarity that had developed over the years and there was no history. Only the present moment, what I felt right now, what her body language was saying, what I perceived from what she was projecting. We could relate on a lot of subjects and whenever she talked, I listened, and it took no effort. I was genuinely interested in what she was saying, getting lost in her dark eyes who were shining sometimes, indicating her passion. Her straight hair flowed back and forth, almost hypnotizing me if I stared too long. She also made me talk about my interest and listened well whenever I did. It appeared like a verbal dance, like everything we said were just movements to lead the other into a mesmerizing choreography. It didn't occur to me I had finished my drink until the waiter came by and took the glass in one swift movement. Violet signaled him to bring me another and I was about to protest until she glared at me and I resigned to let her have it her way. After all, she said she was paying and I didn't want to abuse that, but if she was the one ordering, then surely it was fine, right? It didn't take long until the second pint came and halfway through, I could really feel its effects. My mind became hazy and troubled and, even though I was concentrating on what Violet was saying, some of it got lost before it reached my ears. As the night went on, she was saying very suggestive stuff while looking at me, trying to physically get closer to me and scanning my face for a reaction. She must have been very disappointed as I didn't get any of that until she brought her mouth right next to my ear.

"Want to get out of here?" she asked in a whisper, barely audible to me. Nobody else could have heard what she said. What did she mean by that? And go where? If I was honest with myself, any place with her seemed like a good idea and if she wanted to leave, then I could leave with her no problem. I glanced over at Chloe's seat, but found it empty. Had she already gone as well and didn't tell me? Well, I didn't know any of these other people so nothing was keeping me here. I turned to Violet. She was looking at me with intense eyes, they were inviting me, I thought, and she was blushing a little too. I nodded twice and she quickly got up and started talking to the counter to pay for our drinks. I also got up and was hit by the alcohol I had all at once. I almost fell down on my butt, but held on to a chair for a few moments until I regained my balance. I joined Violet, in the process of paying, and we soon left the bar. The cold air hit my face with a refreshing chill, washing away some traces of drunkenness instantly. I breathed in a few times, enjoying the difference between inside the bar and outside as Violet took out her phone to check something. I stood around for a few moments, eyes closed and breathing in and out. It felt really good. I then realized I had no idea where we were going and turned to face Violet, a bit faster than I would have liked which made my head spin briefly.

"Where are we going?" I asked. She looked at me confused.

"To…my place?" she answered, puzzled as to how I didn't understand that immediately. It simply didn't occur to me that was her intention, and I nodded a few times. "Alright, come on, there's a bus coming in a few minutes just down the street, we should be able to catch it if we hurry." She started walking towards the bus stop and I quickly followed her, not wanting to be left behind. She seemed to hold her liquor a lot better than me, at first glance, but I was still able to keep up with her. As soon as we arrived at the stop, the bus turned the corner of the street towards us. A few moments later, it stopped in front of us, and Violet got on board. I also got on, making sure to grab the rails on the side to help me and scanned my card. The beep somewhat startled me, and I hoped the driver didn't notice it. She was already going down the aisle and chose two empty seats so we could sit next to each other. I joined her shortly after the bus started moving again. I held on to whatever I could on the way to avoid falling over and finally sat down next to Violet. She turned to me. "We should get there in about ten minutes," she said. I simply nodded, staring straight ahead.

Why was I here? Why was I going back to her place? Couldn't I have gone back to mine? I just went along with it, but I didn't understand why she would want me to go to her apartment. If she wanted to talk more, we could have done so in the bar, so what was she planning? I couldn't really think as my head was still a bit shaky. She took me out of my thoughts when her head hit my right shoulder, the weight of it pressing down on me. I didn't know why she was doing that, only Chloe and Camille had ever done that with me before. I remembered the last time Camille had done it and how much I missed that feeling, but soon came back to realize that would never happen again. This girl wasn't Camille and while they may have done the same gesture, it wouldn't quite feel the same way as it did back then. With a sigh, I paid it no more attention and just let her rest for a while. Maybe she was tired and just wanted a quick nap before we would arrive at her place? It only took a few minutes before she notified the driver to let us out at the next stop and she got up. I was blocking the way out and got up as well. We awkwardly walked to the doors and opened them as the bus came to a halt. Getting out, the cold air refreshed me once again. I wasn't sure if it was the fact I had been drinking or what, but the coolness of it hit different tonight. I also realized it had stopped raining and looked up at the night sky. There were no stars in sight, probably all blocked by empty clouds, but they had stopped crying for now, much like me. Their tears had still formed puddles on the ground, a reminder of what had happened earlier, but they had moved on already. I wondered if I could do that too, but Violet tugging on my arm prevented an answer to come. I followed her as she walked down a few buildings until she turned left towards one. We made our way inside and she unlocked door after door, leading me up some stairs to the second floor. In normal circumstances, I always found the railings inside to be irrelevant as I never used them, but I was glad they were here tonight. I held on to them with each passing step. Soon, we found ourselves in front of a wooden door which Violet promptly unlocked as well. She went inside, soon followed by me and closed the door with a loud clunk. I heard a metallic click as she locked the door and I quickly scanned the room. I couldn't see much as it was quite dark and could only make out the faint shapes of various furniture. I turned around to look at Violet, wondering what the next step would be and almost fell as she flung herself on me, her lips locking themselves to mine in an instant. I caught her in my arms, both of us still with our coats on, and couldn't react to the kiss she had given me. Her hands were on my cheeks, locking my lips in place, not letting go and we stumbled backwards a few steps until I hit the wall. Her tongue searched for mine and I was surprised by her forwardness. I had experienced these sorts of kiss before, but never with a stranger and only with Camille. The feeling wasn't entirely new, but there was something exciting about it. I started to feel a bulge in my pants and tried moving my legs a little to give it some space. Violet seemed to catch on and her right hand moved down to feel it. Even through my pants, the contact of her hand made me jump slightly and, as she moved up and down, she smiled a little, breaking our kiss. She backed off slightly and looked straight at me, eyes locking with mine. She bit her lip, grabbed my hand and started leading me down the corridor with enthusiasm. I didn't resist. I couldn't believe this was happening to me of all people. I didn't have time to think for long before we were in her bedroom. It was even darker than the other one and I could only see the faint outline of her silhouette moving around. Before I could even speak, she kissed me again, just as fiercely as the first time, but her hands were frantically moving around my chest and waist, grabbing and tugging on every piece of clothing she could find. Soon, she had unbuckled my belt and dropped my pants to the ground, quickly followed by my underwear, revealing my member. She grabbed it in one hand and pulled up on my shirt. I got the memo and broke our kiss to remove it. I was somewhat distracted by her stroking but managed to chuck it across the room with more force than I intended. With her unoccupied hand, she went behind her back and I heard a little click. I didn't know how she did it, but her bra fell to the floor in one movement, and she also removed her pants, keeping her underwear on. I could tell they were a light color as they stood out in the darkness, and I silently thanked her to have kept it on. Of course, I wanted her to take it off at some point, but it could serve as a guide in the dark.

Violet, without letting go of me, dropped to her knees and took me in her mouth. The sudden warmth made me moan and her constant stroking accentuated the feeling. Her tongue also soon got to work, and I couldn't even process what was going on except the immense pleasure I was experiencing. She felt like such a professional, her hands and tongue working together like a well-oiled machine, lubricating me to the point where some of it was leaking out the sides. She was making weird sounds with her mouth that broke the stillness in the room and my moans joined like an out of tune symphony. While I had received oral before and enjoyed it, it wasn't on the same level as the one Violet was giving me right now. She wasn't afraid to get sloppy, she was putting everything into it while my previous experience with Camille was much different. She used to be assertive in everything related to intercourse and would usually lead me then, but apart from our first time, she didn't seem to enjoy oral much. Violet, on the other hand, seemed to be having the time of her life. However, she was perhaps a little too good and I threatened to bust already. My breathing quickened, and she must have caught on to what was happening as she slowed down and looked up at me to gauge my reaction. I tried to control the rising wave of pleasure by breathing in and out and, with her stopping, managed to calm down. I didn't want her to stop, but she stood up and turned around, her butt towards me. She rubbed against my member with her cheeks, teasing me gently. I couldn't take it anymore.

I don't know what happened. Something in me snapped and I acted out of instinct or pure lust, I couldn't tell between the two. My hands extended and grabbed a hold of her breasts, pulling her towards me. They were soft and not too big, a perfect fit for my hands and I gently squeezed them as she pushed a little startled cry. Her body was now pressed to mine, only a thin layer of fabric between us, but I could feel her warmth on my skin. Her head was resting on my shoulder, and she turned to kiss me. I gladly responded and our lips locked again. Her back was slightly arched so her butt was still on my member. Her hips were moving in circles, gently teasing it. My right hand moved down, across her belly, past her waist and between her thighs, moving aside the underwear she still had on. I felt a sudden wetness on my fingers and knew I had found it. Similarly to her hip movements, I drew circle across the top, making her break our kiss to moan softly. I varied my rhythm a little and she seemed to go crazy about it. Her legs seemed to bend downward and back up, like she couldn't stand any longer. For the first time in my sexual history,

I was leading. I was in control. I was the one acting, and she was reacting. I smiled quietly; I liked this feeling. Since I was inexperienced, I usually let Camille take the lead and she would do as she pleased when we had sex, but this time was different. I wasn't that used to sex still, but I knew enough to know what I wanted, and Violet seemed to go along with it just fine. I saw where the bed was and turned both of us around in one quick movement. Before Violet could react, I pushed her on the bed. She was startled by it and pushed a surprise cry quickly followed by laughter. She moaned seductively and positioned herself to show me her most private part directly. With a swift movement, she removed the only article of clothing still hiding her and tossed it aside with disregard. Her head rested on the sheets, her butt high in the air and her knees just on the edge of the bed. I had seen this exact position before. During my first time, Camille had done the same thing. Then, even if she was inviting me to her, she was in control. She determined what we did and how we did it. Not this time. I was going to be the one to decide. I approached Violet and got right between her legs. She was slightly too high for me, and I pushed gently the inside of her knees to signal her to come down a little. She spread them a bit farther and the tip of my member brushed against her, making her moan. I grabbed it and rubbed it against her folds. She seemed to enjoy that a lot. In the darkness of the room, her womanhood was still very much visible, shining a little by how wet it was. I slid across it with no effort, and it was hard to contain myself to not take the plunge right away. But I wanted to make her wait for it, to beg for it, to want it so much she couldn't take it anymore. After a few moments like this, I saw her hand extend to her bedside table and open the first drawer between moans. It seemed to be extremely difficult for her to concentrate, but she managed to pull out a small package that made a wrinkle sound as she handed it to me. I immediately sighed internally. How could I forget this crucial step again after I chewed out Camille for it our first time? I got too caught up in the moment, too crazed about this power fantasy I had forgotten the most important thing, protection. After all, she was a stranger before a few hours ago and even then, it was always better to be on the safe side. I struggled to open the package, but finally got the condom out and proceeded to put it on. I don't know if it was the nerves or my lack of experience, but I struggled a little to finally get it unrolled completely. Luckily for me, she was as wet as she was when I returned to her entrance, and nothing had changed. After much waiting, I went inside.

Even if it wasn't my first time, the initial thrust always made my knees weak. The warmth suddenly all around my covered member spread throughout my whole body and I moaned softly in tandem with Violet. Of course, the fact I had a condom on made the sensations a little tamer than without, but I was more used to the feeling of having one than not. It took a few moments for me to regain control of myself. I gripped Violet's butt cheeks with both my hands and spread them apart slightly, also pushing down on her already arched back. I began thrusting back and forth, her slit fully exposed for my eyes to see. She was so wet, and I didn't have any resistance at all. The sound of flesh hitting flesh soon filled the entire room, only broken by the sound of our frantic panting. I looked towards Violet to gauge her reactions. Her face was buried in the sheets to cover her moaning, which weren't doing a very good job as I could almost hear her clear as day, and her left hand was gripping them like her life depended on it. Her right hand had slipped underneath her and was making circles across her folds. Sometimes, her hands would brush against me, and the touch of her fingers made me moan every time. I made her go forward a bit and hopped on the bed. I was standing up and wanted to vary it a little, but I wouldn't last much longer at this rhythm. I could have slowed down, but the feeling was too good, and I was finally deciding the pace of the sex I was having. As much as I didn't want to give that up, it felt better to make her enjoy a faster cadence. I stood on the bed, gently lowering myself down to get inside her again. I lingered in front of her, teasing her more, going up and down her folds until I went back in. She moaned a lot on that thrust, and I would be lying to myself if I said I didn't understand. The movement to go in and out in this position was very different and it took me a few back and forth to properly get it, but she didn't seem to mind. I grabbed her by the hips and, every time I would thrust in, I would pull her towards me at the same time. I hit the deepest parts of her insides and our breathing seemed to synchronize through the frenzy. Mine had gotten a lot louder and she could probably tell I was about to give out. Somehow, she tightened up and that proved to be the end of me. With a low grunt, I gave one final thrust, the deepest I could go and let it all out. That was one thing I liked about condoms; I could finish inside with no worries. I rode my high for a few seconds and stayed in that position, breathing in and out a lot slower than moments ago. Violet crawled forward on the bed, making my member exit her and fall down a little. She turned around and I could tell she was smiling at me before she talked.

"I didn't know you would be so aggressive. You didn't strike me as the type," she said with some amounts of teasing in her voice.

"I don't know what came over me, I... I'm not usually like this... Did you like it anyway?" I asked. Violet came right up to my face, and, through the darkness, I could still make out a smirk.

"I loved it. You can take that thing off now," she winked, looking down at my retreating member still wearing a fast-wrinkling condom. I backed up a little, slightly embarrassed I had forgotten to take it off and she laughed silently. "If you need to use the bathroom, it's the first door on the left when you go out the bedroom. But ladies first, so wait for me here." With that, still naked as the day she was born, she walked out, leaving me alone in the dark in a stranger's bedroom. After all that, the bed looked rather inviting and a wave of fatigue crashed over me. It felt like it hit all at once, out of nowhere, and it wasn't long before I got under the sheets after putting on my underwear. I didn't feel comfortable sleeping completely naked in her bed, or in general for that matter, and so I felt it was the best thing to do. Drowsiness soon got the best of me and the last thing I remember is feeling Violet's body pressing on mine as she spooned me. I liked that feeling a lot, but didn't experience it often, even when I was with Camille, and it only made the sleeping process faster.

◊

I woke up in a semi panic, sitting up in the bed and looking around. Where was I? What was I doing? The layout of the room didn't seem familiar, the sheets were clearly not mine. I rubbed my forehead, trying to remember something, anything, and a very strong headache appeared out of nowhere. I grunted a little and bent down forward like it could help me. I remembered getting to the bar, meeting up with Chloe and her friend. We talked for a while and then... went to her place? Was this her apartment? Only then did I notice the weight on the other side of the bed. I glanced over to see a woman with short black hair wearing nothing at all, the moved sheets revealing one of her breasts. I sighed a little. What had I done? Details of the night came flooding back in. We definitely had sex, that much I was certain, but the exact circumstances were still a bit hazy. Why did I do that? For a reason I couldn't quite understand, I was flooded by an immense sense of guilt. Guilt for what, I didn't know, but an image of Camille appeared in my mind to answer the silent question. That's right. Camille had broken up with me earlier. I felt sorry for this girl I couldn't for the life of me remember the name of. I wasn't in any shape to return her feelings, if she had any that is, and this was a mistake. I hadn't realized it, but I had gotten teary-eyed, tears threatening to fall and soak into the bed. I rubbed my face to wipe them off and pushed the sheets aside to get up. I didn't know what time it was, but I couldn't stay here. Why did I feel so bad about this? I wasn't with Camille anymore, why was she occupying so much space in my heart, making me hurt even after she was gone? Would I feel this way for the rest of my life? Was there no escaping her grasp even after she let me go? I gathered my clothes scattered on the floor and put them on silently. I didn't want to wake the girl up, I didn't want to have this conversation right now, not when I was feeling all over the place and overwhelmed already. I gently opened the door and slipped out unnoticed. I was now standing in the hallway leading to some other rooms, but everything was dark, and I couldn't see a thing. I only hoped that nothing would be in the way like stray boxes or something, anything that would trip me and make enough noise to wake her up. Walking a little further, I came across another door that appeared to be the bathroom. I realized I really needed to go, but there was no way I could, not without making some noise. I didn't know how loud I could be, I didn't know how light a sleeper she was, so I didn't take any chances. On the opposite side was a way into the kitchen. The guilt I had morphed somewhat, and I started to feel bad for her. She went to sleep with me and would wake up with me gone, having no idea what happened. She would probably be confused and wonder why. I decided to write her a note explaining everything and walked into the kitchen, looking for paper and a pencil or anything to write with. I struggled to find anything in the dark, but eventually got my hands on a notepad lying around on the table and a pen in a case near it. I had everything I needed, except light. Would it bring too much attention if I turned on one light? What about the bathroom light, they're usually a little dimmer than others? Perhaps I could use my phone as well. I searched my pockets for it. Wallet, keys and… nothing else. There was no sign of my phone anywhere on me. Did I leave it in the bedroom like an idiot? I started to think back to the last evening and realized I never did bring my phone with me. It was probably sitting on my desk back in my apartment. How did I even figure out the bus schedule to get to the bar then? Did I just get lucky or something? I snapped out of my thoughts and returned to the problem at hand; I had to get light to write. A little further down the corridor was the living room extending far enough to connect to the kitchen. I wandered in, being careful not to topple anything over and looked for a lamp I could light. Luckily for me, there was a big one next to the couch and I reached out to turn it on. It was some sort of nub I had to twist, and it took me a few loud clicks before it worked and lit. The sudden brightness attacked my eyes and I had to cover them up for a moment. I soon got used enough to the luminosity to open them and start writing my note. Sitting down on the couch, I tried not to make any noise, but it creaked a little under my weight, making me grit my teeth. I thought of what to say, staring at a blank page for a few moments and no matter what came to me, it sounded bad or made me out to be a jerk. I just wanted to explain myself so she would understand why I left and what happened when she would wake up. The pen landed on the small page and started seemingly going on its own.

Hello,

I'm sorry for what happened yesterday. I don't fully remember everything, but I have a feeling it was a mistake, at least for me. I didn't want to lead you on or give you the wrong impression and my feelings aren't clear at the moment. I'm sorry for wasting your time and I hope you can forgive me.

Jack

As I signed the letter, I remembered her name. Violet, of course. It was so obvious now I didn't understand how I could possibly forget it. I changed my letter to greet her specifically to be a little more personal and stared at the finished product a while before getting up from the couch. I went back to the kitchen and dropped the note on the counter. If there was anywhere, she would be most likely to see it, it would be here, or so I thought. I returned to the living room to turn off the lamp and made my way to the front door, in the dark again. Somehow, it was now worse, and I could see even less. However, I had checked if there was anything in the way before turning it off and walked with more confidence to the wooden door that separated me from the outside of Violet's apartment. I stood in front of it for a minute, staring and deep in thought. Why did I do what I did tonight? Rather, why did I care so much about it? I had answers to neither of these questions and finally turned the handle to get out after quickly putting on my shoes that lay nearby on their side and scattered about as well as my coat. The door creaked too, but I didn't care anymore. I still made sure to close it without making a sound, or tried to anyway, and quickly got out of the building and into the night.

It had begun raining again, nothing more than a drizzle, but an annoyance regardless. I looked up at the sky. At this hour, there were no more buses and, if I wanted to get home, I would have to walk. I had a rough idea of where I was, but nothing precise enough to pinpoint my exact location. If I could get to the main road that crossed the city and passed near my apartment, I could find my way. I briefly thought of going back upstairs and into the bed with Violet, but that was soon chased away from my mind. She was a nice girl, I remembered that, but I couldn't go back. Even if she didn't want my heart anymore, there was another one already occupying it and I couldn't handle any more. Before I left what little shelter I had, I put my hood over my head and my hands in my pockets. I went out the door with as much confidence as I could muster, which wasn't a lot, and started walking. If my sense of direction was still useable, I was going the right way. Raindrops started hitting my coat and my head, making little tapping sounds as they popped. While it was constant and distracted me from my thoughts, it quickly became annoying.

"What a terrible day for rain" I mumbled to myself as I felt my hood slip and held onto it to put it back.

◇

It had been over an hour, or maybe two, before I finally stood in front of my door. I still wasn't sure of my decision to leave, but I had committed to it. On the way, there were multiple times where I doubted myself, wanted to turn back, but something kept me going, walking forward. Rational thought, guilt, or a bit of both perhaps, but it certainly wasn't all planned from the start. If anything, I wasn't going to leave the bar except to go back home so anything past that point was purely a spur of the moment thing after the other. On my walk, I had woken up completely and remembered all that happened. The bar, Chloe, Violet, the conversation we had, her apartment, the sex…That last one was the most problematic. I knew it was mistake deep in my heart, but I couldn't figure out why. Just thinking about it almost made me want to cry. Or was I already crying? With the rain outside, I could barely tell anymore. Even if I had slept a bit in Violet's bed, I was exhausted, both mentally and physically. Emotionally too, I supposed. I felt like I had no more tears to cry, like my reserves had run dry for the day. Was that even possible? Perhaps I wasn't crying then, but who could tell? I slowly opened the door to my apartment building and walked up the stairs, one by one. They felt like immense hurdles, like lifting my feet took such effort even if it was easy. Somehow, I made it to the top and fumbled to get my keys. Suddenly, sensations all throughout my body came rushing in all at once. My feet hurt, my legs were stiff, my coat was soaked, my head seemed to pulse every few seconds, I was very warm, almost sweating and my hands were shaking. I had trouble putting in the key but managed to do it and unlocked the door. I was greeted by another dark apartment and while this one was mine; I felt a stranger to it also. The darkness wasn't inviting to say the least, but I had to go forth and my feet dragged themselves in, closing the door behind me. I removed my coat and hung it on the hook nearby, took off my shoes and went straight to my bedroom. I didn't bother doing anything else. I wasn't sleepy at all, the walk made sure of that, but I was exhausted still. I felt hollow, like a piece of me was missing, a mere husk of the person I used to be. Would I ever find that piece again? Was it hidden or taken from me? I lay in bed for a long time, with not enough energy to get up anymore and stared at the ceiling. I don't know how, but for the first time ever, I thought of absolutely nothing, a completely blank space with no distractions. I lost myself in the dark of the room, unable to fall asleep and unable to move all the same. I didn't know how long it would take for me to do either, but one of them was sure to come before the other. Fully dressed and partially soaked, I somehow fell asleep to a world with no dreams. Would I even want a dream this night? Perhaps it was better to not have any...

◇

I woke up in complete confusion, startled by the sound of a deep rumbling coming from my room. It took me a few seconds to get my bearings and remember where I was. I looked around for the source of the sound, but it had stopped. The sun had just about risen over the horizon and not much light entered the bedroom. I had omitted to close the curtains last night and I wondered how I was even able to sleep for a moment. The sound came back in full force, but this time I was awake for it. I located the source of it to be on my desk and noticed my phone. I rubbed my face to wake up a little more and got out of bed, slowly walking to the desk tucked in the corner of the room. The vibration resonated again, indicating someone was calling me. I didn't look who it was and just picked up. Something heavy was on my heart and I wasn't quite sure if it was only because sleep hadn't worn off yet or because of what happened last night. The latter seemed more likely, but I liked to think it was the former instead.

"Hello?" I answered in a low, deep voice. It appeared my voice didn't get the memo to also wake up.

"What the hell were you thinking, Jack?" she said in a clearly angry tone.

"Woah, who is this?" I asked. I knew it was a girl's voice, but I don't know if it was because I wasn't fully awake yet, but I couldn't decipher if it was Camille, Chloe or if by miracle Violet had figured out my number.

"Are you serious? It's Chloe. What were you thinking?"

"About what?"

"Okay, we're really going to do this, huh? You disappear from the bar without saying anything, you don't answer your phone the whole night, you leave with my friend and then you go and hook up with her at her place? Does that ring any bells?”

“Well, yeah, that’s what we did. I thought you had left; I couldn’t find you.”

“I was at the bathroom for a few minutes, but that’s not the point. Do you realize what you have done? You have shunned me for a year for something like this and then you go and do it behind my back? You’re such a hypocrite, I can’t believe you would do something like this while being in a relationship.”

Her words weighed a ton on my heart. The simple mention of my now past relationship made it stop as if it was pierced by a thousand needles and I had to sit down on the bed. In my ear, Chloe was still going off on me about cheating in a relationship and multiple other things I couldn’t make out. Her voice faded in the background as I stared at the wall, trying my hardest to contain the tears that accumulated in my eyes. I couldn’t do it and they started to flow down my cheeks. I tried to speak out, but my soft voice was drowned by Chloe’s anger. Nevertheless, I managed to get her attention.

“Chloe… Chloe…”

“What?” Her answer came as cold as ice. She was clearly mad at me, and I couldn’t exactly blame her. From her perspective, this was one of the worst things I could have done, and I couldn’t exactly defend against that. Except by telling her everything.

“Camille and I broke up,” I said, my voice shaken by emotion. I tried to not make it apparent, but there was no use. She most likely had heard it tremble even through the phone call. There were long seconds of silence that came and went until she broke it.

“What?” This time, there were practically no traces of anger left. Nothing like that, perhaps more incredulity and concern. If I could have done anything other than cry, I might have smiled, but the tears were overpowering, and I couldn’t contain myself.

“She left me. She… She broke up with me. I thought my heart was going to stop. I got your invitation, and I thought maybe it could make me forget, make me put this pain aside and ignore it. The pain came back, but I hid it as best I could. Then I met Violet, and I didn’t understand what we were going to do until it was right in front of me. I should have known, but I couldn’t think straight last night. I could have stopped, but I had hoped it might make me forget her. It didn’t.” I was now sobbing loudly, trying to get the words off my chest, but it proved harder than I thought. “It was a mistake. I shouldn’t have done that, but now it’s done and I’m sorry. Sorry for her, I didn’t want to lead her on, I didn’t… I was confused, my feelings were shattered and broken and trampled, I… I know it's not an excuse, but I didn't know what to do." I tried to calm down, both breathing in and out, but it took me a while before I could manage. On the other side of the phone, Chloe said nothing and let me take my time.

"I'm sorry, Jack. I didn't know," she said. The sound of her voice helped calm me down, even if just a little. I was glad she was here, even if she was angry at me in the beginning.

"Of course, I didn't tell you," I said through my irregular breathing.

"Why didn't you tell me back at the bar? I wouldn't have left you with someone else then. I would have stayed with you."

"Telling you would have meant acknowledging it. I didn't want that. I couldn't accept it. But now I went and did it with Violet and it's done. I can't take that back, I wish I could, but now it's truly over. My heart aches for her, I want her by my side, even if I know her feeling isn't the same." I paused for a second. "You probably don't want to hear this, I'm sorry."

"Listen, I know how it feels, I have been there. The most important thing for you to do is to avoid keeping those emotions locked up inside your heart. Find someone you trust and let it all out. If that person is me, then I will gladly lend an ear for you anytime, even if I don't particularly enjoy talking about her. Because it's not about her, it's about you. Yeah?"

I let her words resonate inside my head for a few seconds. Her kindness really was something else and I didn't know if I could have done the same had the positions been reversed. Nevertheless, hearing her say all that made me slightly happier, as much as I could be in this situation.

"Thank you," I said in a soft voice.

"Are you going to be okay? Do you want me to come over?" she asked.

"No, I don't want you to see me like this and I don't think I can face you right now anyway. Perhaps another time."

"Okay, no problem. Just… call me if there's anything, okay? It's important."

"I will."

"I'm sorry, Jack. Talk to you later." I didn't answer and just hung up the phone. I let myself fall on the bed and stared at the ceiling, looking for answer. There were none up there. How long would this feeling last? Would it come back every time I thought about her? Even if I had calmed down, the tears were still flowing on my cheeks and soaking the sheets. I felt empty, like a void. I felt like I couldn't breathe, like the simple thought of Camille brought back all the emotions I tried to contain, yet I couldn't stop thinking about her. This bed, this room, this apartment, she had been everywhere in here. We slept together on this bed, we watched movies on the couch, we ate dinner at the kitchen table. Everywhere I looked, memories of the time we spent together appeared, haunting me like a twisted ghost meaning to torment my mind. I couldn't escape them, they were everywhere. I needed to go outside, but I didn't want to do anything. I didn't have the energy or the will to even take a walk. I eventually got up, a few minutes later, and walked towards the bathroom. On the way, I passed the living room. There, on the couch, we had cuddled up and watched multiple movies. I could swear they were still playing on the TV even if it was turned off. I still heard her laugh, I still saw her crying, I still saw her getting angry or scared. I had to look away and turned my head. I continued walking and came across the kitchen next. The sight I saw broke what little drive I was still clinging on to. The supper I was cooking last night was still on the stove, long cold by now, still waiting for us to dig in. We would never do, not together and not in this kitchen. I slumped to my knees and burst down crying. I would never feel her arms around me again. Never feel her lips kissing me again. Never hear her laughing again. Never walk beside her again. Never hold her hand again. Would I ever be able to recover from this? My heart was in pieces, was it even possible to put them back together?

I blanked out for the rest of the day. I don't even remember what I did, but it wasn't much. I could barely exist by myself, the constant thought of Camille bringing wave after wave of tears until there were no more tears to cry. I was exhausted by the end of it and fell asleep in my bed. Even if we didn't sleep together every day, I still felt she was missing, her presence beside me wasn't there and it made me hurt even more. Did she feel the same way as me, I wondered, before sleep took me in for good.

Chapter 15

I dreaded this day ever since I realized I had to go to school. It was now the next Monday and while I had done nothing the day prior, the sudden realization I still had my classes almost made me want to skip. I took a lot longer to get up from the bed, the sheets seemingly holding me there with invisible hands. After a lot of mental effort, I managed to wake up, get dressed and go to the kitchen. I always ate in the morning before leaving for school, but this morning was different. I felt like I couldn't eat a bite, even the thought of food disgusted me. Still, I packed a small lunch to eat later and soon left my apartment. It was the first time I went out the door since the bar two days ago. Walking to the bus stop felt different, like it used to be routine and now it was more a burden. Thankfully, I didn't wait long on the sidewalk until the bus came and I quickly got on board.

The entire trip, I kept thinking about Camille. I tried to hide my face from everyone inside my coat, I didn't want them to see me get emotional. Just the thought of her still brought me to the edge of tears and now that I was going to school, that image was even stronger. I silently thanked fate Camille and I weren't in the same class, or we didn't have a locker next to each other. I couldn't possibly face her, not right now and maybe not ever at this rate. The familiar building soon came into view, and I signaled the driver to stop. As soon as I stepped out, I took a deep breath, the cold air getting in my lungs and refreshing my thoughts. I looked on towards the school as the bus drove away behind me. I had to psych myself up, telling myself nobody really cared about Camille and I, going out together or otherwise, nobody would pay attention to me any more than they already did and while the school wasn't the largest, the chances of me running into her were very slim. I took another breath to calm down and started walking to the front doors. The weight of my backpack suddenly lifted, and my back straightened up. I held my head high instead of looking at the ground. It was a new day, and I was determined to not let my emotion get the best of me.

The inside walls of the school appeared to have changed. The lockers weren't the same, the cafeteria looked different, nothing was as it used to be.

Did they really change everything over the weekend or was I dreaming? The latter seemed more likely, but then again, I didn't dream for the past two days. I stood in the doorway for a moment, getting weird looks from other students coming in on either side of me, but I didn't care. I slowly walked forward, observing my surroundings. It was almost like an entire new building, like everything had changed yet remained somewhat familiar. It seemed weird I would think that, and I wasn't sure why I thought it different, but something was bothering me. I couldn't pinpoint exactly what it was, though, and that in itself was cumbersome. I reached the stairs leading down to the cafeteria and looked to my left down the corridor. Students were walking in every direction, coming and going to and from classes, nothing unusual. If anything, the school seemed busier than normal. I looked to my right and saw much of the same. As I expected, nobody knew, nobody cared, and nobody paid attention to me. I still felt like eyes were constantly staring and judging me for each of my actions, but I breathed a sigh of relief. I was nervous, by all accounts it didn't make sense and to know they were unfounded worries was comforting. I started walking towards my locker to my left. Camille's was on the right side and, while I was bummed out about its location compared to mine a few months prior, I was now the complete opposite. As soon as I started walking, I looked down, true to my habits, but caught myself in the act and lifted my head up. There, down the corridor, I saw her, blonde hair standing out among other students and the monotone walls. There was no mistaking it, it was her. I froze, unable to move and my heart started beating a lot faster. I couldn't take my eyes off her. I wanted to get away, I wanted to leave, but I couldn't. My breathing got heavier and faster and the whole world around me faded until I couldn't see anything else than Camille walking down the corridor in front of me. If I didn't move, she would reach me, and I didn't know what would happen. I didn't want to find out either. If only my legs could move. I felt tears welling at the corner of my eyes. After a few painful seconds that seemed to last an eternity, I regained control of my body and immediately ran away in the other direction. Where was I going? I had no idea, but it was surely away from her. I couldn't face her, not now and maybe not ever, and tears had already started slowly flowing down my cheeks. I tried to rub them as I ran, but it didn't quite work. I didn't want anyone to see me like this, but I couldn't help it. I wasn't looking at where I was going and somehow managed to avoid other students in my way. Until I turned a corner and ran straight into a girl, both of us tumbling to the floor with a loud thud.

"Watch where you're going next time," she said, angrily. The girl quickly gathered her books scattered about and looked at me, her eyes frowning. "Oh, Jack. Wait, are you okay?" She walked up to me, still sitting and looking down.

"I'm sorry I ran into you," I said, without even looking up to see who I was talking to. "It won't happen again."

"I sure hope not. Can you get up?" I lifted my head to see Chloe's face staring at me with concerned eyes. Was it fate or a cruel joke, I didn't know, but I was still a little relieved to see her right now. "What happened? Why are you crying?" I realized the tears hadn't stopped at all the entire time and now they had left visible trails on my cheeks.

"I… I…"

"Why don't we get a little bit of privacy? Let's go over there, okay? Come on, get up," she said, lifting me up to my feet. I looked at her, completely lost like I couldn't process what was going on anymore, and she signaled me to come with her head.

She extended her hand, and I grabbed it, walking with her as she led the way. We soon found ourselves in a little spot way less busy than the main corridor and she leaned on the side of the window's edge. She tapped next to her to indicate I should do the same. I sighed, both to calm down and to gather my thoughts, but it didn't work as well as I hoped. We stood there for a few moments, none of us wanting or able to start the conversation, but it had to be done and Chloe initiated.

"What happened back there? You don't seem too well," she asked, clearly concerned. I sighed heavily and tried to calm down before explaining everything. It was harder than I thought and it took a few moments, but I managed to do it.

"I… saw her and… I don't know what happened. I froze, I panicked. I can't stand seeing her, it hurts too much. It's one thing thinking about her at home and another to see her again, knowing I won't ever be with her anymore." I started crying again, as silent as I could. I tried to hide my face in my hands. I was ashamed, not that I hadn't ever cried in front of Chloe before, but I usually kept my feelings down and I couldn't this time. They were overflowing and out of control. I felt her arms around me as she gave me a hug and brought me closer to her. My head rested on her chest, soaking her shirt with my tears while she slowly moved back and forth to try and console me.

"Everything will be just fine. I know it hurts, I know what you're going through, and it is going to get better. Give yourself time. It's only been a few days."

"How am I supposed to when I'll always see her at school? Every time, my wound will re-open and it's going to hurt again and again and again. How can I heal when she's so close to me all the time?"

"You will. Trust me. You just need to take her out of your mind for a while. Distract yourself with something you like."

"How can you be so sure?"

"I've been through a few breakups myself, Jack. I know how they feel. I don't pretend to know exactly how you feel right now, but I have a rough idea. The pain you have in your heart will go away eventually. Now, I need you to do something for me," she asked, gently pushing me away from her. I looked up, trying to gauge what she wanted on her face and was met with a warm smile. For a moment, I thought her very beautiful, but the feeling went away as soon as it came, leaving me confused. What was that about? Chloe was staring at me directly, not with harsh eyes, but with compassion and something else I couldn't identify. "You need to talk to someone about your feelings, okay? It can be anyone, friends, family, a professional, it can even be me if you want like I told you earlier, but you have to get them off your chest. You can't keep them bottled up like this, it will damage you in the long run. Do you understand what I'm saying? I know it's going to be hard, but believe me, it's for the best."

"Did you do this too?"

"Of course. When I broke up with Max, there was still a period where I felt guilty about it and talked it out with my friends. They made me see clearly through the situation and assured me I made the right decision. They saw how I acted when I was with him and it wasn't the best time of my life, but they didn't want to interfere in my private life unless I asked them about it. A similar thing happened with Kyle. You know, I felt really bad about losing you and it took a long time before I came to term with it. I'm glad we're back to talking, but that's not the point. All I'm saying is, talk to someone about it. It will do you good, I promise."

"Why didn't you talk to me when you broke up with Max, then? We were close, why didn't you?"

"That's a bit complicated, Jack, but it's not important right now. Whether you choose me or someone else, it doesn't matter as long as you choose someone. Please, do it. I'm saying this for your own sake."

"I will. If it's not too much trouble, I'd like to talk to you about it. I don't want to impose, but…well it's not that I don't trust my friends, it's just…" I paused for a while, searching for the right words. I looked at the floor as if it had the answer, but nothing came. I looked back up at Chloe, her eyes filled with kindness and had to turn away slightly. I couldn't hold her gaze, not like this, I was too embarrassed.

"You know, you can talk to both your friends and me, too. I'm sure there are some things guys only want to tell other guys and I understand that. If there's anything you can't tell me, go talk with them. Are you following me?" I nodded in approval, still unable to speak. I had forgotten how kind Chloe was. The whole incident with Camille and her, my relationship with Camille and the fact we hadn't talked to each other in a year before just a few months ago had tucked away those memories. They came flooding back and threatened to come out, but I barely managed to contain myself. "Thank you for your trust in me. It means a lot." Chloe checked her phone briefly. "We should get going to class, are you okay to go?" she asked. Once again, I nodded, but continued looking away. "Do you want to go together?"

"I think I'd like that."

We started walking towards our class. I couldn't tell if it was because we hadn't done it in a long time or something else, but it felt very awkward, and we didn't talk at all the whole time. Everything we needed to say was already said and there was nothing more to add. I tried to calm down on the way there so it wouldn't be as apparent I had cried when we got to class and I didn't know if I hid it well, but nobody paid any attention to Chloe or me. I was glad, in a way, because if everyone had been staring, I didn't know how I would have reacted. I just wanted a quiet class to make me forget Camille and get her out of my mind.

◊

We were now sitting on my couch in the living room. How we got here, I wasn't quite sure, but the awkwardness and the silence between us made it apparent it wasn't planned. Chloe sat straight up, looking forward at a black TV while I was slumped down on the opposite side of the couch. After class, Chloe took one look at me and decided to accompany me back to my place. I wasn't opposed to the idea and simply didn't say anything. I knew I needed to talk, and she was giving me the perfect opportunity, but I couldn't even start. The thoughts in my head were all hazy, it was impossible to grasp one and think it through. I felt her shift a little on the couch and looked over and sighed. She wouldn't stay here forever, if I wanted to talk it out, now was the time. But as much as I wanted to, the words simply wouldn't come out. Maybe if I just started talking, the conversation would flow better? Better than this silence was still and improvement.

"I really feel all over the place right now. I'm glad you're here or else I would probably already be in bed," I said.

"To be fair, your position isn't much better than lying down. You might as well be," she answered with a smirk.

"Perhaps you're right." I waited a little before continuing. The ice had been broken, but now even thinking about the subject at hand made me choked up, like a cold hand squeezing my throat. "You know… I didn't really see it coming at all," I said, looking down. I heard Chloe move on the couch to face me, her eyes weighing down on my shoulders. She was attentive now, that much I could tell, even if I didn't say anything coherent. "It came out of nowhere for me. I don't know, we seemed to have good dates together where we had fun and talked for hours, we always spent time together and did…well you probably don't want to hear this. Anyway, everything seemed fine. I just don't understand it at all, where did it come from?" I said, more blabbering to the ground than to my friend. She readjusted her glasses and folded her arms together. I took once glance over but couldn't sustain the eye contact and went back to staring at the ground.

"Did she ever fault you for anything?" Chloe asked. I took a few seconds to answer.

"Well, she was annoyed at my forgetfulness, but she's not the first one," I said, the faintest of smiles appearing at the corner of my mouth.

"You always forget things, it's genuinely impressive. Remember when you used to forget your pencil case at school all the time and I had to lend you a pencil every time you came over?" I smiled a little.

"Yes, that one I do remember," I whispered, almost as if I didn't want her to hear myself. I didn't know how my mind worked, but there was clearly something I couldn't grasp. There was always only one thought in my mind, constantly changing from one to another, that some of them slipped through and disappeared. I tried multiple things in the past to change it, but nothing worked. The only time it got better was when I was with Chloe, and she would remind me of anything and everything. Back then, it was like she had a sensor for things I would forget. It was uncanny, but very helpful and I still owed a lot to her for that. When we stopped talking for a year, that crumbled, and I started to forget things again.

"There was this one time I messed up really bad," I said. I wanted to continue right away but thinking about it made me stop. The hand had moved on from my throat and was now squeezing my heart in its cold grasp. It hurt as the memory flowed into my mind and I felt myself freeze a little. Chloe snapped me out of it.

"What happened?" she asked. A simple yet effective question. I didn't have a choice now. I had started walking that path and had to continue going forward.

"I… forgot her birthday," I said, slumping down even more. I brought my legs up, my head finding its way between them. I just wanted to hide from all this. But I couldn't, I knew I shouldn't run away, and I needed to get it out, but why did it hurt so much?

"You what?"

"Unforgivable, right?" I paused for a few seconds, searching for the next words. Chloe didn't interrupt me and let me gather my thoughts. "I don't think she has forgiven me for that one still. I just don't understand why she came to me that night. If she was that mad, why would she sleep next to me?"

"Wait, wait, I don't understand, where were you?" Chloe said with a confused expression on her face.

"I went to see her to apologize and try to talk to her. She wanted none of it, but I didn't want to leave so I went to sleep in the guest room. In the night, she slipped in the bed to lie next to me," I explained.

"She came to you? Just like that, with no words spoken?"

"Yeah, she just…climbed in and cuddled with me." I took a deep breath, somewhat relieving the events and finding it hard to contain the sadness overflowing from my heart.

"And did you…"

"No, no we didn't," I immediately dismissed. "But that doesn't matter, I still don't get why she did that. When she came in the night, I thought she couldn't be that mad at me then and thought it was going to be okay. Evidently, she still held a grudge, but how was I supposed to know?"

"You know, Jack, when feelings get confused, they make you do crazy and stupid things. I can't talk for her, and I don't pretend I understand or care for her, but she probably felt conflicted and followed her heart. In that moment, she still chose to be with you," Chloe answered.

"Now that just makes me feel even worse," I sighed. I could feel the tears coming back, but I didn't want to cry again. I had enough of crying, especially in front of Chloe and just wanted to get these feelings out without breaking down at every little thing. Easier said than done, surely, and it took me quite a while before I could gather myself.

"I didn't mean it like that," she said. "I was just saying her love for you was genuine. Even after you messed up, she still wanted to be there with you. That has to count for something, right? I would agree with you it was kind of a mixed message, but I don't think you should dwell on it that much. Did you do anything about it afterwards?"

"Yes, I did. I got her a custom gift I thought she would enjoy and when I gave it to her, she seemed happy. Evidently, that was just a façade. Maybe she had already made up her mind then…"

"Possible, but that doesn't matter. You eventually got her something, right? That's better than just dismissing the whole incident or not getting her anything anyway, isn't it? I'm not saying you didn't mess up, because you did, but you tried to make it right, even if a little clumsily. It's one thing that sets you apart from others." I looked over at Chloe. She wasn't looking at me anymore, instead staring at the white walls ahead. "You always get these weird ideas, and they sometimes don't work, but you put everything you have in them and that's what counts. I'm sure your gift was lovely, and she did like it in that moment."

"Well, it doesn't matter, because she threw it all away. She took our feelings, our thoughts, our memories and cast it aside like nothing. Nothing but garbage to be taken out on the sidewalk."

"I don't think that's true. Memories stay with you forever. The things you did, the time you spent together, the memories you made together, those will always have a place in your heart. It's up to you to decide how much space you give them, but one thing is certain, you will always remember her, even if just a little. Don't disregard the memories you have together. They are as important to you now as they were back then." Chloe still wasn't looking at me and I thanked her silently. I didn't think I could hold eye contact right now, but I needed to look at her face. Her red hair flowing down her back like lava on a volcano, her profile, her face. I never looked at her that way before, but the shy girl I used to know in high school wasn't here anymore. Chloe had gained a lot of wisdom in the short time we didn't talk to each other, and I wondered if I ever would be like her in that regard. Chloe felt my eyes staring and shot a quick glance over at me, enough to make me turn away. With those words in mind, images appeared before my eyes as if I was back there. The café, the hill, the beach, the hike. Everything we did together, perhaps it wasn't all in vain. It still felt like when she left, she destroyed everything we had worked for the past months in one instant, like she ripped out my very guts and threw them to the side.

"When I think about it, I don't think I really knew her. We talked about each other at the beginning, when we started to date, but then we kind of… stopped caring? I don't know if that's the right way to say it, but what's I'm trying to say is, I didn't inquire any more than I had to. Maybe I was more into the idea of being with her instead of genuinely caring about her?" I asked, head in my hands. I didn't want to admit it, if it were true, and didn't want to think any more about it if it weren't.

"Well, I can't speak for you about your own feelings, and I certainly won't do it for her, but you two seemed to have something genuine. I've known you for a long time and I've seen you around her. I hate to admit it, but you clearly liked her. Sure, there were probably things you could have done differently, I wasn't involved in your relationship, so I don't know, but there's no point in dwelling on it. You can tell yourself all the 'should have' and the 'could have' you want, what's done is done and you have to look forward. You can't make progress if you continue looking back. You know, the way you're feeling right now, the heart ache and the tears, do you think you would feel like this if you didn't really care about her?"

I took a moment to take in the full weight of her words. She was probably right, as she always was in these types of situations, and I wasn't thinking straight. My left hand moved on my chest, on top of my heart. My heartbeat was still strong, and I smiled a little. Even through all this pain and emotion, it was doing its duty, as always. I looked up at the ceiling and stared at the white color for a second, thinking on what Chloe had just told me. The conversation, that had started with me slightly depressed and overwhelmed, now shifted to a calmer and more understanding nature. I took a deep breath and closed my eyes, holding it for a few seconds before releasing. The air seemed to purify my lungs and wash away any bad feeling still lingering in me. Opening them up, my eyes landed on Chloe as I turned to face her. She had asked a question but needed no answer. She already knew what I would say, so there was no point in saying it. Instead, I inquired about a different matter.

"This pain, this sadness, how did you get over it? It feels like it will always come back, stronger than ever, every time I forget about it for a moment. It strikes at the worst times, bringing me and my whole mood down with it. How did you do it?"

"You just need some time, Jack," she said, the answer coming easily to her. "It's only been a few days and while your relationship wasn't the longest, you clearly had strong feelings for her. Those emotions, they take time to subside and nothing else will really work. You know they say time heals all wounds; well, they aren't lying. You can't expect to move on in a few days, give yourself room to breathe and mourn the loss you had."

"I don't know how you do it, but you speak with such wisdom, it's impressive. Where did you learn all that stuff?" Chloe smiled and looked down. It wasn't a happy smile and I wondered if I hit something sensitive. I immediately went to correct it. "Anyway, thank you for listening to me, it's been really helpful, and I'll try to do what you told me." She laughed a little at me, still looking at the ground.

"I probably talked more than you did, let's be honest. But I'm glad we could have this conversation and you trusted me enough to tell me of these things. If you ever need an ear again, don't hesitate to tell me. I'll be there for you, no matter what." I smiled at her. Even now, she managed to be kind of cute and I shook my head. She wasn't paying attention to herself, surely, but her fiery hair, the traits of her profile, her stature and her eyes. They met mine as she turned around and I stared into them for the first time in ages. Beautiful blue eyes, as blue as ice or the sky, but gentle as the sea. I felt like I could get lost in them forever, like they reflected an infinity beyond imagination. I snapped out of it when she readjusted her glasses and her hands got between our eye contact. I noticed she was blushing, and she quickly looked away. Was she embarrassed? Before I could say anything, my stomach grumbled, loud enough for the neighbors to hear, I thought, and I froze, hoping Chloe hadn't. But it was in vain, she was right next to me, she had clearly gotten wind of it and when she burst in laughter; I knew she had. I felt like I had to justify myself, for what reason I didn't know, but I did anyway.

"I didn't have much of an appetite these days. Guess it's catching up to me now." She laughed a little and smiled at me.

"Do you want me to cook you something?"

"Oh no, don't worry about that, I'll make myself something. I don't want you to bother doing that right now."

"Come on, it'll be fun! I'll do something quick; you don't even have to do anything. Please, I really want to do it now." I was about to protest more, but my stomach grumbled again and cut me off. Chloe laughed harder and just got up to go to the kitchen. I wanted to say no and stop her, but at the same time, the prospect of her cooking me something was enticing. It had been so long since she did, I almost didn't remember how much she liked it. Ever since I knew her, Chloe liked being in the kitchen, cooking meals for me whenever she had the chance. Over the years, she got pretty good, but even when what she did wasn't the best, it did taste better because I knew she tried her best. I stayed on the couch for a minute, debating if I should follow her or not and finally decide to join her. I might not be of much help, but I wasn't about to let a guest do everything by herself in my kitchen while I sat around doing nothing. As soon as I got in the kitchen, however, she looked at me with bossy eyes, telling me to sit down without a word. I complied, both in fear and amused. She returned to her work, looking around at what I had in the fridge, what spices I had and what cans were in the pantry.

"You really don't have much here, do you? How do you even cook for yourself, Jack?" she complained out loud. I simply smiled in silence. I wasn't a good cook anyway, I felt like if I got all these spices, I wouldn't even know what to do with them, so I generally didn't bother. My meals were usually simple and, as I wasn't very competent, required very few steps or else I would mess something up and the whole meal would be ruined. I preferred when they were easier to make to insure I had things to eat that night.

"Sorry, I don't usually cook much. Do you think you can still make something?"

"Maybe I could do this? Do you have…no, doesn't look like it. Okay, um, let's see… Oh, you have curry? How come you have this and not…? Whatever, yeah, let's use that." It wasn't the first time I watched her work in the kitchen and I was used to her talking to herself at this point. It was like a trademark of her cooking. Some things do never change after all. I let her setup everything she needed until she turned around to face me, sitting at the nearby table with a giant smile on my face. "What? What's so funny?"

"What are you making?" I asked, ignoring her question.

"Butter chicken. I have a real quick recipe and it should be ready in about ten minutes. You like butter chicken, right?" I simply smiled at her. She lifted her eyes up, both in annoyance and amusement as a smirk formed at the corner of her mouth. I folded my arms and stared at her with my head high. She couldn't help but start laughing and I joined up soon after. The heavy atmosphere that followed us in when we first arrived had gone and, for a while, Camille was out of my mind. My heart could feel again, not dragged down by the weight of my emotions, and could let itself be happy in the moment. Even though I was doing nothing, just being in the kitchen with Chloe while she cooked brought me a joy, I thought I could never feel again. When she had her back turned, I caught myself looking her up and down a few times. I had been friends with her for a long time now and I'd be lying if I said I didn't at least think of her in that way before, but this time it was different. There was something about her that changed or perhaps I did? Regardless, seeing her work and manage everything in the kitchen was beautiful, almost like a dance. The meal she was cooking was simple, yet she seemed really into it and didn't notice my staring. Neither of us had said anything in a while, with me being content just admiring her and Chloe being occupied. The whole time, I had a smile permanently painted on my face and I couldn't stop even if I wanted to.

She served the meal later and sat down at the table across from me. Even though it was my apartment, she was doing the serving as well. I felt like a guest in my own home, which was a weird feeling, but it also seemed right letting her do it. Chloe enjoyed it and was also smiling when she sat down. We quickly started eating, my stomach louder than ever, and it hit the spot. I complimented her skills, and she thanked me, almost dismissive, saying it wasn't much at all. Still, I wasn't sure I could pull off something like this myself, so I wanted to point it out to her. The rest of the meal was silent. I was lost in thought about everything we had said previously, and Chloe's words kept bouncing in my head. I didn't quite know how to feel, it was a mix of sadness and hope, like I couldn't decide which one was better. Chloe also seemed in her own head, staring into the distance at nothing. Then, both our eyes met, and I could swear I saw a glint of tears for just a moment before it faded away. I was about to question her about it but restrained myself. This wasn't the time, not right now.

When we finished eating, we both ended up back on the couch for a moment. She had finished first and waited for me there and I joined her a few minutes later. Neither of us could speak. Either the silence was too awkward to break, or we simply didn't have anything else to say, I wasn't sure, but we remained silent all the same. We stared at anything and everything, the blank TV, the bookshelf, the lamp, until she finally decided to say something.

"How are you feeling?" she asked in a soft voice. It almost seemed like she didn't want to be heard.

"I think I'll manage," I answered in an equally low voice.

"Good." She paused for a few seconds, looking down. "Then I'll be on my way." She slowly got up from the couch like she wasn't convinced either. Chloe turned around to face me and smiled. "Take care of yourself, Jack. If anything comes up, don't hesitate to call me." With that, she walked towards the front door, getting her purse sitting on the bench near the entrance. I stayed on the couch, unable to move or say a word like I was completely frozen. Only when I heard the front doorknob turn did I snap out of it, jump out of the couch and turn the corner to see Chloe standing there, door open and not moving.

"Thank you," I said. Such simple words, but they have great effect when said at the right time. I guess that's the case for any words, isn't it? She turned around and smiled again, her eyes a little shinier than they were a few moments ago.

"Anything for you." She walked out the door and closed it before I could say anything else. I wanted to tell her to stay with me, to not leave tonight, but I didn't have the courage to. And now, she was gone. I thought of calling her but stopped that thought before it could settle down in my head. She also needed her space and my clinging to her wouldn't do either of us any good. I had to face this next step alone. I rushed to the window in my bedroom overlooking the entrance to the building. Out she came, her fiery hair contrasting on her grey coat. The wind blew hard, and she had to lean a little into it to continue walking. I followed her until she disappeared from view and was hit by a wave of sadness. Not a sadness of tears, but one of hollowness. I felt she left a hole in me or maybe that hole was left by someone else, and she simply made me aware of it? Either way, I got suddenly exhausted and plummeted to the bed nearby. My thoughts were filled with memories of Camille and I, the words of Chloe and the last supper all mashed together in an incomprehensible cocktail of emotions. I didn't quite know what to feel and staring at the ceiling, like always, brought no answer. I sighed heavily. What to do?

Chapter 16

The passage of time brings many things and when the wind blows colder, snow is soon to follow. Everything was quickly covered in a white veil as the temperature dropped, making everyone wear coats and boots alike. The trees, previously colorful and beautiful, had lost their charms and were now nothing more than bark and branches. The grass had faded and given its place to snow, and rain had turned into snowflakes. There was a stillness to winter, unlike other seasons. There were almost no animals running around, no bugs, you didn't hear the usual birds in the morning, even people seemed to quiet down when the cold air hit.

Winter was my least favorite season with spring being a close second. I liked autumn the most, though the last one dampened my likeness a little. All the events that happened, couldn't they have happened in a worse season like winter? Why did it have to tarnish my favorite one? I didn't like the cold, I didn't like having to wear a big coat to even set foot outside, I didn't like having to shovel my balcony and the entrance to the building. I didn't hate winter, but I felt like compared to the other seasons, there was just nothing to do but stay inside. Walks were unpleasant, nothing grew, and it felt like everyone's spirit was dampened somewhat. Not like it changed much of anything for me as I was already in the dumps on that front.

It had now been a month since Camille left. Just like the first day, my heart ached all the same, yearning for her constantly, even just to hear her speak to me even though I knew I couldn't handle it if she did. The talks I had with Chloe helped, definitely, but there was still a long path ahead of me and I had to walk it alone. My days were filled with nothing but distractions, trying to take my mind off those thoughts, but everything in my apartment reminded me of her. I had decided to move everything around, changing almost every room to give them a new look. The bedroom was entirely different; the bed and the desk had switched places; I transferred a bookshelf from the living room to put it next to the desk and got some night tables as well. I normally wouldn't bother with any of those, I was perfectly fine without them so why spend money on things I didn't need? When she left, I started spending more on furniture, perhaps to fill in the hole she had made. Regardless, I started putting more effort into room decoration which was a little weird to me. I wasn't used to it at all, and it didn't really make sense why her departure triggered it in the first place. The living room had also changed a lot, the TV and the couch had both changed sides and the side bookshelves containing games and consoles had also moved. I had finally decided to buy myself a lamp and put it there as well to have at least a dim light when the sun had gone down. Maybe it was a coping mechanism, but I really enjoyed moving things around in my apartment. It wasn't the first time I had done it, there had been a few times already, but I liked the change every time.

Not a week prior, I received a phone call from Chloe. She wanted to know how I was feeling and dealing with everything, and I was just glad to hear her voice. I could have called her before she did, but phone calls made me nervous, even if it was someone I knew, and I ultimately didn't. After a little chat, she invited me to go skiing with her friends, assuring me exercise was the best remedy to my situation. I had protested, telling her I had no idea how to ski, that I didn't like winter and I didn't feel like going out. After much back and forth, she eventually hung up the call, but showed up at my door later, pressuring me into going. Seeing her in person, I couldn't help but agree. It was like I couldn't say no when her eyes pierced mine, I felt like a kid getting scolded by his mother. It was now the day of the activity, and I was barely awake when she pounded on the door, asking me to let her in. I obliged and she was wearing her full suit when she walked in, pants and all, urging me to go and get on with it. I quickly got dressed but had nothing to bring with me. I had never skied in my life, didn't have any experience or equipment, but she assured me they would have some at the station. I had no choice but to trust her.

A friend of Chloe was driving the car. Chloe was sitting next to her, and I was sitting in the back, alone. I barely greeted her friend as we took off, but maybe that was for the best. I didn't know her at all, I vaguely recognized her from the bar, but since we hadn't talked then, I couldn't see a reason to do it now. So, I tried to make myself scarce, silent in the backseat, while the girls had a conversation between them. It worked, somewhat, and we arrived at the ski station a little earlier than I thought. As I got out, I was blinded by the sun. In the city, the white snow was cut by the black streets and the different buildings. Here, there was nothing of the sort, barely tree bumps in the white veil covering the mountain. I looked around with a hand above my eyes. Even though people were walking around, talking, skiing, yelling, there was some sort of tranquility up here that was missing in the city. There, it was always busy, cars going by and sirens going off. Only silence could be heard here. My eyes stayed on the chair lift a little further away and I followed one chair from bottom to top. A hand on my shoulder snapped me out of my thoughts.

"Admiring the view?" teased Chloe. I turned around to see her. Even with her full suit on, she was still pretty slim, and her long hair went down her coat and stood out in the snow like fire on ice. I took a few seconds to answer, but she didn't seem to mind.

"Yes," I said with a slight smile. "I have never been to one of these. Seeing them in person is nothing like watching movies. You can't feel this atmosphere on a screen."

"You're right, I like the stillness it has, too. Glad you feel the same way!" she said with enthusiasm. "Listen, we're going to get our gear out, but you'll have to go rent some. Do you want me to come with you or are you fine on your own?"

"Well, I have never skied before and I have no idea what to even ask for, so I think it would be best if you joined me," I said, laughing a little. "I'll probably need your help to put it on, too, because I have no clue how to do that either."

"The absolute state of you," she teased again. "Well, I guess it can't be helped. Alright, come on, let's go. Hey, Anna?" she shouted towards her friend who turned around after hearing their name. "We're going to get him some gear!" Her friend nodded in approval, and we started making our way towards the building. I had finally learned her friend's name, which surprised me by how oblivious I was to not even register it in the car. They must have said it at least once, right? The fact I wasn't paying attention to them certainly didn't help, but if someone was giving me a lift somewhere, I could at least have the decency to know their name. Chloe didn't say anything while I rummaged in my own mind. I was glad she didn't, even if the sound of her voice sort of appeased me somehow. Walking beside her in the snow felt nice, even if the moment was but a fleeting instant. The silence between us only made me appreciate it more, somehow. Maybe Chloe was right; exercise was the best remedy in these types of situations. It wasn't long before we reached the main building. We went inside and the atmosphere changed instantly. I took a second to look around, admiring the contrast between the inside and the outside of the building.

While the facades were plain and cold, the interior was warm and cozy. The main door led to an open corridor that cut the room in half. On the right side, the rental box was in the corner, tucked away with a big banner on top indicating what it was. In the opposite corner, a canteen offered numerous food and drinks options to hungry skiers. On the left were multiple tables lined up to allow people to rest and eat. All around the building were countless giant windows that allowed a surprising amount of light inside, illuminating the entire room. At the very back, a fireplace cackled loudly as the flames danced when we opened the door. The weather wasn't windy, but the sudden opening of the door still caused a draft to sneak in. I lifted my eyes upwards and admired the colossal wooden beams that spanned the length of the building, going across the room in a criss-cross pattern, supporting the pointy roof. The whole place wasn't painted, and the natural brown of the wood accentuated by the orange tint of the fire brought out an immediate feeling of comfort. Even if I had never been here, I felt at home straight away.

Chloe was a little ahead, walking towards the rental box. I didn't know if I needed to follow her or not and hesitated a bit before quickly joining her. We still didn't really talk, the surrounding chatter covering up for our lack of conversation. Soon, we were standing in a small line leading to the rental box. Seems like I wasn't the only one coming to the mountain with no gear on. The wait wasn't long and a few minutes later, we were at the counter.

"Hello! Need full gear for this guy," she said, pointing at me. I awkwardly smiled, uncertain of what to do as the man across the counter looked at me. "He's brand new," she added.

"What size?" he asked, still looking at me.

"Um…" I started, but I had no idea what to say. I was glad Chloe helped me.

"What size are your boots?" she asked me.

"They're…10, I think?" I answered, not even sure of the validity of it.

"We'll go with that," Chloe said to the man. He nodded and went to the back. A few moments went by as we stood there, waiting until he finally returned with plenty of stuff in his hands. Some weird looking boots, a helmet, some goggles and, of course, two skis. He gave everything to Chloe and signaled us to move with his head. We quickly moved aside, letting the next person in line rent their equipment. With all our stuff, we made our way to a table on the other side of the building and sat down.

"He didn't seem in a good mood," I commented.

"Must be a rough day already or maybe he's like that all the time, I don't know. Wasn't this guy last time I came here," Chloe said. "Alright, we can put on most of the gear here and finish with the skis later. No point in doing that here. But we can put on the boots right away."

"Ok, is there anything I should know?" I asked while grabbing both ski boots. They looked really weird to me, they had these buckles at the front instead of laces and they looked almost metallic.

"Yeah, so first you want to unbuckle them so pull all of those aside," she explained. I did so and waited for the next steps. "Next you want to pull on the tab at the top. No, the little thing coming out there. Yeah, that one. Now put your foot inside and while you push it down, pull on the tab." I did as she said, and the boot seemed to open like a flower when my foot made its way down. I was a little surprised and fascinated at the same time. Straight away, I could feel my foot being slightly compressed, completely different to how my normal boots felt, but I guessed that was a normal thing for winter sports gear. "Once your foot is inside, tap your heel a few times to make sure your foot is completely at the back of the boot. Good, now make sure that black thing there is at the front. Alright, now you just need to buckle it back on and you're done!"

I quickly executed myself and stood up once I was done. The feeling was way different than I was used to, but it also looked like I had a mechanical foot, and I quite liked the aesthetic.

"Feels a little cramped, but it looks cool," I said.

"Is there any pressure on your toes? You need to tell me, because that means the boot is too small for you," she said.

"No, I think it feels fine. I mean, I don't really know, but it's not hurting so that should be good, right?"

"Yeah, sounds fine. Okay, so just put on your other boot and then we can find the others. They should already be here, but I don't know if they already went up. Maybe Anna would know."

Just as she said those words, Anna entered the building in full gear except her skis whom she carried in her arms. She quickly spotted us and arrived just as I was buckling the second boot. She sighed excitedly when she arrived and looked at me.

"You ready?" she asked.

"I have no idea," I answered, laughing.

"Good."

"Have you seen the others?" Chloe asked her.

"No, I haven't. No chance they would answer their phones even if we called, though, so we might have to wait for them at the bottom and hope to run into them. We really should have organised this part better" Anna said.

"Yeah, well, it's fine. Alright, let's go then."

The three of us, the girls in front and me waddling in the back with my skis in hand, went out of the cozy building back into the cold air of the mountain. I was suddenly glad I put on multiple layers of gloves and socks, because if we were out here for a while and I hadn't done that, surely my toes would have fallen by the end of the day. We started making our way to the chair lift, hoping that we would run into the rest of the group. Walking in the snow with these boots was hard enough, I didn't even want to think about when I'd have my skis on. Sliding on a mountain I could understand, but how did you even walk around with those? We arrived at the chair lift a few minutes later and stood around for a while before Chloe approached Anna and whispered something in her ear. I pretended not to see and started looking around. While the area was mostly clear, there were still numerous trees in the distance, covered in snow, but painting a greener picture. I thought it was very pretty and as far as seasons went, nothing could beat the autumn trees, but winter had gained some points. It was just a shame you couldn't see these kinds of sights in the city. I would much rather have these snow-covered trees instead of black streets and slushy snow.

"Alright, I'm going. See you later, Jack! Good luck!" Anna said, waving at me. I looked at her confused, but she didn't wait for my response and turned around to walk away. I followed her with my eyes for a moment, but soon turned to Chloe instead. I couldn't see her clearly with all her gear on, but the way she was fidgeting, something was clearly going on. Was she that eager to teach me about skiing, but was embarrassed to have her friend there when she did? If anything, I should be the one embarrassed, because I would surely fall numerous times and make a fool of myself. We could have gone to the chair lifts, but we didn't move for some reason. I was following her lead, but since she was just standing there, I had to ask her.

"Are we going?" I said, pointing to the lifts. She seemed to snap out of it at the sound of my voice. I didn't wait for her and started walking towards them.

"Jack, wait!" I stopped and turned around. Chloe had extended her arms towards me, but they quickly returned at her side. "There's…um…something I need to ask" she said. Her hands joined together in front of her, and she was hopping around constantly like she couldn't sit still. The air outside was cold, for sure, but I had a feeling it had nothing to do with that. "I…"

"Hey, guys!"

Chloe and I both turned to the voices clearly intended to us and saw three skiers looking and walking our way, waving. She let out an exasperated sigh and waved back at them as they got closer. I had no idea who these people were, and I couldn't see their faces because of the helmets and goggles, but I could only assume it was the group of friends we were supposed to meet. When they arrived near us, they took off their goggles to greet us. I looked towards each of them, one by one. I didn't recognize the first two, but I had seen the third one's eyes a lot. We had shared a nice conversation and an intimate moment not too long ago. Violet. She looked at me too, straight in the eyes, and I knew there was much to say between us. Another one of Chloe's friends talked out loud.

"Are you guys going to the lift? We already went down twice before you arrived."

"We had to stop at the rentals for him and we got some traffic on the way, too," Chloe answered. The friend who talked turned to me.

"Don't have your own gear?"

"I've actually never skied before. Chloe here is going to teach me today," I said, with a movement of the hand towards her.

"Well, then, I wish you good luck, because she's a strict teacher. Alright now, are we going to stand here long or what? Violet, it's your turn to take the lift alone, right?"

"Yeah," Violet agreed.

"Cool, see you at the top, folks."

The trio put their goggles back on and turned to the lift, walking away from Chloe and I. There was an urge growing in me, a feeling I couldn't ignore. I had to talk to Violet and now seemed to be the best time to do it, but I didn't want to leave Chloe alone, especially since she was supposed to teach me. I turned towards her to ask if I could go with Violet this time and she was already looking at me.

"You want to go with her, don't you?" I looked down, a mixture of both shame and embarrassment.

"Yes. I'm sorry, Chloe, I just really need to talk to her, and this seems perfect. Does it bother you? I don't want to leave you alone if it does."

"Will you be able to concentrate if I say no?" She already knew the answer to that question. Of course, I couldn't. Even if we had all this gear on, she could still read me like an open book. She always was good at that or maybe I was easy to read, but the ability wasn't mutual. To me, she did things that seemed odd all the time and I couldn't figure out why she was doing them without asking directly. She had paused to let me think about it and answer on my own, but since nothing came, she went ahead. "There you go. Go with her, I don't mind, but just this once, okay? Don't mess up."

"Thanks," I ran as fast as I could to catch up to the trio that went ahead, leaving Chloe behind. Two of them had already taken the lift and Violet was next. I quickly snuck beside her and sat down on the lift just as it took off. She, of course, wasn't expecting anyone and turned around to look at me. I took off my goggles.

"Jack? What are you doing here? Aren't you with Chloe?" she asked.

"I was. I needed to talk to you," I answered.

"What about?"

"You know what about," I trailed into silence. The squeakiness of the lift, the increasingly cold air all around and the mountaintop getting closer and closer were all second thoughts. I knew I had to continue the conversation, but now it seemed way harder than I anticipated. Why couldn't I say anything? It wasn't like I didn't know Violet at all, we had slept together and talked for hours, how come I couldn't say a word now? I sighed and tried to gather my thoughts. Violet sat there quietly, letting me take my time and not interrupting in the slightest.

"Violet, I… I'm sorry. About the whole bar thing. I shouldn't have come, and I shouldn't have led you on. I had just broken up with my ex and I was very confused with my feelings and things went a little too far. I'm sorry I led you on," I said, burying my face in my hands.

"You know, when we started to talk, I could tell you weren't feeling well. You briefly told me about your ex, but since we seemed to hit it off pretty good, I let it slide and didn't think anything of it. To me, it was only a casual hook-up. I didn't expect anything to come out of it. Do you regret what we did?"

"I certainly wasn't ready to move on from my ex and I think I subconsciously used you to ease my pain. It was wrong and I shouldn't have done it. I don't regret it, but I do feel a little ashamed. Chloe wasn't happy the next morning, either."

"Yeah, I'll be honest with you, sneaking out of my apartment and only leaving me a note wasn't the brightest idea, especially that night. I called Chloe when I woke up and saw you gone. I'm guessing she called you straight afterwards?"

"She did."

"I thought so. Look, Jack, I had a great time that evening with you, bar and what came after, but it doesn't have to be anything more than that. The circumstances of what was happening at the time are somewhat irrelevant. Were you still with your ex at that time? No? Then it doesn't matter. But you know, I have to come clean as well."

"What about?"

"I… didn't have the full picture when I invited you to my place. I only got it during that call with Chloe the next morning. If it's any consolation, what we did will never happen again."

"You make it sound like I tricked you or something, that was never my intention," I said, on the defensive.

"Oh, no, I'm not accusing you or anything. In fact, it wasn't about you. Well, it was, but…eh whatever. Anyway, I'm just glad she told me, and I got to apologize," Violet continued. The more she talked, the more confused I got.

"What do you mean? What are you talking about?"

"Listen to me, okay, there's a reason why Chloe was so mad at you when she called and why she invited you here today. Well, two reasons, really. You only seem to know one. If I were you, I'd try to get her to talk to you. Alone. She has much to say."

"I don't understand a word of what you're saying, Violet. Why are you so cryptic all of a sudden?"

"She knows what she wants. The question becomes; do you want the same thing?"

Her question lingered as the wind blew in our faces just as we reached the top. The lifts straightened up and we quickly disembarked and moved to the side. I looked at the metal chairs getting dragged and tried to spot Chloe. Violet put a hand on my shoulder and looked at me.

"You're a good guy, Jack. Don't let her down. Catch you later!"

With those words, she left, leaving me stranded at the top of the mountain and hoping Chloe would show up. I had no idea how to get down if she didn't, but before those thoughts could go any further, her familiar red coat appeared in my vision. She also saw me waiting for her on the side and, with much more agility than I, got off the lift to walk towards me. Now that I saw her, I wondered about what Violet had said, that she had something to tell me. It didn't seem appropriate at the moment, but I had to be alone with her sometime later on. She spoke first as she got near me.

"What did you and Violet talk about?"

"Oh, nothing much, we don't know each other very well."

"You already slept with each other, didn't you? Come on, spill it out. Was it embarrassing or something?" she asked. I didn't answer right away and just looked down. Chloe had this habit of unknowingly pressing on the wrong buttons sometimes. Seeing as though I wouldn't answer her questions, she instead turned away from me. "Alright then, never mind. Let's go, this mountain isn't going to ski itself."

I gladly followed as she started walking towards the first beginner tracks. Violet said she had some things she wanted to tell me, so why didn't she do it herself? Why did I have to be the one to initiate that conversation? Plus, the way she said it sounded so mysterious, I almost didn't want to know. Yet a part of me was too curious to pass this up. I just needed to talk to her, rather she needed to talk to me, but how could I nudge her to start telling me whatever she had to? I almost didn't hear her shouting my name, a voice far away that faded in the distance and the wind. I snapped out after she called me a few times and I looked at her, confused, for a second. She looked at me back, equally as confused.

"You okay?"

"Yeah, yeah, no worries. What were you saying?"

"I said, we need to go over the basics first and then you can try to go down the slope. Are you okay with that or are you going to space out again?"

"No, we can go. Sorry about that."

We spent the next few hours together at the top of the mountain, learning how to navigate the slope, how to properly align your skis, how to gain or reduce speed, how to correctly get up when you fall. I faceplanted many times, much to the enjoyment of Chloe who laughed at me every single time, but also helped me back up. Whenever she touched me, I thought back to what Violet had said. The feeling of her hand on my arm, even over our thick coats and winter gear, made me feel differently for some reason. Was it because of what she said or was my imagination running wild again? I didn't have time to think much, because Chloe was always getting my attention back and walking around with those giant wooden boards on my feet already took all my brain power. At the top of the mountain, the wind was colder and blowing more often than at the bottom and, even if we were well covered, we were starting to get cold. She finally felt I was ready to try going down for the first time and nudged me towards it. Even if it wasn't that steep, the thought of sliding all the way to the bottom, possibly while falling many times, scared me a little. I voiced my concerns to her while she pushed me to the edge, but she didn't even acknowledge them. As the slope was getting closer and closer, was heart was beating faster and I started to sweat. Then, she stopped me right before the fall, one more nudge and I was gone.

"You know, I really don't think I can do this," I said with a shaking voice.

"How else are you going to get down? Come on, Jack, surely this is nothing. You'll be fine! Remember what I taught you and you'll make it down in one piece. Probably."

"What do you mean probably?"

She didn't answer my question and instead pushed me, just a little but enough to make me start going down the slope. My surprised cry got muffled in the wind and I tried to look back, but I already couldn't see much as I left a snow trail behind. I noticed my skis weren't aligned properly and quickly corrected it, picking up speed as I continued my descent. A familiar feeling came back to haunt me. A feeling I hated. Whenever I went down from a high point at a certain speed, it felt like a ball started in my chest and fell around my crotch area. It was unpleasant and the main reason I didn't like to go on rides either. Normally, this only happened once and quickly went away, but now it was continuous. I hated this feeling and was a big reason why I didn't like roller coasters and other such attractions. In front of me, there was only snow, much like behind as well, and I had no idea where I was. Was I close to the bottom? Had I just started and still around the top? I couldn't even think right now, the eerie feeling in my crotch and legs and my focus on not falling occupying all functioning thoughts. I don't know how long it took to get to the bottom, but the slope kind of eased a little and I knew that had to be the end of the line. As relief spread through my body, I relaxed my left leg a little too much and my ski started going in the opposite direction. I tried to bring it back towards me but used too much force and it collided with my right leg, instantly making me fall. I tumbled down, sky and snow shifting in my vision as quick as lightning and I finally settled down, my face fully in the snow. I tried to get up, but found I had no strength in my arms as they were also stuck. I started to panic a little but had no time to really wonder what to do when I was pulled off the ground and thrown to the side. I breathed heavily and looked around, the shine of the sun blinding me and forcing me to close my eyes. I put my arm just over my face and looked around for my savior. Chloe, clearly amused, was standing there, towering over me.

"Quite a tumble you had there! Luckily for you, I was right behind you the whole time."

"Thanks for getting me out. I was starting to panic there for a second," I answered.

"You know, that wasn't bad for a first time. There might be a chance for you after all. We'll have to do that again," she said, enthusiastically.

"No chance of that happening," I mumbled to myself.

"What was that?"

"Nothing. Could you help me up?" I asked, reaching out towards her. She pulled me back up and patted me down to remove the snow stuck on my coat. It took me a while to notice my heartbeat had quickened a lot as she brushed the snow all over me. As she rose, we made eye contact, and I was left speechless. I had no clue what happened, but the sight of her at that very moment brought me immense joy. A joy I couldn't fully explain, but I was glad she was here with me on this day. She seemed confused for a second but didn't say anything as we turned around to finish the descent. There wasn't much left to it anyway and I didn't even pick up that much speed as we got to the bottom. Chloe stopped herself while I let myself slide until I stopped on my own. I couldn't remember how to brake with skis and didn't want to make a fool of myself by falling once more. Then again, I had already done that, so who cared at this point? She approached me as I turned around to look back at her. She lifted her goggles.

"So, how was your first descent?" she asked with a smirk.

"Better than I thought, worse than I'd like," I answered while nodding my head. She laughed and I joined her.

"Well, get ready because that was only the beginning. That was a slope for people just starting out, some are much steeper than that one."

"Yeah, well, I don't think I'll be going on those anytime soon."

"Probably not" she laughed again.

"HEYYY!" We heard a shout from behind us and turned around. Chloe's friends were all waving at us and motioning us to come to them. Awkwardly, I started walking with my skis on. It was a lot harder than I thought and I seemed to go at a snail's pace, but we eventually managed to reach them.

"So, how did you like it?" Anna said, turning to me.

"It was…something for sure," I answered. We laughed and my eyes shifted to look at Violet. Hers looked away for just a moment and she made an almost imperceptible motion towards Chloe while raising her eyebrows. I knew what she wanted to say before she even spoke, and I gently shook my head left and right. She raised her eyes in exasperation, but a smile soon covered up her annoyance.

"We were thinking of stopping to eat a bite. What do you say?" said one of the other skiers. Chloe and I looked at her. I shrugged and I saw Chloe do the same at the corner of my eye. "Well, it's settled then. Let's go!"

The six of us went back inside the main building, a moment of respite and heat among the cold air of the mountain. With full gear and coat on, it was already suffocating, and we immediately took off half of our layers starting from the goggles and helmet. One of Chloe's friends stayed behind at a large table to secure a place to sit while we all went to the canteen tucked in the corner near the front door. I stared at the menu for a while, undecided, and multiple people went ahead of me in the line. I wanted everything and nothing at the same time. It was like I felt a pair of eyes constantly watching me and making it very difficult to concentrate and make decisions. Even if I looked around, I saw nobody was even paying attention to me and it made me even more creeped out. Eventually, though, I made my choice and went back to our table after paying. Chloe's friends were deep in conversation, and I didn't want to bother them, so I just kept to myself, snacking on the fries next to my burger. After being out there in the cold for a long period of time, it was nice munching on some hot fries to warm up. Through the multiple conversations in the building, I could still hear the fireplace crackling and, I didn't know why, but it made me smile. I lifted my eyes off my plate and surveyed around us. I didn't have time to do it for long before Chloe, sitting next to me, leaned in my direction to tell me something.

"How's your burger?" she asked.

"It's quite nice, actually. For a canteen so far away from the city, I didn't expect that kind of quality, but I'm happily surprised," I said.

"You find the best in the most unusual of places," she concluded with a smile. She leaned back to her seat, but I wasn't done talking to her, so I tapped her shoulder gently. She turned her head to look at me with inquisitive eyes and, for a moment, I got sort of intimidated and looked away. But I knew I had to say what was on my mind, so, feeling her gaze still on me, I started talking to my food, hoping she would hear me.

"Thanks for today. Thanks for taking my mind off things. The past month has been… difficult, to say the least, but you're always there for me, even after all these years. I don't know if I deserve someone like you, but I'm glad to have you in my life."

"You're welcome, Jack. All I want is for you to be happy and if that means dragging you out here with a bunch of my friends so you can make a fool of yourself on that mountain, then so be it," she said, laughing. I feigned being offended but joined her shortly before she continued. "That's what…" she seemed to struggle to find the word or perhaps saying it was the problem, but she eventually got around to it. "… friends are for." She smiled, but I knew it was a fake smile. What was she hiding? Was it linked to what Violet was insinuating she had to tell me? It seemed important and having that conversation here would be improper in my opinion, so I didn't bring it up. Instead, Chloe swiftly snatched one of my fries and ate it before I could even react.

"Excuse me?" I asked her. She laughed and shrugged. I retaliated by stealing one of her fries as well and held it away from her as she tried to reach for it. She was leaning on me, still sitting in her seat, but practically lying on my chest. Even if we had our coats on still, the physical contact surprised me a little. I hadn't had much or any since Camille left and that night with Violet.

After that, I found myself longing for any type of human contact, even a hug would be fine, but because I lived alone, it was scarce. Chloe took advantage of my distraction to stretch a little bit more and snatched her fry back, eating it before I could do anything. She smiled a content smile, and I looked back at her with amusement. With that kind of expression, she was really cute, there was no denying it. Up until recently, I thought of her as my high school friend, a girl in which I could confide anything and everything without judgement. Lately, though, she appeared different in my eyes. Not a bad different, per se, but something I was both familiar and unfamiliar with. Something I had trouble deciphering and coming to terms with.

"You guys look good together," Anna said. Chloe and I both turned to face her and found all her friends looking at us. Anna was leaning forward, her arms resting on the table supporting her head. She had the biggest grin painted on her face, not unlike all the other girls sitting across from us. Chloe's face immediately turned as red as her hair and coat, and she tried to hide her face in her hands.

"I… um, we… I was just…" I stuttered, trying to think of something to explain what just happened, but the words wouldn't come out. I was hit by a massive wave of heat that took my entire body and I looked down in embarrassment. Did they mean what I thought they meant? Chloe and I were really good friends, nothing more, right? Why would they say something like that, out of the blue? They all laughed and, even if I didn't know these people, I somehow knew they were laughing of the situation, not of me. That brought at least some comfort to my awkwardness, but I still couldn't hold up their eyes on me. I decided to look up anyway and the first eye contact I had was with Violet. Silently, her eyes widened, and she nodded slowly in Chloe's direction. I understood what she meant but couldn't exactly respond so I just decided to let it go and returned to my burger in silence. Gradually, the conversation turned away from us and resumed on the other side of the table. To my side, Chloe also returned to her food in silence, but we both shared a look that made us almost laugh, but we managed to contain it. There definitely was some sort of chemistry there, but when you've done countless homework with the other for years, there's bound to be a minimum of complicity between us.

The rest of the day was spent just like the morning; with me tumbling down a mountain of snow while Chloe smirked at my every fall. As time went on, though, I started getting the hang of it and could almost make it all the way down the slope in one go. Of course, I was still a beginner, but it did make me a little happy to be able to do this. For the past month, I felt like garbage, like nothing could ever go well in my life anymore, like I couldn't accomplish anything. Even if I knew those thoughts were false, they still poisoned me from within. Today, however, they were barely present, and I didn't pay them attention at all. It was good to have a mind free of worry and sadness for a change and I had a lot of fun with Chloe. Physical activity really does help in these kinds of situation, from what I could tell anyway. On the mountain, I was far from home and far from all these feelings, like I had left them behind a locked door, tucked away. Unfortunately, I knew that wasn't going to last forever and I had to unlock that door one day or another, but the experience I had today proved to me that there was still hope for me.

The car ride back was silent on my part as Anna and Chloe talked the whole time. I didn't mind letting them catch up and chat about whatever, if it didn't concern me. I simply looked out the window as the mountain faded in the horizon. It felt like a different place entirely, like I was another person there, and now I was returning to my boring normal self. I was sure Chloe would disagree with that point, but it was true to some degree. I thought back to what Violet said to me on the chair lifts. What was it Chloe wanted to tell me? After lunch, it had slipped my mind completely and now, Anna was here so it would have to wait again. If it was that important, why didn't she say anything the whole day? I debated just mentioning I knew she had something to say, but that would probably make Anna uncomfortable and, given she was the driver and couldn't exactly exclude herself from the situation, I let it go. Surely, there would be another time. Then, she could tell me all about it, whatever it was.

Chapter 17

On days like these, it makes me wonder what the point of it all is. The grey skies covered the horizon and snow was slowly falling to the ground, enveloping the whole city in a sea of white. Some people would find this beautiful, but I couldn't. As I looked to the building on the other side and saw the hanging Christmas lights, shining in bright red, blue, yellow and green colors, I found myself sighing heavily. In my apartment, a shroud of darkness swallowed every inch of light, leaving me completely in the dark. No lamps were lit, no sunrays were getting through the windows and I was sitting on my couch in the living room staring at a wall. The air inside wasn't as cold as outside, but there was clearly a negligence on that front. I simply put on a vest and didn't mind. I was sitting in complete silence with not a thing to break it but my own breathing.

Thoughts of Camille were poisoning my head. The holidays drawing near made me realize how lonely I was even more. I had no family in town to celebrate with and the one person I would have gone to, Camille, had left me just over a month ago. I could ask Chloe, of course, but felt like that would be imposing myself and didn't want to commit to asking that. No, I preferred being in my apartment by myself, in the dark, reminiscing about everything bad that happened these last few months. The feelings I had then were still strong now. I still missed her every day and wanted nothing more than to be held by her again, to kiss her again, even just to hold hands again. I was told time would heal that wound and yet, even if I waited, it still didn't show any signs of closing. What was I supposed to do now? Whenever I looked around, whenever I stopped doing anything for more than a few seconds, these thoughts came back like a crushing wave, washing every other thing aside and occupying my mind. I knew I had to get them out, but the more I thought of getting them out, the more they spread their roots and stayed ingrained in my head. No matter what I did; watch a movie, play a game, listen to music, it didn't matter. She was always there like a ghost haunting me as a punishment for sins I didn't commit. I wanted to do something and nothing at the same time, both feelings clashing and resulting in me staying on the couch, looking at a wall the same color as the sky. It was like I knew I had to do something to get me out of my own head, but at the same time didn't have the motivation to start. Some people told me walks could help a long way in getting you active and letting those thoughts outside. From my own experience, taking walks usually made things worse as the only things I could think of were the ones I was trying to get rid of. Plus, walking outside in this kind of weather wasn't the best and, if I could avoid it, I always would.

I hadn't realized the time I spent blanking out until a soft knock resonated on my door. I snapped out and was lost for a few seconds, wondering where I was and what that sound was. The knock echoed again, and I got up from the couch. Who could it possibly be? Did I have a delivery I forgot about? If so, I pitied the driver, because the weather outside was terrible and he must have had a bad time getting here. I walked to the door and unlocked it without a second thought. I had a peephole, which was pretty much never used, and I could have asked who it was through the door, but that didn't even cross my mind. As the door creaked opened, I leaned to the side to see who it was and was surprised to see a woman with fiery red hair holding two bags of groceries on my doorstep. When she saw me, a big smile formed on her face.

"Hi, Jack! How are you?"

"I'm…" I paused for a second. I was about to say fine, but was I really fine? Did I want to break her good mood with that right now? Should I just answer I was fine and move on or tell her how I was actually feeling? "I'm fine. What are you doing here?" I asked, changing the subject.

"Well, I know your parents aren't anywhere near and you would probably be alone, so as the holidays approach, I figured I could pay you a little visit," she said.

"Okay, but what are the bags all about?"

"Oh, those!" she said, looking at the bags she was holding. "I saw the state of your fridge the other day, so I bought you groceries on the way. Could you help me put them away?"

I was stunned for a few moments. Where did this come from? I never asked her to pick up anything for me at the grocery store, let alone two full bags of stuff. How much did that cost? I'd have to ask her to pay her back. I opened the door further and moved aside to let her in and she promptly entered, switching on the light as soon as she dropped the bags on the floor. She quickly took off her boots and walked straight to the kitchen, bag in hand with me still holding the door. It took me an instant to snap out of it and close it as it squeaked again.

"What were you doing in the dark like this? You need to open some lights in here," Chloe said from the kitchen. Her voice was a little muffled, like she wasn't talking in my direction or inside something. I slowly walked to join her, her energy and enthusiasm contrasting with my demeanor. When I got to the kitchen, her head was almost inside my fridge, and she was placing stuff from the bags in it. "You still don't have anything in here, what are you doing? You need to take better care of yourself, Jack. You didn't even have any vegetables or fruits or anything."

"I don't eat many vegetables," I answered in a low voice.

"You're about to," she said, rising up from the fridge and looking in my direction. I avoided her eyes and looked down. Was it in shame or was I simply overwhelmed about the whole thing? It was extremely generous of her to buy me all this stuff and I didn't feel like I deserved it. It was unprompted, unwarranted, yet very kind and conflicting feelings clashed in my already confused head. I don't know why, but I started slowly crying, a few tears rolling down my cheeks. I quickly swiped them away as Chloe turned around to grab more things from the bags and we locked eyes. I saw her face change just a little. She definitely knew I was crying. She approached me and put a hand on my shoulder. "You okay?" she asked in a very concerned voice. I looked into her eyes hidden behind her glasses. I wasn't, but I couldn't say it and didn't want to be a burden, even if she was in my apartment right now.

"Yeah," I said, nodding and looking away.

"Really?" she asked, doubtful. I took a few seconds to answer that question. "No."

"I thought so. Look, I'm going to put away these groceries and then we can talk about it. Okay?"

"I don't want to talk about it. We already did that last time, and it didn't help."

"It did help, and we'll do it as many times as it takes."

"You don't have to do this, Chloe, really. I'm fine."

"Stop saying you're fine when you're clearly not! You don't have to put up a front with me, be honest with yourself. I don't have to do it, no, but I will and there's nothing you can say that will stop me. I know how you are; you always were like this. Closing yourself off when something bad happens to you and not letting anyone in. I thought you had changed that aspect of yourself when you opened up last time, but I see there are still remnants of that in you. Just give me a few minutes and I'll be there for you, alright?"

There was nothing I could do but nod in approval. She was right about pretty much everything and when she talked on that tone, there wasn't much discussion to be had. As I watched her put away the stuff she bought, I realized I really should be helping her and my legs moved on their own. I started grabbing the first thing out of the bag and putting it away, one by one until we were done a few minutes later. She had really bought a lot of food and I couldn't help but feel bad about the fact she wouldn't want to be reimbursed and would fight me to the end of the day before I gave her a penny. Chloe sighed in satisfaction while looking around and eventually landed on me.

"Thank you for all this, Chloe. You really didn't have to."

"It's no problem, don't worry about it. We'll make use of it later" she said, the last part a little softer than the previous one.

"What was that?" I asked.

"Nothing, nothing," she laughed in embarrassment, the color of her hair slowly appearing on her face. "No matter. Let's get back to you. Do you want to go sit on the couch or just here?" she asked, indicating the kitchen chairs. I didn't even know what to talk about, I wasn't feeling fine, that much was true, but it wasn't like there was anything new she didn't hear before. Wouldn't that just be rehashing the same conversation we had? Actually, there was something else, but it involved her a lot more than me. Would she be upset if I turned it around on her? There was only one way to find out. We sat down on the kitchen chairs, the most unused chairs in the whole apartment. Since I was alone, I usually ended up eating in front of my computer since the kitchen was a little uninviting when I was by myself. I sometimes wondered what other people would think of me, but then again, their opinion wouldn't change anything so why bother? We didn't sit next to each other, she decided to take the end of the table to properly see my face and reactions. Perhaps that would have intimidated me before, but since I knew I wasn't going to be the center of attention, I paid it no mind.

"So, what's going on?" she asked, starting the conversation. I had to find a way to ask my question instead of answering to hers, but in a way that didn't feel forced. I never realized how hard it is to ask those kinds of questions until now.

"Well, my answers are pretty much the same as they were. I miss her terribly and everything reminds me of her. I have to force myself not to look her up online, because I know how it will affect me. I guess the only thing that changed is the ski trip we went on," I said, trailing on the last bit.

"What about it?" she asked.

"I remember you tried to tell me something and Violet confirmed something was on your mind. We never talked about it, because we were having so much fun or because other people were around, I don't know, but she seemed to imply it was important."

"That Violet, huh? She can't stop talking, that one. So, you're turning the questions on me now, are you?"

"Does it bother you? We can drop it if you want," I said, trying to sound understanding.

"No, no, it's fine, I just wasn't expecting to talk about this today. Um…" She looked really embarrassed about it, but I didn't want to rush her, so I kept quiet and simply listened, trying to put on a reassuring smile. Usually, I wasn't the one in this position and hadn't been a lot in my life, so I didn't know how I looked. Maybe my grin was terrifying and making her uncomfortable or maybe my silence was eerie instead of calming. Chloe was looking all around the room, avoiding eye contact, and her leg was fidgeting like she couldn't sit still. Her hands were moving up and down her arms, almost like she was freezing, adjusting her glasses every now and then, resting on the table then back on her arms again. Strangely, I understood her unspoken nervousness as I had been in that position many times before. I knew there wasn't much to do but let her take her time and speak out when she felt ready. Eventually, she sighed and stopped moving so much to look at me.

"I just… really enjoyed our day and wanted to ask you if you would like to go back some other time?" she finally said, more like nervous blabber than a proper question.

"You waited two weeks to tell me you'd like to do it again?"

"Yes! Yes, it was just really bothering me, and I didn't know if you liked it or not, but I really enjoyed spending time with you and thought maybe, if you wanted, we could go back, maybe just the two of us, but it would be fine with your friends, too."

"Right. Well, I wouldn't be opposed to the idea if that's what you want to hear. I had fun, too. Was that everything you wanted to say?" I prodded further.

"Yeah, that was all. What a relief," she said as she sighed exaggeratedly. She quickly got up from the chair and looked around for something. I turned to see what she was looking at but saw nothing other than the white wall. I turned back, confused, but she avoided my inquisitive eyes. "Did you make supper yet?"

"Considering the stuff I had in my fridge, 'I have nothing in here, what am I doing?', then no, I didn't make supper yet," I said, doing air quotes as I said back to her what she said earlier. I only realized once I was done how rude that could be interpreted, but Chloe didn't seem to care.

"Alright, let's make supper, then! You don't mind, do you?"

"No, not at all. You did buy most of what I have now, so make yourself at home. Do you want any help?"

"Of course. Okay, what can we do…?" she said to herself as she opened the fridge. Surely, she knew its content, she was the one who bought it. There were still some things that went unsaid from her part, I knew that, but didn't want to force it. What could she possibly be hiding? What Violet had said, it wasn't about the ski day. Add to the fact we hadn't started skiing yet and she tried to talk to me, her excuse didn't make much sense. Regardless, we would find another time. Everyone had their issues it seemed, but I still wanted to be there for her when she would be ready as she had been for me.

We prepared supper while exchanging the occasional jabs at each other. Making food with someone else was definitely more up my alley than being alone. I knew some people didn't like the presence of another in the kitchen while they cooked, and I didn't understand them. It was way better to talk with someone and separate the tasks instead of handling it all alone, at least in my opinion. I was glad Chloe was thinking the same or else we might have had a problem. As the great cook I am, I handled cutting the vegetables she had just bought, and she handled the actual cooking on the stove. I thought we made a great team, for what that was worth, and supper was ready in no time. We sat down on our chairs again and ate. While it wasn't in silence, there was still something in the air between us, like an awkwardness we couldn't break. Was it because of what I said? Should I not have brought up the ski trip? How could I bring this back now? I tried to make conversation, but they would die out after two or three comments, and I let it go. Maybe she would be more talkative after supper?

She finished before me as she usually would. I was a little bit of a slow eater, but even more so now that I tried to talk the whole time. Regardless, I grabbed both our plates once I was also done and went to rinse them in the sink while Chloe sat there. I could sense her gaze following me around, but when I turned back, she looked away. I was a little confused but felt like I couldn't leave things as they were.

"Do you…want to watch a movie?" I asked, uncertain if that was the right move. Maybe she wanted to leave right away? In that case, she could just decline politely and be on her way, so why did I feel so nervous about this? These questions became irrelevant as soon as she answered.

"Yes, I'd love to," she said, finally smiling for the first time in a while. She readjusted her glasses and looked at me. Her smile made my doubts melt away and I showed her the way with my hand. She quickly got up and walked to the living room, passing right in front of me as she did. Her hair floated in the air and swung near my face. I didn't realize before, but she smelled really good and even if that wasn't my intention, it overwhelmed me a little as she went by. I followed her with my eyes before snapping out of it and proceeding to the living room.

After a brief debate, we settled on a movie and sat down to watch it. I asked to watch a movie, but in truth, I think I just didn't want Chloe to leave so soon. I had minimal interest in the movie, especially since it was her choice in the end, but I stared at the screen regardless. At the corner of my eye, I could see Chloe on the other side of the couch, also watching silently. I guess a movie isn't the most interactive of experience to enjoy with someone else, but I just said the first thing that came to mind. Maybe playing a game would have been a better choice, but it was too late now. It wasn't all bad, though, the movie was a least a little interesting. It was about a guy having feelings for two girls at the same time while he couldn't go out with either of them. When I thought about it, it was kind of tragic seeing him struggle like this and, in many ways, I saw myself in him. Without knowing it, I became invested in the movie and didn't pay as much attention to Chloe who, at this point, had her head resting on my leg like a pillow. I hadn't realized the position we were in, and my heart skipped a beat.

"What are you doing?" I asked, almost in a panic.

"What?" Chloe answered, feigning confusion. "What's wrong?"

"Lying down on me like this is a little…" I started. I hesitated to finish my sentence. What did I even want to say? I was fighting an internal battle against an unknown enemy. Was saying this stuff implying that we…?

"I don't see the issue, we used to do it all the time a few years ago. Does it bother you?" Chloe said, sitting back up next to me.

A few years ago, when we'd finish our homework, we used to watch TV cuddled up like this. It was the highlight of most days for me, but we were young back then. Innocent, barely in high school and inexperienced in the matters of the world. Now, well, she was all grown up and, even if I tried my hardest, I did notice her womanly charms. How could I not? But I didn't want to see her in that way, I didn't mean to, I just couldn't help it and wanted to hide it from her. We were friends, right? If she was so close to me, she would find out and our friendship could end right then and there. What would she think of me? Probably some kind of pervert or something along those lines. I had to find a way to tell her without saying it directly.

"Well, it's just…now things aren't the same as they were back then. They're different now," I answered, looking away in embarrassment. Even I was surprised by my reaction. What was going on with me? I got more and more nervous as the conversation went on and felt like I was just blabbering some nonsense.

"How so?" she asked.

"I don't know…I just…Never mind, just forget it."

"No, go ahead, speak your mind. We just went over this, you need to tell me these things, not bottle them up inside." Chloe was looking at me inquisitive eyes, both pressuring me to continue while trying to be reassuring. It wasn't quite working, but not by a fault of her own. Eventually, I had to turn away, her staring was too intense for me. I just couldn't deal with what my brain was thinking and my heart was feeling right now.

"I just don't think friends should be doing stuff like this, I…" I interrupted myself as I turned around to face Chloe. Tears were welling up in her eyes as they sparkled slightly under the living room light. Why? What did I say? Some of them started rolling down her face and she wiped them off with her hand which stayed there, hiding her face. I couldn't see what was going on, why she started crying all of a sudden and she turned around to avoid me. She slowly got up from the couch and loudly inhaled, her back still facing me. "Chloe, what's wrong?" I asked in a concerned voice, extending a hand towards her.

"I think it's best if I leave now," she said through the tears, her voice trembling from emotion. She walked out of the living room, immediately right next to the front door, put on her boots and coat and reached for the handle. I got up to try and stop her, but she was pretty much already out when I got close enough. I stood there, looking at the wooden door that now separated Chloe and I, wondering what possibly caused all this. Was it something I said? Was it something else entirely? Did she not enjoy her evening? Was it the movie? I had absolutely no clue why, but the sight of her crying made me sad as well. Through the years, Chloe had never cried much, I was the emotional one of the pair and she usually comforted me, not the other way around. I had practically no experience being the comforter and didn't know how to react, especially since I had no idea what the problem was. In the background, the movie had almost finished, and the music was louder than ever, but the sound was dimmed, and I couldn't hear it much. The atmosphere of the whole apartment had shifted from joy to sadness and the walls seemed to turn a light shade of blue or perhaps that was just my brain trying to trick itself. There wasn't much to do but hope she would contact me sometime soon and explain what had happened or else I would stay in the dark for a long time. I don't know how long I stood there, but when I finally turned

back to the movie, the credits were rolling, and it was already over. I absent-
mindedly closed the TV and went back to my bedroom with my phone in
hand, desperate for a text or a call or anything from Chloe. But the phone
stayed silent all evening and, eventually, I had to face reality; I wouldn't hear
from her again tonight. With a heavy sigh, I closed my phone and went to
bed. To make matters worse, I didn't sleep well that night. I couldn't
remember my dreams, but I was constantly waking up, shifting position and
trying to be comfortable, but there was nothing to be done. When morning
first appeared through my windows, I felt like I barely had any sleep at all. I
checked my phone again for the tenth time when I got up, but once again, it
was blank. It was hard, but I managed to sit up on the bed and, eventually,
stand up to start my day. It was not going to be a good one, I could tell.

Chapter 18

"Thank you, have a nice watch!"

The client thanked me back and nodded approvingly before exiting the store. I stretched while grunting loudly. It didn't matter, I was the only one remaining in the quiet shop. I worked at this one for a few years now, but suddenly there had been a real shortage of customers for some reason. Most days were like this; with one person to talk to every hour or so, a little inventory management and the likes to do, but after that, absolutely nothing. I often wondered if the business was failing because of this and if I would lose my job, but I figured they would at least have the decency to warn me if such a thing were to happen. Today was no different than yesterday as the now familiar stillness reappeared when the door slammed shut by the customer exiting. That door really made a ruckus every time it opened. I was all done for the day and there were still a few hours to my shift. I sighed heavily and had a look around the store for the hundredth time today. On the left, there was a little video game section where people could buy used games and some consoles. I often had a look to see what was available, but there weren't many titles to even consider so I didn't pay it much attention these days. Just past that, there were a few rows of movies lined up in sections: action, comedy, romance, horror and many more. I really liked watching movies, it was one of the things I truly enjoyed, be it alone or with someone although I liked to share the experience, and one of the many reasons I initially applied to this movie store.

The job itself was very different from what I imagined back then. I had been here for just shy of four years now and even compared to when I started, the job was a shell of what it used to be. When I got hired, there were many people working every day and we were so busy we almost couldn't take our breaks. People were coming in, renting, buying and business was good. I guess with the rise of digital movie rentals and the likes, customers preferred to stay home than drive to the movie store to rent. There were some that still did, but they were pretty scarce as I found out. The job had its perks, though. I could rent a few movies a month for free, usually the new releases and so I was always caught up as soon as they came out of the cinema. The same benefits applied for the video game section, but I didn't really use that one that often. I really liked the staff when I first started and one of the reasons I stayed as long as I did was because of them. Unfortunately, now my shifts were mostly alone with someone coming in two hours before I was done. I quickly checked my phone. They were due to come in any minute now. Just as I had my head down, the bell that rang when someone opened the door resonated in the empty store and I turned around to look at the customer. As soon as I laid eyes on her, I froze.

Long blonde hair that overflowed from her white tuque and a black coat that strapped in the front. She turned around to face me and we made eye contact. No doubt about it; it was Camille. What was she doing here? I couldn't believe she actually wanted to rent a physical movie, mostly because she didn't like movies that much and she preferred the convenience of digital. Was she here to torment me, then? What good would that do to her? She silently approached the counter and stood right in front of me, not without breaking eye contact for a second. I couldn't bear to do it either even though each passing second made my heart ache more and more. Didn't I have enough pain already, why did she have to come here like this?

"Hi, Jack," she said. The sound of her voice was both music to my ears and a painful serenade. How I had missed hearing it every day...

"Hi," I responded, rather drier than I wanted. My emotions threatened to burst out all at once and I barely managed to contain myself. I was confused, angry and sad at the same time and hoped it didn't show on my face. "What brings you here today?" I finally asked after a few seconds of silence.

"I wanted to talk to you about something," she said. She took off her tuque and stuffed it in her coat, freeing her hair and exposing them to me. I missed passing my hand and playing with them, but now was not the time to be daydreaming.

"I'm on the job, I can't really talk to you right now. I'm kind of busy."

"Are you?" she questioned, looking around the empty store. Her question resonated in the aisles, and I looked away for a few seconds. Of course, I wasn't busy, but I just couldn't really handle talking to her directly, not like this and not right now. What if a customer came in and I couldn't contain myself? I couldn't let that happen.

"I'm sorry, but unless you're a customer, then I can't help you."

"Alright then, I'll rent this one," she said, pointing to a movie just behind me. We had a few on display behind the counters to incite customers to rent them out as well as their movie of choice. It didn't really work most of the time and I silently cursed they were even there. I turned around to grab it and closed my eyes to sigh. I reached out and came back to the counter, movie in hand, to scan it. The beep almost startled me even if it wasn't that loud. I lifted my eyes from the computer screen on my right to tell Camille the amount, but we made eye contact again and the words somehow got lost and I stayed silent. It took me a few seconds to snap out of it and I shook my head.

"That'll be…"

"Can we talk now?" she said, cutting me off before I could finish my sentence. She had this serious expression on her face like this couldn't wait.

"Camille, I told you I can't, I'm on the job. If a customer comes in, I have to be available. You're going to have to leave if you don't take anything," I said, trying to give her a reason to leave me alone. On one hand, I didn't want her to leave, but on the other, just seeing her was enough to make me feel bad about myself. I was conflicted, but I thought it for the best that she just left without a fuss. If she wanted to talk to me, cornering me at my job wasn't the best approach.

"I am a customer, I am making a transaction right now," she said, gesturing towards the movie on the counter. I sighed and looked down.

"You don't have any intentions of renting this movie, we both know that. If you really want to talk, you could have just waited for my shift to end or texted me. Coming in at my job like this is possibly the worst thing you could have done. Now, again, if you're not going to take anything, you have to leave."

Just as I finished my sentence, the door opened, and a guy walked in. He was wearing the same red uniform as I was and lifted his hand to greet me. I was never more annoyed to see him as I was in that moment.

"Yo, Jack! Give me two minutes and I'll relieve you," he said, heading straight to the back room. I sighed and looked at Camille to see a victorious grin on her face. The timing couldn't possibly have been worse. We waited for a few minutes before my colleague came out of the back and joined me behind the counter. "Alright, if you want to take your break, just go ahead, I'll take care of the store. Were you done with this customer?" he asked. I hesitated to answer, but she was quicker.

"Actually, I changed my mind, I don't really want this movie anymore. You can cancel the order," Camille said.

"Alright, no problem. Was there anything else you wanted from us today?"

"No, I'm good."

"Perfect, let us know if you need anything." He turned to me. "Come on, out you go."

Alex smiled at me with the biggest grin on his face. Usually, I liked the guy, and we talked a lot whenever we had work together, which came around pretty often as we were both part-timers working on the weekends, but I didn't like him today. Why did he have to come now, of all possible times? Couldn't he have been slightly late? I wouldn't have minded at all, but he had to be all punctual like a decent worker. I sighed again and went to walk away as he rose his fist towards me. I gave him the slightest bump and he seemed satisfied enough to finally leave me alone. I went around the counter and headed straight to the back room, hoping Camille would get the message and wouldn't follow me. The small hand that landed on my shoulder indicated otherwise. I stopped and closed my eyes to regain my bearings. I really didn't want to have this conversation right now.

"We can talk now, right?" she asked.

"Yes... we can talk. What is it?" I said, trying not to sound annoyed. I probably didn't do a very good job.

"Listen, um, I've been struggling a lot lately. I simply can't focus at school, my grades are going down and I don't know why. Well, I know why, but I don't know what I can do about it. It's really affecting me mentally and now that there's a chance I won't pass certain classes, I'm super stressed out and it's making it very difficult to concentrate."

"Ok and...? You want me to tutor you or something? What does that have to do with me?" I asked, confused.

"I'm getting there," she said, looking down at the ground. Her left leg was hanging behind her right and kicking her boot at regular intervals. I knew that demeanor very well. "See, this all started to happen a few months ago and ever since then it's been really hard. From when we left each other," she said, finally looking up at me. My heart sank. I already had a tough time keeping it together in front of her, but now she was bringing our past relationship into the mix, and I wasn't sure I could handle it.

"You mean when you left me," I answered, both bitter about the truth and wanting to correct her that she had been the one to pull the plug on the relationship.

"You're right. I did leave you then and it was a mistake. From that moment on, my feelings have been all over the place and I've been confused about everything. I didn't realize what we had and threw it away and I regret it."

"It's a little late for that, don't you think?"

"Would you consider giving me a second chance?"

"Camille, do you know how hard these past two months have been? I've been crying almost every day, even seeing you at school hurts me more than you could imagine. When you left me in the rain that day, it was a good thing I had somebody to rely on or else I don't know what might have happened. Do you understand? You caused me all this pain and then when it gets slightly difficult for you, you come back and expect me to agree to get back together?" She hesitated a few seconds, looking everywhere and clearly nervous, before finally saying it.

"Yes."

"Well, I'm sorry, but I can't tell you the same."

"Don't you have any feelings left for me? Can't you help me out when I need it?"

"Were you not listening to what I just said? I couldn't stop crying just thinking of you, what makes you think I have no more feelings for you? You're asking a lot from me, Camille, and I don't know if I can do it."

"But do you want to?" I sighed, both to give me time to think and to hide my growing nervousness.

"I don't know."

"Ok…" she said, clearly disappointed and looking down to avoid my eyes.

I sighed and closed my eyes, trying to make sense of all this. My heart was racing, and countless thoughts were bouncing in my head. I couldn't make sense of them all. What should I do? Should I give her another chance or be resentful and let her experience the same pain I did? On one hand, I was glad she had reached out to me, and we talked again. I had wished for nothing more these past months and our conversation right now made me feel for her again. On the other, I had read about relationships like these where one leaves the other and they eventually get back together. It usually never ended well, but maybe we could make it work. If both of us aren't happy without the other, then surely that means we belong with one another, right? What would we lose to try?

As I was rummaging these questions in my head, I was interrupted by soft lips pressing on mine. I was startled at first, but quickly caught up. I hadn't been kissed since Violet, but the fact it was Camille made it taste even sweeter. Just as I was about to kiss her back, she retreated back in front of me, looking to the side and embarrassed. My heart was now beating faster than ever, and I could feel myself getting excited. I tried to play it off, but she knew the effect she had on me

"When you make up your mind, you know how to contact me," she said, more confidently than before. With that, she turned around and headed out the store, leaving me alone in the empty aisles.

In the background, Alex was pretending to be busy even though I knew there was no job to be done. My break was pretty much over at this point, so there was no use going in the back and waiting two minutes before returning. I slowly walked over to him, sliding behind the counter, deep in thought. He was typing some rubbish on the computer, clearly embarrassed by the situation. He must have wished he hadn't been there at all.

"Your girlfriend?" he asked, without looking away from the screen.

"Ex-girlfriend," I answered with an emphasis on the 'Ex'.

"Right. Not sure I would have kissed my ex in public, man."

"Oh, shut it, she was the one who kissed me, not the opposite."

"That's not what I saw. Anyway, what was up with that?"

"I don't want to talk about it."

"Alright, man, that's cool. Let me know if I can be of any help."

I silently nodded in approval. Alex was a good guy, and we would talk about pretty much anything, but I didn't know if I could have a conversation about this with him. He was my friend, of course, but a work friend and nothing more. Perhaps having another input in this matter would help me make up my mind, but I felt I needed a more personal take on this. Anyway, right now, I couldn't even put into words the numerous thoughts and feelings conflicting in my head, so we wouldn't reach much of a conclusion if we did talk about it. An hour ago, I wanted nothing more than for Alex to come in so my shift could go by faster, and now I actively didn't want to talk to him. Well, that wasn't exactly true. I wanted us to avoid talking about what happened, but how could we? Maybe it was better to stay silent, then. Plus, I only had a few hours left to go. Slow, painful and uneventful hours.

◊

"So, what's up?" Michael asked.

He and Chris were the only two who could make it on such short notice. After Camille had reached out to me again and asked to go back together, I didn't know what to do with myself. I was dragging my feet the rest of the workday and the ride back home wasn't much better. Multiple thoughts kept bouncing around in my head and I couldn't focus on any of them for longer than a few seconds before I was assaulted with another. Texting our group chat, I asked if we could meet up at the bar to talk. From the responses I got, they must have found it unusual for me to ask such a thing and Chris and Michael were quick to say yes. Unfortunately, Sam was busy, and Vincent hadn't seen the message yet. Maybe it was for the best, though; it would be easier to confide in two people rather than four and perhaps I would be able to talk more freely.

I sighed and looked around, searching for an answer. The familiar wooden beams spanning the entire length of the building had me thinking. If we were just like this building, one good swing at the central pillar would make everything come falling. Was this what was happening? Were my thoughts attacking my pillar and taking me down with them? Why would my brain do that to itself, I wondered.

"Alright, um…it's um…" I said, struggling to get the words out.

"Take your time, man. We're not going anywhere," Chris said, reassuringly. I closed my eyes and nodded, gathering all the courage I had to start speaking. The first step was the hardest, I knew that. I breathed heavily to calm down and reopened my eyes, looking straight at Chris and then shifting to Michael. Both nodded slightly and I silently thanked them.

"Can you let me tell you everything and then we can talk about it?" I asked with a more serious tone.

"Whatever works for you," Michael answered.

"Perfect. Ok, so, Camille came to my work today." I could tell Chris had something to say, but he contained himself and instead grasped his glass a little tighter. "She… said she had made a mistake in leaving and wanted to give us a second chance. I think she truly misses me and seemed really disappointed when I said I didn't know if we could make it work again. Just as she was leaving, she… kissed… me goodbye. I know what you guys are going to say, but I still really love her, and my heart was racing the entire time. That has to count for something, right? I'm conflicted, because I know it's probably a bad idea, but I miss her, I miss her laugh, I miss her touch, I miss her kisses and the last one she gave me just…made me want more. I don't know what to do," I said, slumping down on the table, trying to hide my face. I felt like I had just blabbered some nonsense and they would just shut me down completely. It took a few seconds, but Chris eventually answered me.

"Well, you know how I feel about her already, but I think my respect for her has dropped even more. Did she really expect you to go back crawling to her after what she did? She has guts, I'll give her that, but I wouldn't do it, personally."

"I don't have a girlfriend and I never have, so don't take what I'm going to say for granted, but from an outside perspective, I'd say this doesn't look good. You know, she left you once, what makes you think she won't leave you again? I've seen how you were a few months ago, you didn't look well, man. Do you want to go through that again?" Michael asked.

"It's true, she did hurt me a lot when she left. But I still have feelings for her and now that she's back, wouldn't it be a shame to ignore them? How am I supposed to deal with them? Do I just toss them aside and never look back? I can't do that, guys. Of course, she might leave me again, I'm not saying that's not possible, but isn't it worth it to try one more time?" I said.

"I've only ever had my girlfriend; she was my first and we've been together for seven years now. We've had our ups and downs, just like any couple, but we've always worked it out and talked to resolve any issues. What did she do when a problem came up between you? She just left. You know, people can change over the years, but it's only been a couple of months and I very much doubt she did. She's just going to do the same thing," Chris said.

"Yeah, the reason why she left you is still there. You haven't changed in two months either. If you go back together, she'll still find the same issues she had previously and leave again. It's really that simple," Michael added.

"What you say makes a lot of sense, but I just can't ignore my feelings for her. What if we can talk it out at first and make some changes to fix those issues?" I asked.

"That's not how this works, Jack. It takes a lot of time and dedication to fix things and she demonstrated she's not willing to do that when she left you. A relationship is kind of like a vase. When it falls to the floor and shatters, you can pick up the pieces and remake it, but it will never be the same as before, even if you patch it up with gold. Do you get what I'm saying? What you had before with her...you need to let it go. I'm not saying you won't ever experience that feeling again, it just won't be with her. That ship has sailed and won't come back."

I looked up, trying to contain my tears. I knew what they said was true, but there was still a part of me that wanted to prove them wrong. I was aware of our issues, Camille and I, so maybe we could work it out before getting back together. If we fixed what was wrong, then surely it would be better than what we had previously and we could enjoy each other's company again. A hand landed on my shoulder, and I looked down to see Chris staring at me. He didn't look angry or serious and I couldn't tell what he was trying to convey.

"I know it's a hard one to take. Ultimately, it's your decision and I think I speak for everyone in the group when I say we'll support you. Do what you think is right for you but remember what we talked about just now when you take your decision. I haven't been in your shoes, but I can imagine, and I just want to say it sucks, man, and I'm sorry you have to go through this."

"Yeah, if anything comes up, just ring us up and we'll be there for you," Michael added.

"Thanks, guys. It means a lot," I said.

"Alright, let's move on to a happier subject! Check out the girl over there, she has some…"

I smiled a little, the voice of Michael fading in the background. He never changed, that one, but that was reassuring in a way. Do people change following an intense emotional event, or do they change over time on their own? Did it take an outside push, someone to give them the drive to do it? Did they change for someone else or for themselves? Was it even possible for someone to change? I'd have liked to think so and, taking a sip of my now lukewarm beer, my eyes wandered across the room, searching for something and nothing at the same time.

◊

I was pacing around restlessly between the living room and the kitchen, waiting for the doorbell to ring. My brain was going at super speed, thinking of multiple things at once and I felt like it was going to explode. I must have been annoying to the downstair neighbors with how much I was walking on the creaky wooden floor, but I just couldn't help myself. It was physically impossible for me to sit still while waiting for Chloe to arrive. I had messaged her about thirty minutes ago, telling her I needed her advice for something and asked if we could talk face to face. She was a little reluctant at first, but eventually agreed to come see me at my apartment. I didn't even know how or why I was so insistent on telling her everything about Camille. Was it because she had been there after the breakup? Because she was a long-time friend? Or perhaps because I felt I needed a feminine perspective on the whole thing, and she was the most accessible person to me? Was it even right to involve her in all of this? I didn't have answers to any of these questions and tried to calm down to think, but to no avail.

The doorbell rang and I stopped dead in my track. Suddenly, I felt extremely nervous and couldn't move anymore. It was like someone had cast a spell on me to restrict my movement. After a while, the doorbell rang again, and it seemed to get me out of my daze. I rushed to the button next to the front door to let Chloe in. I stood there, staring at it, lost in thought until a knock on the door snapped me out. Why was I spacing out so much all of a sudden? I was a little startled, but I opened the door regardless. Chloe was standing there, a splash of red on the monotone beige walls of the building. A black tuque was hiding the top of her head, but the familiar fiery hair cascaded down on her shoulders, almost camouflaged on her coat. I couldn't stop looking at her and, eventually, we made eye contact as she was trying to get my attention. She looked confused, probably wondering what was up with me, and raised an eyebrow expectantly.

"Are you going to let me in?" she said, both amused and confused at my behavior.

"Oh, yeah, yeah, sorry about that, I'm just a little out of it," I said while moving to the side and fully opening the door. Chloe stepped in and immediately started taking off her coat and boots while I stayed on the side. She hung her stuff on the nearby hooks, right next to my own coat, and turned around. I still held the door wide open and was frozen there.

"You can close the door, you know," she said, clearly amused. I shook my head to snap out of it and closed it, the wood squeaking the whole way. I really needed to grease the hinges of that door. "So, what's up? You seem…pondering. Did something happen?" she asked.

"Um…yeah can we…can we maybe go sit down for this?" I answered with another question.

"Sure, I don't mind." We quickly made our way to the living room and sat down on the couch. We were sitting completely across from each other, both turned towards the other. However, unlike her, I wasn't fully turned, choosing to let my left leg hang from the edge of the couch. She was sitting on her feet and perhaps it would have been better to say she was on her knees. I looked away, trying to gather my thoughts, and eventually got back to her. She had a worried and inquisitive expression on her face and I smiled a fake smile to try and reassure her. It didn't work at all, I was positive, but she didn't say or do anything, opting to let me get my bearings and start talking by myself.

"Okay, so here's the thing. Can I ask that you don't interrupt me for what I'm about to say? It's important, to me, so can you do that? Please?" I almost pleaded, buying time before starting the real conversation.

"Yeah, whatever you want. Seriously, what is going on here? Are you okay? Is this bad or what?"

"I don't know, that's why I need your advice on this. Alright…" I sighed and took a deep breath. "Camille came back to my work yesterday and we talked for a little bit" I started, struggling to find the rest of what I was trying to say.

"You cannot be serious? Jack, is this what I think it is?" Chloe asked.

"Can you… let me finish? It's already hard enough as it is," I said.

"Yes, I'm sorry, go ahead," she apologized, but I knew she was silently very emotional already from the look on her face.

"So, um, she came to my work, and we talked. Judging from your reaction, I think you might have an idea of what we talked about. Um...she... said she wanted a second chance and asked if we could get back together. She said she's super stressed out and can't focus on school and all that stuff and I just don't know what to think of it..." I paused for a while, but Chloe interpreted that as me finishing what I had to say and went ahead.

"What did you tell her?"

"I said I didn't know if we could do that, and I would have to think about it."

"Jack, there is nothing to think about. Things can never work out between you anymore, not after what she's done to you. I thought it would have been obvious. You don't owe her anything anymore, you two aren't a couple. Why should her problems be your problems? Do you really want to go back with her?"

"I still have feelings for her, Chloe. My heart beats faster when she's around, I almost can't control myself. How can I ignore them?"

"You remember the good times you had together, but you also need to keep in mind the bad times, too. Do you remember what happened when she left? How emotionally destroyed you were? How you couldn't stop crying just thinking about her? Do you really want to go through that again?"

Her question echoed what Michael had said to me the day before, but I just didn't have an answer. I wasn't denying the fact it could lead to me getting hurt again, rather that it would be worth it for the additional good times we would have.

"If it means spending more time with her and enjoying myself again, which I really haven't been since then if I'm completely honest, except the ski trip, then I think it's worth it, even knowing I will get hurt again in the future," I answered.

"That is a stupid way of reasoning, Jack. It will never be the same as it was, you need to understand that. You might enjoy each other's company for a few weeks, maybe a month, and then all the things that didn't work out will resurface. Trust me, I've been through a lot with my prior relationships, and I can tell you it won't work."

"Have you ever gone back to one of your exes?"

"That's beside the point."

"It isn't. You never did, so how could you know? I still have feelings I can't ignore, and I just feel so alone without her that I..."

"Are you sure her feelings are the same? Did she say she loves you when you talked again?"

Her question took me by surprise. Looking back at our conversation, Camille never did say she still had feelings for me, only that she wanted a second chance and felt stressed out since the breakup. Did that mean anything or was it just an omission on her part? One thing was certain, I couldn't be sure until I talked to her again. Chloe took my silence for an answer.

"Exactly. I don't know why she's doing this, maybe she wants the comfort of being with someone and you're the most available guy she knows or maybe she's trying to convince herself she still has feelings for you when she doesn't, but…"

"But what if she does, though? What if she does still have feelings for me?"

"Jack…" Chloe sighed. "Maybe she does. Maybe you both still have feelings, it doesn't matter. She broke up with you once, what makes you think she won't do it again for another reason? Things between you didn't work out because of certain things and these things never went away. Look, I care about you a lot, okay, and she will just break your heart again. I don't want to see you like this. Who is going to have to console you when she inevitably leaves you again? Me. I don't want to do that."

"But wouldn't it still be worth it to give it a chance and see how things are? If there's even a possibility, we could talk things out and…"

"Ughhh, you are impossible, Jack. Listen, I've said all I can. You're free to do whatever you want, but if she breaks your heart again, don't come crawling to me for comfort, okay? I'm telling you right now; it won't work. You're free to try, but don't involve me in it anymore."

Chloe got up from the couch and walked back to the front door, putting on her coat in record time. Her sudden movement startled me for a few seconds, and I quickly followed her. By the time I arrived, however, she already had her hand on the handle.

"Where are you going? You don't want to stay?" I asked.

"I think it best if I leave. Before I say anything I might regret," Chloe said, talking to the door. With that, she opened it and walked out, leaving me standing there dumbfounded and wondering if I did anything wrong. Why did she leave so suddenly? I had a feeling she wouldn't be enthusiastic about the subject at hand, but to leave like this was unexpected. At the very least, I thought she would have stayed calm and analyzed the situation from an outside perspective, but she seemed really emotional about it. Why was that, I wondered, before I snapped back and realized the door was still wide open. I slowly closed it, my mind still racing about all the conversations I had over the past two days. Camille coming back at work, Chris and Michael advising me on what to do and now this one with Chloe. Even after hearing multiple opinions, I was still conflicted on what I should do. All my friends were saying this wasn't a good idea, but they didn't have to live with the pain I was feeling since Camille broke up with me and if there was any chance of making that go away then I would gladly take it. Our past relationship was already a little shaky and it would just be worse now, but I still thought we could make it work.

A notification sound from my phone took me out of my thoughts and I looked around, confused as to what the sound was and where it came from. I soon realized what it was and rushed over to check. Was it Camille? Did she text me? I almost dropped it fumbling around, trying to open it and saw it was an email. I opened it up. Junk. Nothing but advertising junk. Did I really get worked up over some cheap email chain ad? Well, now that I had my phone in hand, it was really tempting to text Camille. Almost instinctively, my hands moved to my contacts and hovered over her name. Why did I even keep her contact info? Why didn't I just delete it? Every time I thought about her, it made me sad and angry but, somehow, I couldn't resign myself to erase her completely. Perhaps I hoped she would contact me again, I certainly wished for it on multiple occasions and by keeping her number, I was trying to manifest it into reality. Futile as it may have been, that wish had now come true. But did I truly wish for that? Just under it, Chloe's name was also there, taunting me. Echoes of our conversation resonated in my head, telling me not to go back while my heart was screaming the opposite. I had to sit down on the couch to take a breather, my heart racing the fastest it had ever had. It was like some sort of force field was preventing me from pressing on her name, like I wasn't even in control of my body anymore. I looked up at the ceiling and tried to breathe to calm down. It took a while, but I managed to think a little better and come up with a message to send. It wasn't long, but it took me way too much time to write it and send it. By the time I had sent it, it felt like hours had passed when it was probably closer to fifteen minutes. The familiar sound of the message being sent echoed in the empty and quiet apartment, and I slumped down on the couch. I couldn't believe I was this nervous again, it was like this was the first time I was talking to her. Even back at the end of the school year, I felt better about it than now. What was up with that? Why did this suddenly feel so alien to me, so unknown, when I had talked to this girl as my girlfriend for six months? Was it because I felt guilty of other things or because I was going against what everyone had said? I didn't know, but I stared again at the message I sent. She still hadn't read it yet.

Do you want to go back to that cat café next Saturday?

Chapter 19

I quickly disembarked from the bus and adjusted my tuque as the cold air of winter hit my face, chilling me to the bone. I almost didn't recognize the street; last time I was here, the sun was shining bright in the sky and there wasn't a white coat covering everything. Thinking back, it had been a good seven months since then and I realized how crazy the landscape could change in that amount of time. The bare roads were now replaced with their icy counterpart, the cold wind all around chilled me when the sun had previously warmed me, and I was walking the same sidewalk I had back then. Only now, I had to be careful not to slip on the ice that seemed to have spread everywhere. The street was a lot quieter, there weren't any terrasses or people hanging around having conversations. Everyone was hiding from the wind and keeping to themselves, and all the shops seemed uninviting. Occasionally, some car would pass by and make some noise, but that was it. There were no birds or any other sign of life around. I hated winter, everything looked dead in that season. At least in autumn, even if the trees were losing their leaves, they appeared alive, and you could spot animals running around all the time. Now, there was just nothing but the cold.

I shakingly checked my phone. I still had a little leeway before the agreed upon time to meet with Camille, so there was no rush. Similarly to last time I was here, I looked around at the various shops when I walked pass them. It was a little strange, but I felt differently for most of them. The weirdest one was the odd store I had noticed too back then. It had just appeared strange, but now I almost felt compelled to go inside and check what kind of things they had to sell. What had initiated this change? Why did I pay attention to this now when I had no interest in those things a few months prior? I didn't have an answer to that question, and I found myself a little sad at the thought I would miss out on it again. Well, I could always come back another day if I really wanted to. Just when I had that thought, I noticed a bookstore coming up. That reminded me of what I told myself, that I would try to read more. I didn't even try over the last few months. That could give me another reason to come back here another day in the near future. I could grab myself a nice book and get back to reading, perhaps not every day, but maybe every other day.

The familiar sign of the cat café soon came into view. This time, however, Camille was not standing in front of the shop. I was still a little early and, in this temperature, she would be inside if she had already arrived anyway but seeing the empty spot where she stood still had an effect on me somehow. Would she even show up? I decided to not let it get to my head and walked straight to the door. One thing hadn't changed; the smell inside was still the same as it was back then. But there was some warmth to it and the place, even through the harsh winter cold, was very cozy. I guessed they kind of had to if they had cats walking around; they wouldn't want them to freeze any less than their customers, after all. I went through the same corridor we had, way back then, and I was filled with a sense of nostalgia. That had been my very first date, the first time I went out with a girl, and a wonderful experience overall. Would today be the same or would it tarnish the memory of that time? I found myself both wanting to smile and frown at the thought. It was conflicting and I didn't exactly know what to do with my face. I only hoped the hostess didn't notice when she greeted me and led me through the place back to where we sat last time. I didn't know if that was deliberate or not, but it sure made me smile when she showed me my seat. I sat down and took off my coat, putting it aside on the banquette and now waiting on Camille.

My head was still spinning and chock full of thoughts just bouncing around. I hoped she wouldn't be too late, I hoped things wouldn't be awkward between us, I hoped we could talk it out and fix it. I hoped a lot, but ultimately, it was pointless to wonder and care so much about these thoughts until she was sitting in front of me. I heard some meowing to my left and noticed a small black cat staring directly at me. I scooted over just a little to the right and it jumped right next to me, already starting to purr without me touching it yet. My hand instinctively went to pet its head and flowed down its back. The fur was extremely soft to the touch, and I couldn't help but smile at it and look into his big yellow eyes. They seemed content and happy, and I wondered how my eyes looked to others. Were they sad or happy? Could you really tell so much about a person by staring into their eyes? What would mine reflect, then? Would it be the recent hopefulness of a relationship or the pain of loss that still lingered?

"It certainly seems to like you."

I shifted my eyes from the cat to where the voice had spoken. Those words were familiar and when my eyes landed on Camille standing across the table, I was speechless. She still had her coat on and her signature white tuque which she promptly took off and sat down in front of me. The whole time, I couldn't stop staring at her and felt a growing sense of nervousness within my entire body. Why was it so different from our conversation at work? I felt like this was the first time I was going to speak with her, like this was back on our first date and how nervous I was back then. Why did I regress to that state now?

"Hey, Jack," she said, smiling shyly at me.

"Hey… Camille," I greeted back, still shaken up.

"So, how are you holding up?" she asked.

"I… have been better, but I would say things are taking a turn," I said, hoping she would latch on to that, but she stayed silent. "How about you?"

"Well, I already told you that last week, didn't I? My feelings haven't changed since then."

That was a very odd way of answering that question. It almost felt disinterested or hostile, but I couldn't figure out why. Didn't she want to talk at all?

"Right," I said, trying to come up with something else to say. "How was Christmas on your end?"

"Oh, nothing much. I just saw close family and that was it, not a big fancy party. I wasn't really in the mood for it either, so maybe that was a good thing," she said, looking down. I was expecting a question asking about me and my Christmas experience, but it never came. To be fair, I had nothing to say as I just stayed home and didn't really celebrate it, but it still would have been nice to get asked about it. I didn't have much time to wonder more as the waitress came to take our orders.

"So, what will you two be having today?" she asked with a genuine smile. Sometimes, you can tell customer service staff put on a fake smile, but she seemed to be actually enjoying herself and happy. It made me want to smile too. Wasn't it curious how contagious emotions are? How one happy person can spread it to many others simply by displaying their happiness through their actions? I didn't hear what Camille had ordered, but the waitress was now looking at me and I figured it was my turn.

"A large coffee, please," I asked, with much more confidence than last time I was here.

"Thank you, I'll be back with your orders shortly," she said with a small wink as she went away. I thought it was a fun interaction and was still smiling, but when I turned towards Camille, she was staring at the table and clearly not as happy as I was.

"I've been getting a little more into coffee lately, it really helps get you through the cold months of winter, doesn't it? I used to drink a little, not that much, but now I almost have a cup every morning," I said, trying to start a conversation.

"That's nice," Camille answered, absent-mindedly.

"Is there something wrong? You seem distracted," I asked. Camille lifted her eyes from the table and met mine as I tried to express confusion on my face. She seemed startled, like she had just woken up from a nap and didn't know where she was.

"No, no, everything's fine, I just…" she trailed. I didn't really understand but decided to let it go for now. I kept comparing this conversation to our very first one and wondered what had changed to warrant this much of a difference between the two. Back then, even if we didn't know each other at all, we always had something interesting to say or to ask the other person. Now, she seemed out of it, not the least interested in what I was asking, looking away and answering with vague one-liners. Did she event want to be here? What had happened for her to act this way? Was it the way I was asking the questions? Did she feel uncomfortable or something? As I wondered these questions, I didn't realize we were sat in silence with not a noise coming between us. I looked at Camille without breaking a sound, staring into her avoiding eyes, but she didn't stare back. Just as I was about to try and make another conversation, the waitress came back, all smiles and joy, lighting up the mood from gloomy to cheerful.

"Here is your latte, miss," she said as she put down the cup in front of Camille. For the first time in a few minutes, she seemed genuinely happy. Happier than after anything I had said which made me a little worried and slightly hurt my feelings. Was I less interesting than a coffee to her? Why even agree to come here if she didn't want to talk at all and preferred staring at her drink? "And here is your coffee, sir. Milk and sugar are on the little plate on your right," the waitress said, pointing at the other end of the table.

"Thank you," I answered with a smile, trying to hide the conflicting emotions I was feeling. Either I was successful, or the waitress didn't want to point it out because she didn't bring it up.

"You're welcome. If there's anything you need, just call me down and I'll be right there for you, okay?" I nodded in approval and the waitress went away, leaving me back alone with Camille who still hadn't said a word in ages. She was already sipping her latte, so I went along and opened some sugar to pour into my coffee soon followed by a milk pod. Swirling it around, the metal spoon hitting the sides of the cup resonated between us like a giant gong, piercing the silence and covering up any other noises. She paid it no mind and didn't react at all. It might not be much, but it was starting to annoy me slightly. Why didn't she say or react to anything? It was like sitting in front of an inanimate object that couldn't talk. If I wanted that, I would have stayed home.

"Are you still at your job?" I said, attempting small talk for the last time. If this didn't work out, then I didn't what I would do, but I was ready to give up for today.

"Yes, I am, and things are going pretty well over there. I'm really getting along with Tom, and it almost doesn't feel like a job anymore. Did you ever get that feeling at the video store?" she finally asked.

"Tom, huh?" I whispered to myself. What was she playing at? "I can't say I have experienced the feeling you describe, unfortunately. Things have been slow at my job and shifts are getting excruciatingly long to get through," I answered, trying to move away from the mention of her colleague.

"That's why you need company. The job is kind of boring, let's be honest, but when I'm paired with Tom, it goes by in an instant. When I'm with others, I get reminded why I don't like this job so much."

"I see," I said, taking a sip of coffee to hide my growing annoyance. Why was this the only subject she reacted to? Couldn't we move on?

I was startled by a sound coming from behind me as a cat jumped on the window edge to my right. I turned around to look at it and it seemed familiar. Staring and studying it for a bit, I finally remembered who it was. No doubt about it, it was Luna, the cat that stayed with us the most last time we were here. Who could forget her coffee stains fur patches around her mouth? I extended my hand to pet her, and she approached gently, bowing down a little for my hand to rub its head. She purred loudly, filling the air between all three of us. I looked back at Camille, and she was also looking at Luna with a slight smile on her face. It was good to finally see her engaging in the conversation, even through something as simple as looking at the cat.

"She really is pretty," she said.

"She is," I simply answered without stopping petting it. We stayed like this for a few seconds before Camille spoke.

"Jack, um…" she said, shyly and trying to hide her increasingly blushing cheeks. "Would you want to go back to your place? To…watch a movie or something?"

The question kind of took me by surprise. She seemed so uninterested at the start; I couldn't believe she would want to continue seeing me. It filled me with immense joy she even considered it and, even better, she wanted to go to my place. Plus, watching a movie wasn't so bad even if we would be sitting in silence. At least there would something to talk about afterwards and maybe that could lead to us rekindling the flame that died a few months ago. I had hope it would end better than the last movie I had watched. It seemed like a great idea, and I agreed to her request at record speed.

"Yeah, that sounds perfect! Do you want to go now or...? Because I haven't finished my coffee yet?" I asked, looking at my half-empty cup.

"Now." Her eyes were filled with this emotion I couldn't decipher, but I knew it was best not to argue with her right now. I downed the rest of my drink and flagged down the waitress to get the check. She was surprised at our quick departure, but we reassured her everything was fine, and we simply had somewhere else to go. I paid for both our drinks, and we swiftly put on our coats to get out of the café.

While the coffee had filled me with warmth, the cold air of the outside quickly breezed it away as it hit my face and chilled me to the bone. Even with coats and winter clothing, it still somehow managed to infiltrate and get under your skin enough to freeze you from the inside. We walked to the nearest bus stop and took shelter in the glass cabin there, sitting on the frozen bench inside. Camille immediately cuddled up against me and, even though I was wearing a big coat and multiple layers of clothing, it felt like her body was directly pressed against mine. I felt my heart start to beat faster, and I was glad she was leaning on my right side, or she might have heard it pounding in my chest. The feeling of her head on my shoulder brought me back to when we used to date, all the times she would do that and how much I enjoyed it. They say you don't know what you have until it's gone and if I had to comment on that from my experience, I would be inclined to believe it. I didn't realize I missed it that much until she did it again. Passing my arm over her shoulder and down her back, I gently brought her closer to me. I didn't know how long we had to wait, but my perception of time got scuffed and we stayed like this, two frozen people sitting on the bench, not moving and not talking, for what felt like an eternity and a few minutes at the same time. The rumbling of the bus turning the corner made us move apart as we checked the end of the street for the familiar sight. There it was, approaching slowly. I will admit I was a little saddened it came so fast, and Camille and I had to separate for even a moment. She, however, almost jolted up and was already out of the cabin in record time. I shook my head to wake up from my dreamy state and joined her outside. The bus, eventually, came and stopped in front of us, allowing us to board. She went first and I quickly followed.

How was this bus ride any different than the multiple others we had went on? There was something about this one, I couldn't exactly tell but the atmosphere was clearly different. She sat closer to me than usual, resting her head on my shoulder again. I hesitated to embrace her this time, choosing to restrain myself in public, and it took a lot of willpower to do so. Staring straight ahead, the streets and shops flying by as the bus drove us closer and closer to my place, the familiar yet unwanted nervous feeling I was so used to came back. Why? It wasn't like this was the first time she was coming back to my place, so what was so different about this one? Was it because it was the first time since our breakup? Surely that had a little to do with it, but I couldn't help but feel there was something else at play here. I just couldn't decipher what it was and, judging from Camille resting on me, she wasn't going to help me with that either. Maybe she just wanted to watch a movie so she could take a nap on me which I wouldn't be against the idea, but wouldn't it be better to talk about everything else going on? A few minutes went by, and we were nearing our destination. I gently shook her to wake her up and she stood straight up right away. It almost startled me the way she went from asleep to wide awake and I thought I might have scared her. She looked around and relaxed, realizing we still had another few minutes until we got there. I smiled at her, and she took a few moments but eventually smiled back. I extended my hand towards her, palm facing up, directly on her left leg, and she put hers into mine. I hadn't really thought about it, but holding hands was such a simple yet powerful demonstration of your union with someone. Through it, you can display to everyone else how connected you both are, how you only make one and I found myself happy at the thought we were finally reunited after these past months. The feeling of her hand on mine, even if her fingers were chilly, warmed me up tremendously and I held on to it as hard as I could without hurting her.

The bus finally dropped us off a street corner away from my apartment and we walked the rest of the way. Unfortunately, I had to let go of her hand and put my gloves back on to not freeze completely and longed for the feeling to come back as soon as she let go. We didn't talk much during our short walk, our panting making small clouds in front of us and the ground being uneasy from the snow. There was something pretty about the sight of the city covered in white, but I feel like it was best enjoyed behind a window in a warm home rather than walking on the uneven sidewalk. As we approached the corner of my street, I paused for a moment, looking straight ahead at nothing. Rather, it seemed like it, but the spot brought back some memories, memories I wished I didn't have, but had to live with anyway. It was there, two months ago, in pouring rain and warmer weather, that Camille had left me. I never paid much attention to it, I had walked here plenty of times after that event, but somehow, it made me stop now. Why was it so vivid now that she was back? She stopped behind me, poking her head on my left to see if there was a reason for me to stop.

"What's going on?" she asked.

"Nothing, it's… nothing," I answered as I started walking again. I heard her quickly following behind me.

There was something about that sight I couldn't get out of my head. It was just a sidewalk, was it not? Why did it make me feel the way it did back there? Why now of all times? I wished that we weren't so silent during the small trip to my apartment and that we had a conversation going but didn't know what to say at the same time. It was a weird conflicting feeling, but I chased it away as soon as my front door came into view. We got through the door, went up the stairs and into the comfort of my home. As soon as we came in the building, there was a clear switch between the cold air of outside and the warmth of inside. We took off our coats and hung them on the nearby hooks. I stood in the entrance, looking at Camille the entire time, wondering how to proceed. It usually didn't go like this; I wasn't the one who had to lead. She used to come to my place often, but it was always more of a casual thing. Wasn't this casual too? Why was I so nervous about it, then? It's not like this was a brand-new date or something, we knew each other, she knew how I was, there was no need to impress her or anything of the sort. As these thoughts rummaged through my mind, I snapped back and realized Camille was staring at me with a smirk. She raised her eyebrows in a silent question and even if it was meant to be reassuring in a mocking way, it just made my heart go faster. Well, there was nowhere to go from here but to take the plunge.

"So… shall we go to the living room, then?" I asked, shyly and embarrassed.

"We shall," she answered, having a slight laugh at me. I didn't mind that much because I was clearly out of my depth here and we both knew it. Even if it was my own home, she led the way and sat down on the couch, waiting for me to pick something to watch.

"Um… I have no idea what to watch," I said, more as an incentive for her to pick instead of me.

"Oh, I don't mind. Just put on whatever you want," she said with a smile. That wasn't helpful at all, but I followed what she said regardless. After a few minutes of tinkering on the web trying to find a nice movie to watch, I finally managed to start something I felt we could both enjoy. The whole time, I felt Camille's piercing stare drill a hole in my back, pressuring me to hurry up. It went away as soon as I sat down on the opposite end of the couch, and she instantly got closer to me. I don't know why I didn't just sit down next to her, I probably felt like that would have been too bold and preferred to see what she wanted before making a move. Instead, she made the move herself and was sitting directly next to me. It was exactly what I wanted but was too shy to do it first, so I was glad she took the initiative. The movie hadn't even started yet, and I already felt as nervous as I was the first time I went to her house. Only this time, I couldn't even flee.

I couldn't pay attention to the movie at all. Cycling between watching the movie, suppressing my brain from going too deep into useless thoughts and looking out for any of Camille's movement was too much and I had to ditch one of these. Scenes were passing by in front of me, characters were talking, and music was playing, but none of those things could reach me. My heart was beating so much faster than before, if I didn't know any better, I might have assumed I was having a heart attack. But, of course, that wasn't the reason why I was panicking. The reason was sitting next to me and getting increasingly closer to me. By now, she was practically on top of me. I tried to focus on the movie to calm down, but it didn't work, and I almost jumped off the couch when she placed her hand on my right thigh. I couldn't bear to look at it, but I could feel her hand wander up and down, gently and softly, in a teasing way. I hadn't notice before now, but my breathing had gotten louder and jerkier. Her hand wandered over to my crotch which had already made a bulge in my pants and took a hold of my shaft through my pants. I sharply breathed in, trying to calm down, but it had the opposite effect and my member responded by getting harder. I looked over at Camille and she was also looking at me, asking a silent question with her eyes. She didn't have to say anything, and I knew what she wanted to ask. Was I ready for that? I really wanted to, but it was so quick after we saw each other again, was it okay for us to do that? These past two months, I wanted nothing than to be held again, to be hugged again, to talk with her again, to hear her laugh again. I had the opportunity to unite with her once more, as we had many times before, and who would stop me? No matter what my friends or Chloe had said, they didn't live my life and didn't know my situation. We both clearly wanted it, so what harm was there to give in to our urges? I hadn't stopped looking at Camille directly in the eyes and nodded slightly. A smile formed on her lips, and, in one swift movement, she went from sitting on the couch to straddling me, sitting just above my raging member. The motion surprised me, but she silenced me by putting her lips on mine in a violent kiss.

I had missed that feeling. Last time I was kissed was from Violet and, while it was very nice and enjoyable, it didn't quite get me the same way Camille could. We didn't waste any time and soon, our tongues joined in a battle for dominance. I felt Camille's hands cupping my cheeks and her hips start to sway back and forth in a gentle, almost imperceptible movement. My own hands went straight down her back all the way to her butt and brought her more towards me. I wanted to explore her body again, I wanted to remind myself of what we had before. Her chest was pressing against mine and even if we had two layers of clothing between us, it felt like our skin connected directly. I moved my hands to her side, starting from the hips coming back up just under the arms and stopping where her chest was. I couldn't get a good feel, but I stayed in the area, making circles and occasionally going down only to come right back up immediately. During all that, she had won the tongue battle and had invaded me, but I paid it no mind. Rather, I actually enjoyed it more that way. Our lips scarcely parted, but when they did, they rejoined in a matter of mere moments. The bulge in my pants, previously hard but not totally, was now hurting a little from being contained. Plus, her hips movement certainly didn't help to calm it down. With every passing second, I was getting hornier and hornier, and I just wanted her right now. I probably didn't have to ask her this question; her actions spoke in her stead, and I could tell she also wanted me badly. She backed off a little, our lips disconnecting for a moment and giving me time to breathe. Her head went straight to my left ear, and I don't know how it was possible, but the sound of her whisper made me even harder than I already was.

"Want to take this to the bedroom?" she asked, as silent as she could be, but I heard every word resonate in my very soul. It felt like she sang them, a horny melody only I could hear, and I didn't even have to respond. I don't know what came over me in that moment, but my arms locked themselves around her back and I picked her up from the couch. She let out a small cry, but quickly wrapped her arms around my head and her legs around my waist as I started walking to the bedroom. She kissed me again, this time less violently than before but just as sweet. I almost bumped into the door frame as I was distracted but eventually reached the bed and let her fall on her back. She bounced just a little and looked at me with seductive eyes. I couldn't resist her when she did that and she knew it very well. She turned around to be on her knees and nearly attacked my pants, dragging them to the floor along with my boxers in one swift movement. My member sprung out in the open, the gust of wind slightly chilling the tip as it stood up high and proud. She immediately warmed it up with her mouth and the initial motion almost made me fall to the floor. There was nothing that could quite replicate that feeling and, if I was honest with myself, I had missed it a lot since we broke up. She didn't do it for long before she stopped for a second.

"Why don't you go sit right over there?" she said, pointing to the back of the bed. She didn't look at me, but I had a feeling I knew what she wanted to do so I jumped on the bed and made my way to where she had pointed, putting a pillow behind me to offer better support for my back. She quickly followed, coming towards me from the side instead of the front which I found odd. Camille got her head resting on my belly, facing away from me, and resumed her previous motions. I grabbed her hair and held it in a makeshift ponytail to get them out of her way and give her better access. The warm and wet feeling of her mouth took hold of my member again and I couldn't help but moan at almost every up and down. I was slowly shifting downwards on the pillow, my hips unable to control themselves and sometimes moving around under the pleasure. I could feel every movement of her tongue and couldn't help but marvel at the skill she had. A brief thought traversed my mind, leaving just as fast as it came. She seemed a lot better at giving head than she was a few months ago, but we weren't together, so where could she have practiced? She went down a lot farther than she previously had, and the thought vanished as I struggled to contain my moan. She stayed there a few seconds and came back up, my member now completely covered in her spit, glistening in the daylight.

Camille got up from her position and started undressing, quickly taking away her pants and panties and tossing them aside. I did much of the same and took off the rest of my pants which were near my ankles at this point. Just as I was done, she crawled a little bit forward to position herself just above my shaft. For a moment, her folds passed right by my head, and I almost couldn't contain myself as I wanted to return the favor and give her head too, but she had other plans in mind. When she was in place, she sat down on my member, and it slid right into her with ease. The warm feeling was even stronger there than her mouth and I struggled to keep it together. When we were at my apartment, we had to keep it down in terms of noise or else the neighbors would hear. She made it really difficult to do that and it got even harder when she started moving. Her butt was moving up and down, up and down, and a smacking sound joined our moaning every time she hit my body with hers. I couldn't see most of the time as I had my eyes closed, trying to breathe and calm myself despite the overwhelming pleasure. The bed sometimes squeaked under her movements, and I hoped it wasn't loud enough to hear through the walls, but I didn't have time to think about that enough to get to an answer. Camille took off her shirt and her bra, revealing her chest, and added them to the pile on her side of the bed without missing a single rhythmic stroke.

"Could you turn around, I want to see your chest," I whispered to her between movements.

"Don't you like seeing my butt instead?" she replied in a teasing voice.

"Yes, I do, but I'd also like to give them attention, too," I said.

"Well, you can't have everything, can you?" she said, denying my request with another stroke. I moaned and the conversation was swept away from my mind.

She rode me for another minute or two and I was just about to burst when she got off, my member plonking down on my belly with a wet sound. She crawled forward and stayed there, dangling her entrance in front of me, inviting me, teasing me to come and take her. I tried to silently breathe to calm down, to regain control of myself and keep going before I would finish. I wanted this moment to last as long as I could. I couldn't wait anymore and got up halfway, walking on my knees to get behind her, my hands caressing her back and sliding further and further down until I reached the cheeks and then her slit. She was completely drenched, and I inserted two fingers to gauge her reaction. Her head went down to the sheets and muffled a moan, and I smirked a little. I took out my fingers and inserted myself instead, earning a more powerful moan than before. I was now in control, in control of the speed and the movements, how shallow or deep they were, how frequent, when to stop and when to accelerate; it was all my decisions. I was reminded of the first time we had done this together, back at her house when we had started dating. How inexperienced I was, which I still was but I had gotten better since then. Briefly, a thought about Violet crossed my mind and how different I was during that intercourse. Somehow, that same urge wasn't present with Camille, and I realized I had gone back to how things were, how she was the one leading the charge and I was following. The feeling wasn't unpleasant by any means, but I had experienced another facet of intercourse with Violet and wished I could apply that with Camille someday. Maybe next time I could show her what I was capable of. For now, however, she was right here, and it was up to me to rock her world. I started going back and forth, hitting her cheeks with every stroke as she tried to keep her voice down by shoving her face in the bed sheets. Her voice wasn't loud, but I could still hear everything she was saying, and, in between her moans, I swore I could hear something else, something that sounded like a name. But I was pretty sure it wasn't mine. I chased the thought away, not wanting to break the moment and ruin everything, but it did throw me off a little bit. The pleasure soon brought me back on track, briefly making me forget about it, and I whispered I was soon going to finish. She seemed to lower herself even more, giving me plenty of space to work with, and I got out of her, raising myself on my knees and stroking my shaft just above her butt cheeks. The spasm soon arrived, and I shot my load on her back. A small pool accumulated, and she flattened herself on the bed to prevent it from dripping too much. When I was done, I grabbed some tissues and cleaned her up, panting from exhaustion, but satisfied. As I threw the tissues in the garbage can next to my bed, she silently got up and walked out of the room. Not a word was spoken, and I was left confused as to what she was doing. I put on my boxers and realized I hadn't worn a condom again. I had a thought about it, when we undressed, but I wanted to feel her just like I did on our first time together. Perhaps that was a mistake, but it was too late now. I walked to the bedroom door, my head poking out towards the bathroom to see if she was in there. The door was closed, so I figured she must have been and walked back to bed, lying down on one side and waiting for her to come back. It wasn't long before I heard the door opening and her familiar figure appearing in the door frame. I looked her up and down, her blonde hair flowing down her back, her chest reacting to her every movement, her hips swaying back and forth slightly as she moved, her slender figure. After not seeing her for two months, the sight of her, naked too, was somewhat comforting. She walked to the other side of the bed and started dressing back up. I didn't say anything until she started putting her pants and shirt on like she was getting ready to leave.

"You don't want to cuddle a little?" I asked, lying on my side to look towards her.

"No, I don't feel like it right now," she answered, not even bothering to turn to me to answer. It was almost like she was ignoring me, but I couldn't understand why. The giddy feeling from the moments we had just shared shattered, and a mix of confusion and sadness took its place.

"Will you at least stay for supper? I can make you something nice," I offered, not as confident as I was a few minutes ago.

"No thanks, I think I will leave now."

Now fully dressed, she walked out of the room, leaving me stranded in my own bed, still shocked as to what was going on. It took a few seconds, but I pursued her to the front door where she was already putting on her coat. I was still only wearing boxer and the stark contrast could have amused me in another situation, but I didn't know what to do in this one. Camille opened the door and stepped in the doorframe. She paused and turned around, finally looking me in the eyes for what felt like an eternity.

"Goodbye, Jack." As soon as she said those words, the door closed, separating us once again. What had just happened? Why did she leave so suddenly after having sex, after sharing the most intimate part of yourself? It didn't make any sense to me. Did she use me? A grim thought, one I chased away as soon as I could, but one that still stuck to me for a while. I couldn't answer that question as a part of me wanted to excuse her behavior, whatever it may be, yet the fact remained she had just shown up for sex. Rather, that's what it looked like, anyway. I walked back to the bedroom window that faced the street and saw her walking away on the sidewalk. As she got farther and farther, I realized she wasn't coming back, and I got even more confused. I thought we had something again, I thought we were trying to make things work out, but after this, it felt like I was the only one that wanted that. But she was the one who approached me, how could she not want it just like me? She's the one that came to my work and messed with my brain while I was trying to forget her and now, she pulled something like this?

My mind wandered to us having sex just moments ago. Near the end, she was saying something, words that got muffled in the sheets that sounded like a name that didn't belong to me. Now that I wasn't in the action, this all seemed a little weird to me. I had a bad feeling about it. Perhaps my friends and Chloe were right after all; she was just trying to mess with me and would break my heart again. I couldn't help but shed a few tears, a confused and emotional me staring out the window in his boxers, wondering what went wrong and how he could have prevented it. I didn't want to accept she could be that kind of person; I knew her and went out with her for months. The Camille that left just now was not the same as the one I started dating, it couldn't possibly be. Nevertheless, if that was how she was going to act from now on, then things couldn't continue like this.

I'd have to talk to her one more time.

Chapter 20

For a day in the worst season of all, today wasn't that bad. There was no wind that blew, not even snow slowly falling from the sky, just plain sunshine and dry air. I was sitting on a bench in the park covered in white, waiting for someone to arrive. The snow had reached the height of the bench seat and it was kind of difficult to make my way over there without getting snow in my boots, but I had somehow managed it well enough. Small trails scattered about from every direction; some birds that landed in the snow, some cats probably chasing after them, a path that people made by continuously stepping in the same spots. When looking around, there was a kind of tranquility to the park, something you couldn't exactly get in summer as it was a lot busier, but the stillness of the play area and the nearby soccer field made it appear like a peaceful haven among the constant noise of the city.

A movement out the corner of my eye caught my attention. I turned my head to look at it; a squirrel was hopping towards a nearby tree, leaving small holes in the snow every time it landed. It suddenly turned around to look at me and I stared back. Sometimes, I wished I had the simplicity of a squirrel life just walking around collecting nuts and stashing them somewhere for the winter. Instead, I had to deal with studies and work and finance and love. Love... did squirrels ever have to fight for love? How complicated were their love lives? Surely not as complicated as mine. I sighed heavily and a little foggy cloud formed out of my mouth. The squirrel got scared and ran away, climbing the tree at great speed to hide within its barren branches. Why were stories of love so difficult?

I heard the snow creak to my left and looked towards the sound. A familiar silhouette came into view as she walked to me, her blonde hair swinging back and forth following her every movement. Her familiar white tuque and black coat completed her winter look. Camille. I had asked her to meet up to talk about us and she took some convincing but eventually agreed. Now that she was here, I started getting nervous again. I knew what to say, but not at the same time. What if I fumbled my words and looked like a complete moron? What if I said something but didn't mean it in the way she would interpret it?

What if… I didn't have time to complete my thought as she arrived next to me. I got up from the bench and joined her, walking in my own steps to rejoin the path.

"Hi," she said.

"Hi," I answered in a nervous voice. I was really trying to calm down but having her in front of me still made me anxious, especially when the subject I wanted to talk about was so delicate. "Do you want to walk around the park while we talk?"

"Sure."

We started our small journey circling the entire park. It wouldn't take long, I assumed, but our conversation could be quick as well, so I didn't know if we would even make our way around once. She silently followed me, waiting for me to start, but I couldn't decide on how and the words wouldn't come out. It was like they were stuck in my throat, and I couldn't breathe. Eventually, I managed to get my bearings and start the difficult yet needed conversation.

"This is a little awkward for me and you can probably tell I'm a little out of it, but I really do need to ask; how do you truly feel about me?"

The question seemed to take her by surprise, and she stayed silent for a little while before answering in a hesitant voice.

"I love you, of course. I'm a little confused by your question," she said.

"I'm asking because something seems off to me. Ever since you showed up at work two weeks ago, I've been conflicted on our situation. Like our date at the cat café, for example. You didn't seem that into it and we left in a hurry almost immediately after arriving. When we went the first time, we stayed there for hours. Why was it so different?"

"I… don't know what to tell you, Jack. I just didn't feel like being there for long. Didn't you like what we did after that?"

"Speaking of which, that also brings another point. You're not seeing anyone else, are you?" I boldly asked. Now that the conversation was going, I had my confidence back and managed to dive straight into the meat of the subject. We continued walking, but Camille lowered her head once, just a little, took a breath and turned her head to look at me.

"No, I'm not. The fact you even consider that possibility makes me very sad. We have a lot of things to work on, especially after the break we took, but that's not one of them."

The break we took? We didn't take any breaks; she ended the relationship. As soon as the words left her mouth, I tensed up, imitating one of the branches above our heads. How could she claim we took a break when she was the one who left for two whole months? I tried to play it cool and not let her see how that affected me and I don't know if I did a good job, but she didn't comment on it.

"How do you explain the name?"

"The what?"

"The name. When we were having sex. You said someone else's name in the bed sheets, didn't you?"

"Why are you interrogating me like this? Is this what this conversation is? You asking me questions like I'm a criminal? Listen, I'm not going to stand here and take this questioning anymore. No, I'm not seeing anyone right now, I didn't say anyone's name when we were having sex and the answer is no to any other question of the type. Are you happy now?"

I passed a hand across my face. This wasn't going exactly according to how I thought it would. I never intended to make her mad, but I did come across as pushy in my questions, I guess. Maybe it would be wiser to take another approach, something more personal, speak with my heart rather than my brain. I stopped on the path, the sound of the snow creaking under our weight stopping with me as Camille made a few extra steps before turning around. I looked to the ground as she came back next to me and waited. I could tell she was still a little mad and was waiting for my response.

"Listen, Camille, maybe we started this conversation on the wrong foot. This wasn't meant to be a one-sided interrogation; I'm just trying to voice out my concerns. Can you listen to me without interrupting?" I asked, my confidence way down compared to earlier. I lifted my head up to look at her and she held my gaze, her mouth closed shut and her arms folded. Her eyes were intense, almost like they were shooting daggers at me, but when I looked into them, I was reminded of the first time I had seen them.

They stood out among the other students who mainly had blue or brown eyes. She had the most beautiful emerald eyes of all, her blonde hair completing the scenery. When I saw her for the first time, I was instantly taken aback by her beauty and wanted to get to know her better. Regrettably, I didn't have the courage to approach her, even when we got paired up for a group project. I ended up not talking to her at all. She was even the one who came up to me when we started dating. I was a coward, incapable of doing the simplest task that required the smallest amount of courage, so who was I to talk about these things? Every class we had together, I stayed behind with my friends and looked at her from afar, wondering if there was ever a chance she would notice me.

The Camille back then wasn't the same as the one in front of me. Something about her aura had changed, something I couldn't exactly tell, but her general vibe had shifted along the way, and I was too blind to see. When did that change occur?

"I… don't think this is going to work out." Camille shifted like she wanted to say something. "Please, let me finish. We don't have the same connection we had at the start, the way we talked on our dates and our playfulness, I can tell it's gone. Perhaps there's a way to bring it back, but I don't know it. Our talks became awkward and would die out after a few sentences and… what intrigued me the most was the sex. I don't know what it is exactly, but something felt off last time. How can I put this? It wasn't as intimate as it was before, like you were reluctant to let yourself go completely. Like… something was missing. Add to that the mention of someone else…" I shook my head to try and contain my emotion. I could feel the tears coming up, but now was not the time to cry, not while we were having the conversation. If I wanted to be taken seriously, I had to be serious. "Are you seeing someone else?"

She sighed heavily, wiggling back and forth on one foot, probably wondering what to say next. The silence grew heavier with each passing second, the weight of my emotions piling up on my shoulders that started to slump a little. I had trouble breathing, partly because of the cold air floating around but mostly because I was trying my hardest to repress everything inside for now.

"First, I just want to say, I'm not seeing anyone right now. I… did see someone else, briefly, when we broke up." She paused, uncertain how to continue. "I think some things happened to both of us since the breakup and we simply need to rekindle what was once there. Look, Jack, I still love you, with all my heart, and I… don't want to let you go."

"You did," I said as I looked down. "You did let me go two months ago. If you love me so much, why did you do that? That person you saw in the past months, you started seeing him before that, right? Who was it?"

"That's not relevant to say, Jack, it doesn't matter. What matters is that I'm here, right now, and we're trying to work this out. Don't you want to try and fix things?"

I asked the question, but I already knew the answer. The fact she dismissed it proved I was right. The confirmation stung harshly on my heart, and I had to take a few seconds to recover. She said she wanted to fix things, but her actions didn't speak the same as her words. It was painful for me to come to, but it didn't look like it would be possible for us to continue this any longer.

"I'm sorry, Camille, but I can't go on like this. There's a little too much going on and you broke my heart two months ago, you know. You really brought me down and I thought I could recover quickly if I started seeing you again, but the truth is, I was wrong. The hurt is still there, and I don't want any more."

"Are you serious?" Camille said with an exasperated tone. I sighed and took a few seconds.

"Yes. I think it would be best to end things here, for both of our sake."

"Don't you love me still?"

"I do, Camille, trust me, I do, I care about you a lot. It breaks my heart to have to do this again, but if we can't tell each other everything already and come in with more baggage than we left, how are we supposed to fix whatever this is? I don't have the strength to do that, I can't look the other way to what has already happened, and I don't want to imagine what can come next. These past months have been tough for me, I don't know how they've been for you, but I'm willing to go back to being alone if it means healing in a more natural way. You know, the time we spent together was still good, I hold those memories close to my heart from all the months we spent dating and, while it's nice to see you again, I feel it may tarnish them if we continue like this. I would rather keep them intact than cover them up with something else. Do you understand what I'm saying?"

"You've started seeing someone else too, haven't you?" Camille simply asked. The fact she avoided my question with another of her own surprised me. I didn't know what to answer as well. Was I? Could my time spent with Chloe be considered 'seeing someone' or was it just two friends hanging out? Was it considered dating if none of the parties thought of it as such? Was that just an assumption on my part? How do you define 'seeing someone' enough to be worth mentioning?

"I have not. I told you, you broke my heart, how could I be seeing someone else so soon?" I asked back.

Camille smiled and looked at the ground. It felt like she wanted to laugh, but not of joy or happiness. Something much nastier, like immense bitterness, like she was angry about something. We had been standing still for a while, two frozen statues on a cold winter day and I took a step back from Camille to let her have some space. Maybe that was a bit presumptuous, but I was trying to be considerate of her boundaries. She finally lifted her head back to look at me and saw her cry. She didn't let out that side of her often, so something was clearly affecting her for her to let the tears out. This time, however, it wasn't from joy but something colder. The tears, half frozen, slid across her face in two straight marks all the way to her chin. She wasn't crying heavily, but just enough for the droplets to shine in the sun when she moved a little. She looked at me directly in the eyes and I held her gaze with difficulty. There was something about it that made me deeply uncomfortable. I knew how it felt to be on the other side of the words I had spoken and wondered if she felt like I do now back then. Was she torn between two feelings like I was right now? Was she as awkward as I was? I felt almost frozen in place in the snow, how could she have just walked away?

"To think I would lose to her…pitiful. Well, you know what, Jack? You go have fun with her until you realize how bad of a person she is. But don't come crawling back to me after you do, because I already don't care about you anymore. I never had any sentiment towards you, you know, that was nothing real. I hope she wrecks you, truly. I hope I never see you again." Camille turned around and started walking away, leaving me stranded in the cold barren park.

I followed her with my eyes, her shoulders clearly going up and down. Was it from the snowy terrain she had to walk through or something else? I knew the answer, but I stayed still and stared at her anyway. Before I knew it, I was crying too, some tears falling on the snow and creating little holes. Why did it hurt so much even now when I was the one breaking things up? Why did my heart ache for her when everything else told me to let her go? Her last words… did she mean them? Was it true? I didn't want to entertain that possibility, but even if I tried to shake those thoughts out of my head, they came back like unwanted parasites. Just thinking about it, my heart stung, and I had to really calm down to not break down crying in the snow. Nobody was around, but I was still embarrassed to do it in public, especially after what happened last time. My face was frighteningly cold and snapped me out of it for just a moment, just enough for me to figure out what to do next. I set course for my apartment, running on autopilot as I unknowingly walked as fast as I could, lost in thought and sentiment. I sort of blanked out the rest of the trip until I was lying on my bed and soaking the sheets.

Why was this breakup so hard? We had only seen each other once after she came to my work, so why did it feel the same as the first one? The first one was a shock; it came like the biggest surprise of my life, and I felt betrayed. I felt let down by the one person I loved, like she let go of my hand at the most critical moment and let me fall. This time was different. I was hoping she would extend her hand to catch me from my fall, and she did, but it was only to taunt me and mock me as the void called me from below. If it was the only possible outcome, then I would rather let myself go than live my life getting lied to. It would still hurt when I reached the bottom, but at least I would be free from her grasp. There was one good thing about it if I really tried to look at it from a positive angle. Now that I had broken up with Camille for good, I could finally move on. Ever since the first breakup, I wanted to have her back, I wanted us to fix things and work together to make the relationship work. After the second, I now realize it was pointless to begin with, pointless to even think of that possibility; it was never going to work. I guess it took me way longer than it should have to accept it, I should have known from the start if I was honest with myself, but when Camille came back, even if all my friends told me it was a bad idea, I still felt like I had to try. Meaningless struggle, I now know, but it also allowed me to finally accept that she was gone. She was gone and wouldn't come back. There was no point in longing for her now, was there? Perhaps there was some good to come out of this after all.

Through blurry eyes, I reached for my phone across the bed; I had tossed it aside as soon as I arrived in frustration. I scrolled down my contacts list a little and stopped when Camille's name came into view. How badly I wanted to press that button. Why? She wouldn't answer and I was at fault for that, so why did the button call to me so strongly? It was like an overwhelming force that compelled me to do it, almost forced me to press it. Then what? I would have to write a message and nothing I could say would erase what just happened. Deep down, I didn't want it to either, but I had to concentrate very hard to reject the pull. Instead, I clicked on the contact just under it, still unsure what to do next. I debated writing a text or calling, but since talking on the phone was never my forte, I opted for the text approach.

I… I need someone to talk to.

As soon as I hit send, I felt silly. She told me this very thing would happen, my friends did too, so who was I to ignore their advice and then seek their comfort? They would just tell me to stay in my misery and it could have been prevented if only I had listened to them. They would be right. I let my heart decide what to do and it led me here, in my bed and in tears once again. Perhaps the heart has no idea what the right thing to do is, perhaps it lives only to offer choices the brain has to decipher. I had heard the phrase 'follow your heart' before and never paid it much attention, but now I realized it must have been all lies. I followed my heart, and it only brought me pain.

In my hand, my phone rang, pulling me out of the dark spiraling thoughts I was losing myself into. I quickly checked the name of the caller, Chloe. She was fast, I had to give her that. I hesitated to answer the phone and hovered over the green button, incapable of pressing it. What was it with buttons all of a sudden? Wasn't I the one who told her I needed to talk? Why was I surprised she was calling me, then? What was I waiting for? If I didn't answer, I would look like an idiot, and she would probably rush over here. I didn't think I could handle that right now; I didn't want to see anyone. I finally pressed to answer the call and shakingly brought the phone to my ear.

"Hello," I said, softly and hesitantly. It was the first time I had talked in a while and the words seemed to get stuck at the back of my throat, suffocating me a little. I had to start breathing loudly to recover and I just hoped she didn't hear any of it.

"Told you this would happen," she simply said in a snide tone. I sighed without caring if the phone would pick it up. She was right. She was absolutely right; she did tell me this would happen, and I didn't listen because I didn't want her to be. How hypocritical of me was it to seek her advice now? She must have thought I was pathetic... "You mind telling me what happened?" she finally asked. Her tone had changed a little, like she realized she came off as kind of me. I wouldn't have held it against her.

"I... had a talk with... Camille and, um, we... we broke it off. Well, I broke it off," I managed to say through the emotions. I tried to not let it appear that way, but I didn't do a very good job of it.

"You're crying, aren't you? You know I told you so, Jack. Why didn't you listen to me?"

"I... had to see it for myself, I think. You were right; it was never going to work. But I wanted to know that myself. It just... hurts just as much as last time."

"I told you that, too. Listen, I'm glad you broke it off with her, she was nothing but trouble to you, look at you now as proof. However, I did tell you not to come back to me for comfort when that happened."

I paused before answering. Chloe didn't seem like herself, like she was somehow more involved than before. Why was that? I couldn't think straight at the moment, parts of what she and my friends said bouncing around in my head along with excerpts of conversations with Camille, mixing in a blend of confusion. I didn't know what to accept or reject, what to think and what to disregard, what was real and what wasn't. I cry-sighed and brought the phone back to my ear.

"Do you mean that?"

Now, it was her turn to pause. Was she thinking about it? Why would she need to think about it? Surely, it was a simple yes or no answer, there wasn't any deep thought to give a reflection to. But I waited patiently for her answer, hoping and praying it was negative, and she spoke a few seconds later.

"Tell me exactly what happened."

Her voice was commanding, but not harsh, like a soft demand. I was relieved, briefly, before I plunged myself back into the distressing events that had just occurred. As I was about to start telling her everything, I stopped myself and wondered why I didn't contact my friends first. Did I not trust them enough to keep what I would say to themselves? Did I think they wouldn't understand, or they would reject me for what I did? Did I not appreciate their previous counsel whenever I had a problem? None of those questions had a positive answer. Wouldn't I want them to come to me if they were in trouble? Why wasn't it the same both ways? What compelled me to contact her first rather than my friends I had known for years? Sure, I had known her for just as long or even longer, but we had just begun to talk again a few months ago. Perhaps it was that familiarity we once had that was starting to come back, perhaps there was a remnant of our previous complicity lingering at the back of my mind. Whatever the case may be, here I was, about to pour my heart out again for her and my only thought was hoping she would listen to me all the way through.

She did. Without an interruption or any comment. She listened to me talk about the past two weeks, from the moment she walked out of my apartment to just an hour ago, and if she had a reaction, she managed to contain it or not let it slip through the phone. I was glad she didn't but, at the same time, it was impossible to judge her reaction to any of it from her silence. It was kind of a double-edged sword, and I could only hope she wasn't silently fuming as I spoke. After I finished telling her all the details of the second breakup with Camille, she took what felt like an eternity to answer. Each passing second felt like an hour and I was frozen in bed, rigid like a plank, wishing she would just say something, anything, to let me know she was still there.

"Jack."

Her voice was different now. She seemed… sad, but calm. Like a serene melancholy. Shouldn't I be the one grieving? I didn't think my story was that poignant to convey that much emotion through the phone.

"I'm sorry about how I acted earlier. I know this is a hard time for you and what I said previously… I didn't mean it. I acted out of emotion and said things I regret."

"I'm equally sorry, I shouldn't be talking to you about this stuff. You're probably the last person who wants to hear about her, but I… I don't know who else to turn to. You understand me the best out of anyone. I know it's selfish of me to involve you in all this. I'm sorry…"

"You don't have to apologize. I did tell you, didn't I? Just like all those years ago, if you want to talk about anything, you can call me or text me or whatever you want. I'll always be there for you, even if your words are hard to hear."

I tried to smile through the tears, but my face seemingly didn't obey me and deformed itself into a grimace instead. Her words warmed my heart, but I couldn't let her do that to herself. From her reactions just now, Camille wasn't exactly the best subject to talk about with her and, if anything, it would be better to avoid it. Her offer, though, was really nice yet it sounded oddly profound to me, like it possibly had another meaning to it. My brain was foggy, and I had a hard time thinking straight, so I couldn't figure out what it could be. A few seconds had passed, and I still hadn't answered her. Was it because I didn't have an answer to that offer or because I was too overwhelmed with emotions I couldn't even speak? A little bit of both, certainly, yet I had to respond.

"Thank you, Chloe, I… really appreciate it," I said.

"Are you going to be okay?" she asked, already moving on to the next thing, like she was ignoring my response.

"I think I'll manage…" I sighed, trying to calm down.

"Ok…well, call me if there's anything, alright?" She paused for a few seconds before continuing. "I… Take care of yourself, Jack."

With that, she hung up, leaving me with the dial tone ringing in my ear. I quickly took away the phone and my arm just fell on the bed as I relaxed it, the phone slipping out a little onto the bed sheets. The last words she spoke kept bouncing in my head. It was like advice and threat at the same time, a two-sided coin that always landed on both faces. Taking care of myself wasn't the easiest task, I didn't even know where to begin, and it seemed so daunting to attempt I simply stayed in bed, unmotivated to get up and do anything. Before I knew it, sleep had taken a hold of me and dragged me down to the depths of dreams, a land where anything was possible, and nothing was real.

I don't usually remember dreams at all, but this one was so poignant all the details were still so vibrant when I woke up. I took out the small book I kept on the side of my bed for things like these. Long ago, my dad had given me that leather-covered journal to keep notes of various things in my life. I usually kept it for dreams, but since I never actually remembered them, the pages were nothing but barren except for a few scribbles here and there. I opened it, still lying in bed, grabbed a pencil and started writing.

In my dream, I was sitting on a wooden bench in what looked like a park. I could see a few trails and a little path in front of me, but even a few meters ahead were blurry, and I couldn't tell what was beyond. I couldn't feel the bench under me, which was another aspect of dreams I found quite peculiar. Senses get jumbled up and dulled, sometimes even nullified like this for instance, while others get amplified. I couldn't feel or smell, I hadn't tried to taste anything, but the thought seemed a little silly to attempt. I was about to conclude I couldn't hear as well when the sound of a bird chanting behind me caught my attention. I turned around on the bench and looked up at the tree behind me. It was seemingly moving around slightly, like my dream wasn't stable and it couldn't hold its ground very well. Now that I looked at it, the bench was warping a little too, clearly not made of wood like I thought, but of a much more malleable material I couldn't identify. It was almost see-through, yet my hand could rest on it just fine. The bird singing made me look at the tree again as I tried to find it. I had been looking everywhere, but there was no sign of it. Was it hidden in the leaves or just a figment of my imagination in this crazy instance of a world? Another bird started singing and I turned slightly to my right to notice another tree had suddenly grown, hiding another chanting bird. This one, however, I could see clearly. It was a golden bird with hints of black feather across the wings and face. I stared at it for a couple of seconds before it turned its head to face me. It sang again and I smiled at it. Weirdly, I couldn't decide if I liked the sound of the bird or not, like I heard it but didn't at the same time. I stayed in the same position, frightened to scare away the bird if I did the slightest movement, until eventually it flew towards me and landed on the bench right next to me. It hopped around a little, turning its head to judge me, pacing back and forth. If I reached for it, it could easily hop in my hand. What would it feel like, I wondered? Would the bird stay in place and observe or panic and fly away? I don't know why, but I felt compelled to present both hands to the bird and got up to extend both hands towards it. The bird looked up at me and I swore it appeared confused like it didn't know what to do next. I was caught off guard by another bird flying in and landing in my left hand. Surprised, I stared at it, admiring the red feathers and the pointy plumage of its head. It was beautiful, just like the yellow one, which was just… on the bench? I searched everywhere for it, but there was no trace of the other bird anywhere. I don't know why, but I started to panic and look back and forth frantically, the red bird still in my hand. Despite me moving around, it stood perfectly still and waited for me to stop. Eventually, I had to resign myself, the yellow bird was gone. Even the bench was gone, the trees were gone, the park was gone. All around me, there was only a vague patch of ground and complete darkness. The bird sang in my hand, but it had a different tone this time. It wasn't the normal singing, like it was warped or something else. I looked at it and the bird stared back at me, singing again in its now weird tone. There were a few seconds of silence, then it sounded again, way louder this time.

I woke up in the dark to the sound of the doorbell ringing through the apartment. I blinked a few times, trying to figure out where I was and what had just happened. I glanced over at the clock on my desk. It was 6h34 p.m. Why was I sleeping in my bed at this hour? I distinctly remember waking up already, but that didn't make any sense. Was I in a double dream or something? I thought I remembered seeing a movie about this once, but my foggy mind couldn't recall the title. Images I had just seen flashed in my mind, and I got even more confused. What did it all mean and why did I dream about birds of all things? The sound of a text message coming to my phone added to the doorbell echo and I grabbed a hold of it to check who it was. It was Chloe, unsurprisingly, who was asking me to open the door. I didn't know what to answer and I didn't want to see anyone so I figured I would just let her get tired of ringing the doorbell and she would leave. She must have run out of patience already because it didn't sound again, and I thought I was in the clear. Creaking under my weight as my body shifted, I got up from the bed and slowly walked to the bathroom in just my boxers. I rubbed my face in my hands a few times, trying to wake up faster, and stopped to stare at the stove indicating the time. I had already checked it, but somehow it hit a little different seeing it again. Was it really that late? My schedule was absolutely destroyed now, not beyond repair, but it would take great effort to bring it back.

The sound of the lock jiggling behind me snapped me out of my thoughts. The door handle rotated, and the door opened, revealing Chloe in the frame, staring at me. At first, she seemed relieved and surprised, but her expression soon changed to embarrassment. I looked down and realized I was wearing next to nothing and felt my cheeks becoming redder. I backed off into the bathroom, closing the door with a little too much force as I heard her close the front door as well. I leaned on the wooden barrier between us, wondering what to do next. There were no clothes in here to wear and going out with a towel around my waist would be a little weird. Would it be worse than her practically seeing me naked? Probably not, but, if anything, she was the one who should look away and hide while I get dressed, not the opposite. Plus, why was she even here? How did she get the key to my apartment? Why come now of all possible times and without warning?

"Jack... I'll be in the... living room if you need to get dressed," she shouted to me through the door. I waited a minute for her to sit down and turn away before getting out of the bathroom, rushing to get to my dresser and put on some clothes. I don't know how she resisted the temptation to turn around and see me probably hilariously hurrying up while trying to be quiet, but she didn't. It didn't take long for me to put on a shirt and some pants and join her in the living room.

Sitting on the couch like this reminded me of the movie we had watched together. Back then, she had left crying and I was determined not to let that happen again. I didn't know what she wanted, but I would try my best to avoid getting her upset. Was it from embarrassment on both of our parts, I wasn't sure, but we stayed silent sitting on the couch for what felt like fifteen minutes before someone spoke. Of course, she was the one to break the ice.

"I... didn't see anything if that's any comfort," she said, looking straight ahead and trying to avoid turning around to see me.

"That's good. I mean, not that it would bother me that much, but it just surprised me to see you pop suddenly." I shook my head. What was I even saying, now? That made me sound like a creep, so I decided to quickly change the subject with a question. "What are you doing here, exactly?"

"I was coming to check on you. I thought something might be going on since... you know."

"Oh, well, I'm fine if that's what you're asking. Yeah, completely fine."

"Jack, you haven't showed up to school in three days and skipped work today. I know, I went. Something's going on and you keep ignoring my messages and my calls. Ever since you told me about... her, you've been distant. Tell me what's going on."

I smiled and looked down at the floor, trying to hide my shame. She was so kind to worry about me like this and I felt like a failure to make her do so. I was never good at communicating my feelings, especially when it came to stuff that made me sad, and the whole relationship and breakup side of things was still kind of new to me. I didn't know how to tell even more than I already had, wouldn't I just be repeating myself? What more was there to say? I turned to look at Chloe in the eyes and noticed my vision was blurry. Was I crying? I hadn't said anything yet, why was I crying? I was tired. Tired of holding back, tired of keeping it inside, tired of appearing strong to others. I just wanted to let go.

I did.

I had cried before, I had mourned my breakup, I had talked about my feelings with Chloe and my friends already, but never like this. Before, I put on a barrier and only let certain things slip through, keeping most of what I felt contained, trying to put on a front or keep a certain composure. The only time I had cried as much was the first time Camille had left. But this was different. Then, I cried because my heart ached so much I thought I would die, but now it was because I was tired of holding back and let the flood gates open. I hadn't notice through the tears, but Chloe was holding me in her arms, my head resting on her chest as she was rubbing my back. We were sitting a little awkwardly on the couch, but it didn't matter to me. I was soaking her shirt, but she didn't move. I was sobbing loudly, but she didn't move. I was holding her tightly, but she didn't move. She stayed there, holding me in a calm and reassuring manner, silent. No words needed to be spoken and I felt she understood somehow. She held me for a long time before I parted from her. I wiped the tears off my eyes and looked at her. She had calming and loving eyes and smiled at me.

"You okay?" she asked. I only nodded in response, and she seemed satisfied with that response.

She turned around to look at the wall in front of the couch. I looked at her for a second. She seemed... different, like I saw in another light now. Her face, her hair, her figure, her eyes. I shifted my eyes down, unable to keep looking at her for now. I was still a little embarrassed about what had just happened and wanted to know what she was thinking right now.

"Could you... not tell anyone about this?" I asked in a soft voice, barely more than a whisper.

"Of course," she answered quickly. "This can stay between us."

"Thank you..." I rubbed my face in my hands, wiping any remnant of tears still on my cheeks. "I know this might be a little forward but could you... stay a little longer with me?"

"You want me to stay?" she asked. I nodded positively as she looked at me for confirmation. She seemed to think about it for a few seconds and finally answered. "Yes, I think I could do that."

I smiled and stared in her eyes, hiding behind her glasses. They were so beautiful, so much more than I had realized until now, and while it was a little embarrassing to be looking at her directly like this, it also warmed my heart for some reason. It was little difficult to break eye contact, but I did when she spoke again.

"I'm guessing you haven't had supper yet?"

◊

The rest of the evening was a blur. I remember us doing various things with Chloe trying to cheer me up and me trying my best not to feel or look so sad.

We tried to put on a comedy show, but my heart was simply not in the mood to laugh; I think I just wanted some comfort and staring at a television screen would not bring me what I needed. Things seemed to get better as the hours passed, however, and it had gotten pretty late; the sun had already set and outside was as still as a ghost town. That's when I asked Chloe if she could spend the night with me.

◇

"Chloe, there is one more thing I'd like to ask," I started, not as confident as I tried to make it sound.

"Yes, what is it?" she inquired, eyebrows raised, and head turned towards me. We had spent the entire evening together and, even though I was still feeling a little saddened by the recent events, she had managed to make me partially forget it. It didn't hurt any less, my heart still felt like an exposed wound, but she would sometimes bandage it to try and heal it.

"I know this is a lot to ask, but… could you…would you…stay with me, tonight?" I looked up to see her reaction. She was looking away, her eyes hidden behind her glasses, but I knew she was staring at the ground. Her cheeks became as red as her hair within seconds, and she stayed silent for a while. I avoided staring at her to not pressure her into answering if she wasn't ready, but the growing awkwardness between us threatened to burst at any moment. Should I not have asked that? Was it too forward of me? I didn't mean anything by it, I just wanted to have some company, but maybe she interpreted it differently. I was about to correct myself when she broke the silence.

"We… really shouldn't do that, I think, Jack. You said it yourself last time…isn't it going to be weird?" she asked, trying to voice her concern, but her embarrassed tone made it difficult to take her seriously. She was a lot cuter than she gave herself credit for, but I couldn't think like that right now.

"I just want someone with me; just for this one night. Can't you do that for me?" I pleaded.

"No funny business, right?" she asked.

"None," I answered. She looked down again, thinking it over. I let her take as much time as she needed, hoping silently she would agree. After a few seconds that felt way longer, she rose her head to meet my eyes and I smiled to try and reassure her, but she had already taken her decision.

"Okay…" she said in a whisper.

And here we were, both lying in bed next to each other. It had been around three months since I had someone sleeping with me and, while it was now an unusual feeling, I liked having the thought of her in an arm's reach. She was already asleep, her breathing relaxed and rhythmic, while I was still wide awake. Was it the nerves keeping me up or perhaps I was simply not tired? I wished for nothing other than for sleep to take me, but it wouldn't approach at all. I glanced over at Chloe, lying on her side facing towards me. She originally was facing the other way, but I guess she moved a lot in her sleep. Perhaps she would have been reluctant had she been awake, but she couldn't really protest now. I couldn't see very well, but we had been lying in the dark for a while now and my eyes had somewhat accustomed to the darkness. I could see enough to look at her even in the dead of night. Without her glasses, her face was very different. I had seen her before without them, but that was years ago, and she had changed a lot since then. Her hair still stood out in the dark and flowed behind her back, getting lost under the bed sheets. Her expression, usually cheerful, was now peaceful and calm, just like her breathing, and I found myself longing for something like that. Why couldn't I be this serene while I was awake? Things would be so much better if that were the case, wouldn't they?

I smiled to no one and turned around, trying to get some sleep. For some reason, my heart was beating a lot faster than usual, and my legs felt as rigid as wooden planks. I stared at the wall in front of me, my head spinning with the multitude of thoughts bouncing around. Maybe that was the reason I couldn't fall asleep; my mind was simply not ready yet and I had to think a little more about…everything really. Just as I was about to give in to a much-needed rest, something appeared to pounce on my side. Startled, I turned around to see what it was, and Chloe's hand fell on my belly. I stared at it for a few seconds, then at Chloe. She was still asleep and had no control over it, but that still made me jump a little. Plus, she was dangerously close to…I carefully took her hand and moved it off me. It wasn't that I didn't want her to hold me like this necessarily, but I figured she would be embarrassed if she woke up like this and saved us the hassle of explaining myself to her in the morning. Still, a part of me almost didn't let go of her hand. Her skin was so soft to the touch, even for the moment I held her arm, and I wondered if she would think the same things had the situation been reversed. I turned again, trying to get some sleep once more, but more questions had been added to the already overflowing amount in my head. I did eventually enter the world of dreams for the second time today, but this time I had no recollection of it nor was I aware that I had fallen into it.

◊

I woke up late and the sunlight had already started filling the room despite the curtains being closed. I blinked a few times to chase away the groggy feeling of waking up and turned around to see Chloe. Her spot was empty, and she was nowhere to be found. I sat up straight in a flash, instantly awake, and looked around the room. On my dresser was the pyjama I had lent her along with a note. I slowly got up from the bed and walked over to it. The clothes were folded neatly, way better than anything I could do, and the little piece of paper was filled with her handwriting. I grabbed it and started reading, the blurriness of sleep still lingering.

Jack,

I'm sorry I couldn't stay this morning. I don't regret staying the night, but seeing you sleeping made me feel… I don't really know how to explain it. I know you're probably disappointed if you're reading this right now and I completely understand, but I just… don't know how to feel at the moment. I hope you're still okay, but if there's anything that comes up or you just want to talk to someone, you can always call me, alright?

Chloe

Right next to her name, there was a little scribble, a little rabbit with very long ears. I smiled a little at the sight. Chloe used to draw these everywhere in my books at school and would always do it when my back was turned so it was a surprise when I found them. Those were simpler times, times where we only had few worries, times where it was easier to talk. I couldn't help but draw a comparison between this one and the note I left Violet that one morning. Was she feeling the same way then as I was now? Surely not, the tone of the messages was quite different. Still, I understood a little more how she felt waking up alone after falling asleep next to me. I would have liked to say goodbye to Chloe this morning, I would have liked to see her awaken and slowly regain consciousness. I would have liked to see her face first thing in the morning. Was it normal for me to feel this way for my friend?

I walked over to the bedroom window and opened the curtains to see outside. It was bright and sunny and, even though it was the height of winter, the sun seemed to warm my heart and melt away some of the stress of the past few days. I don't know why, but I brought the note up again to read it once more. Out the reflection, I saw something written at the back of the paper, but I couldn't decipher it. I turned it around to look at it.

I think I have feelings for you.

My eyes widened at the sight of the words written on this little piece of paper. What would have happened if I had just thrown it in the garbage just now? Would her confession vanish, never to be heard from again? Would she have alluded to the fact she had written on the note? What was I supposed to do now? Did I feel the same way as her? Why didn't she tell me face to face? I let the piece of paper go and watched it slowly fall to the ground, turning around as it hit the floor and showing me the bunny drawing again.

How could I face her now?

Chapter 21

The last few weeks were a little strange. With my breakup still fresh on my mind and Chloe's note, I didn't really know what to think. I was emotionally confused and questioning every aspect of the last months, trying to find out what exactly happened between Chloe and I to warrant such a confession. Because I couldn't lie to myself; it was a confession through and through, no doubt about it, but I wasn't wondering why she confessed rather than why that moment in particular? I couldn't understand her reasoning and, being tangled in my feelings myself, it didn't really help me process the breakup healing part.

At school, even though we were in the same class, we tried to avoid each other, for some reason. It was like we both knew it was for the best, even if I didn't necessarily want to. I wanted to understand her, to talk about her feelings with her, but my own were getting in the way. Every time I saw Camille in the halls, it brought back something I tried to bury multiple times. With her being so close to me all the time, it kept reminding me of what we had and even if I realized it was never going to be as it was, a small part of me was still saddened about the whole thing. Maybe if we had taken a different path, we could have stayed friends or maybe…What use was there to wonder these things? It only hurt more like a sharp sting to the heart. Plus, I had my hands full with another touchy subject.

I didn't like that Chloe and I grew a little apart from this. Usually, we talked on the phone on most nights of the week, we texted and told each other what happened during our workdays. Now, we seldom talked anymore, like her note saying she might have feelings for me pushed her away. Maybe she was giving me time to think it over, but then why write it in that moment at all? I wanted to reach out to her to ask, but she always seemed to slip away at the worst moments, and I was too scared to call her on the phone. I didn't like calls in general, but I felt like that one couldn't have been a phone call. It had to be done in person, face to face, I had to see her reaction and see her pour her feelings out. Not in a cruel way, I wouldn't do that to her, but I thought it important we feel what the other was saying, not just hear it.

Sometimes, when it got especially cold at night, I would wrap myself in a blanket and stare at the note Chloe had left. The bunny reassured me and reminded me of simpler times, but it also brought back memories of Chloe and I hanging out and, every time, I would get teary-eyed. Was it nostalgia or something else that made my eyes water? Even so, I couldn't bring myself to throw it away. The thought did cross my mind, but the note stuck to my hand like it was glued or bound by something even stronger. What was this unknown force, I wondered, but I couldn't never find an answer no matter how hard I searched. Perhaps it wasn't a question that could be answered.

I would stare out the window, seeing snowflakes slowly fall to the ground to cover the city in a fresh white coat, a dormant city late at night only lit up by the lampposts scattered along the roads. When dusk came and they started turning on, the colors mixed in a strange amalgamation, painting the sky and ground alike in a constantly changing hue. The duality of the city standing still and my feelings constantly rumbling made me smile whenever I thought about it. The heart has a weird way to heal, and it sometimes is the simple things that alleviates the heaviest burdens, despite us desperately searching for something more impactful. I wasn't an expert by now, not by a long shot, but the best way to cope with losing Camille again, even if it was my fault this time, was to simply invest my time in something else. To take my mind off things; to ease the pain just a little.

Before I knew it, time had passed, and it was already half-way through February. Time was a strange phenomenon. Sometimes, it appeared to flow at the speed of light and sometimes it was excruciatingly slow, but that was only an illusion. Time doesn't care about anything and simply flows forward, like a river pouring downstream towards the lake. Unlike the water, however, one couldn't stop time from taking its course. It had now been close to a month since I ended things with Camille. The burden of the breakup had somehow eased a lot faster than it did previously. If I had to guess why, it might be because I had unanswered questions before that didn't get the answers I wanted when we went back together and, now that they were gone, I had less attachments to her. It didn't mean I didn't care about her at all anymore, I still did, but it wasn't the same kind. Acceptance is a hard thing to come to and I wasn't pretending like I was there yet, but I started to understand how one could come to that, eventually.

A day like any other, a weekend where I had neither work nor school and was therefore completely free, was suddenly disturbed by a text message. My phone vibrated in my pocket and I took it out to check who it was. I was out for a cold walk and couldn't tell from the home screen and had to take out my gloves to check my messages a little closer. Both surprised and relieved to see Chloe's name at the top, I clicked on our conversation to read.

Hey, so I got this reservation at a restaurant tonight. For two. Do you want to join me?

I sighed, forming a misty cloud in front of me that quickly dissolved. I wasn't exasperated, in fact I was quite happy she would propose the idea, rather I was a little hesitant. We had avoided each other for the last few days, conversation was scarce, and now she invited me straight up. It came as a little bit of a surprise for sure, the words seemingly weirder than usual to me. I really wanted to go, but I would be lying to myself if I said I wasn't at least somewhat scared of what the outcome could be. Maybe there was nothing to worry about and it would all be fine, maybe she didn't mean anything else by it, but what if she did? Pointless argument to have with myself, I knew, the only way to know was to either ask or go. Either way, I had to respond.

I would love to, where is the restaurant?

As soon as I hit the send button, a wave of nervousness came crashing down on me. Why was that? It wasn't like this was some new girl I was talking to, had never met before and it was our first date. I had known Chloe for years, we had talked too many times for me to count, so why did it feel so weird sending that text? I stood there in the cold, waiting for a response that didn't take long to arrive. She sent me the address with another text and added a little embarrassed emoji at the end. I checked how to get there with an app on my phone and decided to go get changed at home first before meeting up with her. The whole time on the way back, I kept thinking about Chloe and her sudden invitation. We had grabbed a bite to eat together many times, but something about this one felt different. How did I get that impression from a text message where emotions get completely lost?

My mind wandering off, I almost didn't realize I was home and would have kept going if I didn't get distracted by a passing car that made a lot of noise. I absent-mindedly climbed up the stairs leading to my apartment and warmed up a little inside. As time went on, my heart unconsciously started beating faster and faster, like an increasing music tempo with a stretched crescendo. I tried to calm down, but even breathing slowly did nothing to appease the growing fire inside. I opened my dresser to check if there was anything better to wear than whatever I had on at the moment. I was wearing a pair of jeans I wore for the past two days and a shirt with a few holes on the side; not exactly restaurant worthy attire, even if that kind of thing normally wouldn't bother me. Now, however, I felt compelled to at least show up with some awareness of my clothes. After a few minutes of taking stuff out and checking them quickly, I landed on the shirt I went on my first date with.

This felt a lot like a date, too. It dawned on me at the sight of the shirt and wondered if that was truly Chloe's intention or not? I thought back to that cat café Camille and I went to all those months ago. We had talked for hours, not bothering to know how much time had passed or what others were thinking. I didn't even recall what we said, I just remembered it was a good time and the cats kept us company. Would that feeling ever come back? Would I ever be able to experience getting lost in conversation like that with another girl? I couldn't wear this shirt tonight, there was too much already attached to it, and I didn't want to overwrite that memory with another, even if the previous one was about someone, I had no ties with anymore. I wasn't normally into fashion or paid much attention to my outfit on a normal day; I just grabbed whatever shirt was on the top of the pile and the first pair of jeans or shorts that landed in my hand and that was it. This time was different, I wanted to find something nice, something out of the ordinary for me to wear. I had never put too much thought into my outfit before, so why start paying attention to it now? Even though my heart knew the answer, my mind kept coming to the simplest explanation; I just wanted to look good for my friend. Nothing more, right? After tossing a few more shirts to the side, I finally landed on one I thought was best. It wasn't anything too crazy or fancy, but it was one of the few good-looking shirts I had. It was a dark blue, almost black, plain shirt with three buttons at the top. Admittedly, that was a standard outfit for some people, but since I wasn't into fashion, I never gave much importance to buy any fancier shirts. I also took out some black pants to go with it since that was the only non-jeans pair of pants I had. Trying it on, I could almost be mistaken for a goth if I had black hair and the accessories and makeup to go with it. My wardrobe was pretty much only darker colors, though, so there wasn't much I could do about that. Time was ticking and I already had to leave soon if I wanted to get there early. I hated making people wait for me and, even if it was kind of short notice on Chloe's part, I didn't want to be late. I took the time to get ready still; to smell nice and look as good as I could. Looking at myself in the bathroom mirror, I once again wondered why I was giving so much importance to what I looked like. Most people would probably say that was the least I could do, but I didn't do as much whenever I went out with Camille so why was this any different? I didn't have time to worry anymore and had to go if I wanted to catch the bus, so I grabbed my wallet, keys and phone and practically sprinted out the door.

Luckily, the bus dropped me off directly in front of the restaurant. I looked up at the lit banner proudly displaying the name and stared at it for a few seconds, lost in thought. The cold air outside brought me back down to earth, and I looked down inside the restaurant. From here, I could already tell this wasn't a cheap everyday place, rather something kind of nice, not exactly chic but not far from it. How did Chloe get a reservation here of all places? I had never gone to this restaurant before, the entire ambiance didn't seem like my usual kind of scene, but there was something about tonight that was different. Was it because she had invited me or because I was feeling unusual and wanted to try something new? It was most likely the former and, while I didn't want to admit it to myself, I couldn't possibly deny it. After standing outside for a little longer than would have been best, I opened the door and stepped inside.

Immediately, I was warmed up by the two fireplaces out the back. I didn't know if they were real or not, but the difference in temperature was undeniable and it defrosted my fingers which, unfortunately, had caught cold since I had forgotten my gloves. I had only realized they were missing after leaving and since I was already late, I couldn't go back and get them if I wanted to catch the next bus. Rather unfortunate, but I would gladly get to the restaurant faster if it meant my hands got a little colder. I rubbed them together to warm them up and walked forward to greet the hostess.

"Good evening! Welcome to Vinnie's! Do you have a reservation?" she said cheerfully.

"Hello, yes, would there be one in the name of Chloe?" I asked.

"There are actually two reservations with that name tonight, could you tell me the full name?"

Before I could answer, something caught my attention out the corner of my eye, and I looked to the side to see Chloe waving at me. She was pretty far, but I could already tell she had also taken care of what she wore, and it looked like she had done her hair too. I turned back to the hostess and showed her the table Chloe was sitting at.

"Actually, my friend is just over there. The reservation is in her name," I said.

"I understand, but I don't know your friend's name, so I still need you to tell me her full name so I can cross off the reservation," she said. She was very patient with me; I didn't even know why I was so reluctant to say Chloe's full name. I knew it perfectly well, but somehow, I thought saying it out loud would be embarrassing.

"I understand, then it would be Chloe... Miller," I finally said. Weird how names can carry such heavy tolls with them. The hostess smiled, grabbed a menu and invited me to follow her to the table where Chloe was sitting. She wished me a good evening and left Chloe and I alone, the sound of her footsteps gradually becoming weaker and weaker, fading into the background conversations of the other guests.

At first, I was too shocked to sit down, and I stood there, right next to the chair, unable to move. Chloe was looking up at me, her eyes behind her glasses shimmering with happiness. She had done her hair and instead of flowing down her back like it normally did, it was tied up in a ball behind her head that left only one curly strand falling on her left shoulder. It revealed her face a little more and I, rather rudely, kept staring at her in awe. I could only see the top half of her dress, but from what I saw of the dark cloth, she had to be gorgeous. I was enthralled by her entire aura, reinforced by her smile which just made me melt a little in place, and wondered if she thought the same for me. I had carefully chosen what to wear, but I could never reach that level of...sheer beauty.

Why was I feeling like this? I couldn't remember a time where Chloe had dressed up this way for any occasion where I was present and, while the feeling wasn't entirely new, I had no idea how to approach it. Should I comment on it or keep it to myself? Would that be inconsiderate of me or too bold? Was she expecting me to say something? With Camille, it was much different, but now...

"Are you going to sit down or stay standing for the rest of the night?" Chloe asked. I snapped out and looked at her. She had an amused smile just waiting to come out and I felt my face becoming as red as her hair. I quietly sat down as she giggled a little. She stopped after a few seconds and looked me straight in the eyes. "How are you doing, Jack?" she said with a calm and reassuring tone.

"I'm...better. Better than I thought I would be and better now that I'm here," I answered. Even I surprised myself with that answer directly after she had mocked me. I rearranged my chair to be a little more comfortable and looked around the restaurant.

It was a very large restaurant with tables scattered in a square shape around a huge counter in the middle. There, a man was shaking a little container violently and serving drinks to anyone who would request one. A plethora of different drinking glasses could be seen hanging upside down like the most fragile garland. Waitresses came and went with colorful drinks which contrasted with the more monotone and chicer look of the entire building.

The countertops and the tables were all black and completely stood out among the sea of white tiles that made the floor. Out the back, I could see chefs running back and forth, deeply concentrated on their cooking and laying dishes on the counter that separated them from us. A few lamps hanging over the tables provided each one with a dimmed light, reinforcing the closeness between the guests. The aroma floating around the entire building was invigorating, like the conflicting smells somehow came together to form something wonderful. It made my mouth water and my stomach rumble. It was pleasant, but not too overwhelming either like they had planned this somehow. As soon as I sat down, I felt compelled to get closer to Chloe, like the low light level meant I wouldn't hear her from farther away. Almost every table was taken when I looked which surprised me a little even if it was a Saturday night.

"Sure is busy tonight," I commented.

"Well, considering what day it is today, I'd say that's quite normal," Chloe answered. I didn't know what she meant by that and had no idea what day it was. With school and my job, I would often lose track of the actual date and was so much into my routine it didn't really bother me. However, now I was intrigued.

"And what day would that be?" I asked with a little smirk.

"Valentine's Day," she answered without missing a beat. I was left speechless after her answer. I had no idea we were already on Valentine's Day, let alone that it was today, and she had invited me to a restaurant on that day. There could only be one meaning to all of this, but I had to make sure.

"Is it really? I had no idea, with the job and school, I lose track of it sometimes." I paused, trying to come up with the best way to ask my next question. It was surprisingly hard for absolutely no reason at all, but I still felt nervous to even ask. "Did you...plan this?"

"Perhaps," Chloe answered with a smirk. I closed my eyes and smiled at her response. That was typically her, to do something like this without telling me.

"So that's why there are a lot of couples here tonight. It makes so much more sense now. It kind of makes us stand out, don't you think?" I asked.

"Does it?" We both paused for a few seconds. She was looking straight at me, but I couldn't hold her eye contact for very long and turned my head to look away, my heart beating faster and my cheeks becoming red.

"I guess not," I finally said, more to myself, but I knew she heard it.

"Jack," she called out to me. I turned to look at her once more. "I'm really glad you came," she said with the most genuine smile I have ever seen her make. In that moment, she seemed to shine brighter than a star, like she had a glowy aura about her that illuminated the entire room. It warmed me up and I could feel how happy she was even if there was an entire table separating us. I almost didn't know what to respond to such an emotional declaration, but I decided to keep it simple.

"Me too."

◊

"And then, believe it or not, this woman comes back to the counter with something like fifteen movies to rent and she takes them all for three days. How anyone can watch that many movies is beyond me, but it was also her choices that were kind of weird. There was a mix of horror and romance with some documentaries about the flora of some country I don't remember the name of. Anyway, that was the weirdest rental I've ever had."

Chloe laughed a little and took a sip of her glass. Dinner was practically over as we had finished our meals and waited for the staff to take our plates back to the kitchen. The lights had dimmed even further, yet to me, Chloe shone the brightest she ever had despite her black dress. Conversation was flowing and, for a moment, I forgot about anything else that troubled me; school, my job, Camille.

The evening was very nice, and I could almost touch this sort of weird atmosphere floating around the entire restaurant. The way Chloe looked at me the entire night was different than usual; she held my eye contact for longer and I was the one who had to turn away. She stared with a calm confidence that put me at ease, however, and I sometimes felt off since this was the first time, I had experienced something like this.

"Maybe she didn't have a job? Even then, I can't imagine sitting long enough to watch at least five movies a day, that seems completely mad, doesn't it?" Chloe said.

"Well, that's what I mean, I just don't get it. Did she do like a romance night where she binged all the romance movies and then a horror night? No clue how that worked out for her, but she did bring back all fifteen movies exactly three days later saying they were all good," I continued.

"Wow, really?" Chloe's eyes had widened like she couldn't believe it. I couldn't blame her; I didn't believe that woman either when she stepped back into the store. Which was something even weirder as we had a chute directly from outside. I then guessed she didn't want to put in fifteen movies one by one and opted to drop them on my counter instead.

"Yeah! I'm telling you, weird customer. Did I never tell you about that one? I was so sure I did."

"No, you didn't. I'm pretty sure I would have remembered someone like her," she laughed.

"Definitely," I said with a little smirk that Chloe answered in a similar fashion.

We did have some sort of chemistry going on and I felt at ease for the first time in a while. Last time I was this comfortable was probably when she slept in my bed a few weeks back, though the morning after wasn't quite as nice. The note came back in my mind, and I saw the little bunny clearly as if it was floating right in front of me. If I stretched my hand, I could grab it. Then again, there was a folded piece of paper in my pocket. Maybe I could... but when I looked straight ahead, I only found Chloe's eyes hiding behind her black-framed glasses. They were especially beautiful tonight and my mind wandered into them, getting lost in a dark ocean. Chloe smiled, but I could barely see it, as if my vision was blurred.

"Something on your mind?" she asked, amused. I snapped out and stared at her. She suppressed a laugh and regained her composure as best she could, waiting for my answer. I didn't know if I should be embarrassed or not, but I knew I had to talk to her about it.

"Listen, Chloe, um... about the note you left when you came over last time, I..." I started, rummaging through my pocket as I spoke. I didn't have time to finish as Chloe cut me off.

"That was a little slip-up, don't mind it. It didn't mean anything at all." I paused for a second, taking in her answer, but doubting it as soon as I heard it.

"Are you sure? Because it really looked like it meant a lot to you," I asked, concerned. I took out the paper and held it in my hand high enough for her to see. She looked at it for a second and instantly knew what it was. I could see it in her eyes, even if they were trying to hide it. She turned her head and closed her eyes, smiling a little.

"So you kept it, huh?"

"I couldn't throw it away. Not when it meant so much to you."

"No, don't worry, it's fine. It was a spur of the moment thing, and I shouldn't have done it," she said to try and reassure me, but I felt like she was trying harder to comfort herself than me.

"Kind of like tonight, right?" I asked, staring directly at her. She went silent and stared at the floor. I didn't mean it to come out that way and it might have been harsher than I wanted, but there was some truth to what I was saying. I could tell her eyes had started to water as tears formed just behind her glasses. "I didn't mean it like that, I'm sorry. The note and the restaurant tonight, that was no coincidence, was it?"

Chloe didn't answer right away and tried to smile through her sad expression. I never meant for her to react like this, I simply wanted to address the note and its significance. She tried to deny anything, but I knew even she didn't believe her lies.

"I've known you for years, Chloe. I can tell when you lie about something. You didn't mean what you said earlier, did you? You were so confident at the start of the night, where did that go?" I said to try and prod her to talk to me, but she stayed silent, probably trying her hardest not to cry. I felt some looks from all around us and I tried my best to ignore them, but their weight started piling on my shoulders. I didn't want Chloe to cry, ever really, but especially not now. "Chloe, I'm sorry, please don't cry. Can you talk to me?"

Chloe took a deep breath and wiped out the tears from her eyes with the back of her hand. She readjusted her glasses and looked at me. Even with puffy red eyes, she was still as beautiful as ever. I held eye contact with her to support her for as long as she needed.

"I've been in a few relationships now," she started. "I've always been the one confessed to, however, and I have no experience with the opposite side. I've been meaning to tell you for a while now, but I always ended up cowering out and running away from my feelings. The note and the restaurant tonight were both attempts at confessing, but I realize it might have been wrong of me to assume you would understand. Ever since we rekindled, there's been this growing sentiment in me, something I had suppressed before that was now coming back in full force. Dare I say, I felt like the flame truly died when you told me about you and Camille the second time and perhaps it was selfish of me, but I felt happy when you texted me that you broke up again. I know, I'm a horrible person, right? How could I be happy when you were feeling so sad?" She took a deep breath while I sat there, not knowing what to say. Her words were harsh, and I didn't take her for that kind of person. Did she really have an ulterior motive all this time? Did I hold that against her? "Maybe I should have been more truthful towards you from the start, but I didn't want to interfere with your relationship. I lived with this feeling and suppressed it as best I could to let you live your life like you wanted. And it grew more and more as time went on and we talked to each other until it was a little too much to handle. I tried writing it into words, I tried being subtle by inviting you here, but I guess nothing will work better than simply saying it."

She paused to gather her thoughts and looked away shyly. I continued looking at her, waiting patiently for her to finish to take it all in, but the nervous feeling I was so familiar with had started creeping up to grab hold of my heart. I knew what she was going to say, yet I didn't know what I was going to answer. It was like my mind went blank every time I tried to think about it and there was nothing else to do other than listen to every word she had to say. She looked back at me, staring deep into my eyes. I don't know how long we stayed like this, but she finally broke the silence.

"I love you, Jack. I've been running away from this feeling for a long time, but I can't run anymore. I love you and I have been for a long time. I couldn't come to terms with my feelings before, not until the ski trip. I tried to tell you then, but I couldn't." She looked away and took another deep breath. I was still trying to come up with an answer, but I had a feeling she had something else to say so I stayed quiet until she was finished. "Well, the cat's out of the bag. What do you say?" she asked in an emotional voice. She was clearly trying to keep it together, but it was so precarious I felt like anything I would say would make it crumble, good or bad.

"I..." I looked down at the black table, running away from keeping eye contact with her. I started to think about the last few months and our interactions together. The ski trip and when she came to cook at my apartment, how she was against me going back with Camille, how present she was when I felt sad about both of my breakups. She was always there for me, and it must have been difficult for her to sit through me talking about another girl like that. I admired her strength; I don't know if I could have done the same had the situations been reversed. I didn't want to answer in a positive way and make it seem like I pitied her, however.

How did I really feel about Chloe? Was the feeling mutual and I had disregarded it for so long in favor of another? I always did find her beautiful and, when we were younger, I did have a crush on her, but we were kids and best friends. I didn't think we could be something more, even if I wanted to. Now, the opportunity was there, but did the feelings of the past still linger in the back of my heart, locked away somewhere and just waiting to come out? Through everything that happened in my life, she was always there for me, lending me a shoulder to cry on or bringing me along to cheer me up. What did I ever do for her? Was it right for me to pretend like I was as present for her as she was for me? Did I even deserve to be with someone like her? On the other hand, I couldn't exactly ignore what my heart was feeling right now. When she was close to me, it always beat a little faster and I attributed it to me being nervous around my friend, but what if it was something else?

Now that I thought about it, it was different than when I was with Camille. Then, I was enthralled by her, I wanted to be with her all the time, and she would make me crazy just thinking about being alone in a room with her. It was like an urge, coming from deep within, that compelled me to try and get closer to her, to make her happy. With Chloe, however, it wasn't the same. We had known each other for a long time, and I didn't feel that same urge to please her, rather it seemed like we connected on a deeper level. She understood me and I understood her. Sometimes, we finished each other's sentences, we knew what the other was thinking, we could see through the other's lies. We read each other like open books, at least that's what I thought it was until she managed to hide her feelings from me for so long. But did she truly hide them or was I blind and refusing to see the truth? The pain of losing someone, the joy of finding someone; were they truly opposites of the same coin? Was my heart running away from its feelings because my mind said it couldn't be so as somebody else was already occupying that spot?

I looked up to see her face again. There was no trace of crying on her face anymore, just a serene expression, a calm demeanor just waiting for me to answer. Her hair flowing down her shoulder, her mouth forming a little smile, her cheeks puffing up near her slender nose, her eyes staring back at me in a comforting way. I knew then what the answer was. It was the same all along, and I knew it perfectly well, I was just hesitant for a reason I couldn't exactly identify. Perhaps I didn't want to ruin our friendship if I rushed into a relationship with this girl sitting across from me, but every fiber of my being now wanted to be with her, to experience another side of her that she never showed me and to reveal the same to her. She had waited patiently for my answer, and I didn't want her to wait any longer.

"I love you too, Chloe. I think I have been for a long time too, but I couldn't admit it, both to myself and to you." Chloe started to cry again, silently and with a smile on her face. "No, don't cry, why are you crying?" I asked, on the verge of tears too.

"I'm just so happy," she said, closing her eyes. "So happy we could finally tell each other what we've been feeling all this time." I nodded in agreement with her, at a loss for words. She waited a long time before continuing, pausing to let her tears dry and her voice return to normal. "What do you say we get out of here and go back to my place? I think we have a lot to talk about," she proposed.

I was a little stunned at her questions as I didn't take her for that type of person, but I guessed that was another side of her I knew nothing about. We quickly paid for our meals and went outside to take a bus back to her apartment. The trip was a little embarrassing as we were dressed up nicely and sitting down in a rocky bus and multiple people were staring at us with judgemental eyes, but I could barely notice them. I was holding Chloe's hand for the first time since we were teenagers, but now it had a whole other significance. This wasn't just some normal handholding, this meant a lot more, this was the culmination of our feelings for each other in the simplest gesture possible. After a trip that seemed to take ages, we finally got off the bus and quickly made our way to the building, through the door and up the stairs to her place. She quickly unlocked the door and dragged me inside, telling me to keep quiet. Before I was literally pushed inside her bedroom, I managed to see there was another pair of shoes by the entrance. They didn't look like the type of shoes Chloe would wear and I was about to ask before getting cut off as she closed the door behind her, leaving both of us in the dark of her bedroom. She hastily flung the light switch up, temporarily blinding both of us as the lamp on the ceiling turned on. I closed my eyes shut and waited to get accustomed to the sudden brightness of the room, but Chloe was faster than me and took my hand to drag me away from the door while I was still blind. Gradually, I blinked to regain my sight and saw Chloe's face right in front of me. She was really close to me, closer than I thought she was, and I backed off, surprised to see her appear so suddenly. She laughed a little and kept smiling at me while I was probably staring in confusion.

"You don't have to be so nervous, Jack."

"You're the one that dragged me in here so fast. What was up with that? Were those your shoes?"

"Um... I... No, I live with a roommate," Chloe hesitated before confessing. "Her name is Elizabeth, but everyone calls her Beth."

"Well, I would be glad to meet her, so can we just..."

"No!" I was stunned by the harshness of her response. That was an unusual tone for Chloe, she was always calm and somehow this was enough to break her demeanor. I was intrigued, which probably wasn't her intention, but I would respect her wishes if she wanted me to stay relatively hidden. "No, she can't know you're in here. She... doesn't like when I bring boys over," she whispered.

"So, like, you're not allowed to bring friends either?" I whispered back.

"She is very protective of me on that front. I know, it's weird. She's been like that ever since I knew her."

"Maybe it would be best if we went to my place, then? Why are you breaking the rules all of a sudden? Especially since we have an alternative," I proposed.

"I need to be in my own things to process what we said in the restaurant. Why don't you say we move on to the bed? I think we'll be more comfortable if we sit down to talk. Just keep your voice down," she said, gesturing towards the relatively big bed tucked against the wall. I agreed and took off my boots before climbing onto the sheets right beside her.

Now that I was here, it finally dawned on me what was said back at Vinnie's. In the moment, I said what I said out of pure emotion, even if it took me a while to answer and I had to think about it. It was something in the future, like a ship sailing towards a not-so-distant island. It hadn't arrived yet, but I could see the destination. Now, sitting in Chloe's bed, her red hair overflowing from her shoulder to mine, our thighs touching and the heat of her body warming mine, it felt like I was in a dream. Back when I was with Camille, I would have been a nervous ball and I remembered the first time I was in her bedroom alone with her. I completely panicked and ended up running away from her house. Strangely, I wasn't reacting the same with Chloe; I was a lot calmer and stable than I was before. There was still a hint of nervousness hidden deep inside, just waiting to come out, but I could manage to suppress it if I tried hard enough. I wondered if she felt the same as me or if she was like I was back then. I didn't want to put her on the spot and ask her, though, as I felt this would probably worsen the problem if she really was like me. I hadn't realized, but we had been staring at her bedroom wall for a minute now in complete silence, probably both lost in thought as we tried to figure out where to go from here. She was the one who broke the silence.

"Listen, Jack, I know this is probably a little hasty. You've only just broken up with Camille a month ago and I don't want to force you into anything you don't want to do. I know it affected you a lot and it wouldn't be fair to me if I was just a rebound for you. Do you truly want to be with me right now?"

I had to think about that one for a moment. Not that I didn't have an answer, but I needed to put it in a way she could understand. This probably wouldn't make me look the best way, but I at least wanted to clarify my stand in all of this.

"It is quick in the sense we broke up only a month ago. However, this was the second time and, while I did cry when it happened, I was fine with it relatively soon after. Why is that? I don't really know, maybe it has to do with me having already mourn the relationship and the second time we got together was a desperate attempt to get back what we had. It was doomed to fail, and you told me that. I would be lying if I told you I didn't think about her from time to time, I don't think that is ever going to go away, at least not anytime soon, but if you're asking me if I'm ready for another relationship? Yes, absolutely and even better if it is with you. You understand me better than anyone and you've been with me with every step I took. There couldn't be a better person for me."

"I still think we should...maybe... take it slow for the time being, don't you think? Wait, why am I saying this? I'm the one who brought you here. I'm sorry, I..."

I looked back at Chloe to see her with an expression I had never seen on her face before. It seemed to be a mix of wanting to cry and something else, her eyes were starting to get misty, and her chin had the occasional small spasm, but no tears fell, and no words were spoken. I couldn't decipher if I said anything wrong or anything to upset her and, despite the lamp being directly over my head, I was left in the dark for a while. Finally, she moved, and I was too slow to react. She practically jumped in my arms and before I knew it, our lips had touched, and we were kissing for the first time.

It felt a little surreal. This girl, whom I had met all these years ago and for whom I had some unassumed feelings for so long, was finally in my arms as we were locked into a deep, passionate kiss. Even if she wasn't the first or the second girl I had ever kissed, somehow, her lips felt the best of all. They seemed a perfect match for mine, not too small or too big, just enough for me to truly enjoy exploring them. She tasted sweet and I didn't know if I was imagining that or if it was because of what she ate in the restaurant, but it made me more excited than it probably should have. She was a really good kisser, not that I had a very large frame of reference, but she seemed to have something that neither Camille nor Violet had, something I couldn't exactly explain while under this wave of emotion. My hand instinctively went to her back and started to explore her body. In a way, it felt wrong to be doing this sort of thing with this girl I knew since high school, like in my mind she still had that innocence she had back then, but she was a grown woman now and it became apparent when my hand found her breasts. I froze when I got to them, uncertain if she was okay for me to do that, but she didn't protest at all, still focusing solely on the kiss we were sharing. I resumed my exploration and gently squeezed it, filling my hand with her chest. My other hand went behind her head and played with her hair. She seemed to like that a lot as she muffled a small moan as I continued to kiss her. We separated for just a moment, just enough for us to catch our breaths.

"I'm really glad we're finally doing this. I didn't know how much I wanted this until..." she whispered into my ear.

"Yeah, me too," I agreed before going back for seconds.

I used my body to gently lower her to the bed and, still with our lips locked, she laid down completely with me now on top of her. I backed off a little to admire her. She had brought both of her hands to cover her breasts as her cheeks had become the same shade as her hair. She was looking away like she was embarrassed about it, and I couldn't help but crack an amused smirk. She had spread her legs just enough for me to fit between them and my hand continued exploring her body. Even if she was fully clothed, I could still feel her warmth and every curve with my hands. Starting from her head, I made my way down her neck and chest, making a few rounds on them before moving on down to her belly. She seemed to be a little ticklish as she jiggled a little and contained a small laugh. I didn't want to break the moment and I moved down towards her thighs. Gradually, starting from the knees, I got closer and closer to her most private place, but before I could get to it, she grabbed my hands, gently but firmly. I looked at her with a confused expression and she stared back at me, behind her glasses, with a stern look on her face.

"Can we save that for another time?" she asked, trying to stay as quiet as she could. I leaned in to get closer to her and both of our breaths sort of instantly synchronized.

"You don't want to?" I asked in response.

"No, that's not it. I'd just like to… not worry about my roommate while we…you know."

"Is she the type to barge in unannounced?"

"That's not what I mean. Like I said earlier, maybe we should take it slow. I know, I'm the one who jumped on you, but I couldn't contain myself. We can continue kissing and stuff, but just… not there, okay?"

"Okay, no problem. I do have to say, those lips do look a little barren right now," I said before diving in to kiss her again. Her cry of surprise got muffled as her lips were taken by mine.

She might not have wanted me to touch her down there, but she sure was rubbing herself on my pants. The feeling wasn't entirely bad for me either and I don't know how long we did it for, but it seemed to go by in an instant. If we had no clothes on, I was pretty sure I would have finished eventually, but the constraints kept me from letting myself go completely. My pants threatened to burst at any moment. I understood Chloe didn't want us to go that far yet and figured she wanted us to keep all of our clothes on, but especially the bottom parts. I continued caressing her body, not wanting this moment to ever end, and felt her do the same. At first, she was shy and had let me do it alone, but now she was fully invested and explored my back and my chest. One time, she brought both of her hands to my cheeks and gave me the deepest kiss of the night. It was really hard to contain myself; neither of the two other girls I had been with had stopped me like she did, but I wanted to respect her wishes and kept myself in check. I gave her chest a good amount of attention and it was still weird to be touching and rubbing them when I had seen them grow over the years. She didn't seem to mind it and twitched a little whenever I passed over her nipples. They were rock solid, and I figured she must have been just as excited as I was. I felt like I was caught up in a storm of emotions and couldn't focus on one at a time. Too many feelings were constantly rushing through my entire body, and I wondered if she felt the same thing as me.

We backed off each other after an unknown amount of time, our breathing rough and quickened, my heart pumping as fast as it could and a smile on both of our faces. She checked the time and showed me. It was starting to get pretty late and if I didn't want to miss the bus to get home, I had better get ready now. Reluctantly, I parted ways with her and got up from the bed. Fortunately, or not depending on the point of view, we had kept our clothes on, and I only had my boots and my coat to put on before I was ready to leave. Chloe opened the door to her room and quickly checked before making a motion with her hand to indicate for me to come. I silently joined her, and we got out. She opened the front door and, just as I was about to leave, the door to the bathroom opened and her roommate got out. She lifted her head up and made eye contact with me. I froze and panicked in place. I didn't know how she would react to my presence after what Chloe had said. An arm dragged me and practically pushed me out the door, snapping me out of my trance and I looked back at Chloe who simply shut the door behind me. I knew she wasn't mad at me or anything, but it still felt bad to get literally pushed out like that. I guessed she had other things to worry about now that Beth had seen us, though. I slowly started walking towards the stairs leading down to the ground floor and could only hear a muffled *Who was that?* from a voice I didn't know before the sound of Chloe's apartment faded completely.

I didn't regret what we did at all, and I just hoped Chloe would be fine, but I had no idea the range of Beth's temper. Was she going to take it well? Were they going to change the rules? Was she about to explode on Chloe? None of these questions had answers and, while I couldn't stop thinking about it, worrying would do me no good. I simply walked to the nearest bus stop and waited for something, anything coming from Chloe to indicate she was fine. The bus came and I got on, both anxious about her and glad we had spent the evening like we did. I was completely mentally exhausted, but I couldn't stop thinking about everything; the restaurant, the confession, the evening and now the roommate. Were we official now? Normal friends don't really kiss and caress each other the way we did, but we never actually answered that question. I wanted to ask, but now didn't feel like the right time so I buried that question as deep as I could to try and forget about it. Halfway through the bus ride home, I received a text message from Chloe.

Everything's fine, I managed to calm her down, but we're going to have to go somewhere else next time. She actually asked me if we... did it. That was soooo embarrassing.

I smiled a little and answered we could go to my place next time and she agreed. I hesitated to ask the one question still lingering in my head, but I ultimately decided against it. I just wanted confirmation, but at the same time, her actions spoke louder than words. If she let me do the things I did this evening, then she most likely thought we were official too. She was my girlfriend.

My girlfriend.

The thought still didn't sink in for some reason. Chloe was always there in my life, always right next to me, always walking by my side through whatever was going on at the time. To be now holding hands while walking next to her still felt a little surreal. Passengers on the bus must have thought I was crazy as I couldn't stop smiling to myself for seemingly no reason.

There was a reason. A very good reason and her name was Chloe.

Chapter 22

We both agreed to keep our relationship as private as possible when it came to school. Not that we were embarrassed to show everyone the feelings we had for each other, but we judged it best to not go around and shout it on rooftops either. We would talk a lot during downtime between classes and generally hang out together, but nobody would find us kissing in an alleyway between lockers or anything of the sort. It was both easy and hard to do as every time I looked at her, I wanted to express my love for her, I wanted to kiss her right then and there. The feeling sort of confused me in the beginning because I never experienced that strong of an attraction when I was with Camille. With her, I realized it was more of an extension to the huge crush I had rather than this completely different feeling I was living with Chloe. To have to supress that urge was something I didn't think I would have to do. Seeing as we were in the same classes, we usually tried to sit next to each other. Was that a good or a bad thing? It made it very hard to concentrate sometimes and I would have to really focus on the teacher at the front of the class instead of the beautiful girl sitting next to me.

I crossed Camille a few times in the corridors but we both avoided eye contact and refrained from saying anything. Deep in my heart, I still had a tingle whenever we passed each other, like a fraction of me was still longing for her, but it was a lot easier to let it go than a few months ago. It sometimes amazed me how fast I had moved on from the void she had left, even if I was the one responsible for it last time. It was like we both chose to forget about each other, healing in our own way, and perhaps that was for the best. After all, I didn't want to impose those kinds of thoughts on Chloe as that wasn't fair to her, but they were also damaging to me. When I left Camille, I went back into a very dark place and Chloe was the one who pulled me out of it. I didn't want to go back there, not again and not ever, even if that was probably a little idealistic of me. For now, though, things seemed to go back to what some people would refer to as 'normal'. I didn't think my stories of the heart were that extraordinary and I was pretty sure other students had those problems as well, but it was something we collectively decided to keep to ourselves. I was simply following the trend.

A few weeks had passed since Chloe officially became my girlfriend. I still couldn't quite believe how it happened but smiled every time I thought back on that evening at the restaurant. Admitting my feelings to her took a weight I didn't even know I had off my shoulders and I felt myself relax for the first time in weeks or even months. Since then, we usually saw each other a few times every week, except this one. I had a secret project I was working on, and I didn't want her to see it until it was finished, which annoyed her a lot. She kept pestering to see me, wanting to come over to my place and since things were still a little on the edge regarding her roommate and her apparent dislike of boys in their apartment, I had to keep declining. It pained me as well to not see her, hold her and kiss her for a while, but I figured it would be worth it in the end. She had a hard time seeing it that way.

The final class of the day would end soon, and I shot a glance at Chloe sitting next to me. She noticed me looking and her head turned to look at me. Behind those black glasses, her blue eyes had a glint of mischief behind them. Why that was, I had no idea, but it felt like she knew what I was going to ask before I spoke a word. Regardless, I leaned in closer to her to whisper.

"Would you want to come over tonight?" I asked. A big smile instantly appeared on her face, and she enthusiastically nodded. She extended her hand towards me, and I gladly took it, both of us hiding under the desk so no one else could see.

The final few minutes seemed excruciatingly long. How could time pass so quickly when you had fun and so slow when you waited for something? Of course, it was all about perception, time didn't go faster or slower, but it still took ages for the teacher to wrap up the class and let us all go. Chloe practically floated out of the classroom with me hastily following her. It felt like I was chasing a little rabbit that didn't want to be caught. It made me think of the bunny drawings she made in my notebooks back when we were in high school. She had started doing it again and I would find them in the most unusual of places now. She was way more creative about their placement since we became official, but when it used to annoy me, it now made her cuter in my eyes. I liked that little quirky side of her and silently hoped she would display it even more than she was. We separated for a moment, both going to our lockers to get dressed before going outside. The weather was a little warmer than it was a few weeks ago, seeing as February would soon come to an end, but the cold air was unrelenting. A good winter coat was still very much needed at this time of year, and I longed to be able to go outside in just a shirt, but that would still take a few months to arrive. We met up just outside the school. The oak tree in the center of the small plaza had lost all its leaves, but it still towered over us like a giant looking at a colony of ants. Even with none of them, it still had some sort of charm to it that I couldn't quite explain. For all we knew, trees in winter looked dead and they would only come back to life in the spring. What was so different about this one? I still didn't like winter as a season, but this one wasn't so bad after all.

We made our way through the snow-tapped paths leading away from the school. It wasn't that late, but the sun had almost already passed the horizon and colored the sky in an orange tint, indicating the imminent approach of the night. If there was a time of day I found quite beautiful, it was surely twilight. Everything seemed to change during it, it was kind of eerie but also calm and peaceful. I couldn't quite explain it, but it somehow calmed me when I looked up to see clouds of white turned into giant orange and pink slashes across the blue sky. A muffled voice brought me back down to earth.

"It feels like we haven't seen each other after school in forever! What was up with that, huh?" Chloe asked while giving me a small jab on the shoulder.

"Hey, don't hit me, I had barely anything to do with it. Plus, you shouldn't hit me or else you won't get your surprise," I teased back.

"There's a surprise for me! What is it?" she said, suddenly jumping up and down and clapping with her hands.

"If I tell you…" I started.

"Then it won't be a surprise, I know, I know, but I still want you to tell me!" she insisted.

"Not happening," I answered, not intending to budge even a little to her demands.

"Oh, come on. You had to tease me like this now?" Chloe whined.

"Would you have preferred me to tell you a few days ago?"

"No, I guess not," she grumbled. "You had better deliver, mister, or else I'm going to get mad."

"I could almost be scared by that threat if it wasn't for your adorable tone," I said.

"What do you mean? I'm not adorable," she pouted.

"Sure," I answered with a laugh. She soon joined me as we kept walking to the bus stop.

The bus came earlier than it should have, and we barely caught it in time. Fortunately, there were seats available, which wasn't usually the case at this hour, but we figured it might have been because it was early, and people missed it. Regardless, we sat down next to each other, and Chloe rested her head on my shoulder. Both Camille and Chloe had done so, but there was something different about when Chloe did it. Was it because she was my current girlfriend or was it something else? I wasn't quite sure, but that simple gesture was enough to warm me up in these cold winter days. She would do it more often than Camille too, perhaps it was because she trusted me more than Camille had, but I was glad she did it anyway. The feeling of her head on my shoulder, even if we had multiple layers of clothing on, communicated our love as clear as a kiss or a hug. To me, anyway, it was the same thing, the same symbolic representation of her feelings for me. It made me wonder how I was never the one to do it, she was always the one leaning on me. Did she ever wish for me to or was she fine with how things were right now? It wasn't that I didn't want to, but she was usually faster than me and instantly cuddled up like this whenever she had the chance. My hand went down her side and brought her closer to me. Just touching her and holding her was enough for me. I closed my eyes and let the bus slowly rock us to a calm state. I enjoyed being close to Chloe like this and I was sure she did too as she didn't protest at all until, I had to signal us to get out. She grumbled a little as she grabbed her bag and got up to walk to the doors. They opened soon after and we stepped foot on the cold snow covering the ground. It wasn't a long walk to my apartment, but we still had to make it there.

For Chloe, that didn't seem to be an issue as she instantly recovered her enthusiasm when she remembered I had a surprise for her. She tugged on my arm for me to go faster and I couldn't help but smile. Sometimes, she really felt like a little child in a carnival, but I simply found her cute whenever she did stuff like this. Even if she was a grown woman, she managed to let go and have fun like the little girl she used to be. I wished I could do the same, but my brain could never quite stop thinking like she seemed to be capable of. When we arrived in front of my apartment building, she opened the door so fast I thought it would shatter on its hinges. She climbed the steps at the speed of lightning, three at a time, and was impatiently waiting in front of my door for me to open it. Even if she had a key, she waited for me to get there, and I silently thanked her for it. Through all her eagerness, she kept her principles, and I couldn't help but smirk and laugh a little as I passed her. The door lock clicked, and, with a creak, the door opened. I stepped inside and went forward enough for her to pass. I turned around and she was still in the corridor, jumping up and down slightly, like a dog waiting to be let in. I closed my eyes in amusement and signaled her to come with my head and she couldn't contain her excited voice as she came in. The door creaked again as I closed it, leaving us both alone in my otherwise quiet apartment.

Chloe hung her coat and took off her boots at the speed of light and sprinted to the living room, seemingly searching for something. She spun in place a few times, her head frantically turning to examine every corner of the room. When she realized nothing was there, she went straight back to the kitchen and continued her search there. I couldn't contain a laugh and it made it a lot more difficult to take off my coat and boots to join her. We almost bumped into each other when I turned the corner as she was leaving the room to go scout another. I managed to stop her by holding her shoulders and she looked at me in the eyes. They appeared to be glowing, like a child let loose in a candy store, and I smiled at her. I tried to take an exasperated look, but I don't know if I succeeded because she didn't calm down at all.

"Where is it?" she asked in an overly excited tone. She couldn't stay in place and tried to get out of my grasp. I let go, not wanting to hurt her, and she stayed put waiting for my answer. I was surprised in a way, I figured she would just run off to whatever room she was planning on searching next.

"Want me to go grab it?" I asked back. I was starting to get worried about her expectations of the surprise. She was building it up to be something grand, but it was just a little something, not some expensive gift I had bought. I just hoped she wouldn't be disappointed by it by imagining it was something it wasn't. She nodded excitedly at my question, and I sighed while closing my eyes. A smirk appeared at the corner of my mouth, and I opened my eyes back up to see her looking at me with anticipation. "Alright, stay here. No cheating!" I warned. I started to back away and she kept eye contact with me until I turned the corner towards my bedroom. For some reason, I was compelled to go faster than I wanted and practically sprinted to my closet. Before I entered the room, I peeked over at the kitchen to see if she was coming or not. There were no signs of her. I opened the closet door as quietly as possible and took out a small bag. I took another look at it even if I had seen it plenty of times in the past few days. There was paper stuffed everywhere that concealed what was inside as best I could, but I wasn't the best at that kind of stuff and even I could tell it was clumsily put together. Regardless, I turned around and was surprised to see Chloe standing in the bedroom door frame, staring at me, caught with her hand in the cookie jar. She tried to back away, probably hoping I didn't see her.

"You can come out, I saw you," I said to the wall. Chloe came into the room, not the least bit guilty she was caught, but even more restless than before. How that was even possible, I had no idea, but she kept staring at the bag I was holding. "You couldn't stay put, could you?"

"I'm sorry, but you know me. I go crazy when it comes to gifts, I couldn't just wait in the kitchen for you. Will you forgive me?"

"Depends. Why don't you go sit on the bed for a second?" I said. She almost pushed me to the side as she rushed past and, just as I turned around, she was already sitting, back as straight as a plank, head turned towards me. I smiled and walked over to be just in front of her, slowly handing her the bag. For someone as clearly excited as she was, she took it surprisingly softly from my hands and, before touching anything, she looked up at me as if to ask permission. I nodded silently and she smiled before ripping away the paper covering the top of the bag. I was relieved she didn't pay much attention to it. I didn't have time to think much before she took out a small box wrapped in reindeer-covered paper. She held it, both amused and pondering what the occasion was.

"You've been so helpful to me these past months and I felt really bad I didn't get you anything this Christmas when you came over and helped me so much. I wanted to try and give you something in return for that," I said, answering her silent question.

"Aww, you didn't have to, Jack. I helped you because I care about you, not because I wanted something in exchange," she said.

"I know. I just wanted to repay the favor somewhat. Why don't you open it to see what's inside?" I proposed while gesturing towards the box.

She attacked the wrapping paper easily as I clumsily had left plenty of space around the folding for her to rip it open. A standard brown box was revealed under, and she gently took it out of the paper and examined all the sides. There were no labels of any kind, I had made sure of that before wrapping it, and she was clearly intrigued by its contents. She made short work of the tape used to close the box and practically tossed the covers aside to finally see what was inside. A confused look passed on her face as she took hold of the strange wood contraption and held it over the box.

It was some sort of rack with ten holes in it held up by a pole on each side that allowed it to balance back and forth. A sturdy base made sure it wouldn't move when balancing it, but she seemed to be lost on what it actually was. Chloe looked at me puzzlingly, silently asking me what it was.

"It's a spice rack for… well, your spices. I know you like cooking and you often said you needed something to organise your things better. Well, there you go, now you have something to put them in."

"Oh wow, where did you get this? I've been searching for something like this everywhere."

"I…um… made it myself with one of my friends," I answered, now a little embarrassed about it.

Chloe looked at me as if she was about to cry. Her smile had turned into some sort of grimace which probably shouldn't have amused me, but it did, and I barely contained a laugh.

"You made this for me?" she asked through a wave of emotions that took over her. She looked down and I couldn't see her eyes anymore, but she was clearly containing herself as best she could. I didn't have to answer her question and I put a hand on her shoulder. She lifted her head and I smiled at her, pointing the bag with my eyes. A surprised expression crossed her face, and she turned around to grab hold of the bag she had put to the side. She rummaged inside and took out another small package. This time, it wasn't in a brown box, and she could see directly it was an assortment of ten different spices directly when she ripped apart the paper. Chloe set it aside and took off her glasses to bury her face in her hands. I could tell she was crying and lowered myself to her level. She felt the motion and looked at me with misty eyes. Even when tears had flooded them, their blue color stood out as if piercing my soul and I got closer to her. She hugged me tightly, tighter than she had ever done, and continued crying on my shoulder.

"Thank you so much. It's beautiful," she managed to say between quick breaths. I gently rubbed her back, still holding her in my arms.

"I'm glad you like it. Why don't we put it to the test tonight?" I proposed. Chloe backed off and nodded silently. I smiled at her and couldn't react as she pulled me in for a kiss. Her lips were somewhat salty from the tears that had flowed there, but I didn't mind it at all. This wasn't just a normal kiss like the ones we had been sharing the past few weeks. This one expressed all her love in the simple gesture, it managed to speak without a sound, and I gave myself in to it. I was relieved she liked her gift that much and congratulated myself in my head for a job well done. I was usually the worst at giving gifts, but something had changed that side of me somehow and the last two I had given were both good hits, or so it appeared to be. Was it because they were gifts to girls I loved? Did that element of it change what was given or did it affect what types of gifts I was choosing to give? Regardless of the answers, Chloe enjoyed it, and she made it perfectly clear she did. When our lips finally parted, I felt bad for wanting more when the intent was never to get a kiss in return, but that feeling immediately went away when I saw Chloe's face beaming with joyful tears.

"Shall we?" I asked and Chloe promptly got up, spice rack and spices in hand, ready to cook the best supper she had ever cooked. She ran past me, leaving me alone and smiling in my room. She could never contain herself when she was this excited, but I was glad she was and swiftly followed her to the kitchen. Whatever we would be cooking, it was surely going to be delicious.

◊

I wasn't the best cook, I knew that perfectly well, but seeing Chloe make magic out of nothing made me feel even worse about my skills in the kitchen. I didn't take it bitterly, though, I was helping as best I could by cutting the different vegetables Chloe was taking out of the fridge and putting in front of me. From where I was, I couldn't see her all the time, but I couldn't help myself from stealing a glance every chance I got, both seeing her excited smile on her face and her butt when she walked away. It made me smile as well; I liked her a lot when she was like this. Simply enjoying herself the best she could and doing what she loved the most.

She would have to teach me how she managed to do the best dishes in the world some time. It fascinated me to see her working, she usually mumbled a little to herself and kept going back and forth between the stove and the countertop, grabbing a hold of what I had cut and preparing some other things herself. She was making some steaks I had bought for the occasion along with a pepper sauce, some rice and a little vegetable medley as well. Everything was smelling so good already and I sometimes surprised myself getting lost in thought from the smell alone.

I imagined we would have been talking a little more than we were. Exchanging a few jabs at each other or telling the other a story or an anecdote, anything really, but apart from small comments here and there, nothing was added. It wasn't our first time cooking together, but it was the first time as a couple. Did that affect it somewhat? Surely, we had plenty of things to talk about now, whenever we saw each other on the evenings or when we talked on the phone, the conversation would last for hours, but here it was like she was so dedicated to making the best dish in the world she didn't have time for anything else. At least she was putting the spices to good use as she had already opened four of the ten plastic containers that were in the bag.

"Were the spices a good idea then? I see you've opened quite a few of them," I asked.

"Oh yeah, I'm going to use them all for sure. It was a great idea!" Chloe enthusiastically answered.

286

"Kind of makes me sad I'll only get to experience them once," I said with a false sadness across my face.

"What do you mean? No, I'm leaving them here. That way, I'll have to come over and cook for you more often," she said with a smile while closing her eyes. She opened them back up quickly and pointed a finger at me. "You don't have my permission to use them, though. Don't even try, I know how much is in each one. If you use them, I'll know and you'll suffer my wrath."

"No, anything but that," I said sarcastically while holding my hands in the air. Chloe literally lunged at me and locked her arms around mine, preventing me from using them. I struggled a little, not really putting any of my strength into it, and she held on, bringing her head closer to my right ear.

"I was being serious," she said in a grave tone. If we didn't have an intrinsic complicity, I might have taken it another way, but I knew we were just playing around and I turned my head to look at her. Our eyes met and, for a second, we simply stared at each other, unspoken words being exchanged as my heart started beating faster.

"So was I," I said softly, just enough for her to hear, but the sound soon got muffled as she put her lips on mine in a passionate kiss. If it wasn't for the hissing sound of the meat cooking in the pan, I might have thought we were somewhere else as my mind wandered away, flying through the apartment and out the window into the cold winter night. Just like her meals, she tasted delicious, and I couldn't stop wanting more, coming back after every smooch. My hands drifted downwards towards her butt cheeks and, as I found them, Chloe muffled a gasp, but I made sure she couldn't get away by attacking her tongue with mine. My hands squeezed her cheeks and brought her closer to me. Even with my arms restrained, I could still manage to tease her a little. Eventually, she backed away from me and looked down at my crotch. The obvious bulge must have pressed on her belly, and I immediately felt a little embarrassed about it. She looked up to meet my eyes and I couldn't hold her eye contact for very long. I did see her bite her lips once before turning away as she did the same, returning to the stove to turn the meat and whisk the sauce. I was left standing in the middle of the kitchen, fully on guard, and wanting a lot more from our little interaction. I smiled and repressed a comment; she sure knew how to turn me on whenever she wanted. I started walking towards the kitchen table to set it for us to eat and, as I passed by her, she spoke to me.

"It should be ready in about five minutes," she said to update me.

"Perfect," I answered, taking out drinks and utensils for both of us and setting them down. I stopped what I was doing to look at Chloe standing in front of the stove for a second. She was concentrated on whisking the sauce and keeping an eye on the meat and vegetables. Whenever she was really focused on a task, she frowned a little, but it made her cuter in my eyes. Her red hair was tied at the back of her head and her shirt and pants met her curves well. She was gorgeous, and she must have felt me staring because she looked in my direction and frowned even more, making me look away while trying to contain a laugh and a smile. Nothing could have made this moment better and I wondered why we hadn't confessed sooner.

◊

I got up and took both of our plates to the kitchen sink to rinse them off. As usual, I was the last one to finish eating, but it didn't bother me much at this point. I was used to it and Chloe didn't comment on it. Her meal was exquisite, the perfect amount of seasoning on every single dish, even the vegetables had something to them I couldn't understand. When I did them, they were bland and flavorless, but she somehow managed to bring out every ounce of flavor in them to make them stand out among the steak and the rice, which were both also perfectly cooked. It was so good we didn't even say much during supper as we always had our mouths completely full.

"How was it?" Chloe asked, still sitting at the table.

"Well, I already told you multiple times, but if you want to hear it again, it was delicious," I answered over the running water. "Especially coming from you."

"Aww, thanks, Jack, that means a lot. It's just a bit of a shame the sauce stuck a little to the pot. Guess I didn't stir it enough," she commented.

"And whose fault was that?" I teased while smirking to myself.

"Oh, excuse me, you liked it just as much as I did!"

"Who knows, maybe even more."

"Yeah, I bet you did," she concluded with an amused tone. I repressed a laugh as I finished scrubbing the two plates and rejoined her at the table. I sat back down, both of us looking at the other with content smiling faces, not saying another word and simply being happy to be in each other's presence. After all the hardships of the past months, it felt good to be simply living in the moment and truly enjoying something for once. My mind brought back past events like the breakup and Camille showing back up at my work and I silently chased those thoughts away. Why did my brain have to do this to me whenever I felt happy? Couldn't it just enjoy the moment and stop bringing up the past at the worst times? Chloe put her hand on mine, and I snapped out of it. Her smile immediately cleared the cloudy skies of my mind and brought out the sun, shining just as much as she was. I dreaded the moment she was going to leave for the night, leaving me alone in this apartment of mine. When she was here, it radiated light and joy, but when she left it returned to a sad state of silence and pointless thoughts. I liked having her here, not only to take my mind off things I didn't want to think about, but also because she managed to transform what was around her into a better state of themselves, especially me. I didn't know if she was secretly a mind reader or if she had godlike intuition, but she seemed to know exactly what I was thinking when she asked her question.

"Do you…want me to stay over tonight?" Her cheeks turned red and her grasp on my hand tightened just a little. Could she have read my mind? Did she have superpowers I didn't know about? I could tell she was embarrassed about asking, but it was so relieving to me she did, I didn't really pay attention to what she was feeling after that.

"I would be very happy if you did," I answered. She looked at me with relief as well behind her black glasses and her hand shifted to lock into mine. I motioned towards the living room with my head, and she simply nodded to give her approval. We moved to the couch and sat down next to each other, just as we had before, but now it was different. We weren't sitting as friends, but as a couple and that completely changed the dynamics between the simple action of being beside one another. I slumped down a little and she rested her head on my shoulder. I really enjoyed that feeling and we put on something meaningless on the TV in front of us. Whatever was playing didn't matter one bit to me, it was about spending time cuddling up with Chloe, this girl I knew since high school who was now my girlfriend. I was sure she felt much of the same, but we didn't need to speak another word to know.

As time went on, she started to lie down on me more and more and I kept scooting over to the left to give her more space on the couch. Eventually, she had her head resting on my thigh but hovering dangerously close to my crotch. I tried to play it off, but I would be lying to myself if I said I wasn't getting at least a little excited by it, even if it was nothing. When I was a teenager, I used to get hard at the worst possible times and I silently wondered if I was back in that time. Hoping she wasn't feeling it, I didn't say anything and kept on watching the TV with a blind eye.

"You know, this pillow is pretty comfortable, but there seems to be some sort of rod in the middle of it. Really makes it hard to relax properly," she teased. I froze for a second as the realisation set in; she had clearly felt it and there was nothing I could do about it now. Just to make matters worse, it somehow got a will of its own and twitched a little, thankfully contained inside my pants.

"I'm really sorry about this, I didn't mean to…" I apologized. I was really embarrassed and felt my face getting hotter by the second. She didn't waste any time in responding, however.

"I'm kidding, I know you don't fully control them," she laughed. "Having perverse thoughts about your girlfriend, are you?"

"I'm not having perverse thoughts," I said, defending myself unconvincingly.

"Don't lie to me, I know. It's perfectly fine, I'm not offended by it. I'm just really going to have to…" she stopped herself as she moved her head around back and forth right over my member. I sighed heavily and groaned a little as she snickered amusingly at me. I could have reached down to touch her as well, but I remembered what she said last time, and I ultimately decided against it. I always thought she would tell me explicitly, but was this her way of saying she was ready to take it to the next level? I didn't think it would be wise to press her into doing something she didn't want, not that I could force her even if I wanted to, but I still opted to be cautious about the whole subject. She could tease me all she needed and, even though it took a lot of restraint to not act on any of it, I would manage myself to avoid doing something I would regret.

We went to bed sometime later and, while I normally don't sleep on my back, when she leaned into me and rested her head on my chest, I knew I couldn't move anymore. I passed my arm around her and down her back, bringing her closer to me. The feeling of her skin on mine was still something I wasn't quite used to. She slept in her shirt and panties, but even with a layer of fabric between us, I felt her breasts like she wasn't wearing anything. Her legs had intertwined with mine and our closeness warmed us both in the chill night. Her arm was resting on my chest, but it suddenly slowly went down and kept going until it hit what it searched for. I contained a moan, not wanting to wake her up, but I couldn't help but open my closed eyes. I shot a glance at her head and noticed she had moved to look up at me. Even though she didn't have her glasses, her face was still just as beautiful and, through the darkness, I could only see her smirking at me.

"Why are you doing this to me?" I whispered not to break the stillness of the night.

"I don't know, I just felt like it," she answered in a similar tone. "Good night, Jack," she said as she stretched a little more to give me a quick kiss on the lips as her hand retreated to its previous position. I was left surprised by the gesture and by what just happened.

It was difficult to sleep with all these thoughts rummaging through my mind. Were those signs she was ready or was she just teasing for the fun of it? Now that we were a couple, she could do things to me she wouldn't do before, so was this her way of finally expressing all her pent-up emotions she had accumulated over the years? Was I reading too much into it? She didn't make another movement like that for the rest of the night and, a few minutes after her teasing, her breathing slowed down and was a little more rhythmic, signaling she had fallen asleep. It took me a long time, but I did manage to enter the dream world as well. It was the first time we had slept so close together and, while it made me happy, it didn't affect my dreams at all as they were just as scarce as before.

Chapter 23

I don't know how she managed to do it, but Chloe eventually convinced Beth to meet me in person, properly this time. I was supposed to go to their apartment and have supper with them and maybe spend the evening there before going back home. Classic first meeting, one would assume, but I was incredibly nervous about it. The whole thing about Beth disliking boys coming over made me anxious about being around her. What would she say to me? Would she back out of the evening and push me out? I didn't even want to think about how Chloe felt at the moment. She was stuck between us, living permanently with Beth and being in a relationship with me. If we couldn't agree on anything, it would make Chloe's life a lot harder than it needed to be and I didn't want that to happen at all costs.

On the way there, I kept practicing ways to introduce myself, ways to be quick about it but tell her just enough so she wouldn't be suspicious of me or anything of the sort. It was probably silly and I felt stupid even if I wasn't practicing aloud. At least I could rely on Chloe and lean on her if conversation wasn't flowing right or if Beth had any problems with me. That reassured me a little, but the façade came off as soon as I got in front of their apartment building. Something about it appeared intimidating now. It towered over me, it seemed to lean in to crush me and I couldn't stop staring at it. The walkway to get to the door looked infinite, I couldn't move a muscle and yet, I somehow got inside. I climbed the stairs at a snail's pace, the anticipation growing bigger and bigger and dragging me down along with it. Why was I so nervous about this? Worst case scenario, Beth wouldn't like me and Chloe and I couldn't meet anymore at her apartment. Was that such a big deal? Did I absolutely need to win her approval? I clearly didn't, but there was definitely something hidden deep in me that wanted her to acknowledge me. Maybe after meeting me, she would change her mind about boys and I could visit Chloe whenever I wanted without it having to be such an event every time. I got in front of the door and couldn't knock. I stood there for a few moments, heart beating as fast as it could, with me staring at a plank of wood directly in my face. I had to knock or else they wouldn't know I had arrived. I had to knock, but I couldn't move my arm up. I had to knock, I just had to knock.

My fist hit the wood three times and I backed away, perhaps a little too much, as I was now a few steps away from the door. I heard some shuffling coming from behind it and soon, it opened to reveal a familiar face. Chloe's face radiated as a smile formed on it, melting some of the doubts that had frozen my heart.

"Jack, you're here! Come on in!" She paused and blinked a few times as I didn't move at all. "What are you doing all the way over there?" she asked.

"Oh, I um…" I tried explaining myself, but the words just wouldn't come out right and she interrupted me before I could finish a coherent thought.

"Never mind that, come in," she gestured with her hand to signal me to approach. I managed to put one foot in front of the other and eventually entered the apartment. The smell coming from the kitchen immediately hit me. Whatever she was cooking, it would be delicious, I could already tell. "Alright, just make yourself at home and join us in the kitchen. I already got some stuff on the stove, so I have got to go take care of that," Chloe explained as she was walking away.

"It smells amazing, by the way," I said, taking off my shoes. I looked around the apartment a little, trying to get my bearings.

"Thank you," she said from the kitchen, her voice somewhat muffled by the sound of her cooking.

Last time I was here, it was darker than this and I couldn't really see anything, but now that it was earlier in the evening, the sun hadn't quite set on the horizon yet. It was a completely normal apartment, nothing fancy and nothing weird to report. I don't know what I expected, but it somewhat surprised me. Maybe I thought Beth, with her weird uneasiness with boys, would decorate with a little more girly charm, but that was obviously wrong. I sighed, trying to calm down before joining them. Beth was probably in the kitchen already, sitting at the table, just around the corner. It felt like I was about to be judged for a crime when I didn't even know what I did. Did I even do anything wrong? Perhaps it was simply because I was a guy? After another few calming breaths, I walked over and entered the kitchen.

The smell was even stronger in there. It immediately attacked my nostrils and filled them with the exciting prospect of a delicious meal cooked by none other than my girlfriend. She was standing in front of the stove and whisking some kind of sauce while other things sizzled in a pan next to her. My eyes scanned the room from her to the table on the right and, there, someone else was sitting down, staring at her phone. Chloe noticed me enter and turned around.

"Jack, this is Beth. Beth, this is Jack."

"Nice to meet you," I said towards Beth. She barely lifted her eyes from her phone to stare at me with a look of exasperation and returned to her screen. I stood there, confused at her lack of response to such a trivial presentation, but there was nothing else I could do so I sat down on the nearest chair.

"Supper should be ready in a couple of minutes," Chloe said, having returned to managing the stove top. I silently thanked her for her appropriate timing. Things were already awkward as they were, I didn't want to envision what it would have been like to sit there for thirty minutes waiting for supper to be done with Beth just staring at her phone. She was clearly not receptive to conversation and I wasn't the best at starting one with a complete stranger. Regardless, I had to try and make this a little less weird between us.

"So, what do you do for work?" I asked, trying the first topic that came to mind. It might not have been the best one, but I couldn't think of anything else. Beth just stared at me with intense eyes and didn't answer the question. She eventually looked away in annoyance and returned to her phone. I smiled awkwardly to myself and looked down at the table. It was going to be one of those evenings, I could already tell. Well, when Chloe would be done cooking, she could at least build a makeshift bridge between us so conversation at least flowed a little. For now, though, I didn't want to attempt another ice breaker and just kept silent, occasionally responding to Chloe's brief questions like how my day was and the likes. Beth didn't utter a single word during that entire interaction and I was beginning to think she might have been mute and Chloe didn't think to mention it.

She served us our plates and sat down in between us. I was facing Beth directly and she finally put down her phone to look at the food. With a smile, she turned to Chloe.

"It looks amazing, as always. I don't know how you do it, honestly," she said. Well, there went the mute explanation.

"Oh, it's nothing. This is one of Jack's favorites so I thought this might be a good way to introduce him," Chloe responded.

"Is it? That's kind of a boring dish to have as a favorite, isn't it?" Beth commented.

"I don't think it's boring, as long as it's delicious, right?" Chloe said before I could intervene.

"I… guess," Beth said before starting to eat. I silently started my own plate, reassured by the skill of Chloe's cooking. If anything was comforting on this evening, it would be the quality of the food as it didn't appear to be possible for Beth and I to connect even slightly.

"It's amazing, Chloe. Really good," I said after a few bites. My comment seemed to annoy Beth and she perked up on her chair ever so slightly. Chloe might not have noticed as she was sitting between us and facing another way, but I was directly across from Beth.

"Thank you, Jack," Chloe said with a smile in my direction. "Coming from you, that means a lot."

"I can't believe you managed to cook the dish so well, I mean the flavors all come around beautifully. It's like you make magic when you're in the kitchen," Beth added. She was completely over-the-top with her description, and I was left baffled at her comment. What was she trying to pull here?

"Alright, alright, no need to praise me this much. I'm glad you both like it, that's all that matters," Chloe laughed while taking another bite.

Beth seemed to mutter something under her breath, but I couldn't catch it and Chloe didn't comment on it so I figured she must have not caught it either. I was really confused about the whole exchange. It felt like Beth was trying to undermine my comment with hers, but I couldn't figure out why. What was the point of that? She could have just said she liked the dish too, why did she need to make it appear like I didn't appreciate it the same way she did? I didn't say anything, and I tried to hide it on my face, but judging from our earlier interactions, I was a little weirded out by her attitude and general behavior. What was she trying to prove?

It didn't get better as we ate supper. Beth only seemed to want to talk to Chloe and ignored me whenever possible, answering with the smallest sentences and only when she had to. She kept bringing the conversation back to Chloe, sometimes completely cutting me off. It was really annoying, but since Chloe didn't comment on it, I didn't want to make a fuss either and kept to myself. She tried to bring me into the conversation too, but Beth would always dismiss me when I tried to talk. I wasn't against making some efforts to get to know her, but when Beth did everything in her power to exclude me from literally anything, it was hard to find the will to push forward. I sent a few desperate looks at Chloe which were answered by much of the same and I could tell she was sorry about Beth's attitude, but there wasn't anything she could do except call her out on it. She tried to do just that earlier, but Beth denied it completely and changed the subject. It was tiresome, to say the least, and a part of me was hoping this evening would end as fast as possible or she would change attitude which seemed a little too hopeful. When we were done, Chloe gathered all our plates to put them in the sink and cleaned up the kitchen area from her cooking. Beth resumed her phone scrolling, leaving me alone again. I talked briefly with Chloe about random stuff, just wanting to avoid being silent and ignored. She eventually finished putting everything away and came back to the table.

"Why don't we play something? Cards?" she proposed.

"Sure," I said. Maybe a game would make Beth more talkative and make her open up a bit more.

"Whatever," she said, eyes still glued to her phone.

"I'll take that as a yes," Chloe said as she got up to fetch the cards. I was convinced by now; I didn't like Beth. Not a single bit. I didn't even understand how Chloe could possibly live with her, she was so unpleasant to be around and just disrespectful. Was she always like this or was it because I was here? How could the presence of one guy turn her into this mess? It was like she had two personalities or something. Truly bizarre, but I would still give her a chance to redeem herself. Maybe, just maybe, the cards would make her talk more. That was a long shot, but it was worth a try. She didn't even sound like she wanted to play, why even bother being here when she clearly didn't want to? Just let Chloe and I do our own thing and leave us alone. I was interrupted by Chloe coming back and sitting down, a few packs of cards in her hands.

"So, what do you want to play?" she asked to both of us.

◊

We had played a few rounds already before I ended another one by showing my winning hand. Chloe sounded disappointed as she was really close to winning as well, but I was just a little faster. Beth practically threw her cards at the center of the table with an exasperated grunt. She had been like this the whole evening and since I was winning most games, she got even more and more annoyed after each game. It's not like I was doing it on purpose, I just played the best I could and ended up on top most of the time. Was I supposed to throw the games to make her feel better? Surely, she would notice then and would be even more pissed off at me than she was now. That didn't sound like a great idea to me.

"I'll just make a quick stop at the bathroom. Jack, can you shuffle the cards until I come back?" Chloe said, handing me the cards in a jumbled mess following the game.

"Yeah, no problem," I said, taking them all into my hands to start shuffling. Chloe got up and walked away, leaving me with Beth. At least I had something to do while she was gone. There was an awkward silence that came just as she

296

left, and I had no intentions of breaking it. I started rearranging the cards so they would stack properly. To my surprise, Beth looked directly at me and truly spoke to me for the first time of the evening.

"Alright, listen up." She paused for a moment as I stopped what I was doing, shocked by her intervention "Jack," she said almost with disgust. "I don't know who you think you are, but if you expect to come in here like you own the place, you're dead wrong. I don't like you and I never will. You'd be better off leaving Chloe alone; she doesn't need a guy like you in her life."

"Why are you so hostile towards me? Have I done something wrong or offend you in any way?" I asked, surprised at her sudden attack out of nowhere.

"That's none of your business, okay? You need to back off or else things might get a little nasty," she threatened. I was about to reply, but Chloe came back at the exact moment I was about to speak, and I held back. Beth stared at me for another second, her eyes shooting daggers at me.

"Did you not shuffle the cards?" Chloe asked while looking at me. I realized I had stopped shuffling entirely and cards still stuck out of the deck indicating I hadn't really done anything.

"Yeah, sorry, I was… distracted," I said.

"Alright, well, get on with it," Chloe said with a laugh.

For some reason, I didn't feel like laughing at all. Beth's words kept bouncing in my head, filling me with poisonous thoughts about me, about Chloe, about our relationship. Was it all a lie? Just a façade she put up to make fun of me? That couldn't possibly be it, right? But why would Beth be saying things like this if it didn't come from some kind of truth? Maybe Chloe talked to her behind my back since I wasn't really allowed to come here. They were living together after all. I wanted to hear the words from Chloe herself but wanted to avoid a confrontation at all costs too, so I kept quiet. Chloe gave me a little nudge under the table, and I snapped out of my thoughts, looking at her with confusion. She gestured with her head towards the cards I had been shuffling for a while now and I got the message. I started setting up another game and when I looked up at Beth, she just kept staring daggers at me. I found it odd at the beginning of the evening, but now it made me uncomfortable and anxious. Why did I need her approval so much? If she was against us being together, who cared enough? I shouldn't be caring at all, but the possibility Chloe was in on it shook me a little more than it had any rights to. Regardless, I finished setting up the game and we played for another round.

Why did the cards have to be so in my favor? I was going to win this game as well and I had no desire to. They just kept lining up for me and, quickly, I was one hand away from victory. I wanted to throw it away, I didn't want to win again. If I did, Beth would be mad at me even more than she already was, if that was even possible, and I wanted to avoid that outcome by any means necessary. I was stuck. It was my turn to play, and I could win right here if I just played my cards. I hesitated for a few seconds before passing. I couldn't do it. I looked down at my cards and then at the wall, trying to come up with something to say that would make this less awkward, but of course, nothing came to me. Chloe and Beth kept playing cards from their hands and they were getting close to winning as well. Every time it was my turn, I skipped and let Beth play instead.

"What do you even have in your hand?" asked Chloe. "You've been skipping for three turns now."

"I messed up earlier and can't play on any of your cards. That's what I get for playing too fast," I said, trying to fake laugh, but it wasn't very convincing and even I wouldn't have fallen for it.

"Well, that just means you're plummeting down to the depths of defeat when I play this!" Chloe said, putting down cards on the table. I could play on those and win, but I stopped myself once again and let the turn go to Beth. She only had two cards left, just like me, and played both on Chloe's cards, winning the game. Chloe audibly whined as she was just about to finish as well. She put her cards on the pile at the center of the table and Beth looked at me, not triumphantly like I thought she would, but suspiciously.

"What did you have in your hand?" she asked me. I couldn't tell them the truth or else they would know I threw the game. I had to come up with something convincing that would get her off my back.

"I um… had a 10 and a 2," I lied, hiding the cards I had remaining in the pile.

"That so? Why didn't you play on the 9 I put down earlier then?" she asked with an accusatory tone.

How did she remember all this? I couldn't tell what the last three hands were, how could she possibly recall she put down a 9 and no one played on it? Of course, I didn't really have a 10. Back when she played the 9, I didn't have any single cards, so I didn't play anything because I didn't want to break a good pair. But now, she had caught me in a lie, and I couldn't think of anything to get out of it.

"That's because um…" I said.

"So you threw the game, is that right?" she said, raising her finger at me. I couldn't respond as she continued her verbal attack. "What was your real hand? Why didn't you play like you normally did all night? If there's something that annoys me more than anything, it's people having pity for me. Did you? I bet you did, I bet you threw to make me feel bad, well, guess what? It didn't work and you just made things worse."

"Beth, I…" I tried to say but was interrupted by Chloe.

"Okay, that's enough, Beth," Chloe intervened, getting up and standing next to Beth. "You need to stop."

"Whatever. I'm done."

With that, Beth pushed her chair loudly against the floor and got up, walking past me like a bullet fired from a gun and went straight to her room. The door slammed harder than I thought possible and the sound froze both Chloe and I in place, unable to move, afraid that another one was going to come soon. We looked at each other without saying anything and Chloe mouthed that she was sorry. I didn't know what to do with myself and simply stayed sitting down, trying to process what had just happened. Chloe regained control of herself and went to talk to Beth while I stayed alone in their kitchen, the stack of cards still unshuffled in the middle of the table. On top, a lone King faced up as if to mock me. I certainly didn't feel like a king, that much was certain. If anything, I was a deuce. I distantly heard Chloe trying to talk to Beth, but she had locked her door and refused to come out. Slowly getting up from the table, I had a distressed look around the apartment. These walls, this room, this furniture, it all screamed at me to get out. It was like Chloe and Beth were fighting silently and Beth was clearly winning, chasing me away from this place. The entire apartment exuded Beth's aura, not Chloe's, and it started attacking me. My heart started to beat faster and I audibly breathe louder. What was happening? I had no idea, but I needed to get out. I needed to find the door and get out. I couldn't stay here; I needed to get out. I started walking towards the front door and shakingly reached for the handle. I heard a voice coming from my right and turned to see who it was as I couldn't hear properly. Chloe was looking in my direction and coming towards me.

"Where are you going?" she asked when she got next to me. "You don't have to leave; we can go in my room and hang out for the rest of the night" she proposed. I looked at her with dead eyes, like I couldn't see well.

"I… can't. I can't stay here any longer. I'm sorry."

"What's going on? You don't seem so good, Jack. What's the matter?" she asked, putting a hand on my shoulder. I almost didn't feel it at all. Beth's words resonated in my head. Were they true? Was she just bitter and said things to confuse me? Why would she lie? Was she playing with me? A part of me wanted to tell Chloe right then what Beth had said to me when she was gone, but I couldn't do it. I couldn't bring myself to do it, I didn't even know why, but the words just wouldn't come out even if I wanted to. I looked at her again. Her eyes were concerned, and her grip had tightened on my shoulder like she didn't want to let me go. I absent-mindedly got closer to her and kissed her forehead, something I hadn't done ever before. I backed off and Chloe was clearly confused about the gesture but didn't say anything. We shared another look and her grip loosened as she took her hand off. I turned the handle and got out. I walked forward a little and turned around to see Chloe standing in the doorframe, still probably worried about me simply leaving practically without a word.

"I'm sorry." I apologized again and turned around, climbing down the stairs and disappearing from her view. As I got down to the building's front door, I heard another close upstairs and the sound resonated in the empty staircase. I stood there, contemplating what had just happened and how that affected things. Would it? Would Chloe think less of me because of what I did? I couldn't think straight right now and just exited the building to get further away from all this. I received a text soon after and checked my phone.

Call me when you get home.

That was all she wrote, but I felt her emotions through those words; sadness, confusion, concern. I sighed and continued walking to the nearest bus stop, eager to get back into my own things and have a change of scenery. One thing was made very clear after tonight; Beth didn't like me at all, and I didn't think there was ever going to be a chance to change that. She practically hated me from the get-go, which I still couldn't exactly explain even when I thought about it and wanted nothing to do with me. I felt like I did something wrong, something to piss her off, but I hadn't even met her before tonight so how could I possibly have wronged her before? Was that true? Did I know her from somewhere and forgot? I couldn't remember a single instance, a single memory of her even after thinking about it for a long time. It didn't make any sense. It wasn't fair to me and wasn't fair to Chloe who was stuck in the middle of it. I wondered what could possibly change Beth's opinion about me, but I shook my head. It was pointless to even think about it. Perhaps Chloe would know more and even then, after seeing how she acted just now, that battle was probably already lost.

I got home and sat on my bed, phone in hand and debating if I should call Chloe or not. I didn't have anything to say, nothing to explain, so what would be the point? Maybe hearing her voice would appease me somewhat, maybe she just needed it more than I did. She did ask me to and it wasn't like I didn't want to, but the events of the night still had me a little shook and I couldn't talk about it anymore. Regardless, I dialed the number and brought the phone to my ear.

"You called…" Chloe sighed in relief as soon as the call went through.

"You asked," I answered plainly.

"I was afraid you weren't going to do it. How are you doing? You… What happened?" she asked hesitantly.

"I just couldn't stay anymore. Everything radiated Beth's negativity towards me and it made me have to get out. Can we please not talk about it? I just… want to get my mind off it for tonight."

"Um… yeah, sure. What do you want to talk about?"

"I don't know, you're the one who asked me to call. I just… want to hear your voice."

"If you really wanted to, you should have stayed here."

"I told you, I…"

"I know, I know, I'm kidding. Sorry. Guess that's my way of coping with it, I shouldn't have. Okay, well, let's see. Oh, I know! There was this one guy that came to my shop the other day…" Chloe started.

I wasn't really listening to the story. I just wanted to hear her talk. Maybe I needed it more than I thought as just the sound of her voice calmed me down and washed away the events of the evening, at least for now, and allowed me to think more clearly.

"Chloe," I said, interrupting her story. She paused for a few seconds.

"What?"

"I love you."

"Oh, um, I love you too. Why the sudden confession?"

"I needed to tell you. I'm sorry, continue your story."

"Um… okay, where was I? Right, yes, so the guy looks at me and…"

I fell down on the bed, finally smiling for the first time in ages. I must have fallen asleep on the phone as I woke up some time later, both confused and panicked, still fully dressed in my bed in the dead of night. I quickly checked my phone and the call had ended a long time ago. I only had one new message coming from Chloe.

Think you fell asleep, you pleb. Have a good night <3

I stared at the words for a few seconds. Such simple words that had a very deep meaning. They might have been carelessly written by her after realizing I had fallen asleep, but they meant a lot to me. They chased away some of the doubts that had crept back up with Beth's words and confirmed that she really felt strong emotions towards me. I always knew, at the back of my mind somewhere, but it was hard to truly know it. There was a difference between getting told and knowing something. And now, I knew. She loved me and I loved her. With all my heart.

Chapter 24

And so winter came to pass, giving way for spring and new life to bud. The snow was melting at every street corner and only the most resilient patches still lingered behind. It wasn't that hot outside yet, but a little hoodie was enough to take a comfortable walk around the neighborhood. The trees had just begun regrowing their colors and the green grass finally took over the white veil of winter. Early in the morning, birds could be heard for the first time in a while and life seemed to have come back to the city. I didn't pay much attention to those kinds of things a few months ago, but the breakup with Camille and my new relationship with Chloe made me more sensitive to the little details and admiring the wildlife go on about their day now made me smile. Last spring was very different for me. I had no girlfriend and stuck to my homework and school, occasionally going out for drinks, but that was it. A year later, I was dating my high school friend, broke up with my ex and experienced a whole lot of drama. When I thought back on it, it was crazy how many things happened in the span of a year. Time flies, that was much clearer to me now than it ever had been in the past, and when I thought about all the things hanging precariously in the balance, it was slightly overwhelming. Nevertheless, we march on and continue with our lives.

The days led to weeks and soon, it would be summer again and the school year would be over. It was hard getting that into my head as I walked in the corridor at the end of my class. I still had another one after that and had to get to it as fast as I could as there was only a ten-minute gap between them and it was on the complete opposite side of the building. Whoever decided that was a good idea never actually had to take classes like that, I was certain of it. When students poured out of classrooms, it was impossible to get anywhere fast and I always made it barely in time. A text message made my phone vibrate in my pants and I swiftly took it out to see who had contacted me. I was glad to see Chloe's name pop up on the screen and opened our conversation to read.

Could you stop by the library for a second? I won't be long.

I was already pretty pressed for time, but I figured I could make a quick stop if she really wouldn't be long. Any more than a minute, however, and I would be late for my class. The library slowly came into view as I followed the student train leading down to the cafeteria. I usually hung out on the right side and the library was on the left so I had to cut across the entire corridor which earned me a few annoyed grunts, but I didn't make a fuss about them. I opened the door and entered the quietest room in the whole building. I scanned it from left to right, trying to find a girl with red hair that would stand out among the crowd. Spotting her, I quickly made my way to her side as she lifted her eyes from the book she was reading.

"Hi, Jack," she whispered.

"Hello, what did you want to say to me? I have to be in class in about five minutes so I don't have much time," I whispered back.

"I know, I'll make it quick. I just wanted to tell you to go straight home tonight. I'll have a surprise for you."

"Surprise? Why?" I said, confused.

"You really thought I would forget your birthday? Not a chance."

"You really don't have to do…" I protested as silently as I could.

"I don't have to, but I did," she said, cutting me off. "Now go, or you'll be late."

I was about to protest, but Chloe shut me down with a quick peck on the cheek and returned to her book with not another word. I had to leave and simply grabbed her hand and squeezed it a little, a gesture we had developed in school to signify our love for each other in a silent and discrete manner so people wouldn't get suspicious. I still didn't really know why we kept on doing that; I was fine with it at the start of the relationship, but that was more than a month ago now and I just wanted to give her a quick kiss sometimes. Chloe would have none of it and was adamant we keep to ourselves as much as possible until the school year ended. I guess she doesn't realize it when she breaks her own rules, like she did just moments ago. That wasn't very fair to me, now, was it? I told myself I would talk to her about it because it was really hard to restrain myself that much, even if it was only at school. She smiled at me and signaled me to go with her head. I let go of her hand and walked away, leaving the quiet room behind and returning to the busier corridors. I checked my phone for the time. Class was starting in two minutes and I still had a little way to go so I hurried up in order to get there before the door closed. The whole way, my mind blanked out, but as soon as I sat down, Chloe's words came flooding back in, storming it with some thoughts that made no sense and some that did. I couldn't decipher between the two and it only made me more confused as time went on.

I couldn't concentrate at all on the class. I was physically present, but my mind had wandered into faraway places my fellow students could never imagine. I was unknowingly relieved the professor didn't call out to me during the whole class as I wouldn't have been able to answer anything. Even his words were muffled and faded in the background as thoughts alternated in my head. It's not that I forgot my own birthday, but since my parents left and I was on my own, I didn't really celebrate it. I would go out with my friends an evening on that week, didn't even have to be on the same day, drink a few beers and that was it. To have someone organise something or at least say they have a surprise for me was relatively new, at least in the past few years. I kept thinking and making hypotheses on what it could be. Was it going to be a surprise party? Was it a cake she had ordered from a bakery? Perhaps a gift of some kind, I had no idea what I would even want as a gift either, so how could she possibly have come up with something on her own? Could it be tickets to go to a concert or to go some other place together? The possibilities were endless and so was this class, or so it seemed like it. I couldn't wait to get out of there and find out what Chloe had in store for me. The other students packing their stuff and getting up from their chairs took me out of my head and I looked around confused for a second. I guessed it was the end of class and I just hoped we didn't have any homework related to it or else I would be beyond lost. I followed everyone out of the room and tried to hurry past some slow walkers, but there wasn't enough room and I was stuck behind them. I silently repressed an annoyed grunt, but kept on walking, hoping they would get out of the way soon so I could catch the earliest possible bus back to my place. Eventually, I managed to overtake them in the staircase leading down and almost tripped down the stairs from going too fast. I wasn't used to this kind of enthusiasm in my step and I managed to reach the bottom without breaking any limbs. I left the building through the double doors and realized I needed to put on my vest as the still chilly wind blew right on me. I stepped to the side, letting other people get out and took a hoodie out of my backpack. I had already planned ahead and brought it with me to avoid going back to my locker. Just as I was putting it on, I heard a familiar voice coming from the doors to my left.

"Yo, Jack! There you are!" Michael said. I turned to look at him and saw Chris, Sam and Vincent were also with him. "Look, dude, we're taking you out to the bar tonight, drinks are on us. What do you say?"

"Oh, um, sorry guys, apparently Chloe already planned something for me tonight, so I can't go." The boys all looked at each other for a second before turning back towards me. "Can we reschedule?"

"Something planned with your girlfriend, huh?" Michael asked while squinting. "What exactly are you…"

"Never mind him," Chris said, cutting him off, much to Michael silent protest. "What day are you available then?"

"Well, could be tomorrow, could be Saturday after my shift, I don't mind really," I answered.

"Let's go for tomorrow. Sound good?" Chris proposed.

"Sure, yeah!" I answered.

"Cool, see you tomorrow, then," he concluded.

"Be sure to tell us all about your night, yeah?" Michael said while Chris was dragging him away. Sam smiled at me and put on a hand on my shoulder.

"I hope you have a good evening, Jack. Take care." I looked at him and he simply left without another word. Sam was always a mysterious guy to me, but I liked that about him. You could never quite tell what he was thinking, but he was a genuine nice guy.

"Don't go too hard," Vincent said, winking at me. What was that supposed to mean? I couldn't ask him anything else before he followed the rest of my friends already walking away, leaving me confused. It didn't take long for me to snap out and almost run to the bus stop. There was a bus every ten minutes or so and I usually missed the one I was aiming for because I didn't hurry most days and would go to my locker first, taking it a lot slower than I was now. But if I was fast enough, I could reach it before it arrived and make it home earlier than usual. I just couldn't keep it together and contain myself. The excitement alone could have made me run home if it wasn't for the fact, I was trying to make it there as fast as possible. I kept running, but the bus turned the street corner way faster than I had anticipated and I was still far from the stop. Fate smiled on me that day and the light turned red, stopping the bus and letting me catch up. I quickly got on when the driver opened the doors and made my way to the back, exhausted but restless at the same time. I had done it; I managed to catch it just in time!

The ride was the same as it always was even if it appeared to go on forever this time. I tried to distract myself by thinking about other things, but nothing quite worked and I always came back to Chloe's surprise. Was this how she felt when I told her I had something? Somehow, I understood why she rushed to my bedroom instead of staying in the kitchen like I told her to. I was hyping myself up for something grandiose, and I knew I shouldn't in order to avoid getting disappointed if it wasn't up to what I was thinking, but I couldn't help myself. I almost missed the stop as I was rummaging through different improbable scenarios in my head. I quickly got out and made my way to my apartment, ignoring the cramps in my legs as I was walking a lot faster than I was used to. I climbed two stairs at a time and reached out for the handle to unlock it. Surprisingly, it was already unlocked and I stopped for a second. Did I forget to lock it when I left this morning? I always checked if it was really locked by jiggling the handle before leaving, so I found that scenario unlikely. I slowly opened the door, which announced my presence very loudly in the quiet apartment and gently closed it, all senses in full alert. I quietly took off my vest and hung it on the hooks nearby before a voice came from my bedroom.

"Jack, over here!" Chloe called to me. A wave of relief washed over me. I didn't forget to lock it; Chloe just came in before me. It wasn't a thief that managed to pick the lock, it was my girlfriend calling me from the bedroom. I took off my shoes and hurriedly walked towards her voice, both excited and uncertain about her being already here before me. Did she sneak off her class and come here while I was bored to death in mine? Why did she need to be here earlier than me? I didn't have time to wonder for long as I passed the door frame and saw her, biggest smile on her face and sitting on the bed next to a pretty large present. The sight of her warmed my heart instantly and, like an overexcited child, I almost ran to her side. She quickly got up from the bed as we embraced each other. We kissed, just a small peck, and backed away from the other, observing the other's reaction. She seemed really happy and so was I. My eyes shifted from hers down to the present and she caught my glimpse of it.

"Wondering what that is?" she asked teasingly.

"I am," I answered. "Are you going to tell me what it is?"

"Hmmm," she said, faking thinking about it. "No, I don't think I will," she said.

I made a saddened face and she laughed at me for it. I soon joined her and we both sat down on the bed while she grabbed the present. She turned to look at me and we stared into each other's eyes for a few seconds. Whenever I did that, time seemed to stand still, like she somehow dictated if it flowed or not. Can keeping eye contact really block the river from going down the stream?

"Happy birthday, Jack," she finally said with a smile. "I hope you like it."

She handed me the present and I slowly reached out to grab it. It wasn't heavy, but it was pretty bulky. I examined the paper she chose to wrap it with.

They were also remnants of a Christmas long gone by now, but the wrapping was so beautifully done compared to mine I was almost embarrassed I had given her something so sloppy. I felt bad ripping it apart, but if I wanted what was inside, I had no choice. The tearing sound of the paper resonated in the bedroom as the gift revealed itself gradually. It was a picture frame containing a wide variety of picture sizes. At first, I thought they were the stock photos that came with frames when you buy them at the store, but when I took a closer look, I realized how wrong I was. They weren't stock pictures; they were pictures of us. When we had cooked together, us on the ski trip, at a small coffee shop we went to when we started dating. I lifted my eyes up to meet hers and she smiled at me.

"Do you like it?" she asked.

"I do, I… How did you manage to get all these pictures? The shots are so nice and even on this one, we're both in the frame in my kitchen. How did you do that?"

"That's a little secret," she smugly said with her smile changing to a grin. I stared back at the frame and it sent me back to all those places we went to together. We had only been dating for a month now, but we already did so many things it overwhelmed me to think about all the places we could go in the span of a year. Looking back on it, they weren't these extravagant trips or expensive activities and we still had so much fun simply because we were together. I wanted to make many more of those memories with her, immortalize these moments in my heart for me to remember all my life. As she had said to me once, memories stay with you forever and while that might have been an idealistic way of seeing things, I was beginning to believe it had an ounce of truth to it. I wanted to remember all those places, all those activities and all the time we spent together for as long as possible.

"I have something else for you," she said after a while, bringing me back from inside my own mind. I saw her reach out behind the bed to grab something else. It looked like a wooden stand with some sort of white square on the other side. She handed it to me and I put the picture frame aside to take it. After one second of looking at it, I figured out what it was. A painting. But not of any scenery or random picture, it was of us in that coffee shop. It wasn't expertly painted, but I could still see clearly what it was and I stared at it for a few seconds, incapable of saying anything and just admiring her art. "What do you think?" she asked.

"I didn't know you could paint," I answered.

"I… don't. This is my first piece, actually. I practiced a lot to try and replicate the picture, but it was really hard to do," she explained.

"This is your first? Wow, you did a really good job on it, this is well done," I said, impressed by her clear talent.

"I'm glad you like it," Chloe said, smiling at me while I admired her work. "I wanted to make something for you after you gave me the spice rack and, well, I'm not handy enough to do that kind of stuff so I opted for a more artsy approach."

"Thank you, this is wonderful, I'll have to find a spot to put them on the wall." I set the painting on the picture frame and got closer to Chloe to kiss and hug her. In a flash, she got on top of me and pinned me down on the bed. Shocked, I couldn't react at all and her head got closer to my ear.

"We can do anything you want later," she whispered. I didn't have time to register and process what she had said that she got off me and nearly sprinted out of the room. I only caught a glimpse of the side of her face and it was nearly the same shade as her hair. I stayed lying on the bed for a while, trying to gather my thoughts about what had just happened. Did she mean what I thought she meant? If she was that embarrassed about it, there was no mistaking it. I would still make sure, but this was most likely her way of telling me she was ready. I couldn't help but feel excited at the prospect and had to take deep breaths to avoid the bulge in my pants to grow any further than it already had. Of course, there was no use to it and I resigned myself to hide it as best I could before walking out of the bedroom to look for Chloe. Some commotion coming from the kitchen told me where she was and I quickly followed her. I found her taking out pots and pans and preparing all the ingredients for supper.

"What are you making?" I asked in the door frame. She was surprised and jumped a little, but soon regained her composure only to lose it a second later when she looked at me. Her eyes shifted down to look at the vegetables on the counter and her cheeks returned to a shade of red.

"I was going to make some fajitas with all the vegetables you have here," she said, gesturing towards them in front of her. "You have some ground beef and tortillas so I figured this could work. Is it okay with you?

"Sure, anything you cook will be delicious. Do you want some help?" I said, walking into the kitchen to assist her.

"No! You go sit down at the table and wait," she said with a severe tone. "You shouldn't have to do this on your birthday," she mumbled to herself, but I heard everything.

I smirked at how adorable she was. Even when she tried to be bossy with me, I couldn't help but find her cute every single time. It made her getting mad funny to me which made her madder as well. She knew how to be serious and make her point, though, and I usually could tell when it was one of those moments, but this clearly wasn't it. I looked at her cutting the onions, peppers and tomatoes and put the meat in the pan. In the kitchen, she really seemed like somebody else, like she somehow became more organized and proficient. Not that she wasn't in everything else, but she exuded this aura of knowledge and skill that she didn't have usually. I wondered if I had something similar to that myself, but since nobody had ever mentioned it to me, I figured I probably didn't. Although, Chloe might have a different opinion on the subject. How do you even talk about this stuff, though? Why was I thinking about this right now?

Supper was ready not too long afterwards. Chloe had regained her composure and we talked about anything and everything, how school was going and where we could go on our next date. She wanted to go to an aquarium and I confessed I had never gone to one of those. She excitedly told me we now had to go and I couldn't help but agree with her. Her cooking was still the best I had ever had, even comparable to my mom's cooking. I hadn't eaten at my parent's house for a very long time and I still missed it from time to time. If I wasn't in the presence of a cute girl on my birthday, I could have shed a few tears. Even for something as simple as this, she managed to make it special and I admired her seemingly magical ability to do so. I could make it too, but it could never rival what she could make as she was clearly a step up from myself. Some fifteen minutes later, we had finished our plates and I grabbed hers as well as mine to put them in the sink. As soon as I deposited them, I felt arms crawling up my chest as she hugged me from behind. The contact startled me somewhat and I tried turning around, but she held me in place.

"Is there anything else you want to do tonight?" she asked, her face almost buried in my back.

"Do you really mean it?" I answered with a question, incapable of looking at her as she was hiding behind me. I felt her nod positively.

"Yes, anything, even… you know." Hearing her say it took me a moment to register. I had something in mind, but was debating whether or not I wanted to do it. I finally figured it didn't cost anything to ask and I tried a little harder to turn around. She let go of her grasp, but didn't look up at me, her eyes glued to the ground.

"Then, I have a request." I saw her head move a little and decided to go for it. "Want to take a shower with me?" Her face, barely visible to me, still appeared like it got redder somehow. She fidgeted a little, dancing from feet to feet, seemingly trying to make up her mind. Eventually, she lifted her eyes to look at mine. I couldn't help but find her cuter by the second as she tried to answer me.

"Okay," she finally whispered.

I extended my hand and she shyly took hold of it, leading her to the bathroom door. We stopped in front of it, my heart pumping faster than it had ever been. I was about to have sex with Chloe for the first time and I couldn't contain myself. As soon as she agreed to it, my pants started to feel tight and I just had to free my member from its underwear cage. She buried her head in my chest, surprising me a little and making me take a step back. I instinctively put my hands around her, unsure as to what was going on.

"Can you…go in first?" she asked into my shirt, muffling her question.

The fact she was so embarrassed about it made me smile. She was perfectly fine with us kissing and me touching her entire body, but this somehow was a little much for her. I didn't want to push her into anything she didn't want to do, though, so I had to make sure.

"Do you really want to do this? We don't have to," I said, trying to sound comforting through my eagerness.

"No, it's fine, I just…I'm just a little…Can you just go in first?" she answered. She seemed to debate with herself, like she didn't know if she was fine with it or not.

"Sure."

I opened the bathroom door and closed it behind me, alone in my bathroom. I turned towards the mirror hanging over the sink and looked at myself for a few seconds. No thoughts came through my head for once, not one except looking forward to what was going to happen in the shower. My mind felt blank for once and the feeling was unusual to say the least, but I didn't let it bother me. I turned the shower on and the sound of water hitting the bath soon made enough noise to cover the sound of me undressing. I put my clothes to the side and stood there naked, feeling both uncertain and silly. I was already completely hard when nothing had happened yet and Chloe wasn't even in the room. I felt somewhat disappointed in myself, for what reason I didn't know, but I elected to let it go for now and just get into the shower. The water hitting my skin was good, washing away any doubts I had and relaxing my muscles that were tensed up ever since I entered the bathroom alone. I took the time to rinse my hair before calling out to Chloe.

"You can come in now," I yelled loud enough so she would hear behind the closed door. The wooden door opened and she slid into the room, making as little noise as possible. I looked in her direction through the transparent curtains and saw her starting to undress. Somehow, her silhouette made her extremely sexy and I couldn't help but follow every single one of her movements as she took off her shirt, bra, pants and panties. She stood facing the shower for a moment, letting me admire her curves in a shadowy contour, unbeknownst to her, before she spoke.

"Can you face away from me as I get in?" she asked. I wanted to answer something witty, but she was probably really nervous and didn't need that extra poke of fun right now. When I thought about it, I was nervous as well. I had touched her breasts before, I had seen her silhouette just now, I had explored almost all her body before, but I had never seen her naked in front of me. As much as I wanted to see her, she would also see me. What would she think of me? Would I be appealing to her? With my member already on guard, would she be turned off by it? We knew each other for a while now and even though we had touched each other a little before now, this was taking it to a whole new level. With my heart almost skipping beats, I answered.

"Sure," I said as I turned around, the shower water now dripping directly unto my face. I heard the curtains move to the side and Chloe slipping into the bath. How long did I have to stay like this? When could I turn around to see her? My face slowly started heating up as the water flowed directly on it. The anticipation mixed with the nervousness rapidly spreading across my entire body made it even more unbearable as Chloe kept silent.

"You have a nice butt," she commented in a tone that indicated she was still embarrassed but tried to break the ice as best she could. I took it as a cue to turn around and swiped the water off my face before facing her.

We both stared at each other like we had never seen someone of the opposite sex naked before. Seeing Chloe like this was very different from when I first saw Camille. I had known her for years and finally having her like this, in front of my very eyes, was something I never thought I wanted and could have. She was covering her breasts and her crotch with her hands, still shy about showing me all of her, but, as time went on, her hands gradually parted, revealing what was underneath. Her breasts were just the right size for a handful, her nipples poking out at me just as I was pointing at her with my member. Her curves flowed down to her hips, a little wider than her belly just above, and continued their path to her long slender legs. Between her thighs, I could barely see her slit, hidden behind trimmed hair and the fact she almost had crossed her legs to put it out of view still. I raised my eyes to meet hers and smiled at her. Without her glasses, her face had an entire new look, but I still found her the cutest. Freckles, seemingly invisible as they were so pale, littered her cheeks and her fire hair stood out a lot on the white background of the bathroom tiles. Her blue eyes stared back at me, shifting downwards from time to time to see my shaft only to return to make eye contact. We didn't say a word for the longest time, the sound of water covering up the growing awkwardness between us. I didn't want to make the first move because I wanted her to be at ease, but I didn't know if she would make it eventually, so I opted to go first anyway.

"You are as beautiful as I imagined," I said, smiling at her.

"I... Thanks, you too," she answered, her eyes looking away while she covered her breasts again from embarrassment.

"You shouldn't cover them up. I like them better when they're free." Was that too bold? I hoped not, but as Chloe looked at me, she seemed to relax a little more and stepped towards me, closing the gap between us. Now, she was standing right in front of me, her breasts were almost touching my chest and my member could poke her if she came just a little closer. Droplets of water started landing on her, gradually covering her with the liquid that seemed to make her skin shine under the bathroom light.

"Is it okay if I...?" I asked, lifting my hands towards her chest. She nodded in agreement and my hands landed on her bare breasts for the first time in a while. I couldn't think straight anymore as the excitement of the situation mixed with seeing her naked made my mind go blank. I gently massaged them, squeezing them sometimes, passing over the nipples at other times which made her moan softly. If I was any farther, I wouldn't have heard them over the constant noise of the running water, but since she was so close to me, I heard every breath she took, every quiet moan, every little noise she made while I explored her body once more. My hands gradually left her breasts to wander around in other places, shifting down from her chest to her hips and down to her slit. This time, she didn't stop me and let me do whatever I wanted. I couldn't tell if it was because of the water or not, but she was very wet and my fingers, only brushing against the outside of her folds, were soon covered with her juices. She moaned a little louder this time and practically fell onto me, her hands grabbing my shoulder as she spread her legs a little farther apart, letting me have a little more room than before. I took it as an invitation and pushed one finger inside which made her sharply inhale. She held it for a few seconds and exhaled loudly right next to my ear. The sound of her moaning turned me on even more and, without controlling it, my member twitched and poked her in the belly. Almost as soon as it did, it was grabbed by a delicate hand and started to get stroked. I was startled by the sudden wave of pleasure that hit me and grunted a little which seemed to make her go faster. I had completely stopped pleasuring her as she took over the initiative, much to my liking. She had a lot more experience than me and when the shyness of the first look disappeared, she gained a confidence I never knew she had. I wasn't about to let her do everything, though, and as she continued to stroke me, I resumed fingering her. Her legs gradually bent down as I went faster and faster and her grip eventually loosened on my member. The whole time, she was moaning louder and louder, like a crescendo of pleasure was taking over her. Eventually, she was too far down for me to continue, but she dropped to her knees right as I exited her womanhood and, with too much experience for this being her first time in this situation, took me into her mouth.

My shaft was wetter than usual as the water had flowed down my chest to cover it. I moved just a little forward to prevent it from going into Chloe's eyes as she went to town on me. If there was one thing that really stood out to me whenever I got blown was the sudden warmth of the mouth on my member. Just like all the other times, I grunted loudly and instinctively went to grab her head, opting to hold her hair out of the way instead of pushing. I looked at her going up and down and licking with a passion I never knew she had and felt lucky to see such a sight. She was clearly experienced, maybe even on par with Violet, as she used one hand to cup my balls while the other stroked in unison with her head motion. I was harder than usual, even I could feel that, but I didn't know if it was because of the shower setting, the fact it was Chloe doing all this stuff to me, both or something else entirely. The only thing I knew was the fact I was ecstatic for us to finally be able to express our love in such a deep, physical way. It didn't take too long before I was ready to burst and I reached out to Chloe to let her know. Before I could grab her arm to pull her back up, she took me completely into her mouth. I had never experienced something quite like this during my limited sexual endeavors, but the feeling was unlike any other. She didn't hold it for very long, but I still very much enjoyed every second of it. Chloe backed off with a loud inhale and looked up at me. Her eyes from below somehow aroused me even more and I swiftly pulled her up. She stood next to me and, without a word, turned around and leaned on the wall, exposing her butt towards me. She dangled it seductively in my direction, but I had other plans.

I grabbed her shoulder to turn her around and she looked confused for a second. She didn't have time to wonder about what I was doing for very long as I imitated her previous behavior and dropped to my knees as well, my head directly in her crotch. The shower water started hitting the left side of my face and Chloe lifted her leg up to rest it on the other side of the bath to shield me from the stream. It also allowed me better access to what I was really interested in. Just like when I used my hands, she was really wet and I caressed her for a moment before doing anything else. I heard her moan from up there and felt a hand on the back of my head. She gently pushed me towards her and I started eating her out then and there. She was a little different than Camille and I had more trouble finding the spot that would make her quiver, but once I did, I was relentless and never stopped pleasuring it. The pressure she was putting on my head got me into the groove a lot more and I didn't mind it at all. I wondered if she would like to be pushed like that as well? It would have to be something to try for another time. For now, her legs were shaking every time my tongue passed over the top of her slit and, I don't even know how, she got even wetter than when I started. I pushed my tongue inside, much like I did with my finger, and she pushed even harder on my head. I explored her where I never had before, only taking the shortest possible breaks before delving back into her. She got wetter and wetter and I knew it wasn't the shower stream. Her legs were quivering more and more until she couldn't take it anymore. She pulled me up and towards her, planting her lips on mine with furious passion and attacked me with her tongue. Mine was delighted about exploring another facet of her and battled with hers for dominance. She moved her hands to cup both of my cheeks and mine moved all around her body, starting from her chest all the way to her hips. Her back was to the wall and she couldn't go anywhere. It felt like I was cornering her and, even though I wasn't usually like that, the thought of it made my member twitch in excitement. She must have felt it poke her as her left hand left my cheek to grab a hold of it. She stroked it slowly while still kissing me passionately and eventually parted her lips from mine. Her head moved to my right ear and I heard her whispering.

"I want you to make me yours. Do whatever you want with me."

I was pleasantly surprised and somewhat shocked at her demand. Chloe was usually a little reserved and she didn't seem like the type of girl who would say something like that, but I was more than happy to oblige to such a demand. I lowered myself just a little and my member easily found her entrance. She resumed kissing me and I gladly accepted her lips as I stayed at her entrance, teasing her just a little before going in. She wanted none of that and both of her hands went down to my butt cheeks and pulled towards her, making me enter her as a wave of warmth crashed through my entire body. We both moaned in unison and I stayed inside, not moving, for a few seconds. It felt better than any other I had had before. I almost couldn't stay standing up initially, but I gradually got over the initial wave of pleasure and pulled my head back a little. Chloe reluctantly parted ways with me and stared at me. From this close, her blue eyes seemed to pierce my very soul and I marveled at how beautiful they were. Without a word, I started moving in and out and her mouth opened to moan as her breathing quickened. Mine did much of the same and we were soon synchronized, both experiencing another level of connection we never had before. The sound of the water was tuned out, almost like it wasn't even there, and I focused entirely on Chloe, her face, her eyes, her mouth. Every time I stroked in, she would move just a little, a movement so tiny I would have missed it if I wasn't completely enthralled with her. I felt myself about to burst and this time, I didn't know how I could supress it. There was no stopping it and, just as my breathing quickened, I went faster into and out of her. I reached the point of no return and pulled out reluctantly. She immediately grabbed my shaft and stroked it just as fast as I was going. With the loudest grunt I had ever done, I shot my shot right on her belly and it quickly dripped down, getting washed away by the shower stream. I don't know how much time it took for me to come back down, but it felt like it lasted forever and I somehow wanted it to be even longer. Panting and exhausted, I looked up at her and she smiled at me with a mischievous grin on her face. I smiled back and realized we hadn't even washed ourselves yet.

"That was…amazing," I finally said after a few seconds.

"We definitely need to do that again," Chloe said.

"I didn't know you were so forward in bed," I commented.

"I don't usually tell everyone about it either," she laughed. "I don't know what came over me, but I just wanted all of you over and over. I didn't think you were so aggressive either."

"Was I?" I asked out of genuine concern.

"I mean, I liked it a lot. I just thought you would be more passive and let me take charge, but you lead the way. It was the first time I wasn't completely dictating what was going on and it felt really nice."

"Well, I'm glad you enjoyed it as much as I did. We should probably actually take a shower now, shouldn't we? I think these guys need a little bit more attention," I teased while cupping her chest in my hands. Chloe let out a startled cry that turned into laughter and I soon joined her.

◇

She got out of the shower first and I quickly followed after she moved to the side to make space for both of us. I grabbed a towel hanging on the door and started to dry myself, stealing looks at Chloe who did the same. She eventually wrapped it around herself, covering her chest and going down just like a skirt.

Her nipples were still visible through the thick fabric and they attracted my attention. She caught me looking and raised her eyebrows with a smirk. Her eyes shifted down to glance at my already hardening shaft before coming back up with an even bigger smile on her face. It felt like she was about to laugh, but she didn't and I was slightly relieved at her inaction. Somehow, our roles had reversed. Before, she was the one embarrassed about her naked body and I was confident while now, I was trying to hide myself the best I could while she almost paraded the bathroom in her towel. I couldn't run away either and the only other thing I could do was turn around, so I did. I had never taken a shower with someone before and, for some reason, I was more uncertain about this drying part than the actual shower.

"I'll be in your room," she said with a wink and her clothes in her hands as she turned the door knob to exit the bathroom. A chill breeze entered the still steamy room and made me shiver before quickly fading away. Chloe closed the door behind her, leaving me alone with my thoughts and a shaft I couldn't quite calm down. Just as she left, the events that just happened sort of hit me all at once. We just had our first time together, right there in that very shower. For the first time, I had seen her naked and we expressed our love in the most humane and physical way possible. If there were any doubts in my mind we were dating or already a couple, there could be none now. Would I see her in a different light now? When I would look at her face, would I see the face she did in the bathroom or would the familiar eyes behind glasses stare back at me like they always had? Would she think of me differently now? I finished drying up and hung the towel on the door hook and stood in front of it, my heart now racing at the thought of joining her after what we did. With a resolute sigh, I opened the door, grabbed my clothes on the floor and made my way across the apartment to my bedroom.

The door wasn't closed and when I entered, I saw Chloe standing at the foot of the bed, facing away from me. When she heard me arrive, she turned around. I was still naked, but she had started to get dressed already. The towel now in her hair, she had put on her shirt and panties and had her pants in her hands. She smiled at me and I realized she had her glasses back on. I was so used to looking at her face without them for a while I almost forgot she usually wore them.

"Aren't you going to get dressed? You don't plan on being naked for the rest of the evening, are you?" she teased.

"You are so sexy," I answered, completely disregarding her question. Chloe blushed and went to turn around, but stopped herself halfway through the movement.

"Um…thanks," she nervously laughed while putting on her pants. The motion reminded me to do the same and I started to get dressed as well. Soon, we were both fully clothed again and Chloe approached me, all smiles. We shared a kiss as her arms went around my neck and rested on my shoulders. Mine went behind her back and brought her closer to me. Even though we just came out of a warm shower, her embrace still felt much hotter than the water had been. Feeling her this close to me brought me immense happiness and I never wanted to let her go.

"I can't believe we did that, that was…so good," I said.

"I'm glad you liked it; I had fun too. I had never done it in a shower either. You have to admit, that was pretty unusual for a first time," she commented with a little laugh.

"Yeah, but that made sharing it with you even more special. I couldn't have asked for more." We stayed hugging each other for a few more seconds, both of us not wanting to let the other go. I knew it was because we had just washed ourselves, but she smelled so good and I didn't want to part ways with her. Eventually, though, we reluctantly backed off a little, her hands still on each side of my shoulders and she looked at me directly in the eyes.

"Was there anything else you wanted to do tonight?" she asked. The tone had clearly shifted from before. Where she used to be my lover, she was now my girlfriend. I felt it too and I immediately knew what I wanted.

"Can we watch a movie? Until the end this time," I asked, jokingly. Chloe lifted her eyes up with a smile and let out a little amused sigh.

"Sure, what do you want to watch?"

We made our way to the living room hand in hand with me leading her even if she knew the way perfectly well. I didn't care what movie was playing, I just wanted to spend time with her and be as close as possible to her. We put on something we had both watched before, but it didn't bother us one bit. The movie was more of an excuse than anything else and, when she sat down on the couch, I looked at her with pleading eyes. She was confused, but waited for me to tell her what was going on.

"Can we lie down? I'd like…um… to be cuddled," I asked, blushing and feeling my cheeks get hotter.

"Sure," she answered with a big smile. I lied down on the couch, looking to my right to see the movie and she lied on her side between the couch cushions and myself. One of her breasts rested on my chest with her arm spread across my entire torso and one of her knees lifted upwards to rest on my belly. I felt such a feeling of closeness, love and affection I almost couldn't handle it. I had cuddled with Camille before, but there was never this much weight behind her feelings like Chloe had, there wasn't that deep-rooted passion in each of her actions. Maybe it wasn't much, she was just cuddling with me, but I felt every ounce of love she had with every heart beat that resonated through my arm. Chloe buried her head in my neck and closed her eyes, her breathing slowing down to match mine. She was completely relaxed and it felt good to enjoy being this close to each other without worrying what the other was thinking.

The movie was playing, but I could hardly pay any attention to it. That seemed to be a recurring theme when we were both on the couch. I didn't know if she was doing it on purpose, but her leg kept moving and brushing against my member which, of course, responded by getting harder and harder until the bulge in my pants started to be very apparent. Every time she moved over it now, I had to suppress my breathing to not let it slip that I was enjoying it. Chloe shifted a little, moving her head to be on the same level as mine.

"I think your friend wants to get out," she whispered in my ear. The sudden warmth of her breath on my face made it twitch and she slowly moved her leg out of the way so her hand could take its place. It gradually went from my chest down to my belly, to my waist until finally, it grabbed my member. I couldn't help but inhale at her touch, even if it was through two layers of fabric and I heard her snicker at my reaction. "You weren't done earlier, were you?" she teased, moving her hand up to move my pants down. I wanted to respond, but it was like I was paralyzed and couldn't move or talk. Her hand continued its journey and pulled down on my pants. I lifted my butt a little so she could pull both it and my underwear and when she did, my shaft sprung out eagerly, finally free from its containment. She immediately grabbed it and I quivered at her touch, barely containing a moan from escaping my mouth. She started to stroke up and down and a pleasure I never thought I could experience from hands alone pulsated through my entire body. My breathing had quickened and I felt myself getting harder and harder after every stroke. Her delicate hands were handling me so fiercely, with such raw passion I almost couldn't believe they were Chloe's. She kept breathing next to my face and with each hot breath, I twitched a little. She must have felt it as she moved even closer and started gently teasing my ear with her teeth. It was the first time anyone had ever done that and while I was a little shocked the first time she did it, I soon got over it. I liked it a lot, I loved it, this thing I never thought of doing even once, this completely seemingly random thing to do was turning me on even more. She gradually went faster and I felt myself about to burst a lot quicker than I thought. I slowly turned my head and she backed off a little for us to make eye contact. Her eyes were intense with mischief and there was some sort of glint in her eyes. She was enjoying this as much as I was, I knew immediately just from looking at her. My breathing was rapidly increasing and, any second now, I would finish for the second time of the evening. Without breaking eye contact, I stared back at her with intense eyes of my own.

"Kiss me." She looked surprised at my request, but there was no time. She had to do it now. "Kiss me," I repeated, more like an order than a request. She executed herself and as soon as her lips met mine, it was like an electric current flowed through me in an instant. I immediately started bursting harder than I ever did before. Chloe kept kissing me the entire time, even if I was probably leaking all over her hand, and I was glad she stayed where she was. A few strong pulses later and I finally calmed down, all my muscles relaxing at once. Only then did Chloe move away from my lips and we both looked down at the result of me finishing. Her left hand was covered, but that wasn't the worst. My belly was also drenched. I never came this much in my entire life even though I had earlier on this evening. I couldn't stop panting heavily like I just ran a marathon and Chloe slowly got up, her hand held out as to not drop anything on the floor.

"Stay here, I'll get something to wipe yourself," she said, exiting the room. My head fell back unto the couch and I smiled a content smile. What had just happened?

◊

The rest of the night was pretty tame in comparison. We restarted the movie from the beginning and actually watched it this time with no distractions coming in between us. Both sitting on the couch, she was leaning on me while I had my arm around her shoulders. We occasionally stole a quick kiss from the other, but we didn't let it escalate any further. Flashbacks of the events of the evening kept coming back to me and, of course, I got excited again, but I tried to hide it as best I could this time. Chloe either didn't notice or let me off the hook and I was glad she did. As much as I enjoyed that part of our love expression, I also wanted to spend quality time with her without it getting sexual. I surprised even myself by thinking that, because I normally would have been adamant about getting as much action as I could, but there was something about her that made me keep it in check. I sometimes looked at her just to see the side of her face, her red hair contrasting on my black couch, her eyes fixed on the TV at the opposite side of the room. I still couldn't quite believe we were a couple, like it was still a dream or a fairy tale. Why was it so hard to accept we simply acknowledged each other's feelings after waiting for way too long? It felt too good to be true, like I didn't deserve someone like Chloe, but I was still glad she chose me in the end.

She ended up staying the night. She cuddled up next to me and rapidly fell asleep while I stayed awake staring at the ceiling. The wind outside was making the branches of the tree in front of the apartment building move, casting creepy dancing shadows that seemed to come in and out of the darkness. How was it possible to distinguish shadows in the dark of night? Why did I have these kinds of thought this late? Even so, I was delighted to be able to enjoy such a simple thing as sleeping next to the person I loved. I thought about the next day, when I was going to meet up with my friends at the bar. There was so much I wanted to tell them, but would they care to listen or was it something too private to share? Would they even be curious to know? Could I possibly not mention it? I smiled at nothing; we couldn't possibly avoid the subject after the look they had shared as I was leaving earlier. Looking back on it, they probably knew what was going to happen even before I did. They could have told me, but I was glad they didn't. It kept the excitement of the night as shocking as possible.

For a first experience, it was certainly wild. I wanted to do it a lot more now and also experiment new things. I hoped Chloe would also be willing to try some of the stuff I had only seen in movies until now. I don't exactly know when, but I succumbed to my tiredness and fell asleep in her arms. There couldn't be a better way to dream.

Chapter 25

We had been waiting in line for a little over fifteen minutes by now. From the outside, it didn't seem that busy, but there were clearly a lot of people wanting to come here this weekend. That said, the line was going pretty fast and we were almost at the entrance. Fortunately, we had bought our tickets in advance and didn't have to wait to buy any. That was another queue next to us that went on outside. For some reason, the staff couldn't let us in right away and we had to wait for people to come out before they allowed new people in. It was somewhat weird to me, but I guessed they were pretty busy and that was their way of making sure there wasn't traffic inside and the customers could enjoy their day instead of being packed and confined to one space. Standing next to me, Chloe seemed impatient to finally get in after waiting and she was almost hopping in place to contain herself. I smiled and she must have heard me quietly snicker as she turned to face me, but I looked away guiltily.

"What?" she asked.

"Nothing. I just thought you were cute dancing around like that," I answered, not hiding my amusement anymore.

"Yeah, well, I'm eager to enter and see all the different fish! I've been meaning to come here for so long, but they were renovating and then things kept coming up. But now, I'm finally here!" Chloe muffled a joyful cry, trying to stay as quiet as possible, but she was clearly way into it for that.

The aquarium had been closed to the public for a while now and it reopened not too long ago. Chloe had been pestering me to go ever since, but school exams and my job kept getting in the way. Finally, we both had spare time and we decided to come today. Apparently, we weren't the only ones which would explain the seemingly infinite line to get in. Seems like everyone wanted to experience the new aquarium tour and had the same idea to come today. Normally, I would have been annoyed at this, but there was something about seeing Chloe this enthusiastic about it that made me calmer than usual. She loved animals and it was very apparent as we didn't see any of them yet and she couldn't stay in place.

The dim lighting of the place was very nice. The outside was blindingly bright with the spring sun shining in the sky while the inside was as dark as a bedroom at night save for the few spotlights scattered here and there that illuminated the path to follow. There was a giant banner next to the entrance featuring a multitude of species of fish, I couldn't even begin to name them as I knew nothing about them, but their colors still stood out in the darkness. Chloe and I were mostly silent for the time being, but noises of conversation all around us contrasted with the usually quieter darkness. I wondered if it would continue like this after we had entered or if people would get the message and stop talking so loudly. After a few more minutes of waiting, it was finally our time to enter.

"Hello and welcome to Aquarius! Did you already have your tickets?" greeted the woman working in front of us.

"Yes, I have them here," I said, handing her two small pieces of paper with our tickets printed on it. The woman took them and scanned them quickly before returning them to us.

"Thank you and have a nice visit," she concluded with a nod. She gestured towards the entrance while moving a little to the side and we swiftly moved past her with Chloe leading the way. She was practically running ahead as I tried to hold her back as best I could.

"Thank you," I said to the woman now behind me and she simply smiled at me without another word. I understood that Chloe wanted to go as soon as possible, but would it have hurt her to wait five more seconds to thank the woman properly? I didn't have much time to think about anything else as she was already speeding ahead, eager to see the first tank and the first fish on our day trip through the marine world.

We followed a winding hallway that would eventually lead to the central room of the aquarium. On each side were signs and posters advertising the place which I found rather odd. What was the point of advertising the visit when people seeing it had already paid for it? Eventually, the signs were replaced with small tanks containing the tiniest fish I had ever seen. They were about the size of my fingertip and Chloe eagerly went straight to them as soon as they came into view. I walked up to it, a smile on my face. It was kind of cute to see her that way and while I might not share her enthusiasm completely, I could definitely understand the appeal of such a place. I stopped next to her and we both looked at the tank. The dim light made the sparkling blue water stand out even more and the fish inside reflected some of the projector lights with their scales, seemingly glowing as they swam. Seeing them like this, I understood how Chloe could find them so cute and lovely. I glanced over at her and, through her glasses, I could see she seemed captivated by the swimming fish, her eyes the same color as the water. There were still plenty more to see and I gently nudged her to snap her out. She looked at me and I thought she would get mad about me wanting to move on, but she spotted another tank and immediately went to it, leaving me among a crowd of other people I didn't know. I swiftly followed her, falling behind as people started flooding the hallway and making it difficult to cross without bumping into anyone.

We looked at a few more of these small tanks before continuing on the passage to the main room. Already, Chloe seemed happy with what she had seen so far and it made me happy as well. If she was having a good time, then so was I. Normally, I would have never come here, definitely not alone as well, but being in her company made it different. We held hands in the dark like two teenagers wanting to avoid getting caught and looked at each other with a smirk, probably thinking the same thing. It still amazed me how much of a connection and complicity we had. While we knew each other for a long time, it was as friends and I wouldn't have thought it would have carried over to the romantic side of our relationship, but I was glad it did. I felt like I could truly be myself around her, like she understood me without the need for words, like we knew what we were thinking at all times. I knew it wasn't true, of course, but even now, she managed to make me feel so much by doing so little.

It wasn't long before we reached the main room and stopped walking, impressed by the sheer size of the tank in front of us. It must have been as big as a house or at least it appeared to be. Inside were a multitude of species of fish, both big and small, just swimming around, a colorful and moving rainbow. Once in a while, we saw small sharks coming very close to the glass, their eyes studying each and every one staring at them. There were rock formations scattered about, both to give a feel of the ocean and provide hiding spots for fish who wanted some peace and quiet out of the invading eyes. The tank seemed to illuminate the room by itself, the water a deep blue I could only describe as fascinating, and the movement of it made the seaweed dance to a silent rhythm.

"It's beautiful," Chloe said in a whisper, unable to take her eyes off the sight in front of her.

"It really is," I answered. "Want to get a closer look?"

"For sure."

We went closer, but there were so many people hanging around that we couldn't get a spot next to the massive tank. As we walked up, I looked around the room and saw there were three other ways to go; a passage on the left, a circling passage around the tank that went up and another one on the right. I didn't know where they lead and even though we had a map, it was so dark we couldn't see anything. It seemed to be a little quieter on the left passage as most people were gathered around the main tank, so maybe we could get a better look at another time.

"Hey, do you want to go on the left for now? Maybe let these people clear out and we'll get a better look later?" I asked. Chloe looked around for what I meant by left and spotted the passage.

"Oh, I didn't even see that. The thing is, there were still a lot of people wanting to come in, so are we really going to get a spot later?"

"Can't be worse than it is now if you ask me," I said. "We have the entire day here, I'm sure we'll get better spots when we come back to it." Chloe seemed to think for a few seconds, but eventually agreed with me and we made our way to the left. The deep blue color that dominated the other rooms eased up into a nice turquoise and a literal rainbow of fish soon appeared before our eyes. I took a look to the side and spotted a poster that said it was the tropical area. Most tanks had just one person in front of them, but we managed to find one with nobody so we decided to check that one out.

There were so many different species it was hard to count them all up, but there were at least ten swimming around carelessly. I followed one with my eyes; it was a small but bright yellow one that stood out among the other fish. It seemed really fast and was constantly going in zig-zags instead of going straight like the others. It had two big fins that appeared to have a hard time following it around. Suddenly, it turned around and stared straight at me and, for some reason, I thought it might have known I was observing it. It couldn't have been aware, right? The thought of it still took me aback for a moment. I turned to Chloe to see if she experienced the same thing, but she was obsessed by the lot of them and couldn't take her eyes away from the tank, a giant smile permanently smeared on her face. I gently nudged her to snap her out and she looked at me confused, silently asking me why I did that.

"Which one is your favorite?" I asked, turning back towards the tank.

"Oh, I don't know, they're all so cool. I think I would go with this one," Chloe answered by pointing a slightly bigger blue fish with a yellow fin as a tail. I thought it was an interesting choice, but I had to know more.

"Why that one in particular?" I probed, looking for some more details.

"It... kind of reminds me of you, somehow," she said.

"What?" I asked, slightly offended even though I didn't know why. "What do you mean?" Chloe tried to contain a laugh but she wasn't able to do so completely and her voice resonated a little in the dim and quiet corridor. I looked around to see if anyone had heard her, but it seemed like nobody really cared and were just watching like normal. I turned back to face her and she had become redder than before, trying her hardest not to burst out laughing at my reaction. If anything, it was slightly contagious and now I wanted to join her as well. I managed to stay calm somehow. "Why does it remind you of me?" I asked again, hoping to get an answer this time.

"I don't know, it just… does. It has a flat face and two tiny arms, what's not to love?"

"You're saying I have a flat face?" I said, faking being mad and annoyed.

"Oh yeah, definitely."

"Alright, that's it. Come here!" I said, practically launching myself at her. I grabbed her around the arms, locking hers under mine so she couldn't move and started to kiss her neck violently. She tried to stop me, but couldn't get away from my grip and started laughing from my tickling. At this point, I didn't mind the noise we were making; I was just happy to spend time with her in a place she liked, I just wanted to stay here with her and this day to never end. Eventually, I let her go and she turned around, panting, to look at me directly.

"You're going to pay for that, mister," she threatened between two breaths. She might have wanted to be intimidating, but it wasn't really working, so I simply snickered at her remark and looked back towards the tank. A fish previously hidden came out of a fake sunken boat and rose towards the surface, right at my eye level. It was a lot more colorful than the other fish; it had varying stripes circling across its scales and fins, making it stand out from the crowd by imitating a rainbow. Its fins were long and seemed to dance when it swam, captivating my eyes and almost forcing me to look. It had white spots all over its body that covered its fins as well and I found it a little odd when comparing it to the other fish swimming around it. Some of them had spots, but they never got on their fins and usually wouldn't cover the entire body either. This one was special, I had no idea what it was, but I found it beautiful nonetheless. Chloe joined me soon after seeing me staring into the tank and tried to figure out which one I was watching.

"Which one is your favorite?" she asked me back. I took a few seconds to process the question and answer.

"I was following that yellow one there for a while, but then this other one came out and I just can't take my eyes off it. A little like… you," I said, turning to look at her. Before I could react, I felt her first colliding with my shoulder and I jerked back a little. I lifted my eyes to see her and she was looking away, her cheeks as red as her hair. It was harder to see in the dim light, but the turquoise water next to us illuminated her enough for me to clearly see how embarrassed she was.

"You dummy," she muttered under her breath. I heard it, but didn't comment on it. Instead, I extended my hand towards her and she looked down at it suspiciously, like she was guarding herself against another trick. There were no more tricks, simply me smiling at her.

"Shall we go to the next tank?" I proposed. Chloe nodded and took my hand as we walked to the next available tank in the tropical section.

So many different types, shapes and sizes, how could anyone know all of these? None of the species in the previous tank we had checked were in the next one and the same thing for the one after that. They were all different and I wondered how it was possible to have so many different types of fish. It was a little overwhelming when looking at it farther away and seeing the rows of tanks on each side, all containing unique species. After a good while, we continued walking down the corridor and eventually ended up in another section entirely.

Here, the air was slightly colder and I shivered once which surprised me. We soon arrived in front of a much larger tank this time and it contained some penguins standing on some ice at the farthest corner. From where we were, they were kind of far away, but you could still see them properly. I always found penguins to be funny, waddling around in their fake suits and sliding on the ice like a water slide. They were really good swimmers, too, despite being birds. You wouldn't think so, but sometimes appearances can be deceiving. When Chloe saw them for the first time, she excitedly pointed at them and turned to me.

"Awww, look at them, they're so cute!"

"Yeah, they are," I said, smiling to myself at her comment.

We continued looking at them for a while. I studied their environment a little, but there really wasn't much to it. They had a good chunk of fake ice to stand on, a little ramp to jump into the water which took more than half the space in the tank. It was probably the coldest water possible and you wouldn't catch me anywhere near that. I went swimming in a mountain river once and it was the coldest thing I had ever experienced. I vowed to never do that again and I wasn't about to break that promise. One of the penguins seemed to be arguing with another as they were shouting loudly and moving their wings all around. Everyone gathered was looking at the same thing and one of them decided to leave and jumped into the water with almost no splash. It was kind of impressive. Another one joined in and slid off the icy ramp on the left side, flying in the air for just a moment before diving through the water's surface. Again, almost no splashes. Compared to me, they were really skillful at diving and I would be lying if I said I wasn't slightly envious of their swimming capabilities.

Chloe tapped my shoulder and pointed at something so I followed her finger to see what it was about. A mother penguin and two tiny baby penguins waddled over into view. They were previously hidden by other penguins, but now wanted to move. I was sure Chloe was glad they did.

"The one on the left is the cutest," she said with a resolute voice.

"Hmm, I don't know, I kind of prefer the one on the right," I contradicted just to mess with her. She looked at me with annoyed and amused eyes and I couldn't help but laugh. "They're both cute."

"I want one," Chloe said, resolute in her statement. I simply looked at her funny and she faked being sad. How were we even supposed to take care of a penguin? I would understand a cat or a dog, but a penguin? It made me think about pets in general. My parents had multiple pets as I grew up, but I had never had one myself. I knew I wanted to get one eventually, but it never felt like the right time and I didn't feel like I could give it the life it could have in my tiny apartment. A dog would probably be sad, so maybe a cat?

"Who's daydreaming now?" Chloe asked teasingly. I snapped out and looked at her and couldn't help but smile too. Yeah, maybe I would get a pet soon. I didn't have much time to think about it as Chloe dragged me to the next section. I eventually started walking on my own and she let me go. We exchanged a look, but said nothing as we reached another giant tank. This time, it was slightly different than the previous ones.

The corridor we were in had gradually went down and was now in the middle of a seal tank. To the left and right was one tank that joined up overhead, so we could see the seals swimming over us. On each side of the corridor, benches were set up so people could sit to admire them. I remembered seals liking to mess with people and just being playful in general, but since I had never seen them in person before, I didn't know if that was true or not. A bench was free on the right and we walked straight to it, finally sitting down for a moment. One of the seals passed straight in front of us, going along the edge of the glass before crossing overhead to the other side. We silently observed as they swam around. There were quite a few of them, but they still had a lot of space to go about their everyday business. I decided to break the ice and spoke first.

"How do you like it so far?" I asked.

"I love it! The tropical fish, the penguins and now this? And there's still so much left to see, we didn't even go to that upper section yet. I wonder what's up there. Do you think it's going to be the hardest species of fish to catch? Or maybe it could be other things like turtles or an octopus or maybe starfishes? Oh man, the possibilities are endless." I smiled and snickered a little while looking at her. She turned to me. "What?"

"I just love when you're like this, getting excited about something. It makes you even cuter than before," I said.

"Oh, stop it, I am not cute. I didn't even do my hair today."

"You don't have to do your hair to be cute." I got closer to her on the bench in one swift movement. Our legs were now touching and we both looked down, then at each other. I could tell from just one look into her eyes that she thought of the same thing. I leaned in towards her and she met me halfway, pressing her lips against mine. We probably shouldn't have stayed like this for a long time, but I couldn't resign myself to let her go. She must have felt the same because she didn't move either. Her lips were so soft, like always, but they felt even better now. Time seemingly stood still while we were intertwined like this.

A giant knock on the glass next to us startled me and Chloe both and we backed off from each other, surprised and scared. As soon as we spotted the seal in front of us, we sighed in relief. It seemed to be laughing as it left to go somewhere else. Chloe and I looked at each other, trying to contain our own laughter, but it was in vain. We both burst at the same time, laughing in embarrassment at the crazy situation that just happened. Eventually, we calmed down and the seal that interrupted us came to visit a few more times before we continued our tour of the aquarium. If anything, that would be a good story to tell the guys when we met next. A few minutes later and we had circled back into the main room with the giant central tank. Chloe motioned towards the path leading upstairs and I silently agreed, so we both climbed up. It was a lot steeper than it looked and we were slightly panting when we got to the top. I really needed to get back in shape if something as small as this was enough to make me lose breath. Chloe got over her exhaustion rather quickly and went over to the middle portion of the room where you could see the tank beneath you. She stood in a crowd of people, all looking at their feet, and I joined to see for myself. It was a completely different experience even if it was the same tank and the same fish. Just observing them from another angle meant some stood out more than others and the ones that hung out at the top were more visible now. The coolest one was definitely a mid-sized shark that swam really fast right underneath the glass. If it hadn't been there, I could have extended a hand and touched it. I looked up to see Chloe, her skin a calming shade of blue seemingly moving with the currents underneath, enjoying herself while paying close attention to anything that moved. I couldn't help but smile at the sight. She truly was having a ton of fun and it was all I could have ever asked for. Multiple benches were lined up near the walls and, after a few minutes of intensely observing the tank, we went to sit down at the closest one.

"This was so cool, I can't believe they had ideas like this to observe fish, I never would have thought of that," Chloe said enthusiastically.

"Definitely, I have never seen anything like it either," I added. "The way you could see the sharks passing right underneath you. It was right there, I could have touched it if it weren't for the glass."

"I thought you didn't like the aquarium that much," Chloe teased with a smirk.

"Well, you know, I got around to it," I answered shakingly. Chloe laughed a little at me and put a hand on my shoulder.

"I'm kidding. I'm glad you liked it too. Maybe next time we can go somewhere you really like and you can hope to convert me as well," she proposed.

"That sounds like a great idea," I said with a smile.

I don't know what came over me in this moment, but Chloe's roommate invaded my thoughts. I had been wondering why she was so against me going over to their apartment. I knew they had their rules in place, but why was it there in the first place? I asked Chloe to talk to her, but she told me it didn't lead to anything. It must have transpired on my face as Chloe's voice snapped me out of it.

"What's up?" she asked with concern in her voice. It reassured me to hear her, she could be so nice when she was worried about me. However, I needed to talk to her about this as now that the thought had crossed my mind, I couldn't possibly get it out without mentioning it. Why did I have to think about this now of all times?

"Yeah, I'm fine, it's just...um... I just thought about Beth and how she won't allow me to go to your place, especially after the other night..." I paused for a few seconds, looking for the right words. Chloe didn't interrupt and stared at me with more intense eyes than I would have liked. At least she was listening and not dismissing. I sighed and started back up again. "Will she ever acknowledge me as your boyfriend or will I be unable to see you at your place forever?"

Chloe took an audible breath and looked towards the crowd of people standing in the middle of the room. She seemed hesitant to talk about it, but ultimately, after a few seconds of thinking of her own, plunged into the water of this conversation with me.

"I have talked to her about that. Multiple times. Every time you're mentioned, she dismisses the subject and changes the conversation to be about me. She doesn't want to hear about you at all. It kind of hurts me a little when she does this, to be honest. Like she wants to hear about me, but not all about me, just the bit that she likes."

"Does she hate me?"

"No, I don't think she hates you; I think she just... I don't know, actually. It's just how she is, I guess, we've never had that kind of problem before."

"Has she ever brought her boyfriend home?"

"I don't think I've seen her in a relationship before. Rather, she never mentioned if she was and she never brought anyone other than her friends who were all girls."

"That is so weird to me. How long have you been living with her now?"

"Almost two years."

"Two years! I don't know how you managed to make it this long with rules like that. Does she have other restricting rules like 'must do the laundry on Saturday and no other day' or some overly zealous stuff?"

"Oh, no, she's super relaxed about everything else. But boys? Strictly not allowed. I've asked about it in the past, but she never quite explained why that was such a concern for her. Maybe I should ask again."

"Well, you know, I'm just bummed out about the whole thing, because it feels like she didn't even give me a chance. She disliked me without even meeting me the first time. I just wanted to be able to go to your place for once. Wouldn't it be nice to cuddle and listen to movies in your bed instead of mine one of these days?"

"Yeah, that would be nice." Both of us went silent, seemingly thinking about the possibilities we could have if Beth only allowed me to be there. I had tried to think of reasons why she didn't like me, but they all seemed crazier and crazier and I couldn't believe any of them. I was at a loss and lifted my eyes to see another corridor leading some other place we hadn't visited yet. I nudged Chloe in the shoulder.

"Looks like we have some more exploring to do," I said, pointing at the darkened hallway. Chloe got up, excited, and we walked over together, holding hands. I was glad the previous conversation didn't tarnish the mood and we could continue to enjoy the date like it never happened.

Even if the sun was slowly setting on the horizon, the bright light of the outside still blinded us for a good while and we had to protect ourselves to let our eyes adjust. We had just spent a few hours almost completely in the dark and the sudden change made my eyes burn a little. The slightly glowing snow reflecting the sun rays didn't help either. After a couple minutes of us talking to the ground, we finally were able to see properly and started walking towards the bus stop that would take us home.

"Do you want to go back to my place? We could spend the evening together, too?" I asked on the way.

"I'm sorry, I actually have some other things I have to do and I promised to take care of them today," Chloe answered with a pout. "What about next week?"

"Well, you know you can come any time after school and I'm completely free on Tuesday," I said.

"Let's go for Tuesday, then," she concluded with a smile. I looked at her and couldn't help but smile back. She was so pretty when she was happy like this and it seemed to spread to everyone around her. I was already looking forward to next week and couldn't wait to see her again even though she hadn't left yet. "I'll try to talk to Beth, see if we can't come up with a solution and I'll tell you if anything comes up."

"Sounds good, but don't…um…pressure her into changing the rules, either. Even just knowing why it's there would be a good start," I said.

"Don't worry, it's been at the back of my mind too and I've been meaning to get to the bottom of this ever since she caught us when you came over that one time. She wasn't happy about that one at all," she said, laughing at the thought. I couldn't exactly relate as she had literally pushed me out of the apartment then, but I had no trouble imagining the reaction.

"Yeah, I bet. Okay, well then, see you in a few days," I said with a smile. By now, we had reached the bus I had to take to get home and she would have to walk just a little further. She got closer to me and we embraced each other, both of us not wanting to let go. I peaked at the street corner and saw the familiar sight of the bus turning towards us. I backed off from the hug and looked at Chloe for a second. I couldn't resist putting a kiss on her lips and she happily responded. I didn't want to part ways, but the sound of the bus got louder and louder and I knew it was getting closer to the stop. I finally let go and looked at her again.

"I love you," she said.

"I love you, too," I responded without hesitation. I turned around to get on the bus that had just arrived. I walked to the closest seat next to the window to wave her goodbye and she shyly waved back. I guessed having every other pair of eyes seeing her was making her more embarrassed than usual and I smiled at the sight while, faster than I would have liked, the bus continued on its journey, leaving her behind. My phone vibrated in my pocket and I took it out to see I had a message from her. It was three hearts and I responded by sending three hearts as well. One thing I liked about being with Chloe was we didn't need to prepare something necessarily. We could just hang out, make supper and watch a movie or a show on the TV and we both would enjoy the evening. It was different when I was with Camille, she always wanted to go somewhere specific, be it a restaurant, a café, a mountain to walk, the beach, it didn't matter. It wasn't really possible to simply stay at home for once. With Chloe, we just enjoyed each other's company so wherever we went, it was nice as long as we were together. Maybe that was because we knew each other for longer? Well, there was no real use to comparing the two; one relationship was over and done with while the other was still ongoing. I had to focus on the one I had with Chloe and not dwell on how it was with Camille. I received another text from Chloe.

Thank you for today, it was really nice! Next time, we'll go to somewhere you want, okay? No excuses, I don't want to hear them. Alright, love you <3

People in the bus must have thought I was crazy as I was smiling at my phone. As I read the text, I swore I could hear her voice. The sheer thought of her reprimanding me in advance and telling me to save my excuses made me laugh silently. Even in text, she was still the cutest girl I had ever known and I couldn't wait to see her again.

Chapter 26

“Oh, no way!” I said, eyes widened as I spotted a familiar cover. I quickly shuffled the used games aside and picked one up to check the back. After reading only a couple lines, I knew it was the one game I had been searching for years now. It was an old game, not anything that came out recently and it was the only one missing in my collection. I already had a port of the game on another console, but this was the original and it was rather rare to see it, especially just lying around like this. Working in a video store with a video game section, I usually had first pick when it came to buying used games or whatever the customers were bringing in. I had never seen it then and had been searching relentlessly for years. And now, it was in my hands, just waiting to be bought. “I can’t believe this,” I whispered to myself.

“What is it?” Chloe asked, catching up to me. I turned around and gave her the biggest smile I had ever done. I couldn’t wait to tell her all about it.

“Okay, so you know how I collect the Blood of Battle franchise, right? Well, this is the final piece I was missing to finally have the entire collection! Isn’t that insane?”

“Oh really? That’s so cool. After this one, you’ll have them all?” she asked, getting interested.

“Yup!” I answered enthusiastically.

“Well, then you have to get it, right? How much is it?”

“It’s practically a steal, it’s only 65$,” I explained.

“Wow, rather pricey for such an old looking game. I guess that comes with age, doesn’t it? Is it rare or something?” she guessed.

“It’s not the rarest game out there, but it is pretty rare, yes,” I continued. “This is the first copy on this console I’ve seen with my own eyes. I still can’t believe this.”

“What are you waiting for? Go buy it!” she encouraged.

“I will, I just want to go look around to see if there’s anything else I want to get. I’ll keep it with me, I’m not about to let this one go,” I laughed.

"Okay, well I'll be wandering around not knowing what to do so you know where to find me," Chloe concluded with a smile.

She turned around and started walking away to another section. I resumed rummaging through the bin, looking for anything else that stood out to me. There were a bunch of titles I already saw many times, things that didn't sell very well and were obviously there for a while at this point. Gems like the one I had found were often hidden among less inviting games and you really had to search every corner to find something good. Pretty soon, however, it became obvious there was nothing more of value in there and I turned around to wander into the next one. They were new releases on the brand-new consoles, but being an employee in a video store, I had already seen every single one of these before they were out for sale. We did get new releases, but not all of them which always confused me. Why would you have a video game area that featured only a part of the market? Customers, often gamers, who came in looking for a particular title would leave when I'd say we didn't have the one they were searching for. That was the loss of a sale, every time, and for what? Well, it didn't matter as even looking through the shelves in this section, there weren't many games that interested me and the steep price point of them turned me off from buying any.

I turned around and tried spotting Chloe, but she didn't immediately come into view. I went back to the used games and then in the direction she went in only to find her eyeing up a game cover. Curious, I got closer to her and she quickly lifted her eyes up to look at me as I stopped near her.

"This one looks fun," she said, showing me the game. I read the title aloud.

"Protector of the Gnomes," I paused for a few seconds, trying to decide between laughing and asking for more details. I decided on the latter. "What is it about?"

"From what I can tell, you have a village of gnomes to protect so you have to build defenses and walls, feed your gnomes and train them to build a little gnome army to defend against some threat, they don't say what it is," she explained.

"Oh, so typical city-builder stuff, but with a gnome aesthetic," I commented.

"A city what?" Chloe asked, confused.

"City-builder. It's the genre of game you were describing. I'm sure there are other things to distinguish it from other city-builders, but from what you said it was pretty standard. You like it because of the gnomes, right?" I asked, even though I already knew the answer. Chloe smiled at me.

"Maybe," she said slowly with a smirk hiding in plain sight at the corner of her mouth. She stood there, seemingly waiting for something to happen and time appeared to stand still while I remained silent. Finally, I rolled my eyes a little, closed them and smiled while shifting my head down. I couldn't help but sigh as well.

"You want to get it, don't you?"

"Uh, yes! Of course I do, look at them! They're so cute. Plus, you can play two players apparently, so you'll be able to play with me." The way she said it implied I had no say in the matter, but I didn't mind. Chloe wasn't usually into many games and especially not the Blood of Battle franchise I was collecting, but this game might be the one for her. It didn't look like the type of game I would usually play, but if it meant spending time with her, then I would gladly try it at least once.

"Sure, I'll play with you," I said.

"Yay!" Chloe exclaimed while jumping in the air a little. "Alright, let's go pay, we have many places to do today and if we stay here any longer, we won't have time to do them all," she said, practically dragging me to the counter.

The store was mostly empty and we didn't have to wait in line at all. We quickly paid and got out into the massive shopping mall that would occupy the rest of our day. Chloe wanted to go shopping for anything and everything and the only thing I wanted was to stop at the game store for a quick look. It ended up paying big time for me and I would gladly follow her to whatever store she wanted now. We started walking down a corridor, I didn't know where we were really and it didn't matter to me, I was just glad to spend time with Chloe. I extended my free hand, the other one occupied holding the bag containing the games, and she grabbed it greedily. I could tell she was excited about the day too and it made me snicker a little. She could be so cute in the simplest ways sometimes.

The mall wasn't busy either and we could walk freely unlike previous times I had come here. Sometimes, it was hard to even walk straight there were so many people and getting somewhere took a lot longer than it needed to. I quite enjoyed this, though, as the echoing building wasn't overwhelming with noises of conversation and people walking. It was calm and just perfect to enjoy the experience. I didn't go shopping much, but if it was more like this, perhaps I would more often. Especially if it was with someone like Chloe.

"Let's go in that one first," said Chloe while pointing to a clothes store. Even though it was April, they were already displaying summer clothes and advertising bikinis in the front windows. It always seemed weird to me how companies did this. Halloween wasn't even over and Christmas decorations were already out. Christmas was barely over that Valentine's Day chocolate was on sale. There was like this need to prepare months in advance for something and, while I understood the feeling somewhat, it was sometimes crazy to see how fast stores moved on to the next holiday. I didn't say anything and simply followed Chloe into the store.

It wasn't the biggest store of all; there were barely any cabins to try any clothes, but I guessed that made sense as they mainly sold swimwear. Chloe led me to the bikini section and started looking at them one by one as I stood there awkwardly. She must have seen me fidgeting on one foot to the other as she turned around to look at me.

"What?"

"Nothing, I'm just… a little uncomfortable is all," I said in embarrassment.

"What do you mean? Being in the bikini section?" I nodded in agreement and she smiled at me, containing her laughter. "Don't worry about it, you're fine, people come in with their boyfriends all the time," she said, trying to be reassuring. I looked around the store and no other guys were there which didn't help my cause. I tried to stare at the ground instead, but the redness of my cheeks didn't go away.

"What do you think of this one?" Chloe asked, showing me a bikini. I lifted my eyes up and calmed myself down. There was no reason to be this flustered about this, it was simply my girlfriend trying to shop for a bikini. I had been in this situation before, with Chloe no less, so there was no need to be embarrassed anymore. She put the bikini close to her chest to simulate putting it on and I had to admit she would look pretty cute in it.

"I'm sure all of them would look good on you," I said.

"Come on, I want your real opinion, don't try to be cheesy with me," she said, reprimanding me slightly. "What do you really think?"

"Yeah, it looks good. Wouldn't you get better deals at your store, though?" I asked out of curiosity.

"I would, but our selection is a little… it's hard to say. We sort of have a very specific niche of design that I'm just not into at all, so I usually buy my things somewhere else," she explained.

"That's a shame," I commented.

"Oh, not really. You know, I work there, but I don't have any attachment to the store. I'm perfectly fine with going to another one to do my shopping," Chloe said, still browsing through the many different options she had.

She kept taking some out and looking at them for a few seconds before putting them back in. It was a shame I couldn't see her put any of them on, but I understood the store not really wanting to deal with that kind of stuff. I had heard stories from Chloe about this and they weren't the prettiest things I ever heard. I followed her as she wandered around, occasionally picking one bikini and adding it to the pile she had on her arm. Whenever we encountered another woman in the store, I would always look away as if it were shameful to even be in their presence. I didn't know why, everything was telling me it was fine, but this little voice in my head kept telling me it was awkward and I couldn't ignore it. Still, I walked straight behind Chloe as much as possible so it was obvious we were together. When we had walked through the entire store, she stopped and handed me the entire pile without saying anything. I hesitated for a second before grabbing them all. My awkwardness level had just risen a lot, but I tried to play it off silently. She started taking them one by one and going through them again. Eventually, she only selected two of them and couldn't decide which one she liked more. In her right hand, she had a plain light blue bikini which went marvellously well with her eye color and in her left hand she had a simple darker green bikini that reminded me of the forest trees.

"Which one suits me better?" she asked, putting them over her chest a few seconds at a time before switching to the other.

"Well, the blue one makes your eyes pop out more while the green one seems to go better with your hair. Honestly, I like them both and I think they both suit you," I answered.

"Sure, but which one do you prefer?" she asked again. Now, her question was very different. Both would look cute on her, that much was certain, but which one I preferred was another story. I thought about it for a few seconds which must have appeared an eternity for her before I made my mind.

"I think I like the green one better. It just goes with you the best in my opinion," I settled.

"Let's go with the green one, then," she said with a smile. I was glad she decided to choose mine, but I would have been fine either way. I couldn't wait to see her wearing it and make me look dumb with my swim trunks. Guys didn't have many options when it came to swimwear, but at the same time, I wouldn't have worn anything other than those, so I guess that was exactly why. We made another round through the store to put back all the other bikinis I somehow ended up transporting, but the awkwardness of it had disappeared by this point and I didn't mind it now. After we were done, we quickly paid and got out into the mall again.

"So, where to next?" I asked, curious about our next stop.

"Oh, I don't know. Let's just walk and go into the next store that catches my eye," she said with a smile. I shrugged and went along with it. If even she didn't know what to do next, how was I supposed to know?

We continued walking in the quiet mall, debating what we could do in the upcoming summer and all the places we could go to now that we were together. There were plenty of new stuff I wanted to try like going camping and on a road trip, go have a day or a weekend in another city just for fun and maybe even visit some gardens. I surprised myself with that last one as it wasn't something I would have wanted to do a few months prior, but things were different now and activities I rejected before were now more appealing to me. Plus, I knew Chloe liked everything nature, be it fauna or flora alike, so she would surely be on board with that idea. She must have been into her own mind as we didn't speak until we reached another clothing store, this one a more general brand than the swimsuit store. We both got in without a word, seemingly drawn to this place by an invisible pull that needed no discussion. Shopping wasn't really my thing and whenever I had to go, I always had a precise list of what I was going to buy and where in order to get it over with as fast as possible. Now, I had no idea what I was doing, let alone if there was anything to look for and to consider buying.

"I'll go and have a look over there," Chloe said, pointing to the women's shirt section. I thought she had plenty of shirts already and didn't need any more, but that wasn't really any of my business, so I didn't say anything.

"Okay, I guess I'll hang out in the men's section and try to find something I like," I answered with a shrug.

"You don't absolutely have to buy something, you know," Chloe teased.

"I know, it just…feels weird to me to enter a store and just leave without anything. Anyway, see you in a bit." I turned around to walk to the men's section and found myself among countless pairs of jeans. I started browsing through them, but none piqued my interest and I quickly wandered to another part of the store. They had an impressive section for shirts. Usually, clothing stores were a lot more focused on the women's side, but this one had a surprising balance between the two. There were some that called out to me and I held them up to see them fully before folding them back up. I was getting kind of bored and looked around the store to find Chloe. Before I could see anything, something or someone grabbed me by the arm and started dragging me away. I let out a startled cry and started loudly protesting, trying to see what was happening. They were really holding on tight to my arm and I could feel the pain start to rise around my wrist. The only thing I managed to see was long blonde hair swinging from side to side from the effort of dragging me.

"Camille?" I asked to the person, but they didn't respond. I thanked myself to have put down the shirt as it would have sounded the alarm as we approached the store doors. As much as I wanted out of this situation, I didn't want to make a huge scene about it either. "Hey, let me go! What are you doing?"

The person finally let go of my arm and I rubbed it slightly the ease the pain. They turned around, revealing their face to me and, much as I predicted, it was indeed Camille. She didn't look in her best mood, but after what she just pulled, I wasn't exactly happy either.

"What's your problem? Why are you here?" I sharply asked.

"I wanted to talk to you," she simply answered.

"Yeah, well there are other ways to do that than literally dragging me through a store," I said, angrily. "What do you want?" I stared at her intensely and she looked away. Was it to avoid meeting my angry eyes or was it in embarrassment? It took her a few seconds before I heard her voice again.

"I just wanted to tell you I was sorry and that I made a mistake in leaving you. We shouldn't have broken up, we should be together, things are different when you're not around, I..." she said, trying to put a hand on my shoulder. I shoved it aside with a look of confusion and she was equally confused.

"Camille, we've been over this already," I interrupted, raising my voice slightly which wasn't something I was used to. "We're done. I'm not coming back and you should extinguish any hope you have of that. Move on."

"You were never this harsh before. You've changed," Camille said, backing away slightly and bringing her hands close to her chest.

"Yeah, that tends to happen when you drag people like you did. Look, I'm trying to put this behind me, okay, and you continuously coming back like this is just making it worse, both for you and for me. Can you just stop? Please?"

"You don't get it. I want to make it up to you, I want to make things work between us, I want you back," she practically pleaded while looking at the ground.

"There is no us. Not anymore. There has been no us ever since January. I accepted it when you left, why can't you accept when I left? Matter of fact, how did you even find us here? There's practically nobody in the mall, what were you doing?" I said accusingly.

"I've been...I... I saw you both and..." she stuttered.

"You saw us? Camille, we've been in stores most of the time and I wasn't in view of the door in the men's section back there. There's no way you saw me from outside; you knew I was in there. Don't lie to me now, come on," I said in a slightly disappointed tone.

"Okay, fine! I followed you both since you came in here. I overheard your friends talking about you having plans to go shopping today and decided to come at the same time," she said, gesturing with her hands. Her eyes were starting to water and she looked down, moving them out of view. "I just... I wanted to talk to you," she sighed, still staring at the ground.

"You could have just texted or called me," I reasoned.

"Would you have answered?" she asked, lifting her head up to look at me. Her eyes were accusatory and I felt some remnant of anger in her staring. Before I could answer, I heard another voice coming from my right side.

"What's going on?" Chloe asked in a concerned tone. She stopped in her tracks when she saw Camille, looking both at me and her repeatedly. Camille turned her head and her expression shifted completely. I glanced at Chloe and time seemed to stand still. When I returned to face Camille, I got confused as I didn't expect her to be grinning like she was. Before I could even react, she launched herself at me and smacked her lips on mine, locking me into a deep kiss. Her hand grabbed the back of my head to prevent me from escaping, but I didn't even get passed the shock of her sudden movement.

It took me a few moments to realize what was happening. This wasn't the girl I was supposed to kiss. This was Camille, this wasn't right. Despite having kissed those lips before, I had no desire to do so ever again and, snapping back to my sense, I pushed her away just as Chloe was coming in between us. I couldn't say a word before she exploded with anger.

"What the hell is your problem?" she shouted at Camille.

"How does it feel, huh? How does it feel to be betrayed by your cheating boyfriend? Kissing his ex in front of his current girlfriend, that's bold," Camille mocked while locking eyes with me. I could see her trying to be confident, but they only reflected a deep-rooted sadness in those green eyes of hers. What was she trying to do here?

"Jack is not a cheater. You, on the other hand, are a massive bitch. Why are you kissing my boyfriend?" I had never seen Chloe so angry and, if I had to comment, I wouldn't have liked to be on the receiving end of that stare. She wasn't even looking at me and I could feel the daggers shredding my skin and stabbing my heart.

"I just wanted to give you a taste of your own medicine. After all, there's nothing wrong with that, right? You did it yourself, so I don't see why you'd be upset..." Camille shrugged with a smirk. If I didn't have any principles or morals, I could have punched her then and there.

"What are you talking about?" Chloe said while rapidly shaking her head left and right. I knew what she was referring to, and Chloe would probably come to the same conclusion soon enough, but I wanted to defuse the situation right away. No need to escalate this any further.

"Alright, I think that's..." I started, trying to get in between them. I was stopped by Chloe's hands blocking my way.

"No, I want to hear what she has to say. Go on, then, say your piece!" Chloe said while gesturing with her other hand. Camille, who was previously composed and cocky, shifted to an aggressive look and I swore she exuded fiery tendrils from her whole body. Perhaps I had watched too many movies and was imagining things.

"Don't play dumb with me, we both know what I'm referring to. You did this exact thing to my brother and now I'm simply paying it back. You stole Jack from me. He was my boyfriend and you kept getting in the way, leading him on like a puppeteer and his favorite marionette. Did you like doing that? Do you enjoy cheating on your boyfriends and then stealing them from other people? Ever since you came back into his life, you've been poisoning him with your words, turning him away from me. This is all your fault and I swear I will make you pay for this." Camille's word felt like she had just spat out venom straight in Chloe's face and I could feel her getting flustered very quickly. I tried to get a word in, but she was faster than me.

"I've been poisoning him? I've always been there for him, whenever things got really bad and that includes when YOU left him. We've known each other for years and he's known you for what? Less than one? Jack made his choice when he broke up with you the second time. Why is that so hard to understand in your tiny head?"

"He was confused by your scheming and your meddling of our relationship, that's why!" Camille shouted.

"What scheming? He's free to do his own choice, I had nothing to do with it!" Chloe argued.

"If you hadn't been whispering at him to turn him against me, none of this would have happened. He couldn't think straight because of you. He would be better off going out with me," Camille continued shouting.

"You don't get to decide that, only Jack does, and he's clearly made his choice already. Get out of his life and leave him alone. You need to stay in your lane and stop trying to mess with ours. Get. Out."

"Can we please not do this here?" I said, trying to break off the fight and get in between them to stop the argument.

"I'm not talking to you anymore," Camille said, shoving me aside. "Let me finish talking with this ginger bitch."

The slap resonated in the mall and time seemed to stand still. Camille took one step back from the impact on her cheek and her hand went straight to it. She was shocked and startled while Chloe was definitely pissed off and looking at her with furious eyes, the angriest I had ever seen her. Camille's expression soon morphed to anger as well and she wound her arm back to retaliate. I quickly caught it mid swing with a sharp sound that echoed through the store, much like the previous slap. I looked at Camille and Chloe both in succession.

"That's enough, both of you," I said firmly, any remnant of trying to defuse this situation peacefully now gone. "If any of you have things to say, you can talk to each other outside, but there will be no more violence. If you can't even do that, then I'm disappointed in you both. Is that clear?" When I finished talking, I was surprised at myself for managing to be this bossy as this wasn't my usual behavior at all. Normally, I would try to defuse any situation by talking calmly, but something about these two riled me up a lot more than usual. Why couldn't they just talk to each other? Why did they have to shout every time they saw each other? All this over me, no less. Was I the one causing all this discourse? Camille wrestled herself free and backed away a little, still staring intensely at Chloe who was doing the same to her.

"I have nothing more to say to you. You don't deserve him and he doesn't deserve you. You both should end up alone. That's all you're worth, anyway," Camille said before turning around and leaving angrily.

"Yeah, you better leave!" Chloe shouted.

"Chloe, stop, that's enough," I said, grabbing her by the shoulders and putting myself between her and Camille rapidly disappearing into the mall.

"How dare she come over here and pull this crap after all she's done to you? What where you doing back there? Why did it take so long for you to reject her?" she asked.

"I… I don't…"

"Whatever," Chloe said, cutting me off. She was clearly pissed and I could fully understand why, but I also felt it wasn't totally my fault. I was shocked by Camille's move and couldn't process what was happening. It wasn't like I was enjoying her kiss or anything, right?

I sighed heavily and turned around to see the store manager coming towards us. I closed my eyes. I knew what that conversation was going to be about, and I didn't want to have it, but I guess it couldn't be helped. He soon arrived next to us.

"I'm sorry, but I'm going to ask you to leave. You've been disrupting the customers and making too much noise," he said.

"Of course. I'm sorry about all this, we were on our way out already," I said, trying to grab Chloe and lead her towards the exit.

"Well, if she hadn't…" she started.

"I said enough. Let's just… get out for now," I shut down before she could finish her thought. She grumbled something I couldn't hear, and I turned my head around to silently apologizes to the manager one more time as we were walking out.

The mood had drastically changed after the incident, and we didn't talk much at all during the rest of the shopping. Chloe seemed in a really bad mood and I was just lost in my own thoughts of self-doubt. What if I really didn't deserve either of them? Everywhere I went, they both got hurt somehow and I seemed like a drama magnet at times. I kept hurting Camille's feelings and did much of the same to Chloe when I was dating Camille and talking to her about it. I didn't know, how could I have known? Maybe it would just be best if I stepped away from all this, return to my much simpler life I had a year ago and forget any of this had ever happened. Even the thought of it hurt my heart, but sometimes, if you truly love something, it's better to let it go than hold on to it out of desperation. I had to come to terms with it; I was a bad boyfriend who kept hurting the ones I love over and over again because of stupid things. I couldn't do anything right and kept messing up like me forgetting Camille's birthday and not being able to deal with her appropriately when I broke up with her. I hurt Chloe's feelings when I thought she only viewed me as a friend and commented as such. Even if she told me it was fine, I still felt a little guilty about sleeping with Violet. And now this. She still made me feel like it was my fault Camille had kissed me, but a part of me found that really unfair as I didn't want or enjoy any part of it. The girl launched herself at me, what was I supposed to do? I couldn't have known she would do that, so how was I supposed to…? For the past year, it seemed like everything I did came back to bite me some time later and I was just over the whole thing. Why wasn't it possible to have a normal life dating a girl I loved? Why did it have to be so complicated?

Chloe finally talked again after a while, but I only half-listened to her as these poisonous thoughts kept bouncing in my head. She didn't mention the incident again and, even if I found that a little weird as she usually would, I was glad she didn't. The mood of the day was still completely destroyed, and it persisted through the trip back to Chloe's apartment where we had agreed to go our separate ways for the day. As we got off the bus and walked over to the front door of her building, Chloe stopped dead in her tracks which took me by surprise. I stopped walking right next to her and turned around to face her. She was looking down, hiding her face from my view. I could feel tense energy swirling all around us and, as awkward as it was, I let her decide when to start talking.

"Listen, I think I need time to cool down after what happened today," she started, unsure how to properly say what she wanted to say. I knew this was the direction this conversation was headed in and I couldn't escape it. I had to face it now.

"You know it was all her doing, right? I had nothing to do with that," I tried to explain.

"I know and it's super selfish of me to project my doubts on you, I realize that. But I can't get out of my head the thought of you kissing her and it seemed like you stayed there for so long. I'm sorry, I know this is stupid, but can we just...take a break?" Chloe finally asked.

I was slumped. Never in a million years would I have guessed that was what she wanted. A break? Wasn't this how couples start to distance themselves from each other until they finally cut all contact? I didn't want that to happen! Not so soon after confessing, not ever in fact. She was the one for me, more so than Camille could have ever hoped to be.

"Are you mad at me?" I asked, semi out of fear and out of concern. I had to find out. She took a while to answer which only made the anticipation heavier.

"No. Well, not really. I know this wasn't your fault," she finally said. "But part of me still sees you with her and it doesn't sit well with me, hence why I need a break."

"Are you sure about this? I'm telling you; that was nothing. I don't have feelings for Camille anymore, she's the one who keeps coming back and messing with us. That kiss...was all her doing. If I didn't back away immediately is because I was surprised, not because I liked it. Please, you have to believe me."

"I do," Chloe said, resting her hand on my chest. I looked down and grabbed it with my hand. I could feel the tears welling up in my eyes, but I didn't want to cry in front of her now. "I do believe you, I just...need a little time to process this, okay? Just give me a few days to forget this."

There was no point in arguing further. She had made up her mind already and I knew it was pointless to try and dissuade her at this point. The fact she even proposed a break hurt me a little, but I had already said my piece so it was all up to her now. It wasn't like I did anything wrong; I hadn't been the one to kiss Camille, I didn't cheat on her, I wasn't seeing other people secretly, I told her that much multiple times.

"Okay…" I sighed, holding on to her hands desperately. She pulled them back and smiled at me, a smile filled with sadness and grief, a smile I didn't recognize, a smile I didn't want to see on her face. With not another word, she turned around and got into her apartment building, going out of my view. I had wanted to say the words to her, but my throat blocked up and they wouldn't come out. Would she have responded anyway? I wasn't too sure at this point.

I just hoped I didn't lose her for good.

Chapter 27

The bar had a gloomier atmosphere this time. Where I previously saw dim lights, I now saw fleeting flashes immediately swallowed by darkness. Every color was darker than before and the wood even sounded different. The declining sun on the horizon filled the bar with a seemingly glowing light, but I paid it no mind. No beautiful scenery could appease me now. I was uncomfortable, both physically and mentally. The seat under me hurt just as much as my heart was aching and no amount of sipping my beer would change that.

The chatter of conversation had risen to a level high enough to partially quell my thoughts, but not completely. I kept thinking of Chloe and how I still managed to mess everything up once again. I was annoyed, mostly at myself, for being so stupid and naïve and so clumsy when it came to dealing with personal issues. All around me, my friends were talking enthusiastically between each other and I couldn't bring myself to join their conversation. There was something wrong about enjoying an activity such as this or being out with my friends that didn't sit right with me. I was going over the events of the last week, from when she asked for the break to now, and thinking what I could have done differently. There were loads of things, of course, but I didn't even know where to start. A bump on my shoulder took me out of my thoughts and I looked to my left to see who pushed me.

"Hey, why the long face, man?" Michael said. They knew perfectly well why; I had told them what happened already. "You ought to lighten up a little and join us."

"I'm sorry, guys, I just… I just don't feel like it right now," I answered.

"Still not going better with Chloe, I'm assuming?" Chris asked, bringing his beer up to take a sip.

"No, nothing new since last week. I keep calling and texting, but she hasn't answered anything, she hasn't even seen the messages. That's just what I deserve, though, right?" I said, looking down at the table.

"What are you saying? You know that's not true," Vincent said.

"I should have been more direct with Camille about ending things and none of this would have happened. We're in this situation because of me and, from the looks of it, Chloe won't ever forgive me."

"Woah, that's taking it a bit far, yeah? From what you told us, Camille was the one who jumped you, not the opposite. You did nothing wrong here. Chloe just needs time, that's all. She'll come around," Michael said.

"Even though she asked for the break, I kind of want to go see her and try to patch things up with her."

"Will you?" Chris asked.

I looked at them for a few seconds. I didn't know the answer to that question. I wanted to, of course, but would anything have changed about me to justify that or would I be the same guy that couldn't deal with his issues properly? Camille was my responsibility, after all. If it was just going to be the same then the same problems would arise later, wouldn't they? Their eyes were all on me and their staring pressured me like a ton of bricks on my shoulders. I shrugged and sighed and returned to staring at the wood table we were all sitting around. Perhaps I would find the answer in the weird shapes I could make out of it.

"I want to, but if she's not even answering me, I guess that tells me her answer, doesn't it?"

"It's not a good sign, let's put it that way, but it doesn't mean she won't ever want to listen to what you have to say ever again," Vincent said.

"Did you contact her on something else like social media or whatever?" Michael asked.

"No, I didn't want to come off as insistent or desperate."

"Yeah, I'd say that's probably for the best," Vincent added.

"I'm just fed up with myself for feeling that way all the time. Why am I doubting everything? It's annoying and frustrating, even to me, so I can't imagine how it feels for everyone else. Things were going well with her, why am I feeling guilty about this when I'm the one who got kissed, not the opposite. Why couldn't I just brush Camille to the side and disregard what she said?"

"What's done is done. I think you still care about her, even just a little and not in a romantic way anymore, but you don't want to see her get hurt. You were trying to think of the best approach to the situation and it looked like you were thinking something else," Chris said.

"This is not helping," I sighed.

"Hold on, let me finish. What I mean is, Chloe will realize this. I'm sure of it, even if I don't know her personally. I know what kind of guy you are and she knows it as well. Like Michael said, just give her some time," Chris continued.

"It's already been a week, though, how much longer do I have to wait?"

"I don't know. That's a little hard to answer, if I'm honest," Chris shrugged. He took a sip of beer and paused for a few seconds, staring at the ceiling. It seemed like he was trying to recall something and nobody said a word to distract him. Finally, his eyes came back down and met mine. He was staring at me, resolute, but kind.

"I have a little story to tell you. I don't know if it'll help, but maybe it could clarify some things for you and help you figure out what to do next."

I got back up from the table, willing to listen to him. Chris had always been someone who told things how they were, no matter if the truth was hurtful or not. You could always count on him to give his honest opinion about something and that's one of the things that made him such a good friend to me. He wasn't afraid to call me out on my insecurities and bring me back from the depths of my anxiousness. If he was telling this story, it would at least be interesting and most likely helpful. I was all ears.

"As you know, I met Sarah around seven years ago back when we were in high school. Back then, we were sitting next to each other in most classes as we were seated alphabetically and our last names are very close to each other. We got to know one another quite well and I developed a little crush on her soon after we started working together on homework and assignments. She had her group of friends and I had mine and we usually separated for breaks and lunch and such, but we always came back, class after class. We got friendly enough to start joking about the other's physique and random quirks they had and it was in good fun. Every time I would make her laugh, she would hit me. Not a punch, mind you, maybe a little jab on the shoulder, maybe a light tap with her history book, her math book, that kind of thing." Chris paused a moment, recollecting some parts of the story and letting us process what we had just heard. I thought they seemed like good friends, kind of like what Chloe and I had too. What made them different from us?

"Flash forward a year and a half after we met," Chris continued. "I was tired of hiding my feelings and went to confess to her, knowing it would probably end our friendship if the answer was negative. She actually laughed in my face and mocked me for how long it took for me to do it. She said she had been into me for a long time as well and it turns out her hitting me was her way of expressing her feelings. Might not be the best way to do that, mind you, but it is what it is. That was give years ago and we're still together today. Now, I didn't tell you this story so I could display my relationship status, I do have a reason for it. There was a miscommunication at the beginning, right? I didn't tell her how I felt and she didn't tell me how she felt. After we got together, we made sure to always tell the other if anything was wrong. It's fine to have problems, insecurities, to be anxious about stuff, to want some time to yourself, but you have to communicate properly. Relationships are all about understanding the other's feelings, but also yours as well. How could you communicate what you feel if you don't understand them yourself? What I mean to ask is this; do you love Chloe?"

"I do," I said without hesitation. It even surprised me a little when the words came out, but my heart spoke faster than my head.

"Then you deserve to have your chance. Talk to her. Tell her how you feel. Show her that you're dedicated to your relationship, to make amends and work together through tough times. Say that you only see yourself with her. Just to be sure, that is true, yes?"

"Of course. There's no one else I'd rather be with," I answered directly. There was no hesitation to be had.

"Exactly. Tell her, show her what you mean. Make her understand you want her to rely on you when these things come up, not run away in a corner and bottle it up by herself. You're a team, yeah? Bring the team back together!"

"Yeah, what he said," Michael said, pointing at Chris.

"Oh, buzz off" Chris laughed. "Do you get what I'm saying, though?" he said, looking straight at me. His piercing gaze made me look away after a few seconds. Somehow, in a manner of a few minutes, he managed to make me both embarrassed about myself and resolute to try and fix things. He put it so well into words I was astonished and couldn't answer right away. I always had issues opening up to people before meeting these guys, maybe Chloe was experiencing the same thing right now and didn't know how to talk to her friends about this. Maybe she needed me to lend an ear and a shoulder for her to truly tell me how she feels. Maybe she needed me by her side right now and I was here, moping around about my situation instead of actively trying to fix it. I could be so clueless sometimes.

"Yeah, I do. I'll go talk to her," I said, resolved.

"Good. You deserve it, man, I'll always cheer for you," Chris said with a nod.

"Same here," Vincent said.

"Hey, don't forget me," Michael said.

I looked at all three of them, one by one. I smiled a little and closed my eyes. I was lucky to have such friends; I didn't know what I would do if I had to tackle all this alone.

"Thanks, guys," I said.

They began talking amongst themselves again, but I didn't follow the conversation. I was too busy thinking about what Chris had just said, Chloe and how I would go about telling her how I felt again. Exposing yourself, sharing a part of you that's most vulnerable, is a difficult endeavor for anyone and I just now realized how much these things need to be said and expressed rather than being bottled up. In repressing this part of myself, I was not only causing harm to myself, but also others around me. I looked up at the ceiling and smiled. They say the first step to correcting a problem is recognizing you have a problem. Well, if that was truly the case, then I was one step closer to lifting this weight that dragged me down.

◊

The hot shower water had been gently massaging me for a few minutes already. I had gotten in more as a habit than anything else, but was frozen under the stream ever since I set foot in the tub. I stared straight at the ground, staring at the white bath with water flowing down my face, completely lost in thought and reminiscing what I had talked about the day before with my friends at the bar. Somehow, even though I was really confident at the end of the night, I was starting to doubt myself again. There must have been a reason why Chloe didn't answer any of my texts and calls and what other reason would she have other than she didn't want to talk to me anymore?

I tried to talk to her at school the other day. Seeing her enter the classroom without even a single look in my direction kind of hurt me, but I decided to move past it and approach her at the end of the class. When the professor dismissed us, she almost ran straight to the door and I couldn't catch her. She kept evading me for the entirety of the week, making it impossible to even put in another word to her. Why was she doing this? I just wanted to let her know I wanted to talk, but how was I supposed to do that when she ignored me everywhere? I got that she was hurt by my behavior, but I wanted to correct that mistake. I wanted to tell her everything, but she wouldn't have any of it.

If I went to her apartment, would she answer the door? Would Beth be there? Would she bother answering me or leave me in the hallway, so close yet out of reach? I could just wait for her in front of one of her classes, I knew her schedule, but cornering her at school didn't feel like the right thing to do either. We needed to have a very private conversation and the hallways at school didn't seem like the quietest place to engage in such a talk. No, I needed to see her face to face, alone, somewhere where we could talk freely. In a park, perhaps? How would I get her to come to a park when she didn't answer me on anything? No, that wouldn't work. Everything pointed to her apartment. I knew she would be there; I knew she would be available to have a mostly private talk, but then came the Beth variable. Would she open the door? Would she let me in after what happened last time we saw each other?

I sighed, the sound getting covered by the running water. Even this shower had memories with Chloe. It's where we had our first time together, where we first declared our love for each other's bodies. Now, standing alone under the stream with the water dripping down my face, it felt like I was crying. About ten minutes had gone by since I got in and I didn't even start washing myself at all. I absent-mindedly grabbed the soap in one hand and stared at it like I didn't know what to do with it.

I wanted to go apologize to her and tell her how much she means to me, but what if she didn't forgive me and ended our relationship right then? Could I still call it a relationship? What if she got tired of me and wanted nothing to do with me anymore? Who would I turn to, then? My friends certainly were there, but they weren't Chloe and I couldn't imagine losing her. Just that feeling could have quelled any doubts I previously had. If I was that afraid of her running away from me, surely that meant the feelings I had were very real. Her previous reaction spoke of her perspective, too, so what was there to be unsure about? Why was I so stupid sometimes?

I turned off the water and dried myself off. I needed to talk to her now. Not tomorrow, not the day after. Now. As I got out, I checked the time on the stove; 9h23 p.m. Busses would be scarce at this time, but I was compelled to find a way to get to her apartment. I quickly got dressed and flew out the door, determined and resolved to talk to her if it was the last thing I did.

◊

Cars were going by behind me as I stood in front of the building, trying to gather the courage to go inside. She was right there, a few meters away behind a few doors. I could call out to her and she would hear it. I was confident I could get her to understand and forgive me if I could just talk to her, but that was the hardest part. I walked forward and reached for the door, opening it slightly before stopping myself. I took a deep breath and nodded. I was ready.

I stepped inside. The stairs appeared like mountains to climb, like an insurmountable challenge I couldn't hope to face. Never had stairs intimidated me that much and, as I walked closer, my heart started to beat faster and faster. Every step I took brought me closer to her, she was only a few seconds away. The ascension was painful, not physically, but emotionally. By the time I got up to her door, it felt like my heart was stretched up to its bursting point, like it could rip at any moment. I was breathing faster than I thought, the nervousness enveloping my entire body in a frenzy. If this situation happened last year, I would probably have been shaking by now, but I now had enough control to supress it somewhat. My fist approached the door, stopping before the first knock. Was I truly ready? There wasn't going to be another occasion if I backed away now. I just had to…

Knock Knock Knock

I stepped away from the door a little, looking down at the ground to control myself as much as possible. My breathing had gotten shaky and I could feel my heart pounding in my chest. I tried to calm down as much as I could, to regain control of myself, but had little to no success in doing so. I danced from one foot to another, trying to calm down. I heard the lock turn and stopped breathing for a moment. The door opened slightly. I lifted my eyes off the ground and they met with…

Beth.

Of course, it had to be her. It would have been too easy otherwise.

"What do you want?" she said in a hostile tone.

"Is Chloe there? I need to talk to her," I managed to say, nervously trying to look behind Beth, but she closed the gap in the door even more so I couldn't see anything.

"No, she's not. You had better leave."

"Are you sure? It's really important, I just need to talk to her," I insisted, surprising myself at my forwardness on the edge of panic.

"She's not here, so stop wasting my time and leave," Beth dismissed. She was about to close the door when I interrupted her.

"Where is she, then?" I asked, practically pleading her to tell me.

"You have some balls to come here after what you did to her, you know that? I did tell her she was better off without you and she didn't listen to me. Look where that lead her. You're not a good guy, Jack, you're not good for her. You need to leave. Now. She doesn't need someone like you, not now and not ever."

She closed the door violently before I could say another word. I stood there, dumbfounded and in shock. I didn't expect the interaction to go smoothly, but I didn't expect to get the door slammed in my face either. I was about to turn around when I heard a familiar voice coming from inside the apartment. The sounds were kind of muffled and I had to listen very closely to understand anything.

"Who was that?" Chloe asked.

"Just a delivery guy," Beth answered.

"At this time? What was he delivering?"

"I don't know."

"Where's the package?"

"It was a wrong address," Beth lied.

"Really? Odd..."

I don't know what compelled me in that moment, but I sprang forward and knocked on the door again. Both of them stopped talking and time seemed to stand still for a few seconds. Then I heard the door open again, but this time Chloe was standing in the doorway instead of Beth.

"Jack? What are you doing here?" she asked, surprised to see me.

"I needed to talk to you," I answered simply. Chloe turned around to look at Beth.

"Was he the delivery guy?" Beth didn't answer and crossed her arms to look at me with intense eyes. I tried to ignore her as best I could and focused on Chloe. She turned around to look at me. "Come in, don't just stand there." She stepped to the side to let me enter. Beth didn't like that one bit.

"Are you serious? You're going to let him in after what he did?" she protested.

"What did he do exactly?" Chloe asked.

"He kissed his ex, remember? Does that ring any bells?"

"First of all, he didn't kiss her, she kissed him. Second of all, if he came all the way out here, it's probably to explain himself and I'm ready to give him his chance. I'll decide what to do from there."

"But you told him to never come back!" Beth protested. She did, Chloe did tell me to not come back which only just now hit me. Why do that if she didn't want to see me again? Did she not mean those words when she said them? I was sure everything would get explained later, but for now, I chose to remain silent. I didn't know if it was the right thing to do, but I felt anything else would add salt to the wound.

"Can you stop meddling in my affairs for once? I get to decide who I talk to, when and what I do with them. You don't get to decide anything for me. If I want to talk to Jack, I will and there's nothing you can do about it."

"He doesn't deserve you! You're way better than him in every way, just look at him! He hasn't even said a word since you let him in! He's just pathetic and embarrassing."

"Alright, that's enough from you. You need to leave," Chloe said, pointing at the door.

"You can't make me leave my own home," Beth snickered.

"I can and I am. Get out. Or else things might get feisty," Chloe threatened.

I was about to step in but Beth grunted loudly and walked past me, bumping me hard with her shoulder. I let it go and followed her with my eyes as she stepped outside and slammed the door hard. I winced when the door hit the frame, the sound resonating in my ear for a few seconds before fading away. I turned to Chloe and she had a pissed off expression on her face. Starting the conversation was probably not the right move and I waited for her to break the silence.

"She needs to stay in her lane, I swear." I stayed silent and Chloe turned towards me. "What are you doing here?" she asked again.

"I had to talk to you," I repeated. I sounded like a broken record, but I couldn't think of anything else to say.

"Couldn't you have texted or called me? You didn't even try to contact me for a week and you just show up at my door?"

"I did call and text you. Every day. But you never answered."

"That's not possible, I received nothing from you at all. I thought you had… never mind that. Why didn't I receive anything?" She thought for a second and her expression switched to an even angrier face. "Could she…" she muttered to herself. She aggressively navigated on her phone. I couldn't see what she was doing, but it was clear she wasn't particularly happy right now so I didn't bother her. After a moment, she slightly startled me by how sudden she spoke out. "That double-faced witch! I can't believe she would do something like this!" I risked myself by opening my mouth.

"What did she do?" I asked, almost out of fear.

"She blocked your number on my phone. How did she even get a hold of it? No wonder I didn't receive anything from you. I can't believe she would…" Chloe grunted in frustration and took a deep breath to try and calm down. Her phone started vibrating as all the messages I had sent over the week came flooding in. I looked at our conversation and saw all the previously unread messages were now marked as seen. She started reading them, one by one, as I gathered what little courage I had left after this whole situation and truly spoke my mind for the first time in a while.

"Chloe." She lifted her eyes from her phone to look at me. "I'm sorry about all this. Truly. I didn't mean to cause you any pain, I… I was wrong. I should have dealt with her without getting you involved, she has nothing to do with you. It was my problem and I let you get dragged into it. I thought I was clear enough with her, but evidently that wasn't the case. I didn't mean to make it seem like I still loved her when I didn't react to her kiss, but I was genuinely surprised and couldn't process what was going on. I…" I blurted it all out in a desperate attempt to make her understand my feelings, but everything was jumbled, nothing was making sense and I was so nervous I couldn't stop talking.

"Jack," she said, taking a deep breath. I looked straight at her, waiting for her to continue. "You're not at fault here. It was all on my side. When I saw her kiss you, I was mad at you for a little bit, but I understood you had nothing to do with it straight away. That's not why I asked for a break. I did because I was afraid. Afraid of losing you again, afraid of what this meant for our relationship, afraid that she could be taking her place back into your heart and I would have to see you cry again. I got overwhelmed and ran away. If I'm honest, I'm glad you showed up today or I might never have snapped out of it. Seeing you here tonight, in front of me, I can tell what your heart feels without you having to say a word. And I have to say…" she paused, on the verge of tears. She brought her hands together and closed her eyes for a second before smiling at me. When she opened them again, I got lost into the ocean blue and felt my mind wander deep within. "I feel the same way!" she exclaimed, a single tear running down her cheek. "I'm sorry to have asked this of you. I'm sorry, it wasn't right of me to ask and I know I shouldn't have done it. Forgive me…"

I got closer to her, our foreheads touching. I took a deep breath too, gathering the courage and channeling all the love I felt for her into my next words.

"A wise man once told me a couple is a team. That when things get tough, they rely on each other to get through the hardships, to get through them together. He told me when one person falls, the other picks them back up and they both continue walking forward. I want to be that person for you. I want to walk beside you. Will you walk beside me?" I asked.

"I've never wanted to walk beside another one than you," she said through the tears. She was now crying, but I didn't mind. After all, I was very close to letting the rivers flow as well, but I somehow managed to keep it inside for now. I didn't know how long I would last, however.

We stayed in the apartment lobby for another while, letting our emotions die down a little. I came all the way out there without knowing what to expect. Was she going to be mad? Was she going to end things right then and there? Did she blame me for what happened despite telling me otherwise on multiple occasions? Did I have any right to tell her to move past the incident when I was at fault for not dealing with Camille properly and letting her come back in my life so many times? All these questions, some with answers and some without, but they all didn't matter anymore. Chloe was right here and we each said our piece, reconciled and were stronger by it. I couldn't ask for a better outcome. Despite all my flaws, Chloe accepted me like I was and I did the same for her. We were a team, the best duo, two people stronger together and now more united than ever. After a few minutes of silent understanding, I felt it time to say one more thing.

"Hey," I paused, "I love you." She waited for a few seconds before answering.

"I love you, too. Will you forgive me?" she asked, her voice shaking still.

"I already have."

She brought me closer to her and hugged me tightly. I buried my face in her chest and held her tight. I didn't want to lose her again, I never wanted to experience the last week again. Being away from her was excruciating and now that I was able to be close to her again, I would give anything to keep it that way. I missed her touch, I missed her smell, I missed everything about her. I don't know how long we stayed like this, but she kept me close for as long as she needed to. Eventually, she backed off and smiled at me. She leaned in and I met her halfway into a sloppy kiss. A kiss full of repressed emotions and feelings finally spoken. A kiss I never wanted to end, but we parted ways after a few seconds. I felt bad as my soaked cheeks made hers wet as well. I tried to smile through the tears but it must have come out more as a grimace.

"Can we go to your place?" Chloe asked. "I really don't want to be here anymore tonight." I nodded in agreement, still shaken up by the events that just unfolded. "Cool, let me grab a few things and I'll be right there." She walked away to her room and I heard her pack up from the entrance. I looked around and it felt like the apartment was hostile, like even the walls were mad about me being here. I felt like I was suffocating, the walls were closing in and there was nothing I could do. My breathing had quickened, but Chloe soon showed up and the sight of her brought me such relief that I sighed loudly. Making a weird confused face, she held out her hands and I greedily took it, instantly calming down a little more. We both walked out, hand in hand, and she closed the door behind her. She locked it but left a key under the doormat.

After all, even if she was mad about Beth's meddling, she didn't want her to sleep in the streets either. We left and managed to catch a bus that would bring us close to my place.

During the ride, I rested my head on Chloe's shoulder. Usually, it was the other way around, but tonight was different. She embraced me with both her arms, ignoring the looks from the very few passengers on the bus with us. I closed my eyes and let myself go, cradled by her loving embrace and rocked by the movements of the bus. It felt good to be reunited again, even if I was partly to blame for it happening in the first place. I had to find a way to silence the doubts and anxiousness that whispered in my ear from time to time. It wasn't fair to me and wasn't fair to Chloe to give them such a loud voice. I gradually came down from my emotional state to be somewhat at peace with Chloe cuddling up to me. If I was honest with myself, I was truly lucky to have found someone so understanding and so forgiving as her, as many others would have probably dropped the entire relationship the moment I displayed any semblance of doubt or anything like that. I turned and kissed her head.

"Thank you" I whispered. Either she didn't hear me or didn't have anything to answer as she stayed silent. In a way, that was probably for the best.

As we disembarked from the bus, we made our way to my apartment, climbing up the stairs and opening the door. Here, the walls were much more inviting and I didn't feel unwelcome. We immediately headed to the bedroom. The events of the night were quite enough and since it was getting pretty late, I was completely exhausted. I went straight to the bed and lied down as Chloe started undressing to get into her pyjamas. I looked directly at her and she caught me.

"What are you staring at?" she asked, amused.

"You," I simply answered.

"Yeah, I got that. What exactly, though?"

"You want me to be honest?"

"Yeah, why else would I ask?"

I continued looking at her, my eyes shifting downwards from time to time. She rolled her eyes and shook her head.

"Oh, come on," she said, faking annoyance.

"What? What else am I supposed to do when you undress in front of me?"

"Doesn't mean you have to stare at them?" she grumbled in a mocking tone.

"Would you rather me never look at them then?" I proposed jokingly.

"No..."

"Well, there you go," I answered with a happy tone.

"You're so simple sometimes." I smiled in the dark. We hadn't lost any of our chemistry and it already felt like the events of the past week were already behind us. I silently kissed her on the forehead and she made a smooch sound as I did. Feeling her this close to me was already comforting and with my bed not as empty as it was, I had the best sleep of the entire week.

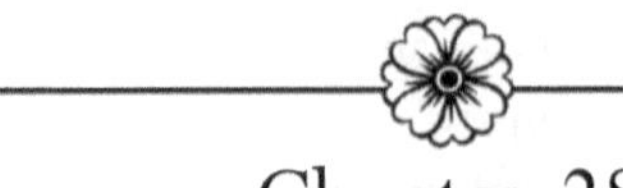

Chapter 28

I had scarcely felt better playing a video game before. I finally had time to pop in the last Blood of Battle game I had bought at the store the other day and was experiencing it for the first time. It was like being brought back several years ago when they hadn't perfected some of the systems in the game yet. The controls felt a little clunky, some of the dialogue was really cheesy and the combat dragged on a little too much. But I didn't mind any of those as I was finally playing the last game I needed for my collection. When I'd finish this one, I could tell everyone I completed the entire series on their original consoles. I was ecstatic to have been able to even find this game at such a reasonable price.

Since I was playing an older game, I kind of already spoiled myself on most of the story as they referenced it in the later ones and I pieced together what happened in this one. It was a little bit of a shame as the twists and turns didn't grip me the way they would have if I knew nothing about it, but I still managed to find it compelling enough to play on. Even if the combat was a little more primitive compared to the latest entry in the franchise, it was still very satisfying and I didn't notice I had been playing for almost two hours at that point.

I heard my bedroom door open and saw a silhouette walk straight to the bathroom out the corner of my eye. I shot a glance in that direction, but quickly returned to the screen, continuing my rampage through hordes of enemies. I was too absorbed by the game to notice Chloe had returned from her bathroom trip and sat down next to me, caving in the couch slightly. I paused the game and looked in her direction as we both smiled at each other.

"Playing your new game?" she asked.

"Yeah, I didn't really have time to sit down and play these past few days so this was the first chance I got," I answered.

"The second I disappear for a nap; I see how it is," she teased.

"Oh, come on, it wasn't the second you went… more like a minute," I said. Chloe got closer and started trying to tickle me and I curled up like a turtle. None could penetrate my shell, but she did try it for a while before giving up.

She returned to her seat next to me and I leaned in closer to her. "Did you sleep well?"

"Oh yeah, I did," she said enthusiastically. "I don't know what made me so tired all of a sudden, but the nap really helped bring my energy levels back."

"I can tell."

"What's that supposed to mean?" she feigned being offended.

"Only that it was quiet before you arrived and now… well," I said, trying to keep a straight face as a smirk escaped and formed at the corner of my mouth.

"Hey!" Chloe tried tickling me again, but I returned to my tried-and-true strategy and became a turtle again, countering any of her moves. We eventually started laughing which made it a lot harder to maintain my defensive form, but I somehow managed to pull through as Chloe's attack got weaker as well. We both returned to our places, panting in slight exhaustion and smiling. I looked at her and she looked back. Instinctively, my head leaned towards her and she met me halfway into a kiss. Our lips touched and it felt like an electric current zapped my entire body as it jolted awake. I leaned more into it, extending myself even more and my hands, seemingly with a mind of their own, went to explore. One went behind Chloe's head and one ended up on her side, moving up and down slowly. Chloe seemed to back away a little and I leaned in more to follow her. It felt like she maybe wanted to lay down and I continued my movement. I soon felt her tongue seeking a worthy opponent and I gladly gave in to the demand. Her hands landed on my shoulders and slowly moved down past my chest. I was giving in to her caress when she suddenly started tickling me again. This time, there was no escaping it and I pushed a startled cry as I backed off her lips. She started laughing and followed my movement as I tried to get out of her grasp.

"Gotcha!" she said.

I struggled to regain my composure and managed to get a hold of both of her wrists. She fought against me, but I pulled them away from me, lifting them higher up in the air. Using my body weight, I forced Chloe down so she laid on her back, her arms extended and pinned over her head. Our faces were mere centimeters away from each other and I stared deeply into her eyes. She had a glint of mischief still remaining, but the blue color stood out more than usual. Was that just my imagination or did I just not notice until now? My eyes moved down to her mouth and saw she was smirking at me. She tried to wrestle herself free, but my weight was entirely on her and I was pinning down her arms enough that she couldn't use them for anything.

"Struggling?" I asked teasingly.

"Still got you, though," she answered.

"Yeah, through deceit and treason," I accused.

"Hey, whatever works," she said, trying to shrug but only her eyebrows made any sort of movement. "What are you going to do to me now, big boy?"

"For your crimes, you will stay in this jail cell for as long as I hold you. Then, and only then, may you atone for your sins," I played along.

"Does atoning for my sins involve your friend in any way?" Chloe asked, making a movement with her eyes down my crotch. I did the same, I don't even know why as I could very much feel it. My shaft was pressing against one of her legs and was very noticeable at this point. "Seems like he wants to join the party," she added in a whisper.

"Prisoners will have no company as they serve their sentence," I said, trying to move away from the fact I got so excited over this little.

"That's a shame," Chloe pouted, making me slightly regret my decision.

"Prisoners will, however, be prone to questioning…" I said, holding down her arms with one hand while another slipped downwards towards her crotch. "… and, in some cases, might be subject to torture," I finished, caressing her thighs over her clothes. I could tell she was into it, but I committed to the bit and only teased her without doing anything else. Her breathing had changed and she was sorely focused on one of my hands, completely forgetting the one holding down her arms. I didn't falter and kept to my objective, which was to make her regret kissing me just to get what she wanted, and when I thought she had learned her lesson, I backed off, removing my weight from her body and allowing her to sit back up. Feeling me going away, she immediately shot up and wrapped her arms around me, her face directly next to my ear.

"Please," she whispered. Her hot breath on my ear felt really good, but I wasn't about to be tempted by the oldest trick in the book, even if my shaft was shouting the opposite.

"That's what you get for kissing me earlier," I answered.

"You're such a tease," she pouted, annoyed but playful.

"And proud of it," I said with a smile. She lightly punched me in the shoulder and I looked at the paused screen for a few seconds before turning back in her direction. "Want to try the gnome game?" I asked.

"Oh, yes! I've been wanting to!" Chloe said, suddenly sitting straight up. I laughed a little at her and got up to change the game. It only took a few seconds before I was sitting back down on the couch, staring into a black screen as the gnome game was loading. Soon, the giant words of the title appeared on screen.

Protector of the Gnomes

It really was a silly title, but it had some sort of charm to it. It described what the game was about, clearly, but just the fact it was gnomes instead of some other classic trope like knights and goblins made it stand out. The main menu soon came after the title and I selected the two-player mode. It was kind of surprising that a game like this would have a mode to play with someone locally and I wasn't quite sure how that would translate to the game as this wasn't usually my thing. How would that even work? Was it going to alternate who plays when the first player lost or something? We only had one controller anyway, which was a bit of shame, but we would have to make do. As soon as the game started, a gnome popped out of the title and plummeted down to the ground, getting carried away by a few other gnomes that came from the edge of the screen. They were kind of cute in their own little way and I couldn't help but smile. It seemed like Chloe thought much of the same.

"They're so cute, look at them go! I'm glad we got this game already."

"We didn't even get to play yet. For all we know, the game could be bad," I reasoned.

"A game with gnomes this cute could never be bad," she argued.

"We'll see about that," I said, turning back to the game.

It proceeded as normal and started showing us how to play. For now, it seemed like a solo game and not a co-op so I was slightly confused. A gnome that looked like he was 400 years old with the longest beard started explaining all these different systems and buildings we could make, some type of resources we had to gather and all sorts of different gnome units we had to train. It was a little bit overwhelming, but Chloe seemed to know what we had to do better than me so I handed her the controller. She started building some defenses on the gnome village outskirts and training some gnome soldiers while managing all of our resources like she had played this game before. While she did play, she wasn't as much of a player as I was, so I was really surprised at how well she processed all this information. I frankly couldn't quite keep up. It was impressive.

"How is this game two players? I know we only have one controller, but what is the second person supposed to do?" I asked, not expecting to get an answer as we both didn't know.

"No idea, maybe you get to play when it's night?" Chloe said. The game functioned on a day and night cycle where enemy forces would attack the gnome village at night. Perhaps the 'second player' had to control the units when night time arrived. Even then, that seemed like a stretch.

"Well, couldn't you just hand over the controller to the other person? This is not two players," I laughed while pointing the screen with my whole hand.

"Alright, I have no idea, then. I'm just glad to be playing with gnomes. Just look at them walk all over the place, they're so cute," Chloe said. I looked at her; she was so focused on the game she didn't take her eyes off the screen. She really was cute when she had this look in her eyes, this fierce resolve that could motivate me to attempt the impossible if she asked. I had a sudden idea. I knew of a way to make this game two players.

"You know what? I know how to make this more entertaining. Come here," I said. Chloe turned around and looked at me, confused.

"What?"

"Come here," I said, gesturing for her so sit down in front of me. She got up and sat back down directly in front of me, blocking my view of the screen. "Alright, now lay back" I said while pulling her closer to me. She was completely lying on top of me like I was her bed. I couldn't see anything on the screen at that point, but it didn't matter. I was going to play another game entirely and she had no idea.

"What are you doing? You can't even see what's going on like this. Plus, this is not that..." Chloe got interrupted by her own moan as my hands grabbed her chest, squeezing her breasts slightly. She sighed a little and her head turned towards me. She couldn't exactly see me as I was behind her. "That was your intention from the start, wasn't it?" she asked.

"No," I lied. "I'm just making this game interesting, that's all," I said, continuing my exploration of her body.

"You're such a bad liar," she said, sharply breathing in as my hand passed over her chest again. Even if we had clothes on, it felt like we were both naked and our skin made direct contact. I could feel her body warmth through my hands and could tell she was getting hotter by the second.

"Continue playing," I said, more like a soft order than anything else. She wanted to protest, but didn't and resumed the game. I only caught glimpses of what was happening from this point on, but I could tell she was less efficient at it than before. Whenever she got too focused on a certain task, I would let my hands do the talking and distract her as best they could. Eventually, night came and it was time to defend the gnome village. She gathered the trained troops and sent them off to attack the incoming forces. I didn't quite understand how the combat worked, but I thought it was time to start the ultimate distraction. My hands wandered down and down they went until I reached her thighs. Chloe instinctively spread her legs to allow me better access and leaned in to me more. She was applying more pressure on my chest, pushing me into the couch, but I didn't move away from my goal. I slowly got closer and closer to her crotch, teasing her and backing off at times where she must have been sure I would have gone for it. Her breathing had quickened a little and I couldn't help but smile mischievously. Of course, she could see none of it, but I was pretty sure she knew exactly what expression I had. Through two huffs, she managed to say one thing.

"Can I count on your spear in the upcoming battle, sir?" she asked before sighing heavily. I was having way too much fun with this.

"I'm not sure it's adequate for this kind of task, I'm afraid," I answered. I moved my head to be closer to one of her ears. I bit it teasingly, just enough so she would feel it and she seemed to really like that as her moan got a little louder. "We may have found a weakness in your defenses, madam."

"That's not fair, you can't... do that," she protested softly.

"I can and I am," I answered with a certain smugness. What was she going to do about it? It was really exciting for me as well and as she kept pushing on me, my crotch pushed back on her, making it more and more obvious how much I was enjoying this. She had clearly noticed it earlier, but now it was even more prominent. I let my hands wander around her thighs a little bit more until I decided to go over her slit once, just to tease. As soon as I did, she grabbed my hand suddenly. I stopped myself, wondering if I took it too far and she held it for a few seconds. She then guided my hand up and over, down her clothes and directly on top of it. Instantly, I could tell how excited she was as my fingers were soaked immediately. I gently started making circles against the top of her folds, making her quiver every time I finished a complete rotation. I started slowly picking up speed and her breathing was getting quicker. With my other hand, I was holding her back and cupping one of her breasts, occasionally giving it a squeeze and rubbing her now excited nipples. She started moving her hips on her own, seemingly not in control of her movement anymore. I dared to push a finger inside her and she sharply inhaled while trying to keep her voice down. This angle was very different from every other time I explored her like this, but I kind of liked having her on top of me in this way. It gave me an impression of control, like she was in my grasp, at my mercy and could do nothing to stop me from taking exactly what I wanted. One of her hands grasped my arm while the other one was clutching the couch. I realized she had dropped the controller and was now focused on nothing but my hands. She squeezed my arm as I pushed another finger to join the other. I continued teasing her like this for a while until we heard some sort of noise coming from the TV. I immediately stopped what I was doing and her head turned to try and face me.

"Why did you stop?" she asked in an accusatory tone.

"You lost," I said, staring at the screen. She turned to look at it and slightly got up from lying on me to look at me in the eyes.

"That's unfair, you never said you would stop if I lost."

"My game, my rules," I answered with a shrug.

"Alright, then, you want to play like that? Now you play. Let's see how good you do," Chloe said.

I grabbed the controller and restarted the game. Chloe got up and went behind me as I moved a little bit forward. With both of her legs straddling me on each side, I could feel her breasts pressing on my back. Her hands immediately reached for my pants and took out my shaft with relative ease. The feeling of her delicate hand on my member almost made me moan right away, but I managed to contain myself. I had to prove to her I could do it, that I could get farther than she did even though I had absolutely no idea how to play the game. I started doing random stuff, preparing some troops and building things I had no clue what they did. All the while, Chloe was gently stroking me up and down, trying to distract me as much as she could. She was starting slow, just like I was, and would finish strong. I had to hurry up and pass the night before it was too late. The sun set and it was now time to defend the gnome village. Straight away, Chloe quickened her pace which made me lean forward for just a moment before I returned to where I was. Her grip had tightened slightly and she was going a lot faster than before. At this rate, I wouldn't last nearly as long as she did. I had to change my strategy and end the night as soon as possible. I led the troops into enemy forces and got a hang of the combat really quickly. It was relatively simple, especially after playing Blood of Battle earlier, but there were so many enemies and time was running out. If I burst before the night ended, then it would be a draw and none of us would win. I just had to make it through. There were only a few enemies left. I sharply inhaled, sensing the point of no return approaching a lot quicker than I would have liked. My shaft pulsated in Chloe's hand; I could feel it twitching and my panting got stronger and stronger. Just a few left, if I could just... No, I would lose. I was going to... As I was about to burst, Chloe stopped everything and it hit me like a cold shower. She brought her head next to mine.

"You lose," she whispered.

I was so confused by what she said it took a few seconds to process the game had proceeded to the next day. I had won the night battle, so why did she say that?

"What? How did I...?" I started asking.

"My game, my rules," she said back to me with a smugness in her voice. I managed to calm myself down. She was so sexy when she got assertive like that. I pulled my pants back up and got up to turn around and face her. I could tell from the expression on her face that, even though she hadn't finished, she was satisfied. So was I, to be fair. She looked up at me with a smile. "We definitely need to play that again."

"Definitely," I answered between two breaths. The sound of my stomach rumbling broke the content silence in the room and we both stared at my belly as it sang for way longer than I would have liked. We both didn't say anything for a few seconds afterwards.

"Hungry?" she asked with a laugh.

"Apparently," I answered, laughing as well.

"Let's go take care of that," Chloe said, getting up from the couch.

In the background, the gnome game was still going on, doomed to fail once night would fall again on an unprepared village. If Blood of Battle always made me feel good while playing, I had a newfound appreciation for Protector of the Gnomes. Unfortunately for them, I only cared if it was two players and the second player had gone to the kitchen with me in tow.

Chapter 29

It was a heavy day of spring as I walked to school for the final week of the school year. It was exam season again and I would be lying if I said I was as prepared as the past years. By now, walking to school had become a habit by the sheer number of times I did it, yet there was still something different about walking to school during exam season. A kind of nervousness that made the building appear larger and taller as if to intimidate the students coming in. Last year, I was one of those even if I was better prepared than most. This year, however, the building couldn't intimidate me. I was still apprehensive about getting good grades, of course, but I stopped doubting my abilities and being anxious about things that couldn't be avoided.

There was one thing I still couldn't quite grasp; the fact we were already at the end of the year. It felt like yesterday, I was walking this exact path to go take some other exams. That was an entire year ago. Where had time gone? I knew perfectly well where it had gone. So many things happened during this year, it was kind of hard to believe when I really thought about it. For instance, I was still in a relationship with Camille when this year started and now, I had been with Chloe for a few months already. I had gone through a breakup as well and experienced multiple feelings with three very different girls. I learned a lot about myself, my limits and what to tolerate, how I loved others and how others loved me. I learned that sometimes it's good to give in to wild ideas and other times it's not. Relationships are very difficult and at the start of the year, I had no idea what I was doing. Sure, it had been a few months since Camille and I started dating, but I was still very much a novice. I couldn't pretend I was experienced now, but obviously; things have evolved since then.

Some people say events are predetermined and meant to be. I wasn't in that academy of thinking and believed we're in control of our own destiny and the choices we make have impact. In their beliefs, there is no real point to live as the path is already drawn, you simply have to follow. When something bad happens, you know it wasn't your fault, it was just meant to be. I thought of this way of thinking as foolish. They just wanted to remove any ownership to their actions as if that could make them feel better about the mistakes they made. Where was the evolution in all of this? Choices manifested in different ways along this path, but one always has options. Crossroads, where to walk, how fast to walk; those were just some of the choices one could make when walking down the path of life. Saying all of it was predetermined was ignorant, at least to me.

For once, the school was quiet and the halls were empty. It was a nice feeling to be able to walk freely in the corridors, but it also felt a little eerie. If the lights were closed, I might have been terrified and ran for my life, but the generous lighting made it much brighter. The dull walls were still dull, yet they filled me with a sense of nostalgia. Why was that? This wasn't my last year here and I had only been through this exam process once, so why did the events of the past make me feel this way? I walked, my steps resonating through the empty building and the thought I had mistaken the day of the exam crossed my mind. It was kind of weird that nobody else was around, but did I really make a mistake or was it normal? I checked my phone, just to be sure, and I was indeed correct on the date. I continued walking, the sound of my steps reinforcing this feeling of loneliness that had started to creep up on me.

At the end of the corridor was an intersection. I was really familiar with it as, once, my locker had been tucked in the corner on the right. I still went over to it sometimes, mostly by force of habit, but this time I was headed for the stairs. Out the corner came someone, their steps conflicting with mine and creating some weird sound amalgamation. I would recognize her among anyone. Long blonde hair, a very familiar white blouse and a skirt she wore every time she could. She was looking down and hadn't seen me yet, but there was nothing to do. We would see each other. I didn't want to make a big deal out of it because frankly, I was over the whole thing. I just wanted to do my exams and get them over with. I continued walking as if I hadn't noticed her but when we came close, she lifted her head up to look at me. I ignored her and went past her. Before, I would have run away at the sight of her like I did a few months ago, but not this time. This time, I wasn't in the mood to be distressed or to worry or to doubt or any of these poisonous feelings. I just wanted her to leave me alone. But, of course, that didn't happen.

"Jack," she called out. I didn't stop walking, thinking maybe she would stop at just one. "Jack!" she called again, this time making me turn around with a sigh.

"What do you want, Camille? I'm busy," I answered, trying to dismiss the conversation. I didn't want to do this right now.

"I need to talk to you," she said, walking closer to me.

"We have nothing to talk about. I have nothing more to say to you after last time."

"I promise it won't take long; will you at least hear me out?" she practically pleaded. I folded my arms and shifted my weight to one leg, tapping the ground lightly with my other foot.

"What?"

"Okay, um… where to start? I… Did you ever wonder why I approached you initially?"

"I already asked this question and you already answered. You said you thought I was weird, but you couldn't stop looking my way and decided to go for it one day." Where was she going with this? We already had this conversation before, what was the point of this?

"That…um… was a lie," she confessed, her gaze shifting to the ground in embarrassment. She started fidgeting on one foot, the other tapping the ground repeatedly. I hated when she did this. The confession kind of confused me as I didn't know why it was even relevant to talk about. We weren't even together anymore, what was she getting at? "The real reason I approached you initially is… I was dared to. By my friends."

They shouldn't have affected me, but the words that came out of her mouth pierced my heart like a sharp needle. Was all of it a lie? The whole foundation of my relationship with her was built on a lie? I let her continue without saying a word, my eyes getting more and more intense as she talked.

"We wanted to pull a prank on you and since we thought you were a virgin and had never been with a girl before, we thought it would be funny to make you think you could get with one of us. I was chosen to go for it and invited you to my house…" She paused, trying to gather her thoughts. I was all ears even if anger started rising up through my whole body. She, however, looked like she was about to cry. There would be no pity coming from me. "After you ran away and left your bag, we found it very funny and made you come all the way to our lockers to get it back. We decided to push the prank a little further and set up a date. After that… everything changed."

"I… thought I was going to run away by going to the bathroom and sticking you with the bill" she continued. "But I ended up having a really good time and… the prank sort of… didn't make sense any more. I didn't want to do it, I wanted to know you for real, but I… didn't know what to do. I kept the prank to myself and my friends, but they pressured me to tell you and end everything before I could get attached. I didn't and… well you know the rest."

As she talked, I remembered certain weird interactions that happened at the beginning of our relationship. The fact all her friends were there when I got my backpack back and they laughed at me, the way they continually looked my way in the class afterwards and stood there when Camille invited me to a date. It all started to make sense. The way Camille was so bold the first time I went to her house, the way she didn't seem too bothered by me running away. The only thing that didn't really click with her story was the date. She seemed genuinely happy to see me even at the beginning of the date which didn't make sense if I was to trust her word. Why was I even listening to this, again? Why would I trust her when all she had tried to do ever since I left her was get in the way of my relationship with Chloe and try to ruin my life? I wanted to give her the benefit of the doubt. Was it because I still cared about her or because I was simply a naïve person? Hard to tell, but here I was, silent and listening to her all the same.

"Then, we continued going on dates and you shared some parts of yourself with me and I didn't know how to proceed. My friends started seeing how I was becoming and pressured me into distancing myself from you. They encouraged me to go after one of my coworkers and... well, I did." Did she do it while we were still together? Did she cheat on me with that other guy? "I never cheated on you if that's what you're wondering, I don't know if you care to know or not, anyway... I left you, because of my friends, and I regretted it as soon as I did. I thought to myself that I should wait and that feeling would go away, but after multiple weeks, I still had this hole in my heart only you could fill. I came back and you soon pushed me away. I couldn't deal with it. When I learned you were now with that other girl, I... I was hurt and just wanted to have you back. But you didn't want me anymore. I guess that's what happens when you play with fire, right?"

She stopped talking and looked to the ground, her eyes clearly filled with water and her voice shaken with emotion. I stood there, angry more than anything, and couldn't bear to look at her anymore. There was a mix of disgust and confusion towards this confession, I couldn't help but wonder why she would do such a thing. Why now, of all possible times?

"Why are you telling me this? What do you hope to do with this? You're just being cruel," I asked, slightly dismissive of her confession like it didn't affect me at all. It clearly did, but maybe not in the way she intended it.

"I just had to tell you, because you should know. Because I still love you and I want you to give me another chance. Because I..." she pleaded.

"Still on that line, are you? You sound like a broken record," I paused and she looked at me, kind of shocked to hear me sound so harsh. "Camille, there is no us getting back together. I told you this multiple times. You need to move on. You're still the same girl I left in January, you haven't changed and haven't learned from anything that happened since then. Your words can't reach me anymore, I have moved past it. I have grown as a person while you stayed behind, trying to come up with a plan to win me back without realizing there was no use to trying. I'm with Chloe now, whether you like it or not, and there'll be no changing that."

Camille started silently crying, her tears falling on to the tiled floor. I always hated that floor.

"You're not saying this to me 'because I should know'. You're saying this because you want to absolve yourself of your wrongdoings and get the guilt off your chest. Your friends didn't make you do anything, they influenced you and you decided to listen to them. They weren't the ones that broke up with me, you did. They weren't the ones that pushed the 'prank' further, you did. They weren't the ones that left me in the streets while it rained with no idea why you ended it, you did. Confessing like this doesn't make you a better person. If anything, I think of you less now than when you started this conversation. If that was your intention, then you succeeded. You're blaming everyone but yourself. You could have stopped it at any point, but you let it go too far, and you're paying the price for your actions." I shook my head, trying to calm down. Camille didn't answer anything and continued silently crying.

"You played with my heart, Camille. You ripped it out of my chest and threw it on the floor before stepping on it. You toyed with me and when you didn't want me anymore, you discarded me like I was nothing. My feelings for you died a long time ago." She lifted her head up to look at me as soon as I said that. "It doesn't mean I didn't care for you as a person. Now, I'm not so sure anymore. There's no excuse for what you did and if you wanted my sympathy by confessing like you did, then I'm sorry to say, but I have none to give you. I don't want to hear from you ever again. Stay away and don't come back."

I started walking away and heard a thud behind me. I turned around to see Camille, on her knees and crying, much like I was when she broke up with me all those months ago. Did she feel exactly this way when she left me then or was she as detached as I was now? Could I even say that after all we went through? I don't know what was real and what wasn't anymore. Earlier, I would have gone to her side to ask if she was okay, but now I didn't even want to be beside her, let alone interact any more than I had to.

"Goodbye, Camille," I said softly. I didn't care if she heard it or not. I just wanted to get her out of my sight. She wouldn't reach me with her words anymore, she couldn't influence me with her sweet talk. I had changed. The confession she said made it very clear in my mind; I didn't love her anymore. There was no doubt about it. I loved Chloe and there was no way she could get in the way again. Not after this. I silently climbed up the stairs to go to the second floor, trying to calm down the anger that had somewhat seeped through as I shut down Camille. I didn't usually get this emotional over things, especially not angry, but the fact she had the audacity to come and try to get me back after saying such hurtful things was mind boggling. How could she even pretend she was doing a good thing? I reached the classroom and entered. There were already multiple people sitting down and Chloe was one of them. She waved at me and I barely responded, sitting down next to her.

"Everything okay? You seem shaken up," she whispered.

"I'll tell you later," I answered in a dismissive way. I didn't want to get into this conversation right now, especially not here in front of all these people. I couldn't see clearly, but I felt Chloe silently look away from me, probably wondering what was up. I wasn't in the mood to talk. The wait for the professor was the longest I had ever gone through. It seemed like an eternity even if it was just a few minutes. He walked in and wrote that we had three hours on the white board before handing out the sheets and allowing us to begin.

I couldn't concentrate at all; Camille's words still bounced in my head and blurred every other thought I had. I tried to ignore them, to discard them, to push them aside, but they occupied every little space they could like a vicious venom spreading through my body. Even when I tried to end things for good, she still managed to impose her presence on me. I just wanted her out of my head. A hand landed on my arm and I turned around to see Chloe. She was looking at me with intense eyes and simply nodded. The sight of her face and her silent comforting words cleared up my head and I nodded back, smiling. She was like a ray of sunshine that parted my cloudy mind. I returned to the paper in front of me and somehow managed to fill out some answers. Perhaps things weren't so doomed after all.

◊

We got out of the exam at pretty much the same time. I waited for Chloe in the corridor, hoping not to run into Camille again as I didn't know what I would do if that were to happen. Fortunately, I crossed no one except my girlfriend who smiled at me as she got out. I was still a little shaken up by my altercation with Camille, but she chased those thoughts away as soon as she came into sight. We waited to get away from the classroom before talking.

"So, you want to tell me what's going on?" she asked.

"I ran into Camille earlier," I started. Chloe stopped for a second and took a deep breath before joining me again.

"What did she say now? I swear I'm going to slap her again if she didn't understand the message," she threatened.

"That won't be necessary, I don't think we're going to be bothered by her anymore."

"Do tell?"

"She pretty much said hers and mine relationship was built on a lie and that she originally just wanted to prank virgin me into going out with her so she could laugh with her friends. Then, she couldn't live with the fact things evolved into something more and, when things didn't work out, tried to end it. But she couldn't live with that outcome either and tried to win me back multiple times to no avail. The end."

"I swear, this family is just crazy. At least we found each other through them. Somehow," Chloe said.

"Another thing in common, huh?" I said.

"I wish we didn't, frankly," she commented, rolling her eyes.

I smiled at nothing in particular, finding the comment rather amusing. We walked outside and the heat instantly pressed down on my shoulders. Weirdly, it seemed way lighter than when I came in. We continued going to the bus stop. Chloe was supposed to join me today and the rest of the week after each exam. We didn't really have much planned in terms of activities or anything, but we were just glad to be able to spend some more time together. While we waited for the bus, I remembered we didn't even talk about the exam we had just done.

"Hey, how did the exam go on your end?" I asked.

"Oh yeah, I mean, it went well, I think I did pretty good. You? You seemed out of it at the beginning," Chloe asked.

"You now know why. After you silently cheered me up, it went fine. Thanks for that, by the way. I don't think I could have done it without you," I said.

"I did nothing, but you're welcome," Chloe laughed.

The bus came to get us and I got on, quickly followed by Chloe. The bus ride felt different this time for a reason I couldn't quite pinpoint. It was some kind of nostalgia mixed with relief. It was a weird feeling to experience while climbing on public transport, but I let it go and just sat down next to Chloe who, somehow, got a seat before me. I guess I just stood there for a while without even realizing it. There were many more exams to go this week and I simply hoped that I wouldn't have an interaction like I did today before every exam or else I was going to have a very bad time. I reminisced about Camille and everything we experienced together. To think that all of this was built on nothing but the drive to make fun of someone else made me sick. She also mentioned that she started having real feelings for me somewhere along the way, but how could she be trusted? I couldn't pay attention to that anymore. I needed to focus on what I had right now, what was real and wasn't built to ridicule me. I turned towards Chloe and she smiled at me while holding my hand. Yes, I had everything I needed right here. There would be no more blonde hair and green eyes to occupy my thoughts; only red hair and blue eyes to comfort me in the night. For the first time in a little while, I rested my head on Chloe's shoulders. She was always the one to do it to me first, but this time, it felt like she knew I needed comfort more than she did. She hugged and pressed me against her. It felt nice to be in her arms again and to be able to do something like this without the fear of being judged by everyone around me. I didn't care what the other people in the bus were thinking. I was just happy.

Chapter 30

"Are you sure this is okay?" I asked as we climbed the stairs to Chloe's apartment. She was practically dragging me along with her. It wasn't that I didn't want to be with her, just maybe avoid the place where there's another girl that actively hates me and wants me to leave and never come back. Any chance of interaction was another chance of her snapping at me and I just didn't really feel like dealing with that today or any other day for that matter.

"I told you; she won't be here. It's fine. Now, come on, you slowpoke," she said, arriving in front of the door and unlocking it. She opened it as I got to the last landing and urged me inside with her arms. I sighed and smiled to myself. How could she be so carefree when walking directly into the wolf's den? We could have just gone to my apartment and not risk anything, so why insist on coming here? That was just asking for trouble to find us while holding a giant flashing arrow sign pointing towards us. Did she want to prove a point somehow? To herself or to an absent Beth? Perhaps I worried too much as I stepped into the apartment.

It was way different than the last time I had been here. It was lighter, more open and less oppressive. Last time I was here, it seemed like even the walls wanted me to leave by choking and suffocating me, but now they were welcoming me with open arms. I took a look around, sort of confused as to why I was experiencing this all of a sudden, and landed on the usual pair of shoes near the front door. There were none, indicating Beth had truly gone away for the night. I wondered if Chloe felt the same thing, this pressure being lifted off her shoulders. I wondered if she always lived in this environment or if it was just my impression of it. Perhaps I was just imagining things and, because Beth didn't like me, I would conjure up some fantasy about her warding me off with spells and incantations. That was definitely taking it a little too far and I silently laughed at myself for even thinking about it. Chloe had turned on the dim light in the entrance and the orange glow illuminated the walls, casting shadows on it. They seemed to dance somehow, even if the light didn't move at all, and I squinted for a second, examining them before they vanished completely. I turned to Chloe as she was taking her shoes off.

"Is your apartment haunted by any chance?" I asked, more as a joke than a genuine question.

"What are you talking about?" she laughed, raising her eyebrows in disbelief. "Why? You think Beth left a ghost of herself to watch over the apartment even when she's gone?"

"Seems like a pretty strange scenario to think about, are you in on it, maybe?" I proposed. Chloe didn't bother to respond and just looked at me with a confused smirk. I started laughing and she joined me as I took off my shoes. She took my hand and pulled me to her. We embraced under the light and stayed in each other's arms for a few seconds, staring into the other's eyes without saying a word. I could have stayed like this forever. Just the feeling of her in my arms was enough for me to never want to let go. Her hands moved down my back and grabbed my butt cheeks. I faked being offended and Chloe hurriedly kissed me, for just a moment, before retreating into her bedroom. I was left standing there, in a state of shock and amusement, and it took me a few seconds of psyching myself up before I joined her. I stopped myself as soon as I passed the doorway. She was lying in bed in a very seductive way and slowly motioned at me to come with her finger. Chloe winked at me and turned to the side, facing the middle of the bed and giving me access to her butt. If she wanted to be such a tease, then I could tease her as well. I closed the door behind me with a creak sound and walked to the other side of the bed. I got on and lied down facing Chloe, looking at her with a hint of mischief. She, however, looked disappointed.

"Why did you go all the way over there? You're so far away," she complained with a pout.

"Well, maybe I just wanted to talk? Ever think about that?" I asked.

"You never just want to talk," Chloe said, getting slightly closer to me.

"You're right about that. But I do want to know how the last week went for you. How well do you think you did?"

"Are you really asking me this right now? We could do so much more than talk about boring exams."

"You have to ease into it is going to be my explanation. So, how was your week?" I asked again. Chloe sighed and rolled her eyes before smiling at me in a friendly annoyed way. I just smiled at her innocently, knowing she hated it when I did that. I was already having a ton of fun.

"Well, if I'm going to fail any of them, it's going to be the one today," Chloe started. "I just couldn't quite concentrate when I thought of us being free to do whatever we want all summer long and all the fun things we were going to do. I just wanted to leave and be done with it, you know?"

"You managed to complete it, though, right? I don't want you failing because of me," I asked out of concern.

"Oh, no, it should be fine. I was just saying it was my worst one, not that I would fail necessarily," she reassured me.

"Good, good. Anything else?"

"Why does this feel like an interrogation? What about you, mister? How was your week?"

"You don't get to turn around and start asking questions before I'm done, that's not how this works," I protested.

"You better believe that's how it works, now. So?" she insisted.

I sighed and smiled. When Chloe wanted her way, I couldn't possibly refuse her. She had a way of looking at me that made her so cute, I just couldn't deal with it and had to give in. She was like that now and part of me immediately thought to trick her and say something outrageous, but I ultimately decided to say the truth.

"After the first one you helped me with, everything went fine. I was excited about the summer too, but I managed to keep my mind off it when taking exams. Which is really kind of a miracle when you think about it. I honestly don't know how I managed to do that," I explained.

"Did you, now? And what's on your mind right now?" she asked teasingly.

"Okay, so you know in Blood of Battle, right? There's this NPC that..." I started.

"You cannot be serious," she interrupted.

"Nah, I'm just joking," I said, laughing at her reaction. "If you really want to know, I was thinking about your eyes. I love them so much, their color, the way they look at me, the way I know it's you when I stare into them. I can just get lost into them with ease and they're...beautiful," I explained. Chloe went silent for a moment and just looked at me. She was smiling, shining in front of me behind her glasses and I couldn't help but stare at her and wonder how lucky I was to have found such a wonderful partner.

"You have some beautiful eyes yourself. You've seen a lot of things, perhaps some you didn't want to, but also some nice things. Even if they're brown, they have a lot of color to them," Chloe said.

"Now you're just making things up," I teased with a laugh.

"I was being serious, why are you joking about this?" Chloe asked, slightly offended I would dismiss her like that. I immediately felt a little bad about it, but I wasn't good at receiving compliments and my first instinct had always been to disagree and dismiss them. It wasn't about humility or not believing in me, I just didn't like the feeling of being praised for something.

"I'm sorry. I just don't… I guess I just don't fully believe that," I confessed, looking away. Chloe grabbed my chin and lifted it back up so I looked directly at her.

"I love you. And I love your eyes. Don't doubt it."

She looked all serious and bossy like she was ordering me to take the compliment. She turned me on so much when she acted this way. I repressed a laugh and simply got in closer to her. Our heads were just centimeters away from each other, our nose nearly touching. She was just there, just a little farther, I could just scoot a little to the left and be directly in her arms again. We didn't need to speak anymore and I moved just a tad closer, not enough to kiss her, making her do the next move. She did much of the same, but stayed out of reach too. I pushed it just a little more, just enough so she would have to do the ultimate one if she wanted to. The back and forth was really exciting and I could tell I was getting harder by the second. Even if we hadn't done anything yet, we were both panting, our hot breath mixing in the little space between our faces, somehow already synchronized. We stayed like this for a few seconds, seconds that build up some anticipation inside me. Was she going to do it? When? Just now? Maybe now? What was taking her so long? Maybe she wanted to…

I was interrupted by Chloe's sudden movement. Her lips violently pressed against mine as she launched herself on top of me, turning me so I was on my back. She straddled me, still lying on top as she kept our kiss going. I was surprised by the attack, but couldn't really protest and just let it happen. She raised herself just a little, just enough so her shirt fell down and I got the hint. One of her hands landed on my cheek while the other started playing with my hair. I never knew I was so much into that before she started doing it a few months back. Ever since then, she did it every time, almost on instinct, and I couldn't get enough of it. It felt like she really cared, I knew she did, but the finesse you needed to do it without being too aggressive showed restraint, love and compassion for the other. She also had smaller hands than me and it fit better when she did it to me rather than the opposite. I had also found one of her sweet spots, a weakness in her defense, but it was currently out of reach. What wasn't out of reach, thought, was her breasts which she deliberately gave me access to. My hands wandered into her shirt, making their way up to find them, imprisoned in her bra. I squeezed them a few times, feeling them out even if they were already so familiar. After a few times, Chloe rose up and released them from their confinement. She removed her bra swiftly and tossed it aside, looking down at me with seductive eyes. She wasn't usually this assertive in bed, but now that she was on top and looking at me like that, I would be lying if I said it didn't have any effect on me. My shaft pulsated by itself, trapped in my pants and I was longing for her to release it. But she didn't and returned to her previous position, kissing me again and bringing her chest back to an arm's reach. I went back into her shirt, now caressing her breasts directly, her soft skin under my hands. I passed over a nipple and she exhaled through her nose, her mouth occupied in another battle. She had attacked mine with her tongue, waging war for control, but I wasn't about to let her win. I fought valiantly, but eventually lost to her offensive maneuvers. I counter-attacked on the other front, teasing both of her nipples at the same time. She retreated, rising back up and making me extend my arm completely to continue teasing her. Her hands went behind her back and found my shaft. It was very obvious as it stood out against the fabric and she started teasing it over my pants. I reached out just a little further and both my hands went down her back as I pulled her towards me, making her lie down on me again. This time, her head went besides mine and I turned around to look at her. She was facing away from me, but that was the perfect opportunity to use my secret weapon. I started teasing her ears and she immediately moaned into the pillow nearby. I softly bit the earlobes, occasionally making my way up before coming back down. I knew she liked it a lot because she started moving her hips on her own and continued moaning right next to me. Even if it was muffled, it still really turned me on and I could feel myself pushing against my pants, wanting to be released. The anticipation was stronger than ever and I desired her more and more by each passing second.

"Chloe, did you..." said a voice as the door squeaked open. Chloe immediately shot up and looked back towards the doorway and so did I. There stood Beth, shocked and frozen in a confused look. Her eyes shifted from Chloe to me then back to Chloe again. Nobody said a word before she spoke again. "What's he doing here?" she asked in an accusatory tone while looking directly at me.

"I could ask you the same thing, what are you doing here? Your parents never told you to knock before entering?" Chloe said, getting off me and the bed to walk towards Beth. Her voice sounded really pissed off and they both looked like they were about to square off. I wouldn't want to be between them, I was instantly convinced of that, but there didn't appear to be much I could do to prevent it either.

"I thought we agreed on no boys in the apartment," Beth said while crossing her arms. "You already brought him here once, wasn't that enough for you? No, you had to sneak him in again, didn't you?"

"I agreed to your stupid policy when I didn't have a partner, things have changed now. What does it matter anyway? Is he harming you? Is he bothering you? We're both in my room and we had the door closed, not anymore thanks to you but I digress. Where is the problem, exactly?" Chloe argued.

"The problem is I set up boundaries and you can't be asked to respect them, Chloe! Is that so hard to understand?" Beth shouted.

"We're both grown adults here and this is as much my apartment as yours. I can do what I want in the confines of my room and it's none of your business," Chloe said.

"It doesn't change the fact we set up some rules for them to be respected. I want no boys in this apartment and you agreed to it. You can't just stop obeying the rules because you don't feel like following them anymore," Beth continued.

"To hell with your rules! Why are you so attached to this one thing? You're like obsessed or something, you need to let it go. It's not like we're doing lewd things in the living room on full display for you to see. We're in my room with the door closed. If you didn't want to see that, maybe you shouldn't have barged in without knocking," Chloe argued.

"Where you do… whatever you were doing is irrelevant, I just don't want any boys here. Simple rule, even a toddler could understand." She turned to me for a brief moment. "You need to leave. Now," she said in a bossy tone. I started to get up, not willing to be opposed to any of them. Chloe glanced back at me with daggers in her eyes.

"Sit back down," she said and I did. "He's not going anywhere. Okay, Beth, we're going to figure this out right now, because I'm not about to have this discussion every time he comes over. We avoided coming here for months now. For you. Because you didn't want to see him here. And that was fine for a while, but we want more freedom now. I'm not saying we're going to be kissing and cuddling in front of you, we're going to stay in my room. You don't have any say in this, it's not up to you to decide. I have had enough of this policy of yours and I'm not going to follow it anymore."

"I just can't stand seeing you like this. I can't stand seeing you with him!" Beth shouted. She immediately looked down to the ground like she couldn't bear to look at us anymore. She then raised her head and stared at me with fiery eyes. It felt like she was trying to burn me alive just from staring. "You!

You did this! It's all your fault" she said, pointing a finger at me. "Everything was going perfectly well before you showed up and messed with her."

"Woah, Jack hasn't done anything, what are you talking about?" Chloe said. I was frankly too confused by the back and forth and was barely following what was happening. I didn't even have time to process what Beth had said to me before they started arguing again.

"Things were going great between us and then he showed up and destroyed everything!" Beth continued.

"What are you saying? He didn't destroy anything," Chloe answered, confused as much as I was.

"If he hadn't shown up, maybe I could have..." Beth stopped herself, emotions starting to get the better of her.

"You could have what?" Chloe asked. "Spill it out."

"Maybe I would have had a chance! There, happy?" Beth shouted angrily.

"A chance for what?"

"You just don't get it, do you?" Beth paused for a few seconds, breathing in and out and trying to calm down. She closed her eyes and looked up before coming back down and staring at Chloe. "I've always wanted to be with you. I've tried to tell you for months, but I couldn't do it. Then he appeared out of nowhere and snatched that away from me. I tried to make him go away, but he just wouldn't and kept coming back. I thought blocking his number would be enough. I thought being hostile would be enough. But like a rat, he survived and just wouldn't leave you alone. It's all his fault."

"Are you serious? Do you hear yourself?" Chloe asked. "You thought that breaking me up with my boyfriend would somehow make me fall for you? Oh, Beth, that's not how this works. Ever since you two met, you've been nasty and mean to him, you've just fallen in my esteem further and further by each passing day. He's been nothing but nice to you and this is how you repay him? I'm flattered by your feelings, really, I am, but you can't win me over by booting out my boyfriend like that. And I'm sorry, but I've never seen you in that light, so it was never going to work out between us," Chloe concluded.

Her words were harsh, but they needed to be said and Beth started crying silently. Some time passed with no words being spoken, all three of us in shock of what had just happened. I didn't say anything during the whole argument and I wasn't about to put oil on that fire. I just didn't know what to say or how to begin that conversation. Beth hated me, there was no doubt about it, and I wanted nothing to do with her if at all possible. Chloe put a hand on Beth's shoulder and she looked up, her eyes misty with tears. It was the first time I had seen her like this and her expression was a lot kinder than any I had seen before. When she didn't look angry, she could have been cute, but the burden of the words she had said to me skewed my vision and I couldn't see her as anything else than the hostile roommate she had been to me all this time.

"Honestly, what were you thinking? You should have been honest with me from the start if you wanted any chance of it working out, but that's never going to happen now. You...disappoint me, Beth. You were my friend, my confidant, my roommate, we used to be able to talk about anything and everything. What happened? Why did you try to stab me in the back like this?" Beth swiped Chloe's hands from her shoulders and her angry expression came back.

"I don't need your pity. I hope you're proud of yourselves, both of you, for destroying my life. I hope things don't work out between you and you have a painful breakup. I can't stand to look at you anymore. You make me sick. Get out of my sight," she said, turning around and leaving.

Both Chloe and I stood there, frozen solid by the coldness of her words. I don't know how much time had passed before we slowly looked at each other, seeking what to do next in the other's eyes, but neither of us knew. Gradually, we regained our movement and I walked up to her. She was so assertive a few minutes ago and now she trembled like a leaf in the harshest winds. It was impressive how she could go from one extreme to the other, but the end result was also devastating. I wrapped her in my arms and she rested her head against my chest. I couldn't tell if she was crying or not, but she definitely needed comfort and we stayed like this for a while before she pulled away. She wiped her eyes and her cheeks before looking at me.

"Can we go outside? I feel like I'm suffocating in here?" she asked.

"Yeah, sure, no problem," I answered immediately.

We got out of the bedroom and saw that Beth was still in the apartment. At the end of the corridor on the left, a door previously opened was now closed, but no sound could be heard from anywhere. Even our footsteps were silent as we approached the front door, put on our shoes and walked out. The few flights of stairs leading down appeared infinite like we were trapped in an endless loop, continuously descending but never able to reach the bottom. We eventually did, however, and walked out of the building into the spring evening. It wasn't the hottest day we had recently, but it was up there and the sun had barely set on the horizon. The heat hadn't fully gone yet and it pressed on our shoulders as soon as we exited the door. Chloe turned towards me, seemingly waiting for me to tell her where to go. I just pointed to the right, at random more than anything.

"Let's go over there." She nodded and we started walking.

Even if the main instigator of the conflict wasn't here, we still went on in silence for a while, processing what just happened and trying to figure out what to do. The main part of the reflection was on Chloe's side, however, and I couldn't do much more than assist her and aid her in coming with a solution. I waited patiently for her to start, but she never did and we had been walking for fifteen minutes before I decided to start.

"Do you think she's going to retaliate?" I asked. "Now that she confessed and got rejected, I mean." Chloe waited for a few seconds before answering, taking in a deep breath to clear her thoughts.

"I'd rather not take any chances. She's clearly unstable and who knows what she's capable of doing now. It's clear to me that we can't keep living together. It's not fair to her to endure her feelings any longer and I don't feel safe sleeping there anymore which is…um…quite an issue." I could tell from her tone she was demoralized and racking her brain trying to find a solution. Fortunately, one had come up recently with almost perfect timing.

"I know I haven't told you this already, but I decided to rent another apartment. If you want, I know this isn't the ideal situation to be in, but maybe we could move in together?" I proposed.

"Wait, really? Why didn't you tell me this?" she asked. I didn't have a proper answer to that question. It's not that it slipped my mind, I just didn't know how to bring the subject and I wasn't sure if moving in with her after just a few months of dating was the right call. After all, things went south really fast with Camille and we were reaching the same amount of time I had been dating her.

"I guess I was afraid of making the commitment. Not that I'm doubting our relationship or anything, but that was before we had our break and before I realized how much I care about you. After that, well, I didn't know if you would want to and didn't want to force you into anything," I confessed.

"Well, I'd be glad to move in with you, if that's any comfort. But you know you can tell me anything, right? Don't be afraid to come to me for how I'll react, we'll deal with it as it comes, yeah?" she said, reassuring me. I smiled staring at the sidewalk in front of me.

"Okay. Now the thing is, I'm only moving in July, so what are you going to do until then?" I asked.

"Couldn't I just move in with you for the next month and then we move in together? That way, all our things are in one place," Chloe proposed. "And to be perfectly honest, I want to get out the door sooner rather than later. I'm not sure I could sleep soundly in that place anymore."

"I think we can make it work," I said, smiling. "I'll ask around to see if people are free tomorrow to move your stuff. For now, though, do you want to get some stuff and sleep at my place?"

"Yeah, I want out," Chloe concluded.

I nodded and sighed a little. What a mess this was. But, if there was one good thing to come out of it, it was Chloe and I finally being able to live in the same space and see each other at home every day. We circled back to Chloe's apartment and she went up to quickly gather some things. I stayed outside, both to avoid further conflict and to think a little more about the whole situation.

Chloe was coming to live with me. I still wasn't accustomed to the idea, not that I didn't want it, but it was going to be a change of pace for sure. I didn't know how she was like to live with, but surely, she wasn't going to be that bad. After all, I had known her for years and she never showed any sign of being that peculiar about cleaning or any of that stuff. Plus, she was an excellent cook and I couldn't wait to make meals with her every day. Maybe I could even learn a thing or two. We could watch plenty more movies together, play some new games and maybe try to finish Protector of the Gnomes one of these days. For a month, things would get a little cramped as she would bring all her stuff in an already furnished apartment, but we could figure out what to keep and what to sell in due time. The thought of waking up next to her every day made me smile, standing alone in the street. If people saw me, they might have thought I was crazy. They say sleeping next to someone you love makes you sleep better. If that was the case, I was about to get the best sleep I ever had on a regular basis and I was all for it. Because I did love her, with all my heart, and even though we went through some hardships together, the journey was just beginning and there would be plenty more along the way. Even if the thought should have been scary, I wasn't fazed at all. I knew we would get through it, together, hand in hand. The front door of the building opened and Chloe came out with a backpack and a small suitcase. She hurried next to me, still smiling at nothing in particular, and looked at me confused as she stopped.

"What are you smiling at?" she asked.

"I was thinking of us being together every day now and it made me smile," I answered simply and truthfully.

"You're so simple sometimes," she teased with a laugh.

At least, we managed to laugh about something on this emotionally-charged evening. We started walking to the bus stop, talking like everything was normal. I couldn't wait to start a new life with her. A life where we were

both in control of our destiny, a life where we could decide where to go next.
The sun may have set in the sky, but it had risen in my heart.

Chapter 31

"And there we go," I said, straining with effort as I dropped the couch in the living room. I rose up to look at Vincent and we both nodded in satisfaction. I skirted around it and sat down heavily, letting a grunt resonate through the messy apartment. Everyone looked at me with a smile and I responded with the same. Taking a look around, I started to realize just how far we had come.

The living room was filled with boxes stacked on top of each other and tucked away in corners to avoid being in the way. Chairs were scattered wherever there was any space and people loudly chatted to one another. Perhaps it was more echoey than normal and that was why the volume of conversation was so high, but I was too exhausted to care. Since this morning, we had been moving from my apartment to this one, the new one I was moving into with Chloe. We had previously taken all her stuff from her shared apartment with Beth and stored it with mine while we waited for the lease to end. It was a lot of stuff and we very well may have duplicates on various things, but we tried to keep it to a minimum by selling furniture and other items beforehand. Still, it took all day to move and since the new apartment was also on the third floor, there had been a lot of climbing. My legs were like jelly and I couldn't lift anything anymore. Even so, everyone we talked to had answered our call; Vincent, Chris, Sam, Michael, Violet, Anna, Caitlyn and Ashley. The last two I had met on the ski trip we went to a while back, but we never actually properly introduced ourselves so it was a little awkward at first. We made it work somehow and I was glad they came. The guys and I took care of most of the moving while the girls prepared the new apartment and Chloe took care to coordinate us when we came in with stuff. I was glad she was there as I couldn't have done it alone and would have ended up with an even messier living room. Even though it was a lot of work, everyone looked like they were having fun and I was grateful to all of them for the help they provided. Chloe turned the kitchen corner, walking up to me as I was lost in thought. I turned to look at her.

"Was that the last thing?" she asked.

"Yeah, it was. We're finally done!" I said with a smile and raising my arms in the air. I immediately let them back down, my muscles silently screaming at me for straining them like that. Chloe snickered and shook her head.

"Perfect, I've already called ahead, so supper should be coming in very soon."

"Awesome," I concluded with a nod. Chloe turned around and started walking away to join her friends. "I love you," I said, a little louder so she could hear. She looked back at me and rolled her eyes while making a smooch in my direction. I turned away, but soon met with Vincent's gaze while he was staring at me with a smirk. "What?" I asked him, confused as to what was so amusing.

"You two look good together. You look better than you were," he commented.

"She's the best. You know, we may have had our hardships, but I'm glad we got there in the end," I said, looking on in the kitchen where Chloe was standing, talking and laughing with her friends. She looked so beautiful even though we had a busy day and I couldn't wait to embrace her tonight and sleep in our new home together.

"I can tell you love her. Sometimes, people think they're in love when in fact, they're just looking for company and can't handle being alone. This…this is genuine. You deserve it, man. Truly," Vincent said.

"Thank you. That means a lot," I thanked him.

"Anytime."

"Hey, what's going on over here, my jolly good fellas?" Michael asked as he plopped down on the couch between Vincent and me.

"Woah, easy there, buddy. You might just break my arm off if you do that again," I warned. Michael started laughing and Vincent smiled.

"Seriously, though, why haven't we met your girl until now? She's gorgeous, man. You landed another good one. Life just isn't fair, isn't that right, Sam?" Michael asked Sam as he was talking to Chris. He didn't respond and didn't even acknowledge him. Michael looked down to feign sadness. "Another loss for poor old Michael."

"Things just got a little busy around us, so we didn't have time to organize something to include you guys. It's not that we didn't want to, but yeah, things kept coming up and we got a little sidetracked," I explained.

"Well, let me just say this, if you ever meet another girl like that, and you seem to be meeting them left and right, just refer them to me, yeah? Like what about that girl next to yours, is she free?" Michael said, pointing with a movement of his head. I followed to where he was looking and saw he was talking about Violet. I silently laughed and snickered and Michael turned around to face me. "What?"

"Yeah, I don't think she's into long-term relationships. You would have better luck looking elsewhere if that's what you want."

"How do you know that?" he asked. "Do you know her?"

"We've met," I answered mysteriously. Michael sighed heavily and dramatically took his head in his hands.

"Why is dating so hard?" he complained.

"You just need to find one," Vincent said. "You just need to get lucky once."

"Yeah, you're both ones to talk, you already have girlfriends. At this rate, I better get a cat to keep me company or else I might die of boredom," Michael joked. A response immediately came to mind, but I managed to restrain myself and keep it together. We laughed a little and looked in Chris' and Sam's direction as they got up from the second couch to join us, sitting down on unoccupied chairs.

"Sup, guys," I said with a nod. They responded with the same. "While you're all here, I'd like to thank you guys for all you've done for me. Not just today, but this whole year. Things haven't been the best at times, but I could always count on you to support me and I'm grateful for that. If you ever need something, tell me and I'll be there as fast as I can," I continued with a more serious tone. I felt I needed to thank them properly for the times we talked, the times they gave me advice on how to proceed, the times where they distracted me when things were going astray.

"You're welcome, Jack. Truly, it wasn't a bother. If you need anything else, just tell us and we'll answer. That's what friends are for, right?" Chris said. Everyone nodded in agreement and I looked at all of them, one by one, and they all smiled at me. My gaze stopped on Chloe, still laughing in the kitchen. "Don't let her go," he whispered to me. I rolled my eyes while smiling.

"I won't. Not this time," I answered. A knock on the door interrupted us and all conversations died down as Chloe rushed to the door. She opened it and started talking with the delivery man. "I better get over there and help her out" I said, painfully getting up from the couch. I didn't want to leave the comfort of my seat, but I knew I had to. Michael gave me an encouraging slap on the back as he helped me get up and I waddled over to the door to join Chloe. I arrived just as they were transferring the pizza boxes from the delivery man to her.

"Here, hold this," she said, handing me the pile. I took them reluctantly, my arms screaming that they needed help. I took a few steps back and used a pile of boxes to help me support them as Chloe was finishing the transaction. She closed the door and looked at me, amused at the sight, and I couldn't help but shrug a little. She laughed a little and joined me. "Want me to take them?" she asked, as a joke.

"No, no it's fine" I said. "I won't drop them."

"You better not," she threatened playfully as she left to the kitchen. I followed her, pizza boxes in hand, and we started distributing the food to everyone.

We thought we had ordered more than we needed, but the slices disappeared fast and soon, we were already through two of the three boxes. Everyone was served, but we were still surprised. Soon, there was only Chloe and me left to sit down and there was one seat left at the table where all the girls were already chatting. I started heading towards the living room, but Chloe stopped me, a glow in her eyes. It looked like she had an idea, but I didn't know if it was a good or a bad one. I was about to find out.

"What if we swapped? You go sit with the girls and I go sit with the boys? Could be fun, right?" she proposed. I didn't know her friends very well, except for Violet of course, but she could say the same for my friends. They had never met before today, so she was in the same situation as I was. Of course, we talked about our respective friends to each other so she knew them in name, but holding a conversation was a completely different endeavor. But, even though all of that was true, I still found the idea to be fun and shrugged at her.

"Yeah, why not? Worst comes to worst, I'll call for assistance and you can come and rescue me," I said playfully. Chloe looked at me with surprised eyes, but soon smiled. She was definitely a little excited about the prospect, but I'd be lying if I said I wasn't too. What a strange way to meet her friends.

"Hey, are you guys going to sit down or are you waiting for your pizza to get cold?" Anna shouted at us. We both smiled at each other and turned around. We started walking towards the table and Chloe turned left towards the living room. I saw Ashley and Anna look surprised, but didn't say anything until I sat down next to them.

"Well, wasn't expecting that," Ashley said with a laugh. "That's a first."

"We thought it could be fun" I answered while taking a bite from my pizza slice.

"Sure, why not?" Anna said. "So, how did you two meet?" she asked, enthusiastically turning in her chair to face me. I felt observed as I chewed my bite, like I was being interrogated for an unknown crime. I thought for a bit as the question weighted harder and harder. Their gaze was pressuring me to answer and I was taken aback by how intense they all were.

"She didn't tell you that?" I asked with confusion. I couldn't believe Chloe hadn't mentioned it at least once during all this time. Surely, they had to know, right?

"She may have, but why don't you refresh our memory?" Anna responded with a smirk while leaning on the table with her head resting on her fists. For some reason, her forwardness was intimidating to me, even if it was similar to Chloe's.

"Um, okay, well, we met in high school a long time ago," I started, uncertain if that was what they wanted to know. "We didn't talk for a year after graduating and recently found each other again. She really didn't say anything about that to any of you?"

"Yeah, she did talk about the whole high school and argument thing, but I meant like, how did you two rekindle after that year gap?" Anna asked again.

"Oh, right, of course. We just happened to run into each other at the park last summer and we... I had a lot on my plate at that time so we didn't talk that much until fall," I explained. I took another bite and looked at them. Maybe this wasn't such a good idea. I hoped Chloe was having a better time than me, because I was feeling pressured by all of them, like they wanted to know everything about me. It was stressful and they had only asked one question by now. What would it be like after thirty minutes of this?

"You guys had sex yet? Is she good?" Caitlyn asked. I almost choked on my food and they laughed at me. What kind of question was that? I was confused by the sudden shift of the conversation and didn't know if I should answer, dismiss the question entirely or lie about it. Surely, Chloe had talked to them about it. Do girls talk about that kind of stuff? I know I mentioned it to the guys, but I didn't go into many details for obvious reasons. If she did, they would know I was lying if I said we didn't have sex and that wouldn't be good.

"Um... we..." I started, uncertain of how to proceed. How much was too much? Was Chloe okay with me revealing stuff about this? How much did she already tell them?

"I know he is," Violet intervened. All eyes shifted on her and she looked at me with mischievous eyes. I gently shook my head no while staring at her intensely and she smirked.

"And how do you know that, per se?" Anna asked. There was a pause during which I silently prayed Violet wouldn't reveal our previous connection. I didn't know if they knew or if she kept it secret, but judging by Anna's question, then they weren't yet aware of what happened between us.

"Chloe told me," Violet finally answered. I internally sighed in relief, but all their eyes shifted back to me as I was taking another bite and I felt silly, like a kid caught with his hand in the cookie jar.

"So, you did have sex. Then I'll ask again, is she good?" Caitlyn reiterated. I guess there was no use hiding the fact anymore, but I could answer without giving too much away.

"We have good chemistry," I said. "That's all I'm going to say."

"Oh, come on, give us more than that," Caitlyn protested.

"I think we can cut him some slack and let Chloe answer that later if she wants to," Ashley said. "I have another question; what's your favorite date you had with her?"

That was a good question and one I felt a lot more like answering. I had many choices to choose from and they were all so great that I had a hard time landing on a definitive one. Of course, there was the Valentine's Day one, the day we both confessed to each other, the aquarium or just one where we cooked together. Any of them could do, I was happy to spend some time with her and that was all that mattered to me. But if they wanted a clear favorite, then I had no choice but to go with this one.

"I'd say it's when we cooked together for the first time as a couple. I gave her a spice rack as a gift and we used it to cook supper together and she ended up spending the night. It was just... a really good time and I'm thrilled to be able to do that more now that we're living together," I said, looking at the table and lost in thought. Anna jabbed me in the shoulder and snapped me out of my trance.

"Stop daydreaming," she said, laughing. "Keep it in your pants," she joked and all her friends laughed.

"Hey, you asked," I said, joining them in their laughter. It felt slightly less awkward now, even if it had only been a few minutes. There was something about them that made me more comfortable than others. I turned around to see how Chloe was doing and she gave me a wink when her eyes met mine. She smiled at me and I smiled back.

"Who confessed?" I turned around to see who asked and Violet was staring directly at me. I guessed she was the one that wanted to know.

"She did. Well, we both did, but she did first," I answered.

"Where and when?" Violet continued.

"In a restaurant on Valentine's Day," I said with a nod.

"That cheeky little..." Anna said.

"She sure knows how to be dramatic," Caitlyn added.

"I'm glad..." Ashley said. All eyes turned to her as it seemed like she had something else to say. "You know, Chloe's been through a lot and she didn't have the best luck when it came to relationships. But you're different. You're a good guy, Jack. Don't ever doubt it and don't ever doubt her. What you have right now, cherish it and you'll be able to keep it forever."

I turned around to look at Chloe again. She seemed to be having a lot of fun with the guys. I couldn't help but smile at them, but she didn't see me this time.

"I will."

◊

We closed the front door and silence landed on the entire apartment. Everyone had left after we thanked them for their help and Chloe and I were now alone in our new home. Our new, messy, unorganized home. But it was ours, a place where we both could build and nurture our relationship, a place where we could come back every night and feel the other's embrace. We looked on at the giant pile of boxes scattered across the living room and I felt a wave of discouragement run through my entire body. Taking these apart and putting them away would take ages to do, but Chloe's hand on my shoulders made me turn around and just seeing her blue eyes look at me, I knew it was going to be okay.

"Man, I am exhausted. I think I'm just going to go to bed," I said, sighing from tiredness.

"Are you too exhausted for one more thing?" Chloe said, getting closer to me.

"I am not opening any boxes tonight," I said.

"I'm not talking about boxes," she said seductively. Her hand slid down to my crotch as she planted a kiss on my neck. Her head moved right beside my ear and her hot breath warmed it up. "Care to break the bed in our new home?" she whispered. My body responded on its own and I felt myself getting harder. Her hand must have felt it too as it was right on top of it. A sudden wave of heat rushed through me and I exhaled heavily. Chloe's head moved again, making a trail of kisses from my neck until her lips landed on mine and I gave myself in to the kiss completely, any trace of exhaustion slowly leaving my body. She soon backed off and smirked at me. "I'll take that as a yes" she said as she turned around and started dragging me to the bedroom. I followed her, amused by her sudden eagerness and equally excited. We dodged a few

393

stacks of boxes in the corridor and finally made it to the room, a gargantuan mess tossed along the walls to allow the bed to fit in the middle of the room.

Chloe stopped and huddled closer to me and started rubbing herself on my crotch. My hands went around her and massaged her breasts over her clothes. She moaned softly and one hand descended to her thighs, gradually getting closer and closer to the main event. I avoided it for now, preferring to tease her and stop right before I reached it as she continued to rub on me. My shaft was getting even harder and it soon became very difficult to contain myself. She expertly unhooked her bra in a fraction of a second and pulled it out of her shirt, half releasing her breasts. I quickly took her shirt off, swiftly pulling it over her head like a shark smelling blood. I attacked her now exposed chest and paid close attention to her nipples, teasing and lightly pinching them. She seemed to enjoy that very much as she sharply inhaled and bent over a little, pushing back on my member which was now fully on guard. My left hand continued the assault while my right hand slipped down her pants straight for the gold. I was surprised by the lack of underwear and I approached her ear.

"Are you not wearing underwear?" I whispered.

"No," she answered as she breathed in. I didn't stop teasing her and she had a hard time answering at the same time.

"Did you just spend the entire evening with everyone while not wearing anything underneath?" I continued.

"Maybe," she moaned as my hand now fully covered her slit and was starting to tease it. I liked her reactions a lot and it brought a smile to my face to hear her like this. I didn't want to stop.

"You really are naughty, aren't you?" I said, accelerating my movements. She couldn't answer me as her breathing quickened and she bent down gradually, her legs starting to give in. She was really wet down there and my fingers were already covered in her juices. Even if I was down her pants, I could still hear the sound of my fingers moving over her moaning. After a while of this, she grabbed my hand and lifted it out of pants, made us turn around and pushed me down on the bed. I fell on my back, my feet still touching the floor and looking forward to how this would play out. Chloe slipped out of her remaining clothes in an instant and then focused on getting me out of my own. She unbuckled my pants and pulled them down, just as I was lifting my butt to allow her to do so. My shaft sprang up once and fell back down on my belly. She took it in her hand and stroked it a few times, making me moan. I could never get enough of that feeling, her delicate and soft hands going up and down. Satisfied, she turned around, facing away from me. She bent down, exposing herself completely to me and my shaft twitched on its own in anticipation. She started backing up, slowly, shaking her butt left and right, silently teasing what was about to happen. Finally, she had enough and took my shaft, lifting it up and sat down on me, swallowing my member whole. The wetness coupled with the warmth almost made me bust right then, but I managed to save myself and moaned louder than I ever had before. My hands went straight to her hips as she started making circles while on top of me.

The real fun began when she started moving up and down. It was different to the normal riding I had experienced before and dare I say this was way better. The only downside was that I didn't get to see her as much as she went up and down, up and down, my shaft moving easily in her from her wetness. It was a surreal feeling, to be finally doing this in our home, both of our home, and the thought of the many more opportunities we would have to connect in such a way aroused me even more. She must have felt it as her moaning got slightly louder and she started going faster and I swore I felt her tighten up even more than she already was. I couldn't take much more of this; I was about to burst, but I couldn't let that happen. I didn't want it to end this quickly and had to figure out a solution. It was obvious once I thought about it for two seconds, which was pretty difficult at the moment. I stopped her movement and lifted her off of me. She stepped forward and turned around, allowing me to stand up. I didn't waste any time and went for the kiss, interrupting her moaning and breathing. She rose one leg to straddle me and the feeling of her skin directly on mine made me grab it to press it down even more. My hands went behind her back and slid down, soon finding her butt and giving it a good squeeze. Chloe's hand went around my neck and she broke the kiss, much to my dismay.

"Carry me," she whispered in my ear, her hot breath teasing it for just a moment. Chloe jumped and her other leg wrapped around me. I was slightly surprised by the movement, but caught her in the air and lifted her up even more. She kissed me again, this time from above me which was a first for me while standing up. But I wasn't going to last holding her like this and I didn't have access to the part I wanted the most. I walked up to the bed, Chloe still in my arms, and threw her down. She bounced once in the sheets and laughed a little, looking up at me while biting her lip. She rose her legs, exposing herself to me again and her slit shone in the moonlight coming through the nearby window as we still hadn't installed the drapes yet. I really wanted to dive right back in and I must have been staring hungrily for a while. "Come and get me," she said seductively while shaking her butt left and right. "If you can."

I didn't have to be asked twice, but just as my shaft was hungry for more, so too was I to give her some personal attention. I got down on my knees and between her thighs and started eating her out. She let out a surprise cry soon muffled by a moan and her hand went straight behind my head as I licked and sucked everything my tongue could find. Normally, I didn't like the taste that much, especially after a day like today, and would have preferred to shower beforehand, but I somehow couldn't care less tonight. She was a little salty and also a little sweet, but I was too busy trying to pleasure her to focus on how she tasted. I started by teasing the top, which she liked a lot. After a few times, I was starting to know her weaknesses and how to exploit them to my heart's content. Her hand pushed me down further and my face was completely buried in her now, but I didn't mind. My cheeks were covered in her juices and there was only one place my tongue could go. She inhaled sharply when it went inside and started exploring her fully and she tried really hard to contain her moaning to a minimum, to partial success. Her moaning made me even more eager to pleasure her and her thighs gradually closed around my head, confining me between her legs. I couldn't go anywhere, not that I would want to. Her butt lifted off the sheets, rising slightly into the air and my head followed, not wanting to waste a single second of pleasure time. I continued for just a moment until Chloe's arms pulled me back up.

"I need you. Now," she said, not even bothering to whisper anymore.

"You need what?" I said, feigning innocence while standing over her, my shaft fully on guard and ready. She was right under it, just there, I could touch it if I wanted to, but I wanted her to beg for it. To want it so desperately it would feel even better for her to get it.

"I need you. Please," she begged, reaching for my butt cheeks and pulling me in closer to her. I bent my knees a little and I swiftly entered her, my shaft sliding in with no resistance. We both moaned at the same time and I was overwhelmed with so many feelings I couldn't move yet. I went all the way in, as far as I could and Chloe didn't stop me. I stayed there for a moment, my legs resting against hers, until she pushed me away to signal me to start moving. And I did. As soon as I stroked, both our breathing quickened and resumed loudly, an out of tune symphony of pleasure. She somehow got closer to the edge of the bed, raising her legs more to compensate. I was now fully on top of her, pressing down on her legs with every stroke, her breasts bouncing up and down every time I hit her butt. She grabbed both my arms supporting me from the bed and squeezed them hard. It should have hurt, but it didn't and only turned me on even more. I looked at her, her eyes closed and completely in the zone. There was only one thing I wanted her to do.

"Look at me," I ordered. I didn't want to be that direct, but I couldn't think straight anymore. She didn't seem to mind and didn't say anything as she stared at me, her blue eyes speaking volumes. She wanted more, she wanted me, she wanted my everything. Looking at her like this, I felt myself getting even bigger and harder, as aroused as I could possibly be, and I didn't stop for even a second. Even her breathing was turning me on, but I felt like I was reaching my limit. My moans turned to harsh breathing then to little grunts and I couldn't go on for much longer. She must have felt it too. She somehow freed her legs from under me while I was backing away from a stroke and wrapped them behind me, trapping me in her. I looked at her for a second, silently asking if she was okay with it. She swiftly nodded and inhaled sharply.

"Give it to me," she whined. "Trust me, it's fine, just give it to me." Before, I might have decided against it. I might have backed away and been selfish, to protect myself and my partner, I might have gone against her wishes to ensure everything was fine before doing something like this. But things had changed. I trusted her, just as much as she trusted me, and if she was saying it was okay, then it was okay.

I felt her grip tighten and that was the end of me. With one loud grunt, I finished inside her, my shaft twitching in rhythmic fashion accompanied by me exhaling loudly. Chloe must have experienced the same thing as her legs unwrapped behind me, shaking a little as she grabbed her chest. Her expression was sort of frozen, like she didn't want to breathe or maybe couldn't, but she eventually came back down and exhaled sharply before her head hit the sheets, soon followed by her arms and legs. She flattened on the bed, panting heavily and I stood up, member still proud for now. I towered over her and, as we both looked at each other, we both smiled.

"That was… amazing," she whispered. "Thanks for that."

"You're very welcome," I said, laughing. I looked down at her, still shining slightly in the moonlight and looked back up. She seemed to know what I was thinking without me talking.

"Was that your first time?" she asked through a few pants.

"Yeah, it was. I…um… never trusted anyone enough to…do that before," I said, embarrassed by it for a reason I didn't know. Why was it embarrassing to put responsibilities over pleasure?

"Well, if you still have any doubts, you don't have to worry. Today is a safe day and I make sure to take my pill every day," she said, reassuring me that everything was fine.

"Oh, no, I trust you on that. It's just…I've never done it before."

"Did you like it?" she asked, rising from the bed to get up.

"Very much, yeah," I answered enthusiastically. Perhaps a little too much which made Chloe laugh a little.

"I'm sure we'll get many more chances, then," she said with a smile. She walked past me to go to the bathroom and I couldn't help but stare at her butt as she passed me. "Stop staring at me," she said to me while still looking forward.

"How could I?" I asked with a smirk.

"Good point," she said, her voice fading away as she got further and further. I turned around to look at the messy room still stacked with boxes. We had a long day ahead of us tomorrow, but I knew it would be okay. Because I was with Chloe. Because she was with me. Because we were together, starting this new chapter in our lives. I sat down on the bed in the dark, my thoughts wandering away deep into the night.

Life is a path that only goes one way. We walk down it, sometimes reaching crossroads and sometimes finding it a very difficult path to walk. Sometimes, someone else's path almost touches yours and you feel like you could reach out to them. Along this path, you make memories, fragments of your life stored in your mind forever. I now feel like this is wrong, memories are not stored in the brain. For the brain can forget things as we reach the end of the path, it can trick you into thinking the path you walked was different than it really was. But the heart never forgets. Just as it was beating faster for Chloe just now, it also beat faster for Camille at some point. That isn't to say that it would if I saw her again, but while my brain could forget the feelings I had for her, the heart and the memories associated with it would never tarnish. Even in the darkest of night, illuminated only by the fading moonlight, the heart would remember and guide me along the path I needed to walk. Some would say that would mean your destiny is pre-written, the path is already made and you only need to follow it. I would disagree, arguing that the destination is the same for all of us, but the journey is what makes us unique. There are many crossroads scattered about, yet they all lead to the same place. Why bother choosing then, you may ask? Why that is the very essence of living; to choose which path to follow.

I smiled and looked up at the moon, high in the night sky, brightest it had ever been. I was happy to have chosen this path. To walk besides Chloe's, to endure the harshness of the stones under my feet if it meant to spend one more day with her. I guess that's what they called 'true love'. My path may have only just begun in the grand scheme of things, but I was looking forward to continue walking, one step at a time, eager to discover the journey ahead of me.

Epilogue
Eight years later

"**P**apa, I'm thirsty," the little girl said while pointing at a café on the side of the street.

"Well, now that's a shame, isn't it?" I answered, smiling at her. She pouted and looked away. "You want to go in?" I asked.

"Yeah!" the little girl answered as she jumped enthusiastically. I laughed and opened the front door to go inside the café. She sprinted past me and ran inside.

"Lily! Come back here, stay with me," I shouted, but Lily didn't stop until she reached a wooden stand where a woman smiled at her. The woman looked up and we made eye contact.

It had been so long since I had seen her, but there was no mistaking it. That blonde hair, those emerald eyes and that smile. She appeared shocked to see me, but wasn't fazed for very long as Lily spoke to her.

"I'm thirsty," she said. "I want a drink."

"Well, now that's not good. We'll take care of that, okay?" Camille said to Lily. She looked up at me just arriving near them. "For two?" she asked.

"Yes," I answered. Camille nodded and took two drink menus before leading us to a table in the corner. She let us sit down.

The café wasn't busy at all, which was surprising for this hot of a day. There was practically nobody inside, just an old man sipping on a coffee in the other corner of the room and a young couple a few tables away. I wondered what the reason was for this low activity, but didn't have time to wonder for long as Lily had already made up her mind.

"I want a lemonade," she said, proudly showing me the lemonade on the menu.

"Alright, we'll get you a lemonade," I said smiling at her. I scouted the many options displayed before me but couldn't choose before Camille came back.

"Have you chosen what you would like to drink?" she asked.

"I want a lemonade!" Lily repeated.

"Okay, a lemonade for the little miss. And for you…" she said, hesitantly.

"Just… a small coffee," I said and Camille nodded. She looked a little sad as she turned around to start preparing our drinks in the kitchen a little further back.

Lily started humming the intro song of her favorite cartoon and I couldn't help but smile at her carelessness. She was so precious, so innocent and I loved her with all my heart. I didn't notice I had been looking at her for a while before she called me out.

"Papa, why are you staring at me?" she asked innocently.

"Oh, I just couldn't take my eyes off such a beautiful little girl," I answered.

"Papa, I want to draw," Lily said while pointing at the bag I had. I nodded with a smile and took out a small colouring book and some crayons and handed them to her. She happily took them like her life depended on it and immediately started filling in the lines to a lion. She started putting some green in its mane and then worked on making the body a reddish pink. Kids were so innocent like that and it was something I had to continue working on. To me, it made no sense to color the lion like that, but to her it wasn't about choosing the right colors or making it look realistic. She just wanted to draw and draw she did. I continued looking at her, heavily concentrated on her drawing, until the drinks arrived. Camille had three drinks on her platter which made me slightly confused as everybody else already had theirs and nobody came through the door.

"Here's the lemonade for the little miss," she said, handing her the drink next to the colouring book.

"Yay!" Lily shouted. "Lemonade is my favorite!"

"You know what, me too," Camille said with a smile. "And here's your coffee," she continued as she handed me my cup. I thanked her and she smiled before pausing for a little while, still standing there, seemingly waiting for something. I looked up at her, confused, and she finally started speaking. "I was hoping we could maybe… talk… for a little while," she asked, clearly embarrassed about asking. I thought about it for a few seconds while looking at Lily. Was it wise to engage in this conversation, especially with her sitting across from me? What did she want to talk about? What did we have to talk about? My curiosity got the better of me and I sighed a little, blinking slowly as I looked up at her.

"Not for long," I said more as a warning than me agreeing to talk. Camille silently nodded and sat down on the chair at the table next to us.

"Papa will only go on the next table, okay? You can continue colouring and drinking your lemonade," I said to Lily.

"Okay," she simply said, not even bothering to lift her eyes from the lion drawing she was doing. I got up and sat back down in front of Camille. She was looking away, perhaps incapable of making eye contact with me after such a long time.

"So, what did you want to talk about?" I asked directly. I didn't want to beat around the bush, I wanted this conversation to end as soon as possible. I even started regretting agreeing to it before Camille started to speak.

"Is she yours?" she asked, as innocently as she could. There was a sadness in her voice and I started to feel bad for her. Maybe I was being too harsh.

"Yes, she is. Her name is Lily," I answered.

"I'm five years old!" Lily said, holding up her hand in the air while looking proudly at Camille. She smiled in response and contained a laugh.

"Five! You're all grown up, then," Camille said.

"Yep!" Lily happily said, continuing her drawing. Camille turned back to me.

"She's lovely… Are you still with Chloe?"

"Yes, I am. We've moved in together a few years ago and started working on our new life. After graduating, we wanted to start building a little family and that's where Lily comes in."

"That's… very nice. I'm glad, truly, for both of you. My luck hasn't been so good lately and here we are," Camille said with a fake smile. I could tell she had been going through a lot and, even with what she had done both to Chloe and I in the past, I couldn't help but feel a little sad for her. "There was something I needed to tell you that I never got the chance," She paused for a second, gathering her thoughts. I stayed silent and listened to what she had to say, hoping it wasn't inappropriate for Lily to hear as she was clearly eavesdropping as well. "I… wanted to apologize… for everything. I was naïve and rash and didn't know how to process my emotions rationally. I did things I regret, I blamed you for everything that happened and that wasn't fair. I made a lot of mistakes, mistakes I can't take back and I'm truly sorry for what I did to you. And Chloe. I'm grateful that you accepted to speak with me today, but I understand if you hate me and never want to talk to me again once this is over."

"I'm talking to you now, aren't I? Yes, it's true, you did do some devious things and you nearly broke Chloe and I up, but I can see that you're sincere about your apologies. I only hope that you learned from what happened and you wouldn't do the same thing again."

"No, I wouldn't, that's for sure," Camille quickly said.

"Then, if you're truly sorry for what you did, I forgive you," I said, looking at her with intense eyes. "I wouldn't want you to live your life wondering if I was ever going to forgive you for what you did and miss out on being happy. I still care about you, Camille, not the same way I used to, but a part of me still wants you to be happy in the end."

"That's enough for me," Camille said with a smile.

"But," I continued. She looked up at me and I stared into her emerald eyes. She still had the beauty she had back then, but I had found something even more beautiful than that. She was sitting at the table next to me, making a green and pink lion and sipping on a lemonade. "We can't see each other anymore. I may have forgiven you, but I don't think Chloe has and she might never will. It's not fair to you, to her or to me to continue this. We won't be coming here anymore," I finished.

"I understand..." Camille started. "I'm just relieved to have your forgiveness. I need nothing more than that."

"Then, we're done here." I looked over at Lily who hadn't even gotten through half of her drink. To be fair, I hadn't even touched mine and the hot cup of coffee sat on the table, still plentiful. "Lily, we're going to pack up, okay? We need to leave; Mommy is waiting for us."

"But we just got here," Lily protested.

"I know we did, but we'll stop on the way to get you another drink, okay?" Lily protested even more, but I finally managed to get a hold of the crayons and the colouring book, putting them back in the bag and holding out my hand for Lily to hold. She grabbed it, still a little gloomy about our sudden departure. I took out some cash and put it on the table next to Camille. She looked up at me and I nodded before turning around. We started walking away towards the door when a voice coming from behind me made me stop.

"Lily!" Camille said. Lily turned around to look at the woman she had barely interacted with. She was holding a lollipop in her hands and smiled at her. "Do you want it?" she asked. Lily's smile came back and she looked up at me to silently ask if she could. I couldn't resist her glinting eyes and nodded in approval. She hurried to Camille's side and took it in her tiny little hands, running back to me, clearly excited about it.

"What do we say to the lady?" I asked Lily. She thought about it for a second before turning back around.

"Thank you, lady!" I turned around to see Camille too and saw she was about to cry. She waved at us as she tried to contain her tears.

"Goodbye, Camille," I said, leading Lily out of the café.

The outside air immediately hit us again as we started walking towards our home. Lily started to get a little tired and I picked her up, sitting her down on my shoulders as she held on to my forehead. She always liked when I did this and she was still young enough that it wasn't too much of a burden on me.

"Was that your friend?" she asked out of the blue. The question caught me off guard and I didn't quite know how to answer her. Kids always had a way to ask difficult questions, to make us really think about them before coming up with an answer. I thought about it for a while, but couldn't come up with a definitive conclusion.

"I… don't know," I answered.

"How do you not know? She's either your friend or not. Kaylee is my friend, but I don't like Caleb very much. He's mean."

"That's not nice, Lily. You shouldn't talk about him that way. Maybe he just wants to be your friend, but he doesn't know how," I said.

"Just like that lady at the café?" I paused and smirked. She was smart, I'll give her that, maybe even a little too much. She definitely took that from her mother.

"Maybe. Hey, I have an idea. Do you want to eat your lollipop right now?" I asked.

"Yes!" she said enthusiastically.

"Okay, hold on tight," I said, stopping to grab it and open it for her. I rose my arm up so she could get it and when I felt it leave my hands, I started walking again. "Don't tell your mom, yeah?"

"I won't, I promise," Lily said. I laughed because I knew it would be the first thing she would say to Chloe, but that was just how kids were, wasn't it? I waited a little bit before asking my next question.

"What's your lollipop's flavor?" Lily thought about it for a while and hummed as she tried to identify the flavor.

"Lemon!" she shouted.

I smiled. Of course, it was lemon. It was her favorite after all.

About the Author

Montreal-based author William Bergeron follows in the footsteps of his father Daniel with his first book, *The Memories We Made*. Growing up, William always had a book in hand and stories in mind. He adored immersing himself in various and compelling fantasy worlds in order to create his own, which makes the complete shift to the romance genre all the more interesting but that is where William found his calling. *The Memories We Made* talks about a young man's first love and all of its challenges in a very personal and intimate perspective. While it is his first book, William has participated (and won!) in the global event *National Novel Writing Month,* a writing event compelling writers to put their pen to work in a self-imposed challenge. Always overflowing with ideas, he is already thinking about what quirky situations his characters will fall into next!